POSSESSIONS:

A Paranormal Thriller

Virginia Renaud

This book reflects the author's present recollection of past experiences. Although it is listed as a work of fiction, this refers to the following fictionalized pieces: the thoughts of some characters, names, and some dialogue. All other content is presented as completely as possible, based on author recollection, interviews with friends and family, and journals kept by the author from that time.

For my daughter, Natassia.

For reasons she will understand.

ACKNOWLEDGMENTS

A huge thank first and foremost to my wonderful husband Dan Renaud.

Dan, your endless patience frankly astonishes me. Thank you for cooking dinner so our family wouldn't starve when I got "into the zone", and although I know you got tired of the editing process, you hung in there with me, and read through the manuscript many times, even though you keep claiming you're 'not a reader'.

I love you for so many reasons, but in terms of this work, I offer you my thanks for your patience, your careful editor's eye, your endless support and your faith in me as a serious author.

Laura Heavens, I'm grateful for your amazing talent in Graphic Design and your instinctive knowledge of book covers. How you ever managed to come up with such a great image for Possessions is beyond me. Good thing you are at least one-part mind-reader!

A big note of thanks to my good friend and kindred spirit, Yvonne Popowich for acting as my Beta Reader. Thank you for your efficiency, your bravery and insightful comments. Your articulate assistance has been a huge help! I look forward to more insightful conversations with you on my next project!

Erin Potter, as a professional editor, your opinion carries great weight. Your high praise inspired me, providing the push I needed to finish this project. Thank you for your honesty and your insight.

And a big thank you to my family for your faith and encouragement. This book was a serious emotional journey, and probably the hardest thing I've ever done. I am delighted that it no longer takes up space in my head.

I truly hope you enjoy the read.

Chapter One

"What the hell is that?" The petite blonde turned on one booted heel and arched delicate eyebrows at the realtor who stood shoulder to shoulder with her, in the small darkened bedroom.

She felt her face growing hotter as she waited for his reply.

A king-sized bed took up most of the room. Fastened around one of its ornate wrought iron bed posts was a pair of fuzzy, pink novelty handcuffs.

An awkward silence hung between them for a moment.

"You know what, Darryl? I think that's enough for one day," the young woman said, tossing her hair back over one shoulder in annoyance. She walked briskly to the front foyer, calling behind her, "Are you coming?"

"Yes," he answered. Taking long strides, he caught up with her quickly. The heels of his patent leather shoes rapped sharply against the hardwood floors as he opened the door for his client. Determined to keep the mood light, he grinned and shrugged sheepishly.

"Didn't see that one coming," he remarked.

Julie didn't trust herself to say anything. This had been such a frustrating day already, and now this? Back inside the realtor's spacious SUV, Julie pulled out some lip balm from her jeans pocket and moistened her uncomfortably dry lips. Darryl re-locked the front door of the house, and smiled again.

Julie resisted the urge to roll her eyes. Now what was he going to think? The man was already convinced of his own divinity, and seemed to think Julie was somehow in his thrall! Whenever their eyes met, he flashed her a confident smile that was all teeth. Darryl had an over-abundance of charisma. Was he like this with all his female clients?

"I am not doing this by myself anymore," she muttered in frustration, staring out the passenger window as the realtor settled behind the wheel.

"Well?" he asked expectantly, before starting the vehicle and re-entering the flow of traffic.

Once again, there was that knowing smile!

"Well what?" she asked irritably.

"I'm sorry about the décor in that last one. I honestly had no idea. People collect the strangest things," he said, hoping to smooth things over. "That's not what 'staging' a home means by the way," He quipped.

"I'm sure," Julie replied tersely.

"So, are we feeling anything here?"

Julie cast a startled look at him. "Uh, no."

"Oh, not about the handcuffs!" he laughed at his own joke. "I'm referring of course to the *rest* of the house," he pressed. "What about it? Spacious floor plan, lots of recent upgrades, new furnace, and a decent yard. And even a garage."

"Yeah," Julie replied hesitantly. "I don't know. It just seemed kinda wrong to me."

She was grateful Darryl had his eyes on the road and couldn't see how much she was fidgeting. Julie knew with certainty that it didn't matter what she looked at now. When she felt like this, there was no point fighting it, she simply had to turn around and go home. In all seriousness, there was something completely wrong about that last house, but despite her best efforts, Julie couldn't put her finger on why.

In a way, she was sort of grateful for the distraction those silly handcuffs provided, so she could get the heck out of there without raising too many suspicions. Looking out the window at the landscape rushing past, she drew a deep breath.

After a few minutes of uncomfortable silence, Darryl glanced over at her. "It just wasn't your style, was it?"

Julie shook her head adamantly. "Not at all."

"You're looking for something more polished, then?"

"Yes exactly, that's what we want," she said, hoping that really was the answer. "Within our budget, of course."

"Ah budgets are always a challenge, but we'll look. If we have to go just a little above your budget, are you okay with that?" He hedged.

Once again, the smile that was supposed to be reassuring and infectious flashed from the driver's seat.

"We'll see," she replied evasively.

A few moments later, they pulled up to a small grey bungalow. Darryl put the vehicle in park and turned to face his client, slinging one arm casually over the back of the seat. "Here we are. Home, sweet home," he announced. "So, are we on for our date Saturday?"

"Date?" Julie replied automatically. Another quick blush tinted her normally fair complexion.

Darryl laughed and amended his question. "Sorry, I meant our house-hunting date. You and Marc, remember?"

"Oh! Of course," she replied, ducking her head to gather her purse from the floorboard in front of her feet. "Marc will be home Friday."

"Exactly," Darryl replied enthusiastically. "I'll put together a more *polished* list and see you then." As he leaned toward Julie, emphasizing the word 'polished', she felt herself lean away instinctively. "What time am I picking you up?"

"Uh, one-ish?" she asked, eyebrows raised. "Marc is usually pretty tired when he gets back, so I don't want anything too early."

"Can do," he grinned. "You said he's coming back Friday, right?"

"Yes, that's right. Friday. My husband will be home Friday." Julie winced at her choice of words. Why had she said it like *that?*

Worried she was going to blush again, Julie quickly got out of the vehicle and made her way to the front door. She felt awkward in her jeans and t-shirt as she approached the house, realizing her impeccably dressed realtor was watching as she fumbled in her pocket for the front door key.

"You got it okay?" he asked. "Need a hand?"

"Nope, I'm fine," she answered, issuing a short wave and a smile.

Darryl's answering grin was once again all teeth as he pulled away.

Julie ducked inside her house and sagged against the door. "Whew! That was work."

She'd only just managed to kick off her boots before a dark blue sedan pulled into the driveway. The woman at the wheel alighted quickly and waved at the house. 'Halloo, we're here!" she announced, turning to open the back door of the car.

And just like that, any thoughts of new houses and narcissistic realtors quickly disappeared.

Julie slipped into her boots again and opened the front door. "Great timing mom, Darryl just left. Where's dad?"

"Oh, grandpa's a spoil-sport," the older woman answered, placing one sun-browned hand on her hip as she leaned casually against the fender of the car. Julie reached into the back seat and began removing her energetic four-year old from his car seat while her mother looked on.

Her green eyes were intense, as she following her daughter's every movement. Would you believe your father is still at the hardware store?" She scoffed. "He wasn't ready to leave yet so I told him I'd come back and pick him up later."

"Yeah, I'd believe it," Julie replied knowingly, as the last strap fell away. Adam slid from his car seat and ran straight for the house, throwing the front door wide open.

"Oh geez! Adam! You'll let the cat out!" Julie turned to her mom as she struggled to remove the car seat. "Mom, could you? My hands are full."

"I'm on it!" she promised, darting nimbly after her grandson, the heels of her dress shoes clicking on the pavement as she hurried inside. Julie followed as quickly as possible, carrying the car seat into the house.

High heels kicked off to one side, Julie's mother was crouched in the foyer removing Adam's shoes.

"Thanks for taking him today, mom," she said, closing the door. "It was easier to focus on the houses."

"You're welcome," she replied. "We had fun!" Her mother's exotic eyes danced as she relived the memory. "He's a ball of energy, but as long as we keep him entertained, we have a great time. How was it today? See anything you like?"

"Not really," Julie answered, trying not to wince as she thought of the last house and its strange decorations. "Nothing my style yet. I guess I'm just picky."

With a peal of laughter, Adam took off running down the hall toward the bedrooms. His white-blonde hair blew back off his forehead as he ran. A moment later, he reappeared, gripping a small book in one hand and a video cassette in the other. Two round splotches of color stood out prominently against his otherwise pale complexion, and his blue eyes sparkled with mischief.

Both women smiled as he stripped the cover from the well-worn children's movie, eagerly feeding the tape into the nearby VCR machine.

"Well, keep your chin up. The right one is out there waiting."

"Thanks mom," Julie replied, turning automatically as her son raced away again. His sturdy legs pounded down the hall at speeds that looked as though he was part of a relay race. A moment later, Julie cringed as she heard something heavy fall to the floor in the next room.

Adam's grandmother shrugged and her perfectly outlined lips twisted into a guilty grin. "Sorry, he had ice cream."

"Yeah, I can tell!" Julie laughed and shook her head. "Sounds like a great day though."

"It's a grandparent's prerogative to spoil her grandson," she said defensively. "He and Grandpa had an ice-cream-eating contest."

Just then, Adam ran into the living room again, and dove head-first into a child-sized foam recliner, that was strategically placed in the center of the room.

"Adam, who won the ice cream contest?" The loving grandmother asked hopefully, her head cocked to one side as she waited expectantly. But as the seconds ticked by, Adam's only response was to wiggle around excitedly in his chair, as he waited for the movie to start. His body was always busy, but he seemed largely uninterested in the people around him. The child's clear blue eyes watched the TV screen in fascination.

Julie cleared her throat nervously. "Do you have time for a quick coffee mom?"

"No, no. I've got to go pick up your dad before he buys more things he doesn't need," she answered, with a negligent wave of her hand.

"Oh, okay. Uh, hey," Julie tried again, hoping to sound casual. "Are you and dad busy Saturday afternoon around one?"

"I don't think so, why? Are you throwing a party?" Her mother's eyes lit up and she turned to her daughter with a hopeful smile.

"Uh ...no. 'Fraid not. We have another appointment with the realtor and we were wondering ..."

"If dad and I would babysit?" the older woman finished with a knowing smile.

"It would be a lot easier to focus on the houses."

The older woman considered the request silently for a few moments, but to Julie it felt like forever! Her mother's penetrating gaze was unnerving.

"Mom?" Julie asked again hesitantly. "If it's not okay I think we can manage," she continued.

"Oh, I'm just teasing you," she agreed, her mouth curving into a gentle bow as she touched her daughter's cheek fondly. "Of course we'll take him! But you have to expect some more spoiling!" Waving to her grandson, she left as quickly as she'd arrived. "Grandma loves you, you little turkey!"

"Turkey!" Adam echoed, his gaze still fixed on the TV screen.

Julie smiled fondly as she watched her mother bustle through the doorway, the hem of her skirt swishing madly as she jogged back to the car in her high heels.

Standing in the doorway she waved as her mom's dark blue sedan disappeared back down the road, wondering why she felt slightly breathless.

"Movie time, huh?" she asked her son, sitting down with him in the living room. Adam smiled and flicked a glance at his mother out of the corner of his eye.

Julie caught her breath and returned his grin. Nice! No words yet, but nice anyhow.

He was already almost five and still not talking. A few words here and there, but she knew other people who conversed with their four-year-old about everything! Adam should have been asking questions and trying to wheedle new toys out of her, but instead, her son ranged from eerily silent to random quoting, repeating phrases taken from favourite TV shows and movies. She and Marc were learning to recognize and appreciate the rare moments here and there when Adam let them into his world, but every time the heartbroken parents were always left wanting more.

The world for Adam was an overwhelming place. He cried and tantrummed more than most children, often ignoring his surroundings with fierce dedication.

As she watched her son, noting his intense focus and the way his short hair curled damply away from his round, little boy face, she wondered if she'd ever really understand him.

The words of the Psychologist came flooding back even as she fought to keep them out.

"There's something wrong with your baby's brain," he'd said candidly, his choice of words blunt as he folded and re-folded his hands on the desktop. It was clear the man was struggling to explain the findings of the diagnostic team. "He doesn't process language the same way you or I do. This is why he seems to exist in his own world. Your words have no meaning for him. The diagnosis is something called Autism. Have you ever heard of that?"

Autism?

Neither Julie nor Mark had ever heard of it before, but now the once-strange-sounding word was part of their daily vocabulary.

"What do we do?" they'd asked.

"There's no cure, if that's what you're asking."

Julie and Marc had been devastated. No cure?

"Will he grow out of this?" Julie had asked, desperation in her voice.

"No, he won't outgrow it. He may improve a little, with therapy but you should make your peace with the fact that your son will always be different."

And with that, they'd been dismissed, driving home from the city in a depressed fog. The words of the specialist didn't sound quite right to them, and yet according to the medical community his word was final.

That was almost a year ago now, Julie thought wryly. And we're no closer to figuring this out. No closer to understanding our son.

The young couple began their exhaustive research almost immediately, and a steady stream of strangers marched in and out the front door. Intake workers, therapists and specialists of every description came and went. The desperate parents wanted answers, and each new person represented hope, but one after another, the only thing they discovered was a phrase seemingly uttered by everyone who met Adam.

They all agreed, he was very *unique*.

Julie made a face at the memory. Didn't every parent want to hear their child was unique? Unfortunately, in their case, unique wasn't really a compliment.

Julie had always been an avid reader, but the books cluttering her nightstand these days had the word 'autism' in their titles.

"Adam, somewhere in there, you know what's going on. Your mind just moves faster than ours, doesn't it?" she spoke as though her son understood every word.

Adam continued to lean forward, staring at the screen, his cherubic face devoid of expression as the favourite show played on. Smiling through the tears that traced silvery lines down her cheeks, Julie took a deep breath and wiped them away briskly with the back of her hand.

"It doesn't matter. One day you'll show them how smart you are!" she said, emotion making her words thick.

Adam suddenly clapped his hands together and an excited giggle burst forth. Fleetingly, he glanced at his mother from the corner of his eye.

Julie sat up excitedly. "Yes!" she said, clapping her own hands and kneeling beside him she held his so they could clap together. "That's my boy! Yay Adam!" Adam laughed and for a moment he was right there with her, but all too soon, the little boy craned his neck and twisted in his chair. The TV was on, and she was in the way.

Pressing her lips together to stem the flood of emotion, Julie backed away. He *does* know what's going on! I must believe that, she told herself firmly. It's all I've got.

~~~~

Saturday began early.

"Wake up, friend owl!" A piping voice at the side of her bed rattled Julie's eyelids open.

The unexpected sound boomed in her ears.

Adam stood next to his mother's bed, winding his fingers in her long hair as he repeated the phrase."

"Wake up, friend owl!"

The alarm clock on her bedside table read 5:01.

Alarm clock, hah! What irony, she thought, as she dragged her eyelids open.

"Hi little man," she whispered, carefully removing his fingers from her hair. "Mommy's up. Ssh, let's go."

Her husband lay on the far side of the bed, where he'd collapsed, exhausted the night before. His powerful chest rose and
~~~~

fell rhythmically beneath the thin sheet. Julie allowed herself a moment to study her husband as he slept. His long eyelashes lay serenely against cheeks that retained a healthy blush all year-round. His blonde hair, the same shade as his son's, needed trimming again. Marc liked his hair short. His strong jaw, accentuated by a well-established moustache, was now covered with a thin layer of stubble. He was home at last!

She wanted to reach out to her husband, to grab him and hold on. He'd been away several weeks this time. The nature of his work took him away so much, the young couple joked that if they based their anniversaries on time spent together, they'd be eternal newlyweds!

How long would it be this time, before he had to go?

The thought made her chest constrict and she caught her breath, turning away.

"Wake up Papa," Adam said, tilting his small head as he looked across the rumpled quilt.

The moment made Julie's unshed tears threaten again. "Ssh," she whispered. Rolling out of bed she took her son by the hand. "Papa's sleeping."

"Not anymore," he rumbled. "I'm up, I'm up."

"Oh!" Julie turned with a jolt. "You scared me!"

Marc rose from the bed and stretched to his full height. It was remarkable how he did that. He was awake almost instantly. He crossed the room and enfolded wife and son in a tight, warm embrace.

"Sorry honey," he mumbled into her hair. Julie couldn't help grinning like a fool, as she felt his hot breath against her skin. Wrapped in his strong arms, she felt like she could take on the world! It was just what she needed after weeks of parenting on her own.

Adam wiggled free and slid to the ground, wrapping his small arms around his father's leg, he sat down confidently on Marc's bare foot. "You got 'em, you got 'em," he announced.

Both parents chuckled.

"Yeah, you certainly do," Marc said to his son. Picking him up easily, he swung Adam up into his arms and carried him from the bedroom. "I see I've been missed," he said, tousling his son's blonde hair. "Whoah! You need a haircut big guy!"

"So do you," Julie quipped.

Despite his obvious fatigue, Marc's blue eyes danced.

Chapter Two

"I don't know, there's an awful lot of stairs," Julie said, as they climbed back into the realtor's SUV. "I love the outside, for sure, but why are those bedrooms so tiny?"

"It's a Victorian," Darryl reminded her. "They're all like that. But hey, if that one's not winning you over, let's see what's next on the list. We've got lots to see today."

As they toured through the next few houses, Julie noticed that Marc held the list in his own hand. She smiled. Leave it to Marc to take the reins, she thought.

As Darryl pulled into the next driveway, he was grinning excitedly.

"Now this is just what I promised you Julie. A more *polished* property."

Marc narrowed his eyes. "Polished meaning above our budget?"

"Asking prices are just a starting point for negotiation, Marc. They never go for that."

"We'll see," he said, as they passed through the front door.

As Marc bent down to remove his shoes and follow his wife up to the main level, a sudden wave of vertigo hit him.

"Whoah!" he said, sitting down awkwardly on the tiled floor.

"Marc! Are you okay?" Julie called. She was already midway up the stairs. "What happened?"

"I'm fine," he answered, slowly rising. "Just a bit dizzy. It's nothing. Let's go on up."

The staircase opened directly off the foyer, and Julie eagerly followed Darryl to the main level. But after only mounting a few of the lushly carpeted steps, the vertigo slammed into him again, and Marc stopped, clutching the railing for support.

"Oh boy," he muttered. "That's not good."

"What?" Julie stood waiting for her husband at the top of the staircase. "What are you doing? Come on up."

"Uh, sure. Be right there."

Reluctantly, Marc climbed to the top, noting as he did so that a pressure was building inside his chest.

Darryl extolled the virtues of the house as he walked, and Marc heard the words 'polished', 'updated' and 'modern' a few too many times. He would normally have been amused at such an obvious attempt to win over his wife, but he found it difficult to focus. The whole thing felt unreal, like he was watching this, instead of living it.

Marc pretended he was inspecting the kitchen counter, as he gripped its hard edge and took deep, steadying breaths.

What's wrong with me? He thought. Have I got flu?

He made his way down the hallway, still following woodenly behind his wife as they peeked into each room.

They were clustered together in the master bedroom before Marc recognised the uncomfortable feeling for what it was.

Heat rushed to his face and his heart pounded.

How could I have been so dumb, he thought. This place is *haunted!*

Protectively Marc put his arm around his wife's waist and pulled her close. "I don't think this is right for us, Darryl," he announced, hoping his voice didn't betray how badly he needed to get out of there. Pulling Julie along with him, he walked rapidly towards the staircase.

"Marc? What wrong?" she asked, hurrying to keep up. "What's going on?"

"We have to go," he whispered urgently in her ear. "Now."

Darryl shot the couple a confused look as Marc rapidly descended the staircase.

Julie hastened down the stairs to catch up with the long strides of her husband, leaving Darryl to re-lock the front door.

Getting back into the vehicle, Darryl swiveled around to face the back seat and his clients. "Is something wrong with the house?"

"I'm sorry, I just don't feel well," Marc replied, running one hand back and forth over his short-cropped hair. "Maybe it's the jet lag."

"Oh, of course," he sympathized. Look, if you're not well, I can take you both home now, and we can re-book."

"How about we see one more, and then call it a day?" Marc replied. "I'll take a nap when I get home. I'm already feeling better just being outside."

"O-ka-ay," Darryl replied uncertainly. "Is this one off the list, or would you like to see it again?"

"Off the list," Marc replied decisively, turning to face his wife. "Right honey?"

"Marc," Julie hissed through clenched teeth. "What's going on? Are you okay?"

"I'm fine. I'll explain later," he whispered, as Darryl turned back towards the steering wheel and started the vehicle again.

As Marc looked into his wife's eyes, he saw question and concern in equal proportions and he knew she wasn't about to let it go. But they would have to be alone to have *this* discussion. He only hoped he knew what to say when the time came. He'd been acting on instinct, and every instinct in his body had screamed: Get out!

Julie flicked an annoyed glance at her husband.

"Sure, yeah that's fine with me too," she said, offering Darryl a fake smile and a thumbs up in the rear-view mirror.

"Where to?" Darryl asked.

Marc cleared his throat and tried to sound calm. He felt a lot better now that he was outside, but the odd pressure hadn't left him yet. "This one at the bottom of the page looks interesting. What do you think?" Marc asked his wife, tilting the page towards her. Receiving a small nod, he sat forward and handed the list back to the realtor.

"Oh yes! That one. Sure, no problem. We can be there in just a few minutes. No appointment necessary; its empty."

"Oh really? Is it new?" Julie asked.

"Practically," Darryl answered. "It was built last year, but the family had to move out suddenly, so no one's living there anymore."

"Great," Marc replied, a friendly grin on his face. "I'll try not to run away this time."

"Don't worry about it," Darryl replied, flashing Marc a toothy smile in the rear-view mirror. "Sometimes houses speak to us, you know?"

Marc chuckled dryly.

"I think you're gonna like this next one. It's again, a more polished style, attached garage and the basement has been roughed-in for an in-law suite."

The couple looked at each other, eyebrows raised. An in-law suite was exactly what they needed.

"How much is it?" Marc asked. 'The price isn't listed here."

"The seller is very motivated, I'm told," Darryl replied. It's in the same ball park as the others on the list, but because it's already vacant, there's definitely room for offers."

"What's wrong with it?" Marc asked suspiciously.

Julie punched her husband in the arm.

"Wrong? Not a thing," the realtor replied smoothly. "They just want a fast sale. I think you're gonna like it. The house is built in a popular, modern style, and has all the things on your list."

"And empty since …when?" Darryl caught a glimpse of Marc's raised eyebrows in the rear-view mirror.

"I'm not sure about that, actually. It's only been on the market a few months."

Marc sat forward as they turned onto the short street that ended in a cul-de-sac.

Darryl pulled up a slanted driveway and set the parking brake. He consulted the paper beside him and scribbled some numbers on the page, handing it back to Marc "That was the list price as of this morning, but I just got word it's been reduced. I don't know what it's dropped to yet."

Marc sat back and whistled, his forehead creased into a frown.

"I know, I know," Darryl replied, holding up his hand to forestall any more comments. "Let's just go in and look. If you like it, I'll do some fast-talking on your behalf. And you never know, right?" Darryl opened his door and turned to face them. "Shall we go in?"

Marc looked out the window. "Okay, what the hell? As long as we're here," he answered, reaching for his wife's hand.

"Over-budget," he whispered to her, as they walked up the steep concrete driveway. Julie's answering smile was guarded.

True to Darryl's word, it was a modern home, with a two-car garage, lots of windows and grand double doors.

Marc shook his head.

Money, he mouthed to his wife.

Julie squeezed his hand and frowned. "Ssh!"

As the three of them walked toward the front door, Julie's stomach tightened.

It wasn't just empty. It looked abandoned!

The front and side lawns where it shared a boulevard with its neighbours could no longer be called a lawn. The grass, sparse though it was, had grown high in places and was going to seed.

"Yeah, I know," Darryl commented, noticing her gaze. "Definitely empty. A friend of mind has this listing, but I think he's been away. Usually he keeps the lawns mowed and things pretty tidy on his vacant listings."

Julie stepped back and looked at the upper floor as Darryl retrieved the key from the lock-box mounted on the front door. The windows were huge! Julie couldn't help shivering just a little. Anticipation perhaps? Her whole body felt as though it were quivering.

She was relieved to see Marc smiling and she squeezed his hand again.

"Why did the family leave so suddenly?" Julie asked, as Darryl swung the door wide and stepped aside for her.

"Relocation for a new job. Apparently, the company is selling the house for them."

"Sweet deal," Marc commented, following his wife inside the foyer.

He almost bumped into her, as she stopped short, a look of dismay on her face as she stared at a pile of disheveled newspapers and advertising flyers that littered the floor. The tiles in the entryway were smeared with dirt and debris in a four-foot radius. Beyond that, the tiles were pristine.

"What's going on here?" Darryl reached out with one shiny shoe to hastily push aside the haphazard pile. "Sorry folks, the listing agent has obviously been away. He usually hires people to clean and stage his empty listings."

"They missed a spot," Marc quipped, jerking his thumb at the pile.

Julie smacked her husband's arm in rebuke. She was pleased to see no sign of Marc's earlier 'jet-lag' and suspected him of trying extra hard to suppress it, just for her. She was quite sure he'd already noticed his wife's keen interest in the house.

For Julie, it was hard to contain her excitement. This house was different from all the others.

She and Marc had been studying houses just like this one online for the past several months, never dreaming they could afford one for themselves.

"Wow, is it ever cold in here," she remarked, rubbing her arms briskly. With a flourish, she pushed open double French doors that opened off the foyer to reveal a good-sized office space.

"Basement entries are always a little cooler," Darryl answered.

"Smells stale," Marc commented. "I wonder how many people have looked at this place."

"For the price it's listed at? Probably plenty," Darryl assured them. "It's a way lower list price than similar properties."

Julie carefully pulled the doors to the den closed. "I love these kinds of doors," she said, smiling.

Darryl pocketed the key. "Feel free to explore," he said.

"Are the cobwebs extra?" Marc quipped, climbing the staircase and waving one arm in front of him as he walked. Long strings of cobwebs festooned the open space.

The realtor coughed self-consciously. Pulling out his cell phone, Darryl waved his hand in front of him. "If you folks are okay to give yourselves a tour, I'd like to just give Jake a call and let him know the state of his listing. He'll want to get this taken care of quickly, I'm sure.

"Ask him the new price while you're at it," Marc said, already eagerly mounting the staircase.

"I hate to say this," Marc whispered to his wife as they climbed together. "But I get the feeling Jake hasn't been past the front door of this place in quite a while."

"It seems that way, doesn't it?"

"Did you hear what he said about the previous owners? They weren't here very long," her husband muttered.

Julie trailed her hand along the oak banister. "It's a gorgeous house, I'd be sad to leave it."

"Yeah, it's pretty nice," Marc agreed. "And it's new. That's what I like."

"It seems big, but that's probably the layout. It's definitely bigger than what we've got now," he said. "I have to go outside to change my mind!"

"Har-de-har-har," Julie replied sarcastically.

"Look at how wonderfully it's been staged, Jules," Marc muttered sarcastically, waving his arm at the empty rooms.

Julie rolled her eyes and walked into the kitchen, where all thoughts of sarcastic come-backs quickly left her. Gleaming floor-to-ceiling cabinets and flawless countertops stood out in contrast to her own woefully cramped kitchen. "Ooh, a pantry," she commented appreciatively.

"Hey Marc," she called to him. "Come see this!"

Marc quickly rounded the corner and nodded. "Nice," he said.

"Nice?" she asked incredulously. "Think of what we have now."

Marc smiled, but quickly put a finger to his lips. Rapid footfalls could be heard as Darryl jogged up the staircase, his call obviously finished.

"I have excellent news," Darryl said as he joined them. "Not only was the price reduced last week, but there was another drop again, today."

"What? Why?" Julie blurted.

"I don't know," he said. "It's not my listing. But that's good news for you, right?"

"What's the new price?" her husband asked.

"Subtract fifteen from the last price I showed you."

"Are you serious?" Marc asked, grinning. "Fifteen thousand?"

Darryl nodded and Julie spontaneously hugged her husband.

The realtor grinned. "Did you see everything yet?" he asked.

"Not yet, Julie was just drooling over the kitchen," Marc replied.

"Thanks," she muttered dryly.

"Yeah, it's a quality home, for sure," Darryl agreed. "Check this out." Walking into the family room that flowed off the end of the kitchen, he flipped a nearby wall switch with one finger, and instantly, blue and orange flames sprang up behind the glass doors.

"Marc grinned, "A gas fireplace? Nice touch."

"Let's go check out the master," Darryl suggested, turning to lead them back down the hall.

"Not so fast, what about the backyard?" Marc's hesitation made Julie catch her breath.

Marc smiled disarmingly at his wife. "Don't panic honey, I just want to have a look, and see if there's enough room back there for a growing family with a dog. Adam's getting bigger. Next year it'd be better to have his birthday in our own backyard instead of a fast food joint, right?" He drew open the wide, sliding glass doors to the back porch and stopped.

"Oh no," he said, his voice falling. "Is that it?"

Julie's face fell as she joined her husband on the back porch.

"Oh no," she echoed, sadly.

Scrubby tufts of grass grew haphazardly in a yard that was much smaller than their current one. It was cordoned off from its rear neighbour by a short, ugly chain link fence, while a high retaining wall separated the property on the right side. The left side of the yard was open and stared, unabashed into their neighbour's spacious, manicured yard. A lush vegetable garden formed a natural barrier between the two properties, in stark contrast to the sickly state of its neighbour.

They must hate this eye sore, Julie thought, looking at the other homes that bordered this one.

A lone pine tree, the only example of healthy greenery seemed to stand guard at the center of the yard, while the skeletons of long-dead Christmas trees lay scattered at the far edge of the property.

"A Christmas tree dumping ground?" Julie wondered aloud.

"The previous owners were planning to put a pool in," he said. "But there wasn't time."

"Right," Julie commented. "Cuz they left in such a big hurry."

Darryl ignored the comment.

"Well, at least now we know why it's going so cheap," he said. "This yard isn't really big enough for a pool. What were they thinking?" He slid the glass door closed behind him and shrugged at his wife, who was eying him suspiciously. He grinned and turned her by the shoulders. "We have more to see, honey. This way."

Julie allowed herself to be led, daring to hope that this time, they'd found the right house.

"There are four finished bedrooms, a den and three full bathrooms," Darryl told them, his voice echoing as they walked down the hall. Julie followed, trailing her right hand along the smooth oak of the railing cordoning off the stairwell.

Walking into the master bedroom, Julie knew she was sold.

Spacious and elegant, sunlight streamed in through double French doors that led out onto a spacious front deck, overlooking the cul-de-sac, with a view of the distant, snow covered mountains.

The happy young woman turned in a complete circle, taking it all in, while her husband opened windows and doors, stepping out confidently onto the deck with a smile of his own.

"Check this out," he said. A light breeze wafted inside, carrying the scent of freshly mown grass.

A small sigh escaped Julie's lips. "I've come home," she muttered.

"Pardon?" Darryl asked.

"Uh -nice home," she said simply, looking at her husband apologetically. He turned away, covering his mouth with a hastily raised hand.

Darryl grinned. It was no secret his clients were sold.

Darryl and Marc quickly descended the staircase to view the unfinished suite area while Julie lingered for a few more minutes, checking out each bedroom, before following the men downstairs.

This was the longest she'd cared to linger in any of the houses they'd seen. She could see their family living there. Now if only the downstairs space was big enough, it would be a perfect fit! It was already a huge coincidence that the house was now priced exactly within the high-end of their budget!

This house was falling into their laps! As though it's meant to be, Julie thought, as she reached the foyer.

Marc and Darryl's voices were muffled inside the unfinished suite.

It's about time, she thought dryly. I'm so done with house-hunting! Marc's supposed jet-lag seemed to be gone. She resolved to find out more about that later when they were alone.

Julie ducked through the partially open door and followed the men inside. The first thing she saw was a long, shadowed hallway, and concrete floors. Marc and Darryl were standing in an open space at the end of the hall. They appeared to be examining the rough two-by-four framing.

Before she could join them, a sudden wave of dizziness hit her and she leaned heavily against the wall. Spots danced in front of her eyes, and she found herself wondering how long it'd been since she'd last eaten.

Lots of light though," she heard Marc say, as he and Darryl strolled into view. "But who did this framing? What a joke!"

Darryl nodded in agreement.

"Hey! Honey you okay?" Marc walked toward her quickly and held out his hand.

"Fine," she said. "Just lightheaded."

"I'd offer you a chair if I could," Darryl said "Are you ready to go? You look a bit pale."

"Well," she said, trying to make a joke out of it. "I'm *always* pale, but yes, I am a bit tired." This house-hunting business was wearing her down, which was all the more reason to make an offer on this one as soon as possible. Good thing Marc was being thorough. She hoped he wouldn't miss anything important.

Julie accepted her husband's arm gratefully.

Marc settled into the car beside her and squeezed Julie's hand.

"Well?" he said anxiously, peering through the windshield as Darryl re-locked the front doors and stashed away the key once more. "What do you think? Did you get a good look at it? I think it'll work for us. Oh sure, the construction in here wasn't done right, but I'm gonna haul it all out anyways."

Julie raised her eyebrows at her husband.

"Did you buy it already?"

"Well, uh," he replied sheepishly. "Not yet. I guess we'd better make an offer," he laughed. "If you like it, that is."

Darryl re-entered the vehicle just then, and turned to his clients, a knowing smile on his face. "Well folks? What do you think?"

Julie smiled at Darryl and for once, she wasn't annoyed by his over-the-top enthusiasm. In fact, she shared in it.

"We love it!" she said. "Let's do it."

"Shall we use your table or mine?" Darryl's smile was all teeth as he waited for their reply.

"Let's use yours," Marc said. "Ours is probably covered in toys," Marc replied, reaching into the front seat to shake the realtor's hand.

Marc and Julie just grinned at each other. Their search was finally over.

Chapter Three

"Hello? Oh, hey Darryl, what's up?"

Julie heard Darryl's booming voice clearly through the phone, even though Marc was holding the receiver and she stood some distance away. "The sellers accepted your low-ball offer. Frankly, I'm amazed."

"Excellent!" Marc replied excitedly.

"Yeah, but the complicated bit is that they want a clean offer, with no subjects."

"Okay, what does that mean?"

"That means they're fine with the price, but they're saying: no appliances, no draperies, no subjects."

"That's silly," Julie protested. "There aren't any of those anyhow. But what do they mean no subjects?"

"They don't want any reasons for you to break the deal. Like for instance, subject to sale or a house inspection. They've said no to both, but I think if you agree to the 'no inspection' clause, they'll loosen up on the 'subject to sale' so you aren't trapped if your house doesn't sell in the time frame they've asked for."

"What?" Marc and Julie answered together. "That's a bit extreme, don't you think? Who are these people?"

"I haven't told you the best part," Darryl continued. "They want a really quick possession date. June 15th."

The line went quiet as Julie and Marc tried to absorb the information. What Darryl couldn't know was that the young couple were staring at each other with wide eyes.

Damn! Julie thought. It had been such a perfect idea.

"Oh geez," Marc replied slowly. "I knew it was too good to be true."

"Oh now, just hold on a sec," Darryl responded. "It's not done yet. As I said, I think they'll agree to a subject-to-sale, and 60 days' completion. What do you think? That's still pretty fair. You okay if we try that?"

"Well, it seems fair enough to them, but not to us. No house inspection? Isn't that kind of risky? How do we know we aren't buying a money-pit?"

"Unfortunately, they made it quite clear that a 'subject to inspection' wouldn't be accepted."

"Why?"

"They didn't say. Could be they've had some deals fall through because of that. They kept saying they'd dropped the price low enough that they didn't feel they needed to make any more concessions."

"Is that legal?" Julie asked.

"Oh sure. You don't have to accept their terms, of course."

Julie and Marc looked at each other. A heavy sigh passed between them.

"So, we either accept it as is, or we walk away?"

Marc mouthed the word sketchy, while Julie frowned.

"What would you do?" Marc asked his expression grave as he pressed the phone to his ear.

"Me? I'm not buying it. You are."

"Well," Marc looked at his wife, and seeing her small shrug and supportive smile, he plunged ahead. "The house is almost new. It's in good shape, so we won't be faced with aging plumbing or a leaky roof, right?"

"Go on," Darryl urged.

"And you think they'll go for that subject-to-sale with a two-month completion?"

"I think so, yes."

"And you said they're definitely fine with the price we offered? No counter-offer on that?"

"No counter-offer," he confirmed. "I'll be honest, I was a bit embarrassed to pitch it, since you're a pretty bold guy, coming in even lower than their twice-reduced list price. But heck, they approved it!"

"If we don't buy it now someone else will get it," Julie whispered urgently, tugging on her husband's free arm. "It's a good deal, Marc. Think of it. Twenty thousand dollars less than it should go for. What an opportunity!"

Marc nodded at her and walked slowly away into their small kitchen where he peered out the window into the back yard, the phone still pressed to his ear. He had a clear view of his son, contentedly digging in his sand box.

"Okay, go ahead and pitch the 60-day completion, and subject to sale." Marc was frowning and running a nervous hand through his hair again.

"Consider it done," Darryl replied. "Getting this much house at this kind of price is good news all around. You'll see. As soon as the market turns, you'll be sitting on a gold mine! I'll call you as soon as I get word on the offer."

Marc and Julie exchanged a long look. Identical lines of worry creased their foreheads.

Replacing the phone in its cradle once more, Marc took a deep breath and looked around at their tiny living room. The little plush chair still sat in front of the television and the contents of their son's large, but now virtually empty toy box lay strewn everywhere. Children's books, videotapes and scattered Lego covered the modest coffee table and spilled onto the floor.

"I can't wait to have a play room," he muttered.

"Me too," Julie agreed, automatically picking up the toys and placing them back into the bin.

"I hope Darryl is quick with this," Julie said, her arms full of children's books. "Are we doing the right thing?" She asked.

Nervously, Marc glanced at his watch and parted the gauzy curtains to peer out the front windows. "I don't know. I'd like to say it feels good, but all I feel right now is sick."

Julie laughed. "Me too," she agreed. "Maybe that's because we're about to spend a LOT of money."

Marc sighed and turned around. "Don't remind me."

~~~~
~~~~

"Finally!" Marc banged down the phone receiver. "That was Darryl. The sellers accepted our counter-offer, honey. We just bought ourselves a house!"

Julie let out the breath she was holding and allowed herself to smile.

"They agreed to a longer closing date? And the sale of our house too?"

"Yup. The paperwork now says July 13th and subject to sale."

"That still doesn't give us much time."

"That's real estate," Marc said. "Nothing's perfect. At least we know the house is ours. No more surprises."

A month later, Marc would remember that statement and wince at the irony.

~~~~

Julie looked down at the package of photos in her hand. Darryl had left them for her at the real estate office, along with a copy of their contract.

"It's common practice for us to take photos these days," he told her. "The listing realtor is a friend of mine, as I mentioned. He dropped these off for you guys, as it doesn't make sense for us to keep them."

~~~~

Back in her minivan, she looked again at the plain, brown envelope on the passenger seat. Soon, curiosity got the better of her, and she opened the package, spilling out several color photos of her new house! It was quite a collection, and Julie was pleased to see there were photos not just of the house, but also several shots where the realtor had tried to capture a favourable view of the back yard. Julie smiled as she leafed through the photos, until she came to one that made her frown. The center of the picture was obscured with something round and white. It was fuzzy and indistinct, as though the photographer had tried to take a picture of a light bulb at close range.

Thinking it was just a fluke overexposure, Julie eagerly looked through the rest, coming across three more pictures with similar white blotches. In each one, a part of the photo was still visible, and Julie could pick out the partially obscured window arch from the formal living room, and in another picture, she recognised the double doors from the master bedroom. The third affected photo, of the upstairs family room, appeared to have a million-watt light bulb suspended from the ceiling! Julie frowned in wonder. That room didn't have any overhead lights, as she recalled. What a strange thing! Lost in thought, she continued to flip through the photos, imagining where she would place each piece of her furniture.

Suddenly, a car horn blared behind her. As Julie hastily checked her mirrors, she saw the driver raised her arms in question and call through her open window, "Excuse me, are you leaving or parking?"

Julie glanced at the clock and threw the photos back on to the seat beside her. "Crap! I'm late to pick up Adam again. They're gonna kill me!"

"Leaving!" she called out, throwing the van into reverse.

~~~~

I miss you," Julie spoke softly into the receiver. "How are things going?"

"Good! We should be out of here on schedule. How are you holding up?"

"Well it looks like things are finally falling into place. Darryl brought a couple through the house yesterday for a showing, and he's planning an open house for Saturday. My challenge is to keep it looking nice, with little mister trying to tear things apart every second."

"Well, we're gonna wrap things up here and head for home tomorrow afternoon."

"Music to my ears," she said.

~~~~

The next morning, Julie's eyes popped open in alarm. Oh no, she thought. Not today!

The smell was unmistakable.

As she rounded the corner of her son's bedroom, her shoulders sagged. Adam, naked from the waist down, was finger-painting. Instead of paper, he had used the walls and carpet as his canvas.

What's worse, it wasn't paint he was using to create this masterpiece.

He was almost five! When was he going to be potty-trained? The thought made her want to cry.

Adopting what she hoped to be a neutral expression, Julie separated her son from his artwork. She would now have to make several adjustments to the events of her already fully-planned day.

First, there was breakfast, then preschool and now she'd have to rent a carpet cleaner, to somehow get the house ready for the open house that had seemed like such a good idea only last week.

The list mounted in her mind as she hurriedly drew a warm bath for her son, while keeping one arm clamped around his wiggling body.

"Oh, no you don't," she said as he strained against her grip. "I'm not chasing you again."

"Stop that noise! Whoosh!" her son shouted. Another movie quote, no doubt, she thought wearily as he lowered him into the bath. Julie watched in wonder as her son's expression relaxed. "The station master came in," he quoted.

Julie smiled. "Oh, did he? And then what happened?"

As her son happily played out the rest of the scene that ran like a movie in his head, Julie shook her head in wonder and scrubbed the little boy clean. She didn't dare take her eyes off him for a second. Adam was truly unpredictable.

As he stepped from the bath, Julie wrapped her son in a fluffy green towel.

"All done," Adam said proudly, his blue eyes dancing.

"Yes, all done," she repeated, smiling at the comment. His little arms clamped around her neck like a vice as she towelled him dry.

She hugged him hard and closed her eyes, wishing that moments like these weren't so rare.

"You rascal," she teased. "Good thing you're so cute, so I forgive you for everything."

"Rascal," Adam copied, wriggling free of her arms and racing out to the living room.

"Come back here!" she called. "You can't go to school naked!"

Minutes later, as the two made their hurried exit Julie flung open the front door, to find her mother standing on the doorstep, reaching for the doorbell.

"Oh! Mom!" she cried out. "What are you doing here?"

"Oh! My goodness, you scared me." Her mother replied, one manicured hand pressed to her chest. "I was in the neighbourhood," she answered. "So I thought I would stop by. But oh dear, are you going out?"

"Yeah, preschool. And then I gotta rent a carpet cleaner."

"What? Why?" Her mother's frown was instant.

"You don't want to know," she sighed. "But one more step inside and you'll find out."

"Uh-oh," her mother sympathized, with clear understanding. "He's been at it again?"

Julie nodded.

"Adam, you mustn't do these things," she said to her grandson, her voice stern as she frowned at him.

Adam averted his gaze.

"Are you okay? Do you need help?" She said, looking back at her daughter, her green eyes inquisitive.

"Well, aside of being frustrated, angry, tired and running late, yeah I guess I'm okay," she joked. "In all seriousness though, I could use some help if you're volunteering?"

The older woman nodded, her expression serious.

"Great! But right now we're late for preschool."

"Okay, don't let me stand in the way," Julie's mother replied. "You take this rascal to school, and let me get the carpet cleaner. We'll meet back here, okay?"

Julie let out the breath she was holding and pulled the door closed with finality.

"Yes. That's great, mom. Thanks."

"Rascal," Adam copied, straining against his mother's hand.

"That's you alright," his grandmother called out, climbing gracefully back in her blue sedan.

Half an hour later, Julie was back at the house. She only had time to unlock the front door and make some coffee before her mom and dad arrived, the trunk of the big blue sedan popping open as her father pulled the e-brake. A self-satisfied smile on her mother's full lips and she held a large shopping bag in one hand.

"This should help," she said, coming inside, and placing the bag on her daughter's kitchen counter. Inside were several big jugs of cleaning solution and some rubber gloves.

Julie frowned.

"Not so fast," she said, reading her daughter's expression. "Come with me, there's more outside."

In her father's strong arms, Julie was surprised to see a large cardboard box, with a picture of a shiny, new carpet cleaner on one side!

Rather than renting one from the local department store, Julie's parents bought a brand-new machine! Julie hugged her mom enthusiastically.

"Now then, let's get this show on the road," she said, shooing her husband back to the car with a knowing smile. Julie's mom was suddenly all-business as she tied back her chestnut hair with a flowered scarf she pulled from her purse. "Your father will go pick up the mess-maker from school and keep him occupied til supper."

Julie and her mother worked shoulder to shoulder, putting the new machine to good use. Gradually, the house retained its cute-factor and Julie allowed herself to hope it would stay that way at least until the Open House was over.

"How long is dad staying with Adam?" she asked.

Brushing a stray strand of hair out of her eyes, the older woman pursed her lips. "Five, I think he said."

Predictably, at five o'clock sharp, Julie's doorbell rang.

As soon as she opened the door, Adam went into motion, heading straight for his favourite chair.

He was stopped only by Julie's automatic reflexes. "Oh no you don't!" She said, snatching him back before he could run across the still-damp carpet.

"Thanks dad," she said over her shoulder as she manipulated her squirming son out of his jacket and shoes.

"No problem honey," her dad replied, looking around. His heavy brow knitted as he took in the recently scrubbed bungalow. "Mother said your house was a wreck but it looks okay to me."

"Arthur!" his wife admonished sharply, emerging from the hallway. Stripping off her rubber gloves, her green eyes bored into his forehead but Julie's father happily ignored the comment.

"Well, thanks to mom, everything's fine now. Thanks for taking him this afternoon dad."

"My pleasure," the older man replied, chuckling warmly. Julie's dad watched his grandson with interest as Adam made minuscule adjustments to his favourite chair, ensuring it was in the precise center of the room.

"Well mother," he addressed, the corners of his eyes crinkling as he grinned at his wife. "Are you done fooling around here?"

"Fooling around?" Julie's mom echoed, in the midst of re-applying her lipstick.

Julie's dad turned and winked at his daughter. His ice-blue eyes sparkled with repressed mirth as he kept a straight face and looked pointedly at his watch. "It's dinner time. Let's get a move-on."

Moments later, Julie's father backed the sedan carefully down the driveway. As Julie locked the door, the TV was already on.

"I don't have the energy to argue," she sighed, flopping down on the couch to rest for a moment, as the preschooler fed another videotape into the machine. "At least you're occupied."

Julie looked around and groaned with fatigue. "Ooh! Will this day never end? Mommy has one more thing to finish. You be good," she said, wagging her finger at her oblivious son.

Adam was just beyond her line of sight where she crouched in the hallway, scrubbing away the last vestiges of that morning's disaster. Julie couldn't help feeling nervous as she circled her cloth over the paint, hoping that the label was true and this paint truly was 'scrubbable'. She did not have the time or energy to re-paint before Saturday!

As she checked on her son for what felt like the hundredth time, she wondered how old Adam would be before he stopped doing these wild things. He got upset by certain textures against his skin, but this? It was almost too much to take.

The thought of a quick cup of tea and a moment's peace was at the forefront of her mind. Despite the smell that still lingered in her nose, Julie's stomach rumbled. With all the excitement, she'd missed lunch, and now it was approaching six o'clock and she hadn't even thought about dinner.

But sadly, the tea and her dinner would have to wait.

Wet rag still in hand, Julie dashed into the living room to check on her son.

But instead of a peaceful scene, what she saw made Julie grind her teeth in frustration and anger.

Adam was crouched in front of the fireplace, his arms and hands covered in soot. Julie quickly realized he'd been playing in the ash like he was in a sandbox! The centre of her living room carpet, ordinarily a pleasing shade of smoky blue, was now hopelessly smeared in black ash!

"Aaaaaaaaah!" She screamed.

"AAAAAAH!" Adam screamed too.

"Adam!" she shouted. "What did you do?"

"NO-NO-NOOOOO!" Adam screamed. The child's voice pitched higher, making her eardrums pound.

Another bath for her son, and another bath for her sad, sad little house.

When was this day going to be over?

Grabbing her ash-coated child around the waist, she cast a rueful glance at the mess. Was it even possible to clean this?

Breathe Julie, just breathe, she told herself, fighting back angry tears. You'll laugh about this one day.

Drawing in a deep shuddering breath, she blew it out hard and ran another bath. She just had to pull herself together, and quit crying over stupid stuff. Autism is life-long, her Behaviour Consultant had said. There will be lots of things Adam just won't understand, but with repetition and training he *would* learn.

Julie gritted her teeth and felt the answering pressure in her jaw. He had to learn! Please God, he had to learn!

Adam looked up at his mother for a moment, his normally fair complexion covered with a fine coat of ash. "Uh-oh," he said seriously.

Despite everything, Julie started laughing.

She had a lifetime of teaching ahead of her and somehow, she had to get tougher if she was going to survive it.

The trick was to never take her eyes off him.

Take it one day at a time, her mom said to her.

The trouble with that sentiment was, every day seemed to have a million hours in it!

Later, as a very clean Adam happily munched down a makeshift dinner of peanut-butter sandwiches at the dining room table, Julie allowed herself to think about that indulgent cup of tea once more. Dinner would have to come from a box tonight, she thought.

She watched wearily as her son slipped out of his booster seat, the crusts of his sandwich forgotten on the place-mat. With peanut-butter fingers, he began methodically emptying each toy onto the still-damp carpet.

Julie ground her teeth in frustration.

Just then, as though there wasn't enough going on, the phone rang.

Maybe it was the realtor, Julie thought. Good! I'll tell him in person that the open house is off! Adam was hell-bent on making the house a disaster!

"Hello?" She answered breathlessly, wiping her son's hands at the same time. Adam protested loudly as she shrugged the cordless phone up against one ear.

Let whoever it was hear that, she thought. It would only strengthen her case.

"Julie," the voice on the other end was not the realtor and she felt a quick stab of disappointment. "Hey sis, I really need your help. I'm planning a birthday party for Dad, and whoah! Is that Adam? Yikes, I was gonna ask if you can you give me a hand, but it sounds like yours are full at the moment."

The voice belonged to her older sister Laura and although Julie loved her sister, and she loved her dad, all she had left were tears.

"Oh, oh, oh! Don't cry!" her sister responded as Julie tried to hiccup her way through a garbled sentence. "Never mind. Sorry I asked. Obviously, I called at a bad time."

"It's been a pretty chaotic day," came her mumbled reply. "I'll be fine."

"Oh yeah, cuz you totally sound fine," her sister answered with heavy sarcasm. "What's going on?"

"World's worst mess," Julie answered. "Look, I'm sorry. I don't even know where to start. The house is a wreck, Marc's due home tonight and there's a real estate Open House here tomorrow. You know that kid poured ashes from the fireplace all over the living room carpet?" Julie had warmed to her subject and her voice was escalating with every sentence. "And he chose today of all days to paint with the contents of his –"

"Oh geez!" Laura interrupted. "Do you need help? How does everything look?"

"Well, if I can get him to stop messing it up, it should look okay. How it'll smell I don't know. I'm exhausted, and I have stink permanently embedded in my nostrils. The carpets should be dry by tomorrow, I hope."

"You're gonna look back on all this and laugh someday," her sister said, deliberately trying to lighten the mood.

"I can't wait that long," Julie retorted. "Look, I'm sorry sis I can barely hear you over Adam. What's this about Dad's birthday?"

"Nevermind," her sister replied. "Sounds like little mister has been jumping up and down on your last nerve."

"Totally," Julie agreed.

"Birthday plans can wait for another day. Are you okay?"

"Yeah."

"You sure?"

"That's not really a fair question."

There was a pause, then both sisters laughed together.

"Alright my sister," came the doubtful response. "Make yourself some tea and put on a movie for that rascal, so you can relax a minute. Everything will be fine."

Julie laughed, wincing at the sound of her high-pitched giggling. I've gone crazy, she thought. It's really happening. Right here, and right now.

Casting her eyes around in search of Adam, Julie leapt to her feet again, cordless phone in hand. All other thoughts took a back seat as she flew into action.

"I'm sorry sis, I gotta go. That kid disappeared on me again."

"Call me if you need help okay? I have rubber gloves, and I'm not afraid to use them," Laura laughed good-naturedly. All Julie could manage in answer was a weak chuckle as she marched through her home, phone still pressed to one ear, in search of her troublesome son.

She still had her thumb on the disconnect button when she finally found Adam, sitting calmly in his tiny, round laundry basket, a small book in his hands.

The absolute soul of serenity, he carefully examined each page.

Suspiciously, Julie heaved a deep sigh, and another wild giggle bubbled forth.

What irony!

"If I'm lucky," she muttered. "I can probably throw something edible together for dinner and make that tea. You never know, I may even get to drink it." Julie hurried into the kitchen.

Unfortunately, what she didn't see was the thick layer of clear dish soap that coated the dark linoleum, turning it into an ice rink.

With a startled cry, Julie landed painfully on her backside, the momentum carrying her through the kitchen and out the other side!

Somehow, it seemed a fitting end to a very trying day.

The young mother sat there, in a pool of dish washing liquid, trying not to cry. But seconds later, she heard the front door open, and her husband's familiar voice greeting their son. Realizing help was there at last, a dam broke inside of her, and nervous laughter spilled out.

Seconds later, Marc found his wife huddled on the floor, hugging her knees to her chest and rocking back and forth. Exhausted tears rolled down her face, and although she was smiling up at him, giggling uncontrollably, there was no mirth in her eyes. Obviously, he'd come home just in time.

"I don't even want to ask," he muttered.

Chapter Four

"You're never going to believe this Marc," Julie exclaimed into the phone a few days later. "They actually made an offer, and it's a decent one! I think we should take it."

"You're kidding?" He scoffed. "After all those things Adam did to the house? Someone actually wants to buy it?"

"Yup." She was grinning ear to ear and wished he could see it, but he wouldn't be home for hours yet. Even though he was technically working in town and would be home for supper, she couldn't wait that long to tell him the good news.

"Well you're some kinda miracle worker then, hon!"

"Thanks," she replied. "The place smells like lemons but I guess that's better than the alternative."

"Definitely," he chuckled. "This calls for a celebration."

"You mean I get to sleep in?" It was Julie's turn to laugh.

~~~

"Honey, can you come in here please?" Julie called from the bedroom a few days later.

Marc peeked his head inside the doorframe. "Halloo," he replied, a smirk on his face. "Being summoned to the bedroom now? Alright!"

"I've got something to tell you."
~~~

"Okay, what is it?"

"I'm pregnant."

"What?" Marc's already handsome features came to life in an instant, registering first shock, then excitement. "Honey, that's fabulous! Are you sure?"

"Well yeah, as sure as I can be with a drug-store test." She held up the test wand for him to look at. "See there? The indicator has a line through it. According to the directions, that means 'pregnant'." Julie turned to face her husband. He was beaming at her.

"Oh Marc," she continued. "Now, of all times? We're moving! I mean, I know we wanted another baby, but now I don't know. I'm more stressed right now than ever!"

"None of that matters," Marc assured her. "Nothing's ever perfect. Besides, we agreed that Adam can't be an only child. That's why we're buying a bigger house remember?"

"Yeah, I know. I guess I'm just worried."

"Well stop," he said, breaking into another wide grin. "It's not good for the baby."

"Get outta here!" Julie smiled and tossed a pillow off the bed at her husband.

~~~~

The visual schedule was working!

Thank you, Ariel, she thought fervently as she watched her son move his finger methodically over the squares of his very own count-down calendar. He was counting down to their big move, and instead of the raging storm that always accompanied change of any kind, Adam was calmly counting how many days until he got to see his new house!

The Behaviour Consultant who'd been working with their family suggested it, and took the time to train both mother and son on how to use the visual tool. Now the home-made poster-board calendar was Adam's first stop every morning and several times throughout the day. There was a photo of the new house, glued to the July 13th square, and another photo, one of Marc was glued to a space two weeks afterwards!

Her husband had been called away again.

It wasn't fair!
~~~~

Marc had tried to soothe her. He would do everything in his power to get home early, he said. All his brothers were committed to helping, he told her.

"You won't even miss me," he lied.

"Just get home as soon as you can," she said. It was all Julie trusted herself to say.

~~~~

"Ass-ho," Adam muttered as he wandered down the hallway. "Ass-ho."

Julie's eyebrows shot up as she followed her son to the living room. Had she heard that right?

The young mother plucked the chart Ariel had given her from its place on the fridge, and dutifully recorded the incident. She followed Adam, working valiantly not to laugh. What a strange life I have, she thought. My non-verbal four-year-old starts swearing and here I go, creeping around like a detective! Laughter was out of the question, but Julie couldn't help feeling ridiculous.

As if on cue, she heard Ariel's words of caution in her head.

Remember to write it down, but don't draw attention to the behaviour. He'll soon tire of it, and move on to other, more appropriate words.

Following her son back to his bedroom, aware that the toddler cast sidelong glances at his silent mother, she watched him stretch out on the carpet beside his train set.

Again, he repeated the contentious word, flicking glances her way as he did so. Julie kept her expression neutral as she placed another checkmark on the page.

"Ass-ho … ass-ho," Adam chanted happily to himself, while he moved the small toy in his hand back and forth along a piece of railroad track.

"Looks like fun," she said at last, still leaning against his doorframe.

Adam, focused entirely on the toys in his hand, didn't respond. Not even a flicker of recognition crossed his beautiful face.

"You have such a sweet face," she said to her son, shaking her head and turning away wearily. "So how come you only want to say the bad words?"

"Ass-ho," Adam responded, looking up at her.
~~~~

"Nice," she muttered, dryly, placing another checkmark on the page as she left the room. "Ten to one he's going to use that little gem next time we're in church."

~~~~

"Call him again Julie," Maurice encouraged her, his expression stern. "Be persistent. This is a real problem."

Marc's eldest brother was right, she thought ruefully. The moving drama had kicked up another notch.

Her hands shook with suppressed anger as she put through the call on her cell phone.

"'lo?" came the curt reply. His voice sounded far away and Julie could hear a car engine.

"Finally!" She exploded. "Darryl, it's Julie. Where are you with my keys?"

"Excuse me? Your what? Who did you say this was?"

"It's Julie, and I need my keys! It's moving day, remember? Where are you?"

"Uh … Julie, that's tomorrow. Not today. I can't give the keys to you until completion day. I know you're anxious, but–"

"WHAT?!" The pent-up emotion of a night with no sleep, constant packing and worrying had taken their toll. She was through being nice. "What do you mean tomorrow? What's going on? We agreed on the 13th, and that's what it says on my contract. That's *today* Darryl."

"Look, I'm driving right now, so why don't we pick this up when I'm back in the office?" Darryl chuckled into the phone. "You can't expect me to break the rules and give you the key when the money hasn't technically transferred yet. Check your paperwork, I'm sure you'll see that it actually completes on the 14th. The money transfers at midnight."

"I know very well what the completion date is," Julie replied, her voice low and deadly calm. "You apparently do not."

There was silence on the other end of the phone. "What do you mean?" The realtor's usually confident voice had grown quiet and suspicious. "Where are you right now?"

"I have a rented truck sitting here in the driveway of my new home, and my brothers-in-law have begun unloading my living room furniture all over the front lawn, since my realtor has failed to show up with the key that he promised to deliver over three hours ago. The
~~~~

paperwork that my husband and I signed said July 13th, 1995. That's today."

There was no way the man could possibly mistake the outrage that was so close to bursting through the telephone.

"How could this have happened?" she heard him breathe into the phone. "Someone must have processed the wrong copy, somehow …"

The silence was awkward, but Julie waited. Let him figure it out, she thought. This is his mess!

"I'm gonna have to call you back once I get this sorted, Julie. I don't know how this happened. All I can think of is that somewhere there's a typo on the documents."

"Listen," she growled into the telephone receiver. "You are going to fix this, because the contents of my house are in the back of a rented truck that's got to be returned by tonight. My antique piano is arriving soon, and the movers are going to expect an *unlocked* front door. Oh, and another thing. The purchaser's realtor has shown up twice today at my old house, to see how I was coming along with the move. So, whether you think the completion date is tomorrow or not, everyone else seems to think it's today. I don't have another option, Darryl. And just in case you forgot, Marc is out of town. So, this is what you are going to do: You're going to get over here NOW, and place those keys into my hand, unless you'd like all my furniture unloaded onto your front lawn, and some very irate house guests spending the night. See you soon, Darryl."

Julie didn't wait for a reply. She punched the button to end the call and stuffed the cell phone back into her pocket as she took a deep, shuddering breath.

"Wow! Atta girl!" Maurice praised her, a smile on his face as he clapped his hands together in gentle applause. "He can't fail to understand that."

"Let's hope so," Julie replied. "If not, I don't know what I'll do."

Ten minutes later, a black BMW screeched to a halt and double-parked in front of Julie's new home. Six people watched its arrival from a mock living room set up on the front lawn. It was complete with sofa, love seat, area rug, a coffee table and accent lamps. The entire set up was staged by Marc's brothers, for the benefit of Julie and the panicked man inside the car. Biting his lip nervously, with a wary eye on the crew who lounged idly in the mock living room, he handed an envelope to Victor, Marc's second older brother, who had stepped forward to confront the man.

"You must be Darryl," he said. "I wouldn't let Julie see you. She's pissed. We wanted to avoid bloodshed, so we sent her to get food. I'd get outta here before she gets back if I were you."

"Make sure she gets this, with my apologies? I still don't know how this happened."

"Sure," Victor answered. "I'll give her the key, but I doubt she'll accept the apology. You should invest in a calendar."

Darryl gathered the shreds of his dignity and jogged down the driveway to his waiting car. He was gone in seconds.

When Julie pulled up, a few minutes later, the scene they'd staged for the realtor was still in place.

"What are you doing!?" she screamed, nearly dropping the plastic bags full of food and drinks.

"You like it?" Victor spoke up. "Well, we thought, since you don't have the key, and it's summer anyways, this'll do for now. Think of it, you don't even have to vacuum."

Julie just stared, open-mouthed.

"You don't have to thank us; your breathless silence is thanks enough."

Maurice, shoving his younger brother aside, took pity on her. Stroking his bearded chin, he draped an arm around her shoulders and squeezed. "Relax, sis. It's a joke. Your realtor was just here, but he left fast. I think you scared him. He left something for you. Here." Maurice handed the envelope to Julie.

"Thank God!" Julie breathed, tearing open the envelope. There was no note, nothing to explain or apologize. Just keys.

"That's just as well, I didn't want to talk to him anyways," she muttered. "But did you really do all this just for a joke?" She swept her arm in the direction of the front lawn.

"Of course," he answered. "We had time. Pretty good, eh?"

"You guys," she muttered. A weary chuckle soon turned into an almost hysterical laugh, and Maurice, with a strange expression, plucked the key from her hand.

"Let's get going, shall we? This way everyone! Moving day is back on!"

~~~~
~~~~

Julie knew the walls were there, but with all the boxes, she couldn't see them anymore. It was strange and overwhelming, being hemmed in by cardboard. There was so much work ahead of her!

She had to stop thinking like that. Marc would be home in a few more days and he'd get right in there to help. She had to shake this off.

What a day. Emotionally exhausting, culminating with an Autism meltdown! Adam had been so carefully prepared, she thought ruefully. Walking trips around their new neighbourhood, larger-than-life calendars posted in their old home, personalized stories to explain what was happening.

They'd done everything in their power, but it wasn't enough.

As she closed her eyes, her face tightened at the memories that flooded in. She could still see him kicking and screaming, his little face beet red and contorted in a frightening expression of rage. My poor little boy, she thought.

Autism didn't care if you were tired, overwhelmed or busy. Her little son saw and experienced the world in a different way, but it seemed to Julie as though it was never the same way twice.

"Fingers crossed, you stay asleep," she mumbled. Yawning deeply, she stretched her tired arms over her head and let them fall back against her sides, as she stood in her son's doorway. As tired as she was, Julie couldn't help smiling. Even in sleep Adam still gripped his favourite toy in one hand. His tousled blonde hair curled damply across his forehead in the after-effects of his tantrums, but the rhythmic rise and fall of his chest said that the storms were over and he was finally asleep for the night.

"Good thing you're so cute," she whispered. "When you look like that I forgive you for everything."

Making her way back towards her own room, she paused. Had the staircase just creaked or was that her imagination?

Listening intently for another noise but hearing none, Julie chalked it up to imagination and went to bed.

~~~~

Julie grinned as she pulled the hood of her rain jacket further over her head. The rain continued to pour from the sky, but she stood out in it anyways, smiling as she watched the efforts of her son.

The grass they both stood on was sparse and scrubby, with bare patches of earth showing through like some kind of patchwork quilt
~~~~

gone horribly wrong. In truth, there was more mud than grass but Adam, happily played in the puddles that dotted the small yard. Now, the only clean part of the child seemed to be his teeth, which gleamed white against the dark brown mud caked over his face.

"Mud puddles," she muttered. "Hundreds of dollars in toys, and here we are playing in the mud."

With a grin, she raised the camera to her eye and clicked the shutter. "Awesome," she said, shoving the camera back in her pocket. "That's a keeper."

As usual, Adam didn't say a word as he attempted to dash past her. Julie, with a practiced hand scooped him up as he ran, large chunks of mud falling off in the process. "Not so fast," she said. "You're destined for the bath."

Adam squealed and wiggled in her arms, but she held tight. Mother muscles, she thought wryly, tightening her grip and mounting the stairs. It had already been two weeks since the big move and Marc was finally coming home. Julie wanted everything in readiness.

Thinking of Marc made her smile. This was the first time her husband would see the new home as theirs. The last time Marc was there, it was just another house for sale.

"You'd better give me directions so I don't get lost on my way home," he'd joked during their evening call the night before.

Julie smiled as she reached the sliding glass door and pulled it open.

CRASH! TINKLE. CRASH!

"What in blazes?!?" she cried.

It was the unmistakable sound of breaking glass.

That was inside the house!

The cat?

A quick darting gaze around the family room where she stood revealed their Siamese, blinking sleepily at her from the couch.

Julie's heart clenched. There was no one else home.

"Oh my God! The door!"

Julie rushed inside still clasping the toddler to her body.

She pictured the inset windows in her double front doors, smashed beyond recognition, while someone with bad intentions reached inside to unlock the door and step inside.

Cautiously Julie tried to peer down into the foyer from the top of the stairs. Adam resumed his struggling, but she held him tighter.

Too dark. Too many shadows.

Reaching behind her, she flipped the switches that illuminated both the giant chandelier hanging over the stairway and the one for the front hall below.

Even with the increased light, her view was still blocked.

"Damn!" she whispered. Heart hammering against her ribcage, she pulled the child down beside her.

She was torn between hiding and screaming. The good thing was that with her neighbours so close, she could simply scream for help. Someone would be sure to call 911.

If only she could see better!

Lying flat on her stomach in the hallway, Julie pressed her face close to the railing and craned her neck for a better view. Despite the earlier crash there hadn't been any other sounds. Either the intruder was waiting her out, or there was no one there, which was scary for a whole *other* reason.

Twisting her neck painfully, she finally caught a glimpse of the front doors.

Slowly, Julie stood, her heart rate returning to normal. No broken glass in her front doors, and no intruder.

"Ow! Adam!" she admonished. Adam, desperate to make his mother let go of his hand, had started biting her knuckles.

"Ma-Ah!' he screamed, the high-pitched tone felt like it would pierce Julie's ear drums. She released the squirming child, and watched him run for his bedroom.

"Well, it might be another mystery but at least it's not someone trying to break in," Julie muttered. "I guess I'll take it."

The top step creaked loudly as she set her foot down on it, and she winced. Despite her earlier statement, she knew she couldn't just trust that everything was okay. She still had to check.

Julie's breath caught in her throat and her foot froze just inches from the second stair tread.

Why was she looking at shadows? What happened to the light? Hadn't she just turned them both on a few moments ago?

A cramp in her thigh reminded her to keep going. Light or no light she had to see what was happening down there.

The staircase squeaked again. Oh perfect, announce me, why don't you?

Each sound was magnified in the abnormally quiet house.

Julie rubbed her ears, conscious of a dull ache and an odd sort of pressure building there. As she reached the bottom of the stairs, the pressure had sound as well. It was an odd, booming type of sound that she felt in the pit of her stomach. Julie frowned in concentration. It was as though waves crashed against an invisible shore right in front of her! It seemed to be coming from all around her. The impossibility of what she heard and felt made her grip the railing harder.

"What's going on? There's nothing there," she said, her voice barely above a whisper. "There has to be nothing there." The sound of her own voice lent an air of normalcy to a bizarre situation.

So, if everything was normal, why was she so afraid?

The word *paranoia* screamed in her brain.

What about the light? She reminded herself. A light doesn't just switch itself off. That was hard to dismiss. Julie rubbed her ears again, willing the annoying sounds to stop.

The sound of broken glass had been so loud, so unmistakable. Was it possible she was still adjusting to cul-de-sac life? Could it have come from outside?

The muted light from the overcast sky spilled through the oval windows in her beautiful front doors. Peeking through into the den, she saw nothing amiss there, either. Everything was as she had left it. Straightening, she walked purposely to the front door and stepped outside.

The instant her foot cleared the threshold, the roaring sound ceased and she breathed a sigh of relief.

"Finally!" She exclaimed, shocked, but relieved too.

Bewildered, Julie carefully remounted the stairs and went in search of Adam. Drying mud was smeared up and down the hallway carpet, and half the spindles of the railing were smeared with streaks of mud where they had crouched together, worried and afraid.

Julie just looked at the mess. She considered leaving it, and then realized that if she didn't clean it up, no one would.

"But not right now," she commented. "Right now," she continued, following the trail of mud that led to her son. "I'm gonna get you cleaned up, young man. At least that's something, I can see, and fix."

Chapter Five

Marc walked up the drive towards his new home.

Wow! He thought. I own this?

Well, he amended, technically the bank does, but who cares?

Marc and Julie embraced warmly, their kiss lingering.

"I've missed you so much," she told him, hugging him tighter.

"I missed you too. You've been busy since I saw you last." Grinning, he leaned away from his wife and waved his hand at the house.

"Yeah, it's a good thing that you come from such a big family," she told him. "Your brothers were amazing!"

"As they will no doubt remind me for many years to come," he joked. "But I'm glad they were here to help. Did you happen to ask them how much beer I owe each of them?"

The couple laughed together as they walked through the front door.

"Well, don't worry. There's lots of stuff that needs doing, but I'm here to help you now. It's good to be back, but it's gonna take some time before this place feels like home. I don't have the faintest clue where all my stuff is."

"Pick a box, any box," his wife answered with a light-hearted grin. "Your guess is as good as mine."

~~~~
~~~~

Ponderous. That's what she'd be. In no time at all.

The thought consumed her, as it had done for days.

Already, she couldn't fit into her favourite jeans, and that was just the start.

As she stared, ashen-faced into the ensuite mirror, willing her stomach to settle down, she heard the distinct sound of a child, crying.

"Oh fabulous," she muttered. "I don't even get time to be sick, now." The sarcastic comment came easily to her lips. She paused only just long enough to swig a shot of mouthwash and wipe her face. Marc had left early for work, so that left her on full-time duty with their son, but at least he'd be home for dinner.

Dinner. Ugh. The thought made her stomach want to heave again, but she clamped her teeth together and straightened her shoulders.

The wailing had grown louder and Julie's footsteps quickened to her son's door.

"It's okay sweetie," she called out, pushing open her son's bedroom door. "Adam!" Rushing to his side, she stared in horror at his arm, pinched between the edge of his closet and the partially open closet door.

In horror, she dropped to her knees and began pulling at the door, trying to free her son's arm, but soon realized that something was wedged against it from the inside. It wouldn't budge either way.

Her son's wails increased in pitch and volume. The sound tore at her heart. "I know, it's ok. Mommy's got it, mommy's got it," she chanted, hoping desperately that she did.

Running to grab a chair from the corner of his room, she stood atop it and with desperate fingers she pushed at the mechanism that would undo the top pin, and release Adam's arm.

"NAAAAH!" he screamed, his round face beet red.

"It okay, it's okay, almost there," she chanted.

The spring-loaded release was stiff. Julie pushed harder.

How had this happened? Something was obviously jamming the door from the inside, she thought, but how did his arm get in there?

At last, the pin gave way and the door pivoted open on one hinge, revealing nothing inside but a few boxes still sealed with packing tape.

But Julie only had eyes for her son. His arm was still impossibly wedged, his face contorted in agony.

"This is ridiculous! There's nothing there!"

As soon as the phrase left her lips, the door shifted again, the panels folding back on themselves, and with the gap between wall and door now a little wider, the child fell backwards, his arm finally free.

Julie wasted no time. She clutched him to her body, his cries filled with pain.

The young mother was too relieved to speak. Adam's blonde hair lay plastered against his head with sweat and tears. Julie examined the angry, red welt on his upper arm and carried him quickly to the kitchen, where she wrapped his arm in an ice-filled tea-towel.

Adam's cries finally reduced to sniffles, as he lay cradled in his mother's arms. In curiosity, he plucked insistently at the make-shift ice bandage Julie had tied around his upper arm.

Settling him into his bed with a favourite book, she turned to examine the closet door in detail. "I don't get it, there's nothing here, nothing to cause this."

The two boxes in the bottom of the closet were small. There was plenty of room for the door to swing open and shut.

And while clothing hung from tiny child-sized hangers above, there were no obstructions on the carpeted floor. Re-engaging the pin mechanism, Julie tried the door, which swung open with ease. The frustrated mother tried it twenty, thirty times, certain she would figure this out with pure logic.

Each time, it swung open and closed smoothly, the top mechanism firmly in place, the space between the door and the wall that had somehow allowed her son's arm inside, now impossibly narrow. At most, the space was barely enough for her index finger.

Julie shook her head. It defied logic.

Another mystery?

No! She wouldn't think that way. The door was simply defective, somehow. It didn't matter that she couldn't re-create the incident. It was simply defective.

The statement felt good. Yes, a defective door. Well, she knew how to handle that.

Within minutes, Julie was carrying the door down the hallway, to the garage. Let Marc deal with it, she thought. It's safer this way.

Adam watched his mother with interest as she manoeuvred the awkward item down the staircase.

"Enough of this nonsense," she said angrily, feeling the rage fuel her muscles. "Nobody gets to hurt my son!"

Julie let the spring-loaded garage door close behind her with a bang. That door would stay there, she vowed, until her husband could have a look at it. Re-mounting the stairs, she was startled to see Adam's tear-streaked face pressed up against the spindles of the upstairs railing.

"Mommy's here sweetheart," she said, feeling her eyes welling up with tears of her own. She hated seeing her child so afraid. "That bad door can't hurt you anymore."

It wasn't until she lay in bed that night and her thoughts began to slow down that she realized the implications behind her vehement statement.

'Nobody gets to hurt my son' is what she'd said. Now why had she said that? It should have been 'nothing gets to hurt my son'. It was semantics of course, a turn of phrase and yet, the thought bothered her so much that she couldn't let it go. Julie listened to her husband's contented snores and smiled. It was good to have him home. Maybe she'd finally be able to get some rest with two parents on the job.

Opening the book that lay on her bed stand, <u>A Parent's Guide to Autism</u> she took a deep breath and began to read. She'd only gotten through the first paragraph, however, when a small movement caught her attention. She turned automatically to look at the doorway, expecting to see her son but it was empty. The door stood open, and shadows draped the hallway as they would in any house.

Casper, their Siamese cat, lay curled at her husband's feet.

Everything was as it should be, and yet she couldn't shake the feeling that something was wrong.

Julie frowned. The air around her had turned ultra-cool. In the summer heat the temperature difference was welcome, albeit puzzling. She squinted up at the ceiling fan but noticed it wasn't moving. That was on when they went to bed, wasn't it? Marc was usually so meticulous about those things.

A cool breeze brushed the exposed skin on her legs. Wriggling them back under the sheets, Julie shivered, despite the temperature. She felt vulnerable, as though she'd been put on display.

Marc suspected this paranoia was due to the closeness of their neighbours and the thinness of their walls, but Julie wasn't so sure.

It was a long time before she could stop staring at the shadow draped hallway, and longer still before she turned out the light and allowed her eyelids to close.

~~~~

"Marc, I need to talk with you this morning," Julie said, her voice slurred with fatigue.

"Go back to sleep, Adam's not up yet. It's early." Her husband soothed as he shut off the alarm and swung his legs out of bed.

"No really, I mean it. We have to talk."

Marc turned to his wife for a second look and saw her solemn expression. "Oka-ay," he said, his easy grin becoming a frown.

"That closet door yesterday," she began, sitting up in bed, she shook her head slowly, trying to clear her thoughts. ""I can't figure it out. There's nothing wrong with it, is there? Did you look at it last night?"

Marc cleared his throat, and went to the dresser to pick out his clothes for the day.

His shoulders slumped slightly as he faced her. "No, I can't see anything wrong with it, but there could be something with the track in his room. I'll look when I get a minute, but I don't have time right now."

"I wasn't gonna suggest you look at it now," his wife answered, folding her arms.

"Okay, well if that's all you wanted to talk about, I gotta get in the shower. I'm doing a job at the far end of the city today, so I have to leave early."

A deep sigh escaped Julie's lips as she watched her husband disappear into the ensuite washroom. A few moments later, she heard the shower start.

"Well, that was a productive conversation," she muttered angrily, tossing aside the covers. "I might as well go make some coffee. There's no way I can go back to sleep now."
~~~~

Chapter Six

"Woof, woof! Woof-woof-woof-woof-woof!"

The insistent sound resonated in the quiet neighbourhood.

Keisha was loyal and strong and of course, being part Samoyed she was also a beautiful dog, with snow white fur and long, elegant limbs. Julie wasn't convinced the beautiful dog was all that bright, but she was certainly a loving pet.

Her incessant barking was a real problem, however.

"Sorry," Julie called softly to the annoyed neighbours who gathered on their back porches to direct dark looks at Julie's house. It was the time of night when young children had been put to bed, and weary parents were trying to relax.

Keisha's fierce barking was definitely not welcome.

Julie clomped down the back porch stairs in Marc's runners, the only thing she could find in a hurry. "As if this will do any good," she muttered. "Damn dog doesn't know what she wants!" Julie and Marc had been repeating this process for days. In a frenzy, the dog barked to be let outside, and then once in the backyard, safely clipped to her lead, the normally social dog would cower under the porch, whining and howling until they brought her in again.

At first, they thought it was merely a bid for attention, that maybe the dog wasn't adjusting to her new home as well as they'd hoped. But lavishing her with affection hadn't altered her behaviour in the slightest.

"What do you want?" Julie asked the excitable dog when she reached the yard and found the animal straining at the end of her lead, barking and pawing the air. "Settle down, now, settle down," she soothed, stroking the dog's silky head. She felt the animal press up against her hand, grateful for the human contact. Under her hands, she could feel that the large dog was trembling.

"Silly dog," she said, un-doing the lead she allowed the young animal to scamper up the steps. "What could you possibly be afraid of out here?"

Back inside the house, Julie commanded the dog to sit beside her. Petting and speaking in soothing tones, Julie was hopeful the animal might finally relax, but a moment later, Keisha's eyes widened and rolled to one side. Fearful once again, she raced into the living room and tried to burrow underneath the sofa.

"Keisha! Get back here!" Julie raced after her, worried that the big dog would hurt herself. "You're too big!"

Obviously confused and frightened, Keisha dashed back to the kitchen and sat, quivering at Julie's feet.

Her head jerked side to side as though she expected an attack to come at any moment.

"What is it girl?" she asked. "It's safe in here. This is our home."

Keisha took off again, barking and yelping, pawing excitedly at the staircase gate.

Quickly, Julie opened the gate and watched as her dog raced down the steps two-at-a-time, then turned around and bolted back up a moment later! As though she was being chased, the big dog nearly knocked her owner down as she ducked behind Julie's legs! As Julie stood there, gripping the railing Keisha peeked her head around Julie's knee and growled fiercely down the staircase.

"This is crazy," she muttered. "You're acting nuts! I wish Marc was here." Julie petted the silken head and tried not to allow the animal's obvious fear to affect her own emotions. "It's late, time for you to go to bed, missy. Maybe you'll feel better in there."

The vet had told them that inside a proper animal crate, a nervous dog would feel more comfortable, as it offered her a sense of security, and this was obviously missing in Keisha's life.

But why was it missing? She'd been a happy, well adjusted dog in their last home. So why was it different there?

Marc was working a night shift, something he rarely did, but he reminded her that it wasn't his place to question it. He simply had to go. Oh, of course he'd apologized for the crappy timing, but that didn't make it any better.

With one last look, around, Julie doused the family room and kitchen lights, grateful that the hallway was still well-lit. It was time she sought her own bed. Adam's contented snores made her smile as she walked down the hallway to the master bedroom.

I locked the front door, right? She thought sleepily, as she got into her pajamas. *Yes, yes I'm sure I did.* The thought of traipsing back downstairs in the darkened house was an unwelcome one. Whether the door was locked or not, she wasn't going down there!

If only night time brought actual rest, she thought. Dousing the hall light, she climbed quickly under the covers and pulled them up to her chin. The design of the doorway in the master bedroom was flawed, she thought angrily, looking once more at the shadows that congregated there. Even the lamp by her bedside, casting a muted glow over the entire room, could not erase those unnerving shadows. Although Adam was tucked in by nine, and fast asleep shortly after, there were unnerving sounds that echoed through the house when all else was quiet. Through it all, the dog whined and yipped in an annoying counterpoint, insistently pawing the front of her crate.

Julie's eyelids burned. The dog had been difficult all day, and Adam was only slightly less so. All Julie could think of was getting some sleep and yet the insistent barking and whining continued. She counted her blessings that Adam seemed to be just as sound a sleeper as his daddy.

It was nearing midnight when inspiration struck.

"The garage will have to do for you tonight, miss," she said to the excitable dog.

Keisha looked contrite on her doggie pillow, as Julie let the garage door fall closed. She hadn't managed to carry the awkward crate down the stairs. It was just too heavy.

"So there. Time to put this weary body back to bed," she commented, grasping the oak handrail to pull herself up the carpeted steps.

Exhausted, she lay down and tried to relax. Julie's eyelids soon slid closed and the house was finally quiet.

She awoke with a start. For a moment, she wasn't sure if she'd slept or not. The red LED numbers said 12:45.

Forty-five minutes? Is that all?

Julie sat up quickly, suddenly aware of a startling noise. What was that?

As her sleep filled brain tried to identify the distant sound, Julie mentally rejected each suggestion. A siren? No. A baby's cry? Not that either. A child in pain? Maybe ….

The sound intensified, until she was certain it came from within her own house!

Instantly, she was fully awake.

But something about the sound wasn't right. When Adam cried, he shrieked and there was usually anger and pent up frustration in the tone of it. This sounded almost soft and musical by comparison. And while it was still pitiful, like the person was intensely sad, it made Julie pause in the act of shoving on her slippers. What if it wasn't Adam? Who could it be? Was it possible the neighbours were that close?

The weary mother waited to see if the sound would repeat. Maybe this was another puzzling thing to add to the growing list of puzzling things. Julie's lips twisted as she thought about it. Yet another thing that Marc wouldn't want to talk about, she thought.

She'd only just laid back down when the child's wail came again. The tone was different this time. More insistent.

Bone weary, but knowing she couldn't just ignore it, Julie dragged herself out of bed. It didn't hurt just to check on Adam. Remembering the incident with his closet door gave her new purpose. As her footsteps quickened, the cries seemed to intensify. What would make him cry out like that? As she drew up outside the closed bedroom door, she realized there was no mistaking it. The desperate sounding cries were coming from inside his room!

Oh, my poor son! She thought, feeling instant guilt at having taken so long to reach him. Julie seized the doorknob and burst into the room, already calling to him. "It's ok Adam, Mommy's h–" Julie clapped both hands over her mouth to stifle the rest of the sentence as she stopped abruptly in her son's doorway.

Adam was fast asleep.

The noise of the crying child, so desperate a moment earlier, now inexplicably silenced. As she stood there, adrenaline coursing through her body with nowhere to go, her arms and legs trembled. A cold chill raced up her spine, and she cast a frightened glance behind her, down the length of the darkened hallway. Shadows played in the corners, as they normally would in the middle of the night, but to Julie, those shadows were sinister. The darkness seemed to press in on her with a physical touch. There was no reason for her paranoia, she told herself.

C'mon Julie, she thought. *Snap out of it! For goodness sake! This is my own house.*

Taking a steadying breath, the frightened mother pulled her son's door carefully closed and backed away. As soon as the latch on the door re-engaged, the anguished wail came again! Close, but certainly not Adam. She'd seen that with her own eyes. Casting a frightened glance at the shadows, her heart pounded as she realized the sound came not from her son's room, but downstairs!

Did she dare ignore it?

Julie's heart hammered in her chest as she tip-toed guiltily back across the hall. Her eyes huge, she huddled in her blankets, too afraid to turn off the light, and disgusted with herself for feeling that way.

As the minutes passed, the wailing grew louder, as though whoever this was, they need help desperately! Julie clutched her knees to her chest and rocked her body, her thoughts racing.

It couldn't be a child. The only child in her house was fast asleep! Even if this was, it was her neighbour's child, right?

But those pieces refused to fit either. Her nearest neighbours had no small children.

Her logic was sound, she thought, willing the grating sound to stop. So why did she feel such intense guilt just trying to sleep in her own bed?

Biting her lip, Julie wished for the millionth time that Marc was home.

But … wait! What if it wasn't a child at all? What if it was the cry was coming from an injured animal?

Yes, that had to be it! Nothing else made sense. And besides, animal cries sometimes sounded human, she told herself. *Keisha! My poor puppy, I left her down in the garage and she's gotten hurt somehow.*

Knowing she couldn't simply cower in her bed while their dog needed help and now more convinced than ever that it had been the dog crying the whole time, she shook off her fear and bolted out of bed, throwing on lights and charging down the staircase. In the same state of excitement, Julie hauled open the awkward door, but before she could turn on the light, a heavy body hurtled towards her with a fierce snarl and snapping teeth!

"Oh, my God! No! No! Keisha, down girl!" She squeaked, backing up quickly. The heavy door had already fallen closed, so Julie ducked behind the only thing she could find. A pile of cardboard boxes from moving day, stacked three high created a barrier between her and the dog.

Julie called out soothingly to the animal whose growls were intense and awful.

"Keesh, sweetie its mommy, keeshy, keeshy," she soothed. Tears flowed down her cheeks as she spoke, hoping that somehow the frightened animal would recognise her master's voice. In pitch-black, Julie groped along the roughly plastered wall, hoping her trembling fingers wouldn't encounter anything else as she searched for the light switch and found nothing. "Keeshy, keeshy, Keisha," Julie chanted. "Mommy's keeshy, keeshy." It was ridiculous, but it was all she had. Impossibly, her dog continued to snarl. She didn't know her! With the menacing growls seeming to grow louder by the second, Julie realized it was now or never.

She felt desperately along the wall for the light switch she hoped was there. With a sense of relief, her fingers touched cold plastic and the overhead light came on, mercifully blinding both dog and human for a few precious seconds, while their eyes adjusted. Julie peered through her fingers, as recognition slowly caught up with the startled dog.

Her snowy body, mere inches from Julie, rose from its deadly crouch and the bushy tail began to move. The eyes that Julie knew so well widened and softened.

Julie allowed herself a sigh of relief.

The dog's velvet-like ears pricked forward and she thrust her muzzle towards Julie's hand.

Instinctively, Julie jerked her hand away, before realizing the intent. With hands that shook, she reached out and stroked the soft head.

"Yeah," she said. "We're okay now. It's me girl." Julie's breath came in short, ragged gasps as her body dealt with the aftermath of terror. Keisha's snowy body was trembling too, the muscles still bunched with tension. Julie realized with sudden clarity that if she hadn't found that light switch, this could have been a very different outcome.

Woman and dog stood together in a circle of debris. Cardboard boxes all around them were tipped over and ripped open, the contents flung in a wide arc. Julie looked around at the mess. How could one dog do all this? Had she been in a fight with someone down there? The thought was ludicrous, but Julie couldn't deny the facts. A fight might explain the sounds she'd heard, mixing and muddling with sleep deprivation. Clearly, when she'd come bursting in there, the frightened dog mistook her for the intruder and she'd gone into attack mode to defend herself. Logic told her Keisha was already amped up before Julie had even arrived.

"Oh, I don't know anymore," she muttered wearily, suddenly more exhausted than she'd been in her life. "All I know is, I can't live like this." Julie took a moment to inspect the soft fur for injuries before picking up the dog bed and shaking it free of debris. "You're coming with me," she said. Settled back under the covers, her bedside lamp on, she directed a wry smile at the dog, curled nose to tail beside the bed. Julie's vision blurred with tears. "Marc's right," she whispered. "I'm a paranoid wreck."

She should have been able to take comfort in her dog's presence. The slow regular breathing told her the animal was fast asleep. But even though her house was quiet once again, and ridiculously, Adam was still asleep, Julie lay shivering underneath her covers, afraid to close her eyes.

~~~~

The conversation was tense, to say the least.

"Marc, why do you have to go again?" she wailed. She was aware there were tears spilling from her eyes, but she made no move to wipe them away, thinking they might help her cause. If he saw how upset she was, maybe he'd change his mind and stay with her.

"Why can't someone else go?" she continued. "You only just got home. I can't be alone again. Don't you understand that?"

Marc looked away as he packed his suitcase in silence. What could he say? He knew he didn't have a choice in the matter. The boss said go, you went. End of story. He wished she would just understand that. Instead, she was standing there crying and making him feel like shit for doing his job.
~~~~

"Julie, cut it out!" He exploded, whirling around. "Do you want to pay the mortgage or let the bank take our new house?"

"What?" Julie's face reddened with embarrassment.

"I have to work. I … have … to." Marc enunciated the words with exaggerated care. "If I don't, I'm gonna get fired. Or maybe you want me to quit, is that it? Did we suddenly become wealthy and I don't need to work?"

"Of course not," Julie replied, her voice barely above a whisper. "I'm sorry, it' just ... well, it's just that you only got home a few days ago."

"Of this, I am aware,'" he snapped, turning back to the suitcase. "Don't you think I want to be here with you and Adam? Especially now with the new baby coming? I just don't happen to have a choice."

"Not at all?" Julie asked, her voice coming out as a squeak.

"No. Not at all," he answered with finality. "This is a job I'm specially trained for." He turned back to his wife and took a deep breath. "I'm sorry honey, but it's got to be me. There's no one else to do it. I'll call you when I get there, okay?"

Silently, Julie nodded.

Marc watched his tiny wife straighten her shoulders and wipe the tears from her face with the back of her hand. He wished he could make her understand. This was something new in their relationship. Even though neither of them enjoyed the time they spent apart, Julie had never acted this way before. It wasn't the first time he'd been called away for work, so this should be no big deal.

Marc zipped up the suitcase and lifted it off the bed, convincing himself that his wife's odd behaviour was just a side effect of the pregnancy. He cast a quick glance behind him as he wheeled the luggage from the room. Strange how the master bedroom gave him chills on a beautiful sunny day.

Julie had retreated to the kitchen, and was absently wiping the counter as Marc arrived. Adam lay on the family room floor, moving tiny cars back and forth, along lengths of bright yellow plastic race track. It was eerie how his son played, he thought sadly. There were none of the usual sounds another child his age would make. There was no 'vroom-vroom' and no dramatic smash-ups with explosive sound. Sadly, there was no attempt at interaction, either. The only sound a rhythmic 'swoosh' every time the tiny plastic wheels travelled over the same piece of track.

What he wouldn't give to have his child say: Look daddy! Look at me!

Marc could feel his wife's eyes on him, but instead of turning into it, he crossed the carpet and hugged his little son to him as hard as he dared. The child clung to his neck and squeezed back, automatically.

That was the best feeling in the world, he thought. At least I know *he* loves me.

The sun was still high in the sky, but a quick mental calculation revealed he would be driving the last stretch of this trip in the dark.

"I'll call you when I get there," he said.

"Uh-huh, okay," she replied, dropping the wet the dish rag back into the sink and walking over to him. "We'll be here."

As Marc kissed his wife goodbye he tried hard to think of something else. This was work, he had to go. It wasn't like there was any choice. If they wanted money to pay the rapidly mounting bills, he had to go. After all, he reminded himself defensively, he'd been making trips like this for years. None of this was new. In the old house, they'd treated it like a crazy kind of routine, joking about being eternal newlyweds.

But all that seemed like a million years ago.

"Be safe," Julie whispered, hugging her husband harder.

Marc wished he could think of something fantastic to say, but nothing came to mind.

<div style="text-align:center">~~~~~</div>

An angry growl resonated through the house, and Julie nearly dropped her coffee cup.

"Casper?" she called. This was the distinctive howl of a Siamese. They could be quite vocal when they had something to say, but this was different. It sounded like …pain!

"Casper?" she called again, going from room to room.

After a half hour of searching, and no further noises, Julie had determined that the opinionated Siamese was no longer in the house.

Realizing she was simply mistaken, and the cat had obviously let himself out through the cat door in the laundry room, she glanced at the clock. Time was cruel and unforgiving. If she didn't leave right that moment, she'd be late to pick up Adam from school.

It was seven days before Julie saw her cat again.

She was just putting a load of laundry on, when she heard a faint scraping sound. Looking up, she saw Casper, pawing at the cat door, mounted in the window.

"Oh!" she sighed gratefully. Opening the window, she received the normally affectionate cat into her waiting arms. But Casper was not the same animal as he'd been before.

Julie opened his favourite canned food and carried him upstairs to eat it, but as soon as his feet touched the kitchen floor, he raced back downstairs to the laundry room and pressed himself into the far back corner, where it was impossible to reach him. Despite bribery, repeated calling and offers of catly comfort, Casper continued to hide. Realizing her efforts to draw out the frightened cat were fruitless, Julie moved his food dish and cat box into the laundry room, hoping that one day he would revert to his normally social self.

The cat was never the same again. Half-wild, the normally confident feline ran and hid at the slightest noise, quick to use teeth and claws on anything that moved near him. He resisted Marc's attempts at play, and withdrew into himself, becoming eerily silent.

Marc and Julie were animal lovers, but the evidence spoke volumes. Their pet had been abused, somehow! The thought was deeply disturbing. Worse still, they didn't know who the culprit was or how to protect their beloved animals.

Julie's thoughts strayed to the frightened, painful howl she'd heard only week ago, and how she'd been sure it came from inside the house. Could it really be coincidence?

Chapter Seven

"Keisha!" Marc called, placing the food dish on the floor in the kitchen, he smiled as the dog raced up the back steps and ran into the family room, tail wagging.

It had taken the dog several weeks to recover from her scare in the garage, but aside from seeking out human company more than she had previously, the dog appeared to be herself again.

"Okay girl," Marc soothed. "Settle down now, and eat." He stroked the soft, white head and Julie saw the love in her husband's actions.

Keisha skidded to a stop, and sat down obediently at Marc's feet, but a moment later, she turned, the food in her dish forgotten. Facing the fireplace, her head tilted in fascination she stared at the ceiling in the family room.

"Keisha, here!" Marc commanded, trying to get her attention as he pointed to the dish.

But instead of obeying him, the big dog seemed not to hear.

Julie watched in amazement as Keisha kept staring at the ceiling.

It was an odd scene. Julie chewed her lip in wonder and walked over to stand next to Marc.

"Keisha," she crooned, "There's nothing there, puppy."

Keisha's gaze flickered towards Marc, then Julie, and back again to the spot on the ceiling, but she still made no attempt to move.

"Marc, what's wrong with her?" She asked.

"Beats me," he said. "She doesn't even care if there's food in her dish.

"Crazy," Julie muttered, turning away.

"Yeah," Marc agreed. "Well, I'm not gonna waste my day off just sitting here watching dog tricks all day. I'm gonna see if I can get some stuff sorted in the garage."

Julie smiled as her husband turned away.

But a moment later, she reached out to snatch at his arm before he could descend the staircase.

"Marc, look! You'll never believe it!" Julie whispered urgently.

Casper and Keisha now sat side by side, their posture identical. Both animals, their muscles stiff with concentration appeared to be staring with rapt attention at the ceiling, as though awaiting a command.

"That's creepy," Julie whispered.

"What in the world?" Marc muttered. "The cat too? What do they see? Is there something there? Maybe a bug?"

Carefully, Julie approached for a closer look, but shook her head, frowning a moment later. "There's absolutely nothing. I don't get it."

"Those two normally hate each other," Marc muttered.

As the stunned couple watched their pets in equal fascination, Keisha raised one front leg as though someone had just asked her to 'shake a paw'. Julie jumped in surprise, but Casper continued to sit, transfixed, at the dog's side, his attention still riveted to the ceiling.

Other than Keisha's one elevated leg, neither animal moved a muscle.

Just when Marc thought it couldn't get any weirder, both dog and cat, as though released from a spell, stood up and walked away. Keisha buried her snout into her food dish with relish, slumping and chomping the same as she always did, while Casper, tail held high, the tip in the shape of a question mark, stalked haughtily down the hallway.

It was ridiculous to fathom, but the couple had the distinct impression both animals had been 'dismissed'.

"We aren't telling this story to anyone," Marc said quietly. "They'll think we're nuts."

"Absolutely," Julie agreed. "My lips are sealed."

~~~~

"Again?" her plaintive response was a familiar one but this time he was glad the conversation was being held over the phone. That way, as mean as it sounded, he didn't have to deal with any drama. Julie was once again over-reacting to the fact that he was called out of town for work. It wasn't like he had any choice in the matter. Technicians were in demand these days, and usually the locations were remote. The reality of his job was, when they called, you went. End of story.

"It's only for a few days, and then I'll be home again," he said, bracing for the usual onslaught.

But instead, Julie merely sighed. "Okay. I assume you'll be coming to pick up a suitcase?"

"Yeah, I'm on the way now. I'll have a co-worker with me." He thought it only fair to warn his wife there would be a stranger in tow when he arrived. "I'll just have a few minutes to pack and then we gotta hit the road. It's a twelve-hour drive."

"Okay," she replied dispassionately. Good thing I just did laundry." Her voice was so soft Marc had trouble hearing the words. "I left some folded clothes in a basket on the bed. I have to take Adam to speech therapy, so I have to go now."

"Um, okay," Marc replied suspiciously. This certainly wasn't the response he was expecting. It wasn't that he wanted his wife to be upset or anything, but this was just weird. "You okay honey?"

"Sure, just tired."

"I'll call you when we get there," he promised.

"Sure."

As Marc hung up the phone, he was still frowning.

"Trouble at home?" his co-worker asked both hands on the steering wheel.

"I'm not sure," he replied truthfully.

~~~~

Julie was startled out of an exhausted sleep by the intense noise. She wasn't sure which sound was louder. The furious pounding on her front door, the dog's frantic barking or her son's terrified cries, but the combination sent panic racing through her body.

"What the hell's going on?" she screamed angrily. Her frightened mind thought back to her terrifying encounter in the garage. She was too tired for these bullshit games.

The pounding continued, now punctuated with insistent peals of the doorbell as Julie quickly checked on Adam. He was sitting up in his bed, his cheeks bright red as he cried. He was obviously just as startled and angry as his mother. Julie went to her son and gathered him to her body for a moment as she perched on the edge of his bed.

"It's okay," she said, hoping that it really was. "Stay here for mommy."

Grumpily, she stomped down the hall. The peel of the doorbell continued.

"Alright! Alright!" she growled. "I'm coming!"

Despite her instructions, she saw Adam out of the corner of her eye, coming out of his room and along the hallway towards the stairs.

"I said stay in your room, young man," she said sternly, pointing at him.

Adam stopped. His face contorted into a miserable frown and he screamed with all his might.

"Perfect," Julie fumed. "Of course, right? He never listens."

With a strange detachment, she flipped on the lights at the bottom of the stairs, throwing the foyer into full illumination.

"There better be someone there this time," she muttered. Keisha, sensing the chaos, barked furiously from inside her crate in the family room.

"And you're staying there," she called. Julie blew stray hairs out of her eyes as she approached the door and threw on the front porch light.

As light filled the space on the other side of the door, Julie let out a startled scream.

Given the impossible scenarios she'd lived with thus far, the exhausted woman was convinced that all she would find would be nothing, but instead, Julie staggered back in fright as the porch light revealed a tall shadowy shape on the other side of the door!

She watched through the wavy glass of the inset windows in the door, as the shape reached with an indistinct arm and pressed the doorbell again and again, pounding the door with an angry fist in between peals of the bell.

"Who are you? What do you want?!" Julie screamed, realizing belatedly that not only had Adam followed her all the way downstairs, but she stood in a well-lit foyer clad only in pajamas without even a telephone.

Her mind whirled as she watched the shape outside her door with wild eyes. He appeared to shake his huge fist at her and in her panic, she thought she heard an animal-like snarl.

Damn those beautiful, horrible front doors!

She was grateful for the sturdy deadbolt, but wondered at the same time if it was enough to keep this madman out.

"You'd better shut that eff'in dog up, or I will! Permanently!" He snarled. "You hear me?!" Julie recognised the thick speech of someone heavily impaired by alcohol or worse. The indistinct arm rose again, something that looked shockingly like a shotgun clutched in his hand. He shook it at her with emphasis.

"Hey! She was fine til you came along. She's barking because you're trespassing!" She shouted.

"That dog does nothing but bark. Are you so stupid you can't hear it?!" he shouted. "Day and night, nothing but noise coming from this place!"

The insulting words made Julie see red.

"What's wrong with you? Are you drunk or just an IDIOT?!" she screeched, unable to hold back her anger. "It's the middle of the night and this is my house! You'd better get out of here, I called the cops you know!"

"With what?" he scoffed. "Your magic finger? You forget, I can see you."

"Go home!" she yelled, determined not to allow him to see how terrified she was. "Don't you have anything better to do than come over here and yell at me?"

"Sure I do. It's called sleeping, but I can't do that with your stupid mutt carrying on all night. SO SHUT IT UP OR I WILL! I MEAN IT! I' M AN EXCELLENT SHOT!"

Julie just stared at the figure behind the glass. Was this really happening?

"You'd better get the hell out of here," she managed, her voice shaking as she tried to sound ominous. "Look, I already called the cops from upstairs," she lied. "YOU HAVE ONE MINUTE TO LEAVE!"

"Go ahead! You think I'm scared of cops? They'll be on my side!" he yelled.

"GO AWAY!" She screamed. She realized with a start, that Adam had come up behind his mother and was cowering behind her, clutching her legs. With startled eyes his gaze flitted between his mother and the man behind the door.

The stranger shifted his position as though to leave, and the glow from her porch light illuminated the questionable object he held.

A shotgun.

…I'm an excellent shot, he'd said.

Oh my God! It really was a gun! Julie gulped and backed away, her eyes riveted on the figure behind the glass as she clutched Adam against her. If he hit the glass with the butt of that gun, would it hold? Julie felt stupid all over again. Why was she so dumb? She should've kept her mouth shut and just raced upstairs to call 9-1-1. That was the smart thing to do, right? Now, the phone was beyond her reach and the police didn't know any of this was happening. She was all alone with this madman.

The man-shadow stood there as the seconds ticked by, belligerence and anger making him seem huge. He growled again, muttering some more choice words. Finally, just when Julie was certain he'd break through, he lowered his voice to a hoarse whisper and leaned close to the gap between her two front doors.

"This is my neighbourhood. It was just fine until you showed up! We don't tolerate people like you here. You and your freaky kid better watch it, and make sure that mutt stays quiet. I won't warn you again."

"You can't just go around threatening people," she retorted.

"Lady, I can do whatever I want," he threw back at her, as he turned away.

Julie pressed her back against the foyer wall and allowed a shaking sigh to escape her lips as she watched the shadow retreat.

The young mother stared at the well-lit entryway. Fear had robbed her legs of even the most basic muscle control. She slid to the floor, still clutching Adam against her body. He stared up at her, his little face frightened, but serious.

Julie didn't know how long they sat there like that, but eventually she realized she had to get up and call the police.

Pulling herself up the staircase, she watched her son climb the steps ahead of her and hoped that the police would care. The danger was past, after all. Should she still call? What did they do about stuff like this?

With her cordless phone in hand, her fingers hovered over the keypad.

Just then, Adam let out an ear-piercing scream. Running at top speed she arrived in his room in time to see her son gather breath for another shriek, his fists balled up by his sides in a show of rage, he beat his fists against the wall beside his bed.

"Shit!" she muttered angrily. "I might have known this would happen." He was obviously just as upset by the experience as she, but he was a child without words. Tantrums were all he knew.

Julie shoulders slumped. She knew this drill. If she didn't want that madman back in her doorway, she had to deal with Adam and do it now. Glancing down momentarily at the phone in her hand, she grimaced. She'd have to call in the morning and report the incident. There was simply no choice here. Adam took top priority.

Adam's eyes were angry as he yelled at the top of his lungs. She was grateful her parents hadn't moved in yet.

Dashing quickly to the family room, Julie snatched her son's favourite video and ran back, waving it at him, to get his attention.

The child stopped suddenly, his bottom lip still stuck out in an enormous pout, but at least he'd stopped screaming.

Feeding the tape into the machine, Julie shook her head. "What a life I have," she muttered, as she tucked them both onto the couch with her son's favourite blanket. "What the hell? Why not watch TV at three in the morning?"

She looked down at the child, now nestled securely against her, his cheeks still wet with tears, and bright red with fatigue.

Julie wondered what new surprises morning would bring. Her son's usual wake up time was 5 AM.

It's probably that now, she thought, yawning and rubbing her own eyes.

"My husband will be home Friday," she whispered to herself. Saying it aloud always made her feel better, somehow.

She'd talk to Marc about this whole stupid mess when he got home. There was no point in telling him sooner. What could she say anyways? And it would only worry him. Yes, that was a good idea. And the police? Yeah, she should definitely call them in the morning. That was the plan.

Julie awoke the next morning with a pain in her neck, realizing she and Adam had fallen asleep on the couch.

As she went through the tasks she performed every morning, Julie's thoughts returned to the phone call she needed to make.

Sure, I'll do it when Adams' at school, she promised herself, with one eye on the clock.

Because of their wild night, both had overslept, and now there was no time for the usual walk to the school. Today, she'd take the van.

It was just as well, she thought. One of her neighbours was a raving lunatic, and it was clear he hated Julie and her family.

With Adam safely delivered to school, and her son's Teaching Assistant aware that they'd had a rough night, Julie headed back home, her hands already sweating on the steering wheel as she thought about her call to the police and what that would entail.

What would they say? Would they believe her? Would they question her neighbours, looking for witnesses, or searching for this man? If they did, what would that do? It might make things worse, she realized.

She felt like crying but instead her expression hardened. She'd better not start, or she might never stop.

By the time she returned home, Julie had her mind made up.

Chapter Eight

"Julie, why didn't you call the cops?" Marc asked, frustration and anger evident in his voice. "You were in a lot of danger. That guy had a gun!"

"I know that," she said, her voice small. "Marc, you don't understand, I could barely function. I hadn't slept properly in days and it was almost three in the morning …" her voice trailed off. She knew he wasn't buying any of her excuses, and if she was honest with herself, they sounded lame to her own ears. Her eyes jumped to the digital readout on the microwave. They were well past their allotted time. She hoped Marc wouldn't get in trouble for going over the time limit the company set for him. Silently she cursed her decision to tell him during their mid-week phone call, but as soon as she'd heard his voice, it had just come spilling out.

"That's bullshit," he protested. Julie could hear his voice change and she knew he was pacing. "I can't believe you're just gonna let him get away with this!"

"Marc, look, I'm not the bad guy here," she told him. "Don't act like I did something wrong. I'm worried it'll make things worse for us here. You know what things are like with the neighbours already. And besides," she continued. "I don't know which neighbour it was. The fact is, I didn't call, and I'd appreciate it if you'd stop blaming me."

"I'm not blaming you. Look, I know you were scared. To be honest, I'm scared of what could have happened." Marc blew his breath out with a large, heaving sigh. "But what I'm trying to say is that 9-1-1 is there for this reason. The fact that you didn't even think to use it–"

"Of course I thought of it!" she snapped. "The phone was upstairs. I never thought there would be a psycho at our front door!"

"Well who did you think it was, ringing the bell and pounding on the door at three in the morning? Welcome Wagon?"

Julie didn't trust herself to speak so she just glared at the phone.

After a few moments of dead air, Marc took care to make sure his voice was neutral before he spoke again. "Look I'll be home soon and we can discuss it then, okay?"

"We've gone way over time," she reminded him, hoping to change the subject.

"I don't care," he said. "Just let somebody complain. This is important. They're lucky I don't just chuck this whole thing and head home right now."

Julie's eyes widened. Although she knew it was sheer bravado, and he could never actually do such a thing without being fired, his words were music to her ears.

"We both know you can't do that," she replied softly. "We're okay, honest. The crisis is over."

"I'll see you soon," he promised.

~~~~

The next morning, Julie prepared her son for another fun -filled, action packed day of school. She winced at the thought, realizing it was sure to be action-packed, but how much fun they would have remained to be seen. It was already clear that the school staff tried their best to understand Adam, but came up short most of the time.

Adam loved the short walk to his new school, mostly because they made a point of going early, so he could have some time in the playground before the bell rang. Julie wished she could share her son's enthusiasm, but the memory of her encounter with that terrible man at her front door was stamped on her mind, and she could think of little else.

Julie wasn't looking forward to this part. This required a different kind of bravery. True, she'd been practicing it ever since her son was born, when senior citizens turned to her and said,
~~~~

"What's the matter with your boy? Doesn't he have any manners? Why don't you spank him?"

Apparently, they thought this was good parenting advice.

If they only knew that it took every ounce of self control Julie possessed to simply grit her teeth and look away.

They knew nothing of her world.

It was the same scenario when she took Adam to the pool. The other children his age, recognizing his awkwardness, called him names, thinking they were far enough away that no one heard.

But somehow, they always heard.

Life had to go on, though. There wasn't time to wallow in the unfairness of an uneducated world.

The corners of Julie's mouth twitched at her melodramatic thoughts. Was she composing a monologue or taking her son to school?

She stood up as straight as possible and squared her shoulders. It felt like she was going into battle, but really it was just a simple walk.

"Hah!" she mumbled. "Nothing is simple with Adam."

Julie was careful to fit the newly purchased muzzle onto the dog, locking her securely inside her crate, knowing that somewhere in their normal-looking neighbourhood lurked a man who hated her family, and her dog most of all.

Glancing through the glass doors into the den, Julie allowed herself a moment to look again at the collection of favourite things, arranged attractively on the wooden bookshelf. She drank it in for a moment longer, before grasping Adam's hand firmly and stepping through the front door.

The sun shone, and somewhere high up in the trees that dotted the concrete landscape, birds were singing happily. Even the wild strawberry plants that dotted her sickly-looking garden were showing some signs of life. It was a bizarrely beautiful day.

Heart beating uncomfortably at the task before her, Julie gripped her son's hand and started out for the school grounds.

"Sidewalk please," she cautioned the insistent child. "Walk with mommy, no running."

Julie couldn't bear to look around at all the picture windows she passed. Was he watching her? That crazed shot-gun toting stranger lived around here somewhere, but where? Many of her neighbours went to work during the day, but it was impossible to tell which ones. The houses looked the same, day or night.

It made her blood boil to think of the experience, and she silently berated herself for not reporting it when she had the chance. Somehow, she'd allowed the circumstances to dictate a plan of non-action, and now she lived in fear that it would happen again, panicking every time her dog barked or her child let out a scream. It was no way to live, but what else could she do, especially now? If she called the police at this point, they'd just want to know why she took so long to report it. Worse still, the answers Julie could give would sound lame to someone who didn't live this kind of life. Besides, she thought wryly, they probably wouldn't believe the incident was real. Lost in her own thoughts, Julie nearly tripped over her son, who'd become fascinated with a rock garden in a front yard they were passing. Quickly she regained her balance and pulled him away before he could dislodge all the carefully placed stones. "Come on, here we go! Walking feet, let's go to school," she added in a sing-song voice. Snatching a laminated card from her pocket, she showed Adam the two picture symbols on it. One showed a silhouette of a person walking, with a big number one above it. The other, labeled number two showed line drawings of park equipment like the swings and slides that were his favourite.

Adam glanced at the cards briefly, taking in the details in the blink of an eye. Julie used to think he ignored things if she didn't belabour each point, but lately she'd come to realize that Adam understood visual cues like this a lot faster than most people.

Once more, his body leant forward and he strained against his mother's arm. Julie kept her eyes on the sidewalk, concentrating on the pressure she felt in her palm. That firm grip reassured her Adam was safe. It was only a short distance to the school, but it seemed to take forever. Her son's blonde hair glinted in the sunshine, the tiny backpack he wore jiggling around as the little boy bounced across the concrete on the balls of his feet. Julie smiled politely at the highly focused joggers or pedestrians they passed.

Just a normal day folks, she wanted to say. Nothing to see here!

At last the school and its colorful playground lay ahead. Grateful to relieve the pressure on her arm, she took the backpack from his shoulders and released his hand. She watched him run through the short, enclosed path that connected to the school yard. Adam, with single-minded purpose, ran straight for the swings.

There were other children in the playground, but she knew Adam didn't really see them.

By the time she caught up, Adam was seated, his strong legs kicking back and forth in a fruitless attempt to achieve momentum. Julie grasped the seat of the swing and gave her son a big push.

"There you go! Pump, Adam, pump," she called, mimicking the motion with her arms. "Back and forth, remember?"

Although she could see the other children out of the corner of her eye, and she knew they were staring, she ignored them. Her son didn't have the skill-set to socialize with these kids, and she didn't have the energy to explain.

At last, Adam swung his legs with enough rhythm that the swing continued on its own and Julie clapped her hands, grinning excitedly. "Good job!" she called. His answering smile was so genuine Julie felt a thrill in her chest. Quickly, she glanced over at a cluster of parents gathered by the giant slide, a hopeful and friendly smile on her face.

As a group, they avoided her gaze.

~~~~

Grasping the doorknob, Julie paused to take a deep, steadying breath.

Adam, anxious to go inside, pushed past his mother and ran for the stairs.

Julie caught her son just as he mounted the bottom step.

"Sit," she said, pointing. "Shoes off." Releasing his hand, she watched as the child dutifully removed each shoe only to turn and fling them one at a time, back towards the door.

Julie ground her teeth. "Oh well," she sighed. "Don't sweat the small stuff, right?"

Julie picked up her son's shoes as Adam pounded up the staircase with single minded purpose. As the familiar theme song of Adam's prized three o'clock cartoon played from upstairs, however, Julie tossed both running shoes behind her, neatness forgotten.

"I know I closed these," she whispered. Julie pressed her lips together as she cast her memory back to the hasty departure of an hour ago. She'd wondered at the time, why Marc had been so careless as to leave them wide open like that.

And now here they were again! Wide open.
~~~~

She and Marc were both extra vigilant about the den. Now that the new computer was set up, and their precious collections had finally been unpacked, they couldn't afford to have their son messing around in there.

And now, the confused young mother stood in front of the doors she remembered closing, wondering how the hell they could have popped open on their own!

Was something wrong with the hinges, maybe? Or the pressure-mechanism that kept them closed? As she moved forward to investigate, she caught sight of something else.

"Oh no!" she cried, rushing forward. "My collection!"

Julie had been collecting blown glass animal figures for years, but with the birth of their son, the prized collection had remained in a box, until now. Shaking her head sadly, Julie scoured the jumbled heap of items that lay on the floor, looking for the pieces of delicate blown glass she was sure to find amongst it.

"I'm pretty sure I would have felt an earthquake," she mumbled irritably.

Cleaning up the spilled items, while still searching for the remains of her collection, she couldn't help thinking how unfair life was, sometimes.

Suddenly, she stopped.

Beneath a layer of jumbled picture frames and books, stacked as though they were still on the shelf, lay her husband's collection of music CD's. It was literally impossible! The plastic cases were stacked atop each other, the edges lined up with a precision that defied logic. No earthquake had the ability to do that!

As Julie sat back on her heels, something else caught her eye. At the back of the seemingly empty shelf, one tiny blown glass figure remained. An elephant, his miniature trunk raised, glittered from the shelf triumphantly.

"What the hell?" she muttered. "Hello little guy," she said, taking the ornament in her hand. "Where are your friends hiding?"

Chapter Nine

The renovations were supposed to be simple and straightforward. At least that's what the first contractor told Julie and her husband as he strolled through the unfinished basement, making notes on a tiny notepad with the stub of an HB pencil.

"Of course, all this will have to come out," he said, waving one arm at the roughed-in walls and electrical cables. "I don't know who did this, but they didn't have a clue."

Julie and Marc exchanged knowing glances.

A short time later, they shook hands at the front door. "I'll call you tomorrow with an estimate," he promised.

Unfortunately, that was the last time they saw or heard from the man.

~~~~

"I wish I knew what it is about this job that keeps spooking these guys," Marc said as they stood together in the open space that would one day be a beautiful in-law suite.

"What do you mean 'spook'?" Julie asked, narrowing her eyes.

"I don't know what else to call it," Marc said. "Every one of them that's come here has started out telling me how easy a job it would be, and then inside of a few minutes, they're either making excuses they're too busy, or they don't return my calls."
~~~~

"Doesn't make any sense," Julie agreed.

"Did you hear back from the guy your dad suggested?"

"No. Not yet, I left him a message though." Julie rubbed her aching temples. "Hey, can we get out of here? I don't like it down here."

"It'll be nice when it's done," Marc said. "Can't you picture it?"

"I can't picture anything with this splitting headache," she retorted.

"Fine," Marc ceded. "Well, sooner or later we've got to find someone to give us a hand. Dad and I can't do all the work ourselves."

~~~~

Julie was a frustrated journalist.

The local paper had been slow to accept her as a freelance writer, but accept her they had, and now it was all she could do to eke out enough time to generate the copy they had come to rely on.

Julie made a face in the rear-view mirror, as she put the van in reverse. Her first piece had flowed quickly and easily. She'd been elated by the deep feeling of satisfaction she got from writing again. It made her come alive!

Her story was run in its entirety, which was a rare occurrence in the newspaper business. She knew that the fact they'd gotten the piece for free probably had something to do with it, but it felt good nonetheless.

And now, the article that was to be her sparkling debut back into the work she loved had become her enemy.

The paper had saved her a spot in the entertainment section of the weekend edition, dangling it like the proverbial carrot. They talked about taking her on as a contract writer, which meant getting paid! They were counting on her to meet the deadline, and once she showed she could do this consistently, they'd make it official.

Her thoughts strayed often to the unfinished piece, and she grew increasingly frustrated as the days sailed by with little or no progress.

Adam needed constant care, and because of the Autism, he had a busy therapy schedule that meant Julie was often in the car. It seemed the only time she had to work was at night, after he was in bed. Unfortunately, the thought of spending time alone in the downstairs den made Julie fearful. An involuntary shudder rippled
~~~~

through her body as she tightened her grip on the steering wheel. She couldn't shake the feeling that she was constantly on display, as if she were watched every second. Julie told herself that maybe Marc was right and it was the proximity of the houses that faced and surrounded theirs that made her so nervous all the time, but given the strange occurrences of late, even that didn't sound as plausible as it once had.

How ironic that the house they'd both fallen in love with still didn't feel like home?

The deadline was tomorrow, and Marc was in town. No more excuses, she told herself. She would simply have to put a brave face on and get to work. No more distractions.

Marc encouraged his wife gently that evening, noting the fiercely determined expression she wore all through dinner.

"This is your thing," he reminded her. "Just start typing. It'll flow, you'll see. It always does."

Julie smiled at her husband and trekked down the stairs to the den. Once more, that same feeling that someone was watching her every move made each step a huge effort.

Her long hair blew gently away from her neck with an icy breeze, and Julie turned to shut the window, only to find it was already firmly closed.

"Oh, bugger off!" she hissed.

As soon as the words left her lips, she felt different, almost like she'd been experiencing a different kind of writer's block and now she was free of its grip. She began to type, slowly at first but building speed rapidly as the ideas flowed. The old familiar feeling of being 'in the zone' asserted itself and just as Marc had predicted, she felt the article come to life under her fingers, pausing only to brush strands of hair out of her face.

With an automatic action, Julie took a hair tie from her wrist, tied back her long hair and kept writing.

How easy it was to manipulate this woman, he thought. Her mind was putty in his hands.

Her fingers danced over those keys. He was fascinated by this strange device. It was not quite a typewriter, but appeared to be a device of pure energy! Tentatively, he reached out to place his hand on top of the TV screen. Jagged lines shot across its surface as his energy mingled with its own.

"What the hell?" she muttered, pulling her hands away from the keyboard she stared at the warped images on the screen. "What the heck's going on?"

Jerking his hand back, he watched it return to normal. This was useful, he thought. Standing silently at her back, he noted with amusement her small shrugs and stretches. With pure delight, he touched her exposed skin and watched it respond to his icy touch. With an automatic gesture, the woman rubbed at the spot that now danced with goose bumps. How accommodating she was to put her hair up! He laughed.

Julie wished she could just switch the machine off and leave. This was torture! She was uncomfortable and paranoid.
"This is ridiculous!" she fumed.

It was much more convenient when they couldn't see you, but with this one it was more than that. No, this one is different, he thought. She senses me, but she doesn't want to.
He wanted to laugh out loud as he watched the young woman pressing a key labeled 'Del' over and over, erasing words she hadn't intended to type.

~~~~

Adam's favourite movie blared from the TV Julie peeked her head around the corner to see her son lying on the floor, half-wrapped in a blanket, seemingly hypnotized. She smiled, ducking back into the hallway to methodically roll more paint over the walls. Hair tied back with a scarf, she wore a pair of her husband's old ripped jeans -rolled up several times at the leg. Her expanding middle made his jeans a better fit than hers, these days. The worn denim, her face, oversized t-shirt, and of course, the length of her arms and hands were highly decorated with paint splatter. Her bare feet stuck to the plastic sheeting as she moved, reminding her again that she should have started this project with shoes on, but it was too late now. The pair of flip flops she was using to walk on the rest of her non-spattered floor lay in a heap to one side of her drop-cloth.
~~~~

She moved quickly, determined to get it finished before she ran out of movies and time. Marc would be home soon and she wanted to surprise him.

Julie grinned despite her feverish pace. She remembered their last house and all the changes they'd made. That was the feeling she wanted to recapture here! Julie was certain that by the time she was done, this place would finally feel more like home.

She looked off towards the end of the hallway where it dog-legged, toward the nursery. It was always a little shadowy at the end of that hallway, even during the day. Had she missed any spots down there?

The expectant mother laid one hand protectively over her belly. The room where they would soon welcome their tiny little girl was at the end of the hallway. "You're going to have your very own room," she said. "I hope you like it as much as I want you to."

Julie rubbed her tired eyes. What was that? A quick glance into the other room verified that Adam was still watching his show.

"Oh geez, Casper again?" She muttered. Striding down the hall, her eyes were drawn to the window in the nursery. The change table that sat beneath it apparently made a wonderful cat bed. A small amount of light filtered through the closed blinds, as the day drew to a close. More than enough light to find that renegade cat and boot him out, she thought. But as Julie got closer, she realized the change table was clear and the cat was nowhere in sight.

"Huh," she shrugged. "No cat." As she spoke, a cold chill shuddered down her back, and as her eyes tried in vain to make sense of what she was seeing, an elongated shadow seemed to block the light from the window for just an instant.

Was her mind playing tricks on her? Maybe she was too tired.

No way! When she was in mid-project, she was her most relaxed, rejuvenated self! Besides, Autism was something she'd been living with for years, so why crack up now?

Damn! Logic was supposed to help, not shoot your theory full of holes!

Resolutely, she turned away, determined to put such things out of her mind.

But there are some things you can't ignore.

Cre-ak. Slow and drawn out, the sound came from the baby's nursery. This simple sound told Julie that despite what logic dictated, someone was walking around in that room.

Leaning forward with narrowed eyes, her heart thudded wildly as she searched in vain for an explanation.

Cre-ak.

Somehow, the new floors in their new house were creaking all on their own.

"Fabulous," she muttered sarcastically, wiping her hands on a paint rag. "Is that all you're gonna do? Just stand there, watching? The least you could do is pick up a brush and help."

Bravado, and sarcasm. It was all she had left. Besides, even though Adam seemed to be watching TV, she couldn't be sure what the child noticed and what he didn't. This made it even more important that she not draw attention to it or seem afraid.

Ever since his ordeal with the door, he'd been more attached to his mother than normal, sometimes following her from room to room as she went about her daily chores.

Looking down at the wall in front of her, she noticed two small smudges in the fresh paint.

"What the heck?" she said, moving quickly to re-coat.

"Don't think about it, don't think about it," she chanted to herself. She couldn't help but notice the shape of those smears bore an uncanny resemblance to child-sized handprints.

~~~~

Shrugging into her windbreaker, she left for the short walk to pick up her son from school.

"I wish we could walk everywhere," she muttered, enjoying the rhythmic sound of her runners hitting the concrete. Looking around, she couldn't help still feeling impressed at the amount of detail had been put into the development of her new neighbourhood.

She'd been impressed from the beginning. Manicured grass, lawn ornaments, sculpted sidewalks and street lights too!

Yes, they'd been impressed alright, she thought wryly. Maybe too impressed.

~~~~

Marc was away again. She pressed her lips together and tried to put a brave face on it. He'd been home for a longer stretch than normal, and she shouldn't feel like this, but the moment he'd left the house, the noises she couldn't explain started anew.

Whatever this was seemed to know Marc was leaving and Julie would be all alone again.

Julie bit her lip and tried hard to think of something else as she mechanically circled a tea towel over the dripping plate she held in one hand.

A tell-tale click in her hands made her look down at the dish. A hair-line crack was just visible down the centre.

"Well, shit," she muttered. "Another broken plate."

Washing dishes was certainly not her favorite, but it was the first chore that slipped when Marc went out of town and she was determined that this time, the house wouldn't be a wreck when her husband came home. Looking down at the broken plate, she sighed. Maybe she should listen to music or something while she did the dishes. These intense thoughts were emptying her cupboards!

Behind her, a familiar sound made Julie freeze, her breath catching in her throat.

Footsteps on the staircase. Slow and measured.

Marc had left early that morning and wouldn't be back for weeks. It was just her and Adam in an otherwise empty house.

The sounds came closer.

Julie wished she could believe that any moment, she'd hear the squeak of the gate at the top of the stairs, and see Marc's handsome face appear around the corner as a welcome surprise, but somehow, she wasn't quite as convinced as she wanted to be.

"Marc?" she called hopefully. "Why are you back so soon?"

Rounding the corner, Julie looked down the staircase, finding it empty.

Adam, ran to the gate to stand beside his mother.

"Da?" he said.

"No sweetie," she said softly, not knowing what else to say. "No Da."

Adam turned to his mother, confusion evident on his young face.

Redirection was her best defence, and as she'd done so many times before, she placed firm hands on Adam's shoulders and wordlessly guided him back to the playroom, when all she really wanted to do was pack up her son and leave.

There was no longer any doubt in her mind. She and Marc had unwittingly purchased a haunted house.

But what could they possibly do about it? They'd sunk every penny into it and then some, just to buy the thing! If they left now, just as the previous owners had done, they'd be selling at a loss. And while the attractive purchase price should have meant they'd be ahead of the game, in the months since they closed the deal, housing prices had fallen to near record-lows.

"Casper, the friendly ghost," she sang to Adam, as she settled him back amongst his toys and sat on the carpet next to her son. Adam brightened at the familiar song and joined in, his garbled language skills making the best of the lyrics. Automatically, Julie began handing him lengths of bright yellow race track from his toy box so he could piece them together. She needed something normal to re-establish what was real and what wasn't.

"Sounds are just sounds," she reasoned, smiling at her son. "Sounds can't hurt us. Nothing to get worked up about, right, partner?" She gave her son a thumbs-up sign.

Adam held up his own thumb and grinned but as usual he didn't answer. Wordlessly, he continued to connect the pieces of track his mother handed him, with the patience and precision of an engineer.

~~~~

"Marc, I'm telling you what I heard. Adam heard it too!"

Marc pressed the phone closer to his ear. "You actually heard clomping sounds, like someone climbing the stairs? Was this while you were watching, or when you were still in the kitchen?"

"What difference does that make?" she asked, clearly exasperated. Marc's desire to hear all the facts was natural, but did he have to harp on these little insignificant details?

"I'm just trying to get a clear mental picture," he said.

Julie sighed. "I was still in the kitchen when I heard the sounds. Adam was playing in the rec room. He and I both came to the stairs to check. We both thought you were home."

Marc was at a loss what to say, but it was clear his wife was severely upset. Her previously flat emotions had swung in a complete opposite. Marc could hear the panic in her voice.

"Is it possible the sounds you heard could have come through an open window? Like maybe through the living room or something? You know that guy across the cul-de-sac is always making projects in his garage. I saw him over there last week, working with a
~~~~

grinder. If he were hammering something together, it could easily sound like footsteps on the stairs. Couldn't it?"

Julie's first instinct was to reject her husband's patient, though far-fetched explanation, but she quickly realized that if their roles were reversed, she would be having just as hard of a time wrapping her brain around this, too.

"You know what Marc?"

"What?"

"It doesn't matter," Julie said with finality. "Whatever it was, it's gone now, and we're fine. No harm done, just a bit of a scare. Maybe it was just those weird acoustics you mentioned, who knows? After all, our realtor didn't mention anything about uninvited house guests."

The glib comment seemed out of place to Marc, but he laughed along with his wife anyhow.

Anything to get her through the week.

Chapter Ten

The suite was finally taking shape. They had seen enough delays already, and fall was rapidly approaching. Just when they thought they'd have to do the renovations on their own, Julie's dad announced he'd found a contractor who would get the job done for less than they'd budgeted, and in a fraction of the time! It seemed too good to be true, but Julie trusted her dad, and knew he was a practical man so she tried not to worry.

When the man arrived to take measurements and talk about supplies, Julie was grateful her father was there to greet him.

"Fred?" Julie's dad inquired as he opened the door to an older man with a salt and pepper moustache and broad shoulders. He wore a baseball cap and a thick plaid shirt, tucked into faded blue jeans, a worn leather tool belt, complete with framing hammer and measuring tape hung loosely from his waist.

"Arthur," the gruff carpenter greeted Julie's dad, as he held out his hand. The two shook hands firmly, and Julie marvelled at how opposite these men appeared to be.

While her father was clean-shaven, Fred wore a few days of grey stubble on his chin, and his eyes, though crinkled in the corners with age and sunshine, seemed able to pick out every detail, while her father had worn eyeglasses since his early twenties. Fred appeared to be sizing up her dad as they stood together in the foyer for the space of a few heartbeats.

Arthur wasn't afraid to swing a hammer or get his hands dirty and in truth, his carpentry skills were good, but this project required speed and accuracy. Julie hoped Fred was the type of man who could understand and appreciate that, but somehow, she doubted it.

Her father backed away from the door. "Good to meet you. Come on in and meet my daughter, Julie. She and her husband live upstairs."

Fred looked Julie over with an appraising stare that made Julie's face burn, before tipping the brim of his cap. "Ma'am," he said.

With that, the gruff carpenter walked quickly past her and into the unfinished suite without waiting for an invitation.

With a startled look, Julie's dad quickly followed, leaving his daughter to close the front door and retreat upstairs.

It soon became clear that this man might have amazing carpentry skills, but he lacked all the usual social graces, seeming content to share his chauvinistic opinions without being asked. Julie heard him joking to her dad, that a woman's place was in the kitchen and never with a hammer in her hand. Comments like this were frequent, and so, in the days and weeks that followed, when Julie heard the rumble of his truck engine, she would race down the staircase to unlock the front door, and then race back up again so she wouldn't have to speak to him. The tell-tale bang of the two doors, as he entered her home like he lived there, meant that work had started for the day. Although his presence made her nervous, she was just grateful he showed up every day. The man knew his craft, even if he didn't know how to use a doorbell!

The move-in date for her parents loomed large on the calendar. Fred doggedly stuck to his own ideas, insisting that his design was the best, and no one knew his craft as well as him.

Julie bit her lip and wondered how much longer her mother would tolerate Fred.

The man foolishly scoffed at the drawings her mother had patiently created, throwing them on the foyer floor as he disappeared back into the suite.

Julie and her dad both winced, expecting the worst but instead of becoming incensed, Anne had calmly picked up the drawings, brushed them off, and made some adjustments. Three times she had similar interactions with the grumpy contractor, until one day she seemed to have had enough. These latest set of plans were labeled with the word FINAL and they'd been signed by both Anne and her husband, clearly indicating they were done talking about it. The couple brought these same drawings in to Fred, where the affronted chauvinist was busy laying out his materials for the day. Julie hung back in the darkened hallway, where she could see but not be seen by the cranky man.

As the carpenter turned, ostensibly to chase Anne out of what he considered his domain, the older woman simply smiled and picked up Fred's hammer, banging a nail through the top of each page, effectively pinning the plans to something the carpenter couldn't fail to notice.

Whether Fred was impressed with Anne's ability to wield a hammer or he finally realized he was being an idiot and these people were paying him, he finally backed down and finished the suite to Anne's specifications.

He, of course, was loath to admit it, but it soon became apparent that her mother's design made clever use of the square-footage.

And now it was finally all coming together.

Fred managed it all, and slowly the suite took shape. The ever-present baseball cap darted in and out of the house, carrying all manner of supplies, cautioning them each day that he wasn't a miracle worker and things take time. They shouldn't have given him such a tight timetable.

But no matter how much doom and gloom Fred heaped on them about the construction timeline, Julie couldn't bring herself to be upset. She was happier than she'd been in weeks, knowing her mom and dad would soon be living under the same roof and that meant she would have some much-needed back-up when Marc went out of town.

Funny how it was all working out, she thought. And even better, was the fact that while all the building and renovating was going on, there had been no more incidents of strange, unexpected noises or creepy shadows. Could it have been her imagination after all? Perhaps it was a side-effect of being too overwrought for too long? If that was the case, she thought, I'm not going to let it get to me.

The pressure over the move-in date mounted day after day, until Julie's mom made a startling announcement. It seemed she'd had enough of it too. She and her husband were going on an extended vacation in their new fifth wheel trailer, leaving Julie in charge of the last few details.

"Just use my sketches, dear," she'd said. "And don't let that curmudgeon boss you around."

The driveway looked bare without the trailer parked there. With the trailer gone, Julie had a clear view of the snowy mountains, visible over her neighbour's rooftop. She remembered the plans she and Marc had made while staring out that same window.

"Maybe this place can be all we imagined after all," she muttered.

Below her vantage point, she could see men and women with long ladders and buckets of paint marching up her driveway like a procession. A small thrill traced its way up her back. Yay! The last of the details were finally coming together! Now it was just the kitchen cupboards and the trim pieces and then her parent's home would be ready!

Just in time, she thought. They were due home soon. Just in time for Halloween!

Marc would be so happy when all their stuff was finally out of the garage, and moved into the suite. He had big plans for 'his' garage.

Julie wandered away from the window, lost in thought. Cutting through the kitchen, she absently grabbed a cloth and went to wipe the top edge of the staircase gate. Adam was constantly trying to vault himself over it, and his hands were usually sticky.

Suddenly, a thumping sound caught Julie's attention and her heartbeat tripled before she realized what it was.

Fred was back. He'd caught sight of Julie at the top of the stairs on his way into the suite, and had banged on the wall to get her attention. As she looked down at him, he touched his fingers to the brim of his battered baseball cap and nodded. A small smile twitched at the corners of his mouth as he disappeared through the door.

For a moment, she was puzzled by his strange reaction, until she looked down at herself and realized the picture she presented to a man like him. Standing barefoot, wearing a large, white maternity shirt and a wet rag in her hand.

Barefoot, pregnant and cleaning stuff.

"Hi asshole," she muttered through clenched teeth, fluttering the fingers of one hand at the already closed door.

No matter what, don't piss him off now, she thought, as the sounds of people hard at work below her filled up the silence.

Ah, Fred. He was nothing if not predictable.

~~~~

Marc picked up a long-handled screwdriver in one hand, while he searched through boxes to find the rest of what he needed to re-hang Adam's closet door. It was always like this, he thought. Finding the tools he needed to fix something seemed to take longer than doing the repair!

There were so many boxes, he thought. It was a bit like making his way through a complicated maze. A narrow walk-way snaked in between the stacks of cardboard. He'd be grateful when his in-laws were finally moved in. Maybe then, he'd be able to sort out this mess of cardboard and finally locate all the tools he needed for the jobs that kept piling up.

Marc stood looking at the nearly empty peg board in front of him, grateful for that small bit of organization in a sea of chaos. He wondered how much more time it would take, until he had all his tools hanging there. He'd made some progress already, but the unopened boxes labeled 'Marc's tools' surrounding him made it clear he wouldn't be finished for a while.

Crouching to cut open the box nearest him, he hesitated. Julie had written several words across the top instead of just the usual 'Marc's stuff'.

"Random bits of metal shaped like curlicues?" he read aloud. "What the heck does that mean?" Marc chuckled to himself as he dug into the box, discovering various clamps as well as the parts to assemble his bench vice. "That's what I get for letting Julie pack my stuff," he muttered ruefully.

But as Marc straightened up in search of a more promising box, he heard a loud bang on the other side of the wall. The tools on the board bounced with the force of it.

"What the hell?" It was just like a heavy fist or maybe something bigger had hit the wall sharply from the other side. But who was in the suite? No one was supposed to be working today! The heavy silver wrenches that hung so neatly on their metal hooks continued to sway gently as Marc carefully stepped around the half-opened cartons and made his way to the door.
~~~~

On the other side of that wall, was where his mother-in-law's kitchen would soon be.

Was Fred back already? The cupboards weren't supposed to arrive for another few days. Marc frowned. That guy never knocked or used the doorbell, so that was probably it. Friggin jerk, Marc thought, as he shook his head and took a moment to slow his erratic heartbeat. He could have given me a heart attack!

"Who's in here?" he called, quickly entering the suite. He was certain the heavy sound could have come from nowhere else.

But instead of finding the gruff carpenter hard at work, the suite was empty.

"Hello?" he called. "Anyone in here?"

The suite was well laid-out, with an open-concept floor plan. There was nowhere for anyone to hide.

Marc stood in the area that would soon be the kitchen and looked thoughtfully at the wall where he'd heard the noise. Soon there would be cupboards there, but right now it was just a bare wall. Nothing there but a few pencil lines to indicate where the cupboards would be placed when they arrived.

How was he going to explain this to Julie? He thought. What would she think?

By the time Marc carefully remounted the staircase, he'd made up his mind.

He would keep this to himself. Besides, things had settled down over the past several weeks. The last thing he needed was for his wife to get worked up just in time for him to go out of town again.

~~~~~

"Man, it's hot."

"Yeah, and the humidity's just making it worse. Weird weather for the end of September."

"Well, at least my parents are cool. They have air conditioning in that rig of theirs. Do you think they're in Arizona by now?"

"Yeah, probably."

Marc and Julie sat together, their matching lawn chairs drawn close as they watched their son play in his new sandbox.

"I'm glad you built that, honey, he loves it."

"Yeah. It was kind of fun, even though it took forever. I was half worried Fred was gonna intervene and tell me I was doing it all wrong."
~~~~~

"That would have been interesting," she laughed.

Julie opened the small paper fan she'd brought outside and waved it quickly in front of her face. She sighed deeply, thumbing through the book her sister had given her. "This sucks. My preggo book here, says I'm gonna feel hotter than everyone else by the end of this. I'm only going into my second trimester, for goodness' sake! Good thing we don't live in Florida. I'm hot enough now. I don't remember having this problem when I had Adam."

"Hmm," her husband commented. "But remember, doc says baby's nice and healthy. Probably already getting a tan in there too," he joked. "Besides I knew you were hot when I married you." He smirked at her and winked.

Julie shot an irritated glance at him and fanned herself again.

"Okay," he said. "I surrender." Marc held up both hands in a pose she knew well.

"Sorry, I don't even have the energy to smack you for that comment. I just don't feel very chipper."

"I know. Still feeling sick?"

Julie wagged her hand back and forth. "So-so."

Suddenly, Marc stood up. "Tell you what? Let's take the rascal and go get some ice cream. Would that sit ok on your tender tummy?"

Julie nodded gratefully.

"Awesome! That place is freezing every day of the year. Should feel really good today, with this heat wave."

"Alright. You're on," she agreed, the prospect of air conditioning giving her purpose. "I might not eat much ice cream, but I'll take a dose of cold air to go!"

As they settled onto the hard, plastic seats, Marc handed Adam his ice cream and grinned as the child bent his blonde head over the cup and began spooning it in without pause.

"Slow down partner," Marc chuckled. He looked up to see if his wife was enjoying the spectacle as well, only to find her absently poking a red plastic spoon into her own dish, a strange expression on her face.

Something was wrong.

"Jules, you okay?" he asked, hauling out the coloring book and crayons they'd brought from home. Adam was rapidly finishing his ice cream and would soon need a distraction.

Looking up at her husband, it was clear she'd been lost in thought. "What?" she asked. "Sorry, I wasn't listening."

"You're unusually quiet today," he said. "Anything on your mind?"

"A few things," she admitted, not looking up. "But I don't know how to say it."

"You? Since when have you been at a loss for words?" he joked.

Julie looked up at her husband and smiled. "Thanks," she replied dryly. "It's just ... you know those things we talked about before? Those things we both agreed weren't really happening?"

Marc noticed the emphasis on her words and the easy smile left his face as he darted a quick glance at their son. "Maybe we shouldn't talk about this here," he said.

"Humph," she replied, returning her attention to the table. "You asked."

Her husband looked up from wiping Adam's sticky fingers and frowned.

"What?" she replied testily. "Okay, so perhaps this isn't the right time or place to talk about it, but when and where will it be the right time Marc? We're a pretty busy family, ya know."

Marc tried to smile reassuringly but Julie was having none of it.

"I know it probably feels like we travel in opposite directions most of the time," he said.

"Okay Marc, here' a logic-based question for you then. What would cause the garage door to open if no one's near it?"

"What? This sounds like a riddle."

"I'm not joking," she said seriously.

"Did you see it happen?"

"No, I heard it from upstairs. It makes a very distinctive sound and shakes the house when it closes. So, what could do that? The wind?"

"Oh. Well, I don't know, the only way the wind could blow that door open would be if we had gale forces," he said frowning. "We know your parents are away, so it couldn't have been them."

Julie nodded encouragingly.

"I don't know, that sucker's spring-loaded. It shouldn't even wiggle." Marc rubbed his chin thoughtfully. "Maybe if it didn't close all the way the last time someone went through, then all it would need to re-settle would be another bump in the house, or a change in air pressure. You could have caused that by simply opening or closing another door in the house. Do you remember if you were doing that at the time?"

"I don't remember," she answered truthfully. "I guess that could be it." Looking down into her bowl of melting ice-cream, she stirred it absently, wondering why it was so hard to talk to Marc about this stuff. She knew what she'd heard. Someone had opened that door to its fullest capacity, and let it fall closed again. She'd lived in the house long enough to recognise that sound. The thing that chilled her more effectively than a bowl of ice cream was the fact that contrary to Marc's theory, she'd been alone in the house, sitting cross-legged on the floor, unpacking boxes, not opening and closing random doors.

"Do you want me to take a look at it?" Marc asked.

"What? No, that's okay," she replied, wishing there was some way she could ask her husband about the hundred or so other things that were on her mind. There was just no way to say that stuff in a normal way.

"Ready to go back?" Marc had one arm around Adam who was once again wiggling in his father's grasp and doing his best to slide himself under the table to escape. "I think we've reached our time limit here."

Ready? That's a loaded question, Julie thought. Smiling half-heartedly, she slid out of the booth to follow her family back outside into the summer heat.

~~~~

The incessant ringing of the doorbell brought Julie's head up sharply. Now what? Was Fred locked out? Or was it another door-to-door salesperson or someone else raising funds for something? One of the first things she and Marc learned about their new neighbourhood was that houses like this one led people to believe they had money.

Peal after peal of the doorbell chime told her that whoever it was, he or she was in a hurry.

Probably Fred," she thought irritably. Great! He finally learns how to use the doorbell and this is what he does?

Stomping down the steps in irritation, she was muttering choice phrases about the cranky carpenter. The renovations were basically done, so no doubt he was anxious to collect his money and start his next job.
~~~~

As the doorbell continued to ring, Julie resisted the urge to shout at him. What was so blazing important that he had to keep ringing it?

"I hear you, I hear you," she muttered, undoing the dead bolt and flinging open the front door at last.

But to Julie's surprise, there was no one at the door. The concrete apron stood empty.

Taking a few steps outside, she looked around, wondering if Fred had gone back to his truck in a fit of rage at having to wait, but the driveway was empty too.

Frowning, Julie wondered fleetingly if their neat and tidy neighbourhood harboured a prankster. Julie had only just closed the door again and turned around when the doorbell sounded again!

BING-BONG, BING-BONG, BING-BONG!

Julie jumped in surprise, but a moment later, a ripple of fear cascaded down her backbone.

She had a clear view of the space in front of her doors. There was no one there!

Julie drew closer to the inset window in her door. She could clearly see the button, mounted on the side of her house that controlled the doorbell. Nothing touched it and yet, defying all logic, the ridiculous chiming began anew while Julie stared, ashen faced at the empty space on the other side of the door.

BING-BONG, BING-BONG, BING-BONG, BING-BONG!

The impossibility of what she saw washed over her.

Taking her courage in both hands, Julie straightened her back and hauled the door open again.

"Cut that out!" She shouted.

As though she'd been speaking to a naughty child, all sound stopped. Only the sound of Julie's frustrated shouting still echoed through the deserted cul-de-sac.

At the home next door, Julie noticed a young woman with shoulder-length hair hauling a full trash can to the curb. She was looking at Julie with eyebrows raised.

"Everything okay?" she called kindly.

With an awkward wave of her hand, Julie replied. "Yeah, it's okay. I think the doorbell got stuck, that's all. Darn thing wouldn't shut off. I thought it was someone playing a prank. You didn't see anyone out here, did you?"

"No, I didn't, but I did hear the bell. It's pretty loud."

Yeah, Julie thought. No kidding! She turned back towards the button, wishing she knew what to do.

"Please don't come over, please don't come over," she chanted to herself. The people in her new neighbourhood seemed to be warming up to them, but the memory of her night-time intruder still loomed large.

Julie crouched in front of the device as well as she could without toppling over. Her sense of balance was worsening as her middle grew. Perhaps there was a short in the wiring, she thought, feeling dumb that she hadn't even considered the possibility before. But how was she supposed to check it? She was no technician. Experimentally, Julie pressed the button again, and heard it chime once only. Pressing it again, it still only chimed a single time. She had just opened the front door to go back inside when a deep voice came unexpectedly from behind.

"Everything okay here?"

"Aah!" she yelped, pitching forward in surprise as she lost her footing.

"Whoah!" the voice responded. A strong male arm shot out and caught her by the hand, another pressed to the small of her back as she regained her balance.

He was a man of medium build, with brown, wavy hair. He wore a pair of sunglasses perched high on his head and even though fall was already upon them, he was dressed in athletic shorts and a light t-shirt. His skin was sun-browned and Julie guessed he spent a lot of time outdoors.

"Hi," she said, still a bit breathless from the shock, but happy that at least this neighbour looked nothing like the man with the shotgun.

"Hi," he answered. "Sorry about that. My wife said you were having trouble over here, and since Marc's out of town, I thought I'd see if you need a hand."

"That's very kind," she stammered. "I – I don't think we've met yet. You know my husband?"

"Oh geez, sorry again." He made a face. "My name's Steve. My wife Shawna and I live next door, here. I guess I haven't met you, but your husband and I have talked quite a few times. Sorry I scared you. I thought you heard me coming. I'm not noted for my graceful moves," he said, showing straight, white teeth as he laughed as his own joke.

Julie grinned too. "Nah, that's okay," she said. "Thanks for catching me. I'm not noted for my graceful moves either," she said, patting her mid-section.

He rubbed his clean-shaven jaw as he turned to get a better look at the doorbell, pressing it once himself. "You said this thing is stuck?"

"Well," Julie coughed self-consciously, as the chime rang out a single time. "It doesn't appear to be now, but a few minutes ago, it wouldn't shut off."

"Weird," Steve noted.

"Hey Steve?" she ventured.

"Yeah?" he said, still examining the bell at close range, running his fingers around the perimeter.

"There aren't any, uh, pranksters living around here, are there?" Julie wrinkled her nose and cocked her head to the side, aware of how awkward the question sounded.

"Oh! No, nothing like that." Thankfully, Steve seemed to the think the question was funny instead of awkward. "Just a few adults who refuse to grow up." He turned and grinned again. "Well, as you said it seems fine now. If it acts up again, or you need any help with other stuff, you just give us a shout. Marc said he travels a lot, but we're usually around. We believe in being good neighbours."

"Thank you," she replied with a warm smile. "That's very kind."

"No problem," he said, returning to his own yard. "And good to meet you by the way."

Julie waved and darted back through the front door, breathing a sigh of relief.

"That went better than I expected," she congratulated herself. "At least I can cross one neighbour off my list of suspects.

Chapter Eleven

"Our first Halloween together," Marc enthused. He was working on the large pumpkin in front of him. "What do you think?" He turned it around to show Julie.

"He looks drunk," she commented, turning her head first to the right and then left again. "And lop-sided. Definitely lop-sided."

"Who asked you?" Her husband replied defensively, turning the pumpkin back around. "You like it don't you Adam?"

Adam paused in the act of getting off his chair and came over to where his dad sat with the pumpkin.

"You like it, don't you?" he repeated to his son. "Here," he put the open marker into Adam's small hand and guided his son toward the face of the pumpkin. "Your turn."

A thin snaky line appeared across the pumpkin's face.

"Good!" Julie said, smiling and clapping her hands. Adam turned slightly and smiled. His reaction was more valuable to her than gold.

"Sure," Marc replied uncertainly. "Every jack-o-lantern has to have a scar, especially a pirate."

"Oh, you're terrible," Julie joked.

Adam grinned at his father, and Julie's heart soared. She often wished it was possible to bottle these rare moments and save them up for when she felt so sad.

"Knock, knock," came a sing-song voice from the bottom of the stairs.

Julie rushed over to the stairs and smiled down at her mother, who was just emerging from their newly renovated suite.

"C'mon up mom, we're making a jack o' lantern. You're just in time. We need an artist's eye."

Julie's mother climbed the steps, her smile widening as she saw her grandson.

"There's my boy," she said. Gaining the second floor, she crouched and scooped him into her arms for a short hug.

Catching sight of the pumpkin with its happy, toothy grin and jagged 'scar' she laughed. "Wait 'til Grandpa sees this," she said. "He'll love it!"

As trick-or-treaters flooded the neighbourhood, Pirate Jack-O-Lantern sat proudly in the front window, sporting a huge, jagged scar. Marc turned up the volume on the stereo that he'd set up on the dining room table. Eager to have their first Halloween be a huge success, Marc had purchased a special effects CD for the occasion. Grinning like a kid himself, he adjusted the speakers that now sat on the window ledges that faced the cul-de-sac, treating all who drew near to ear-piercing shrieks, low, terrible moaning and the sharp cackling of a witch or two. Julie watched the approaching hordes in colorful costume and pulled her sweater tighter against the chill. Smiling at her husband's absurd dedication to Halloween, she hoped her parents would be okay with all the extra noise. It was only their third night in the new suite.

Her dad was still putting the finishing touches to the suite himself, being a frugal man of many talents, but thanks to a contractor who didn't run away, her parents had been able to move in on time, and seemed happy in the relatively small space. And now with the addition of a large fifth wheel trailer, they had plans to do lots of travelling so they wouldn't be home much.

Julie's parents had made this move to help her and Marc both financially and emotionally, and she loved them for it. It felt good having someone else in the house she could talk to.

Catching sight of an especially large pack of kids meandering down the sidewalk, she worried about her stash of candy. Would it hold up to all these kids? There were a lot of them out there, she thought, hurrying to the stairs.

She was half-way down when a figure wearing a long black cape emerged from her parent's front door.

Julie froze for a second in a mid-step, her heart racing

"What?" She gasped.

"Oh, hi there," the figure turned and Julie breathed a sigh of relief.

It was her father, sporting a black hood and a mask that depicted the lined, misshapen face of an incredibly old man with spooky, mirrored eyes. "You like my get-up? Think this'll work?" he asked, his voice muffled as he swirled his cape with dramatic effect. "Your mother hates it."

"It's perfect, dad," she said. "You gonna answer the door like that?"

"That's the idea."

"Great! I just saw a big pack of kids coming this way. I put the bowl of candy here, on a stool by the door. Since you're having so much fun I'll let you be."

Her dad flashed his daughter the thumbs-up sign and headed to the door.

"Let me know when you run low," she called, jogging back up the stairs.

Cries of "trick of treat" sounded behind her before she reached the top of the stairs, and she imagined how much fun her dad would be having, as he doled out candy in his ridiculous mask.

She chuckled. "Happy Halloween!" she called out through the open upstairs, as streams of children ran back down her driveway, shrieking happily.

Moments later, as she crouched in front of the pantry, looking for more candy, several more sounds came from the foyer. Julie frowned momentarily, realizing these sounded more like screams of fright, until she remembered her dad and his hideous outfit.

Moments later, her father called to her from the foot of the stairs. "How about that Julie? I guess I'm too convincing," he said, shrugging. "Did you hear the screams? They took off before I even got the door all the way open. At this rate, we might have to eat the candy by ourselves."

Julie smiled and gave her dad a thumbs up, before continuing down the hall, in search of Adam.

She found father and son in the ensuite bathroom, putting the final touches on Adam's costume.

"Isn't it great hon?" he asked. "Those sound effects are awesome! Listen to 'em scream!" Marc was grinning as they went to the front deck for a better vantage point. "Look at all those kids! They think the effects are real! See how scared they're pretending to be? They're acting like it's a real haunted house. This is too good!" Marc rubbed his hands together in delight.

Julie had to laugh. He was such a kid.

"Don't fool yourself. They know it's fake. If they were that scared, they wouldn't keep lining up for candy at our front door! If they keep up this pace, we're gonna run out. Better get going before our neighbours run out too!"

The doorbell rang and several children called out in unison.

"Trick or treat!"

"Julie!" Her dad called out as she reached the foyer with Adam. Several smiling, costumed children were jostling for position in the open doorway. "Give me a hand here? My mask is slipping."

Julie laughed and doled out the candy to the waiting children, smiling as her dad tugged his zombie mask back into place and spread his black cape with a creepy-sounding laugh. The teens at the door seemed to appreciate the effort and several chuckled, enjoying the corny atmosphere, despite their horror-genre costumes.

One of the teens, a girl dressed in black rags, with a blue long-haired wig, black-rimmed eyes and black lipstick, spoke up. "Nice effects you got here, totally believable," one teen complimented as she turned away. "Happy Halloween!" That seemed to be the popular look for teens. Anything hideous was AOK. No wonder they liked her dad's costume!

Marc watched his wife slip the padded shirt over Adam's head. He had to admit Julie did a pretty good job of re-creating one of Adam's favourite movie characters, using layers of cloth to ensure warmth as well as style. Adam wasn't thrilled about wearing a coat any time, least of all at Halloween. One look at Adam and Marc could tell his son was eager to get started. He had learned about trick-or-treating in their old neighbourhood, and in the previous few years, he'd become better and better at it. Once Adam understood that he wasn't supposed to go inside when they opened the door, things were much smoother. Now, the child enjoyed it tremendously, running with his parents from house to house in breathless excitement in his search for candy.

"Alright, let's move!" Adam proclaimed loudly, rushing for the open door.

Marc switched on his flashlight and grabbed his son's hand. Adam already had a firm grip on the handle of the pumpkin-shaped bucket that would soon be full of treats.

"Did you hear that?" Marc laughed. "He's already in character!"

"He's never *out* of character!" Julie reminded her husband with a laugh and a fond wave at the two as they set off on their adventure, hand in hand.

~~~~

Adam's costume had been put away and most of the chocolate treats stashed in the freezer. Halloween was over for another year and Julie was glad to be rid of it.

Adam, although he'd come home with lots of candy, had become moody, his language overly repetitive. Julie could only guess the line was from a movie, but it was one she didn't recognize.

"He's a monster!" the child shouted, over and over, as he made explosive noises with his mouth, that he obviously thought resembled thunder.

Both Julie and Marc felt responsible. They hadn't stopped to think that all of these outlandish decorations would affect their son like this.

Truthfully, being new to the neighbourhood, they couldn't have known how 'all out' her neighbours would go when it came to decorating for the annual spook-a-thon.

On his travels through the neighbourhood, Marc and Adam saw a smoke machine, fake tombstones, fake cobwebs, and even watched a brief dramatic re-enactment of a 'mummy', who was obviously one of their neighbours, wrapped in toilet paper, sporting a baseball cap and tennis shoes. The man rose eerily from a lawn chair with a dramatic moan as children raced up and down his driveway, shouting "Happy Halloween!" Several home owners who answered the door for Adam had been dressed in costume, but all were extremely kind. A few, recognising his costume, sang him a song from the movie, earning a delighted smile. Marc and Adam danced down the last stretch of road as Julie watched their approach from the front deck. Strains of "monster mash" echoed through the cul-de-sac as one of her neighbours pumped canned music out into street.
~~~~

The smiles on both of their faces had been memorable and Julie grabbed her camera fast, capturing several images of a smiling happy Adam, proudly displaying his loot.

~~~~

But that was yesterday, she reminded herself. Today, he's a different child.

"How are you doing over there?" Steve called out from his front yard, as he caught sight of Julie, plucking the last of her fake cobwebs from the doorframe. He was carrying armloads of decorations to stash them away in his garage for another year.

"Oh, we're doing okay, we don't have as much to put away as you do," Julie remarked.

"The spookier the better, I just can't help myself. I get into it!" Steve pulled three very realistic-looking headstones from his front yard and walked them up to his garage. "The kids love it, and to be honest, so do I."

"It's a bit overwhelming that the whole neighbourhood gets into it so much," Julie commented. "I had no idea. Unfortunately, Adam got a bit scared."

"Aw, poor kiddo. Too much for him?"

"I think so, yes. He was up most of the night, talking about witches and vampires."

"Oh geez!" Steve looked down at the remaining decorations on his lawn. "Would it help if I showed him it's all just fake?"

Julie paused in the act of winding up another cobweb and turned to smile at her neighbour.

"Steve, sometimes you have the best ideas! Wait there, I'll be right back with Adam."

~~~~

"So you see Adam," Steve said as he encouraged the child to touch the tombstone made of Styrofoam. "Completely fake. Not scary, right?"

"Not scary," the child repeated, grabbing the tombstone with one hand.

With a crunch, Adam closed his fist around one corner, snapping off a chunk of the decoration.

"Oh no!" Julie cried out, her face falling. "Steve, I'm so sorry. Adam, you can't wreck it."

"Nevermind," Steve replied. "I think it looks better now, to be honest." Chuckling to himself, he picked up the remaining pieces and quickly put them away.

"Thanks," Julie called out. Adam plucked at the fake cobwebs that still clung to their house and jumped with all his weight onto the automated doormat with its tinny laugh. The sound made him laugh, and he jumped over and over. "Hey I think it worked. He's feeling better!"

"Sure, no problem. You guys had some great special effects over at your place too. Make sure you show him that stuff's not real. The teenagers were even scared. You're the talk of the neighbourhood."

"What?" Julie replied, startled. "What effects?"

"And while you're at it," Steve continued, oblivious to her question. "How did you rig it? The 'shadow man' in your downstairs window, I mean. I know it wasn't Marc, cuz I saw him out with Adam, and your dad was answering the door. So, who did you convince to creep around in your den? It was great, but you must have had lots of candy leftover."

"Well we did have lots of candy leftover, but I don't understand …"

"Didn't you see the kids avoiding your place? I heard the screams from my place! So, who was that anyway?"

"I wish I knew," Julie replied, her face reddening. "It was a spooky night. Maybe they were all just keyed up." She knew the answer was lame, but she wasn't about to mention her suspicions to a neighbour, no matter how nice he was. She didn't want him putting two and two together.

Steve narrowed his eyes briefly, before continuing up his driveway with another armful. "Well, anyway it was cool! Good job!" Julie watched him go, hoping her expression was still neutral.

~~~~

"You know what, Dad?" Julie asked her father, as she carefully re-filled his mug.

"What?" he answered, settling into a kitchen chair. They were enjoying a small bit of peace and quiet, with Adam at school and her mother already off at work. Her dad was newly retired and he enjoyed spending time with his daughter.
~~~~

"I think I must be cracking up," she said, sitting down beside him with a sigh.

Her father's brows raised in question. "What makes you say that?"

"We-ell," she began. "It's gonna sound crazy and paranoid. Are you ready for that?"

"Your mother and I raised you, remember?" he said, a smile tugging at the corners of his mouth. "You still think you can shock me?"

Julie laughed. "Okay, here goes. I don't know if it's the pregnancy or what, but I'm seeing odd things in this house, and hearing sounds I can't explain."

"That's just your mother," Arthur replied with a straight face, taking a careful sip of his black coffee.

"Dad!" Julie said, stifling a laugh. "I'm serious."

"Houses makes strange sounds all the time, Julie. You know that. It's called settling."

"Yeah, but this is different."

"Okay," he replied cautiously. "Tell me."

"It started right after we moved in. Bangs and thuds when I'm alone in the house. Footsteps on the staircase when no one else is home. And …"

"Footsteps?" her father prompted.

"Yeah," she said. "I told Marc about it, but he said it might just be the noises from the neighbours coming through the windows. Cul-de-sacs make strange noises, apparently, but I don't remember that from when I was a kid. We lived on a cul-de-sac when I was a teen, remember? I don't remember having to get used to any weird noises like this. Do you?"

"No, I don't remember that," he said. "Is that all?"

"Well, no. I was … well, I was wondering," she hesitated again, not sure how to word this so it didn't sound like an accusation. "Uh, the TV. You and mom turn it off when you go out, right? And the computer too?"

"Absolutely," he replied with emphasis. "Electricity is costly. You know how I feel about that. Why do you ask? Is Marc worried about the light bill?"

Julie could see she had her dad's attention now.

"No, it's nothing like that. Last week, remember you and Mom went to that retirement lunch? I heard something from your suite, so

I went down to check." Julie stared into her mug of tea as she spoke. "Both the TV and the computer were on."

"Are you sure?" he asked.

Julie nodded. Her father's blue eyes looked troubled.

"They were both off when we left. Adam must have gone down there. Little bugger's obviously figured out how to open the lock on our door."

"Oh! I don't think so dad."

"Okay," he said. "What's your theory then? Adam's an active kid."

Julie clasped and unclasped her hands nervously as she spoke. "There's more if you want to hear it."

"In for a penny, in for a pound," her father replied. Julie could see his expression had changed, but she plowed on. "I was doing laundry yesterday and … dad, would there be any way that my washing machine lid could pop up on its own?

Her father stared at her.

"What do you mean pop up?"

"I mean up. Open, all the way."

"You mean when the wash was already started?"

Julie nodded.

"No, I – no, I can't think of any way it would do that on its own," he replied. "It had to have had help. I'd say Adam is interested in more than you realize. You know how kids are. A lot of these things can be chalked up to human error, honey, and you do have a curious youngster. You're getting yourself all worked up for nothing. Did you think there was a ghost in the house or something?"

"Dad," she protested weakly. "It's not like that. I'm concerned." This wasn't going at all the way she'd hoped.

"You do know," he continued. "That you live with an Autistic child who is faster than thought, right? Despite all our best efforts, he gets into everything."

Julie opened her mouth to speak and then closed it again. She knew with certainty that Adam had been in school when these mysterious things occurred, and part of her wanted to explain that, but her dad would never understand. He didn't want to.

"Well?" he prompted, as the silence lengthened.

"Yes, dad of course," she replied. "So you think he's doing all these things?"

"Marc's away and it's not your mother and me. What else can it be?" Her father's eyes narrowed slightly as he spoke, almost daring her to say more.

Julie sighed and looked away, realizing she didn't dare bring up Steve's comment about the mysterious figure in their den on Halloween night. "I guess it's nothing then. You're right, I'm just tired I guess. Forget I said anything."

"That's my girl," Arthur rumbled, draining the last of his coffee. "Well now that the mystery's been solved, I had better put a dead-bolt on that door, so we can keep sticky fingers out of our place when we're not there. If you need me, you know where I'll be." He turned and disappeared back down the staircase.

Chapter Twelve

The countdown to Christmas had officially started. Julie didn't even mind that it was still only mid November. She and Marc agreed to get started way earlier than normal to appease their son, who still spoke endlessly of vampires and witches.

Standing in her living room, Julie had to admit, the effect was beautiful! The special red and green throw pillows that lay at each end of the sofa added a festive flair, but it was the Christmas tree that would truly be the focal point. For the first time, they would be able to get a real tree!

Julie had created the image over and over in her mind of what it would look like, with its perfect shape and impressive height. It would make the room look that much bigger, and the glowing angel at the top would cast a warm glow across the pristine cathedral ceiling, welcoming all who came near and filling the house with a sense of peace that the troubled couple had been trying to create since they moved in.

Julie breathed deeply and allowed herself to revel in the thought. This Christmas was going to be awesome! It was already their favourite time of year.

~~~
~~~

"I love dis Christmasey time a year," Adam sang as Marc carefully parked the van in the gravel driveway at the local Christmas Tree Farm, just minutes from their house.

"We can get a really big one this year, honey," Marc announced excitedly "The living room is perfect for it, and your parents aren't even interested in having a tree they said, so it has to be big enough for everyone. The guy here says these ones are called 'Grand Firs'. I like the look of them, what do you think?"

"Sure," she smiled at his enthusiasm. "They look good, but how much do they cost?" Julie kept a wary eye on their son, as he happily muttered to himself.

Marc led his son by the hand between the rows of trees.

Julie looked around. They all looked the same to her.

But to Marc each one was a little different. He wandered off with Adam in a jagged line, their trail easy to follow through the ankle-high grass that grew in between each tree. The little boy wove effortlessly past the tangle of branches, as his father looked for exactly the right tree. Julie tried to follow, but the best she could manage was an awkward, slow pursuit. She was now in her last trimester and balance was an issue. To make matters worse, the ground was soft from the recent rains, and her boots sank deeply in the mud.

"I'm gonna be so happy to deliver this kid," she muttered. "I get bigger every day," she muttered. "Marc," she called to her husband, as he came to a stop and looked back at her. "Honestly they all look the same to me. Just pick the one you like. If it'll fit in the house, I'm good." She looked around and sighed deeply. "Oh great. Where's Adam? I thought you had his hand?"

"Crap!" Marc fumed. "I only let go of him for a second. That kid needs a tracking device."

Later, after Adam had been successfully recaptured, and the perfect tree was finally selected, Julie hoisted herself into the van and enjoyed a few moments of peace, while Marc tied the Grand Fir atop the minivan with a length of yellow rope.

Once they got the mighty tree back home, and brought it inside, Marc had to admit he'd gone a little overboard.

Julie covered her smile with one gloved hand as her husband got out his hand saw.

"I'll just take a few inches off the bottom and it'll be fine," he said confidently.

It was quite some time before Marc came back inside with the tree.

"Had to give it three haircuts," he mumbled, dragging the massive tree into place.

As the adults gathered around the mighty tree, Adam ran from the room. Julie heard her son's feet pound down the hall and back to the doorway of the family room, where he stopped short.

Julie glanced behind her and saw Adam, frozen in the doorway as though something barred his way.

"AAAAH!" He screamed the sound echoing through the hallway and down the empty staircase.

"What the heck is he doing?" Anne asked, her hands full of jumbled tree lights.

"I haven't the faintest clue," Marc replied, as he climbed a small ladder to secure the angel on the topmost branch. "He just started that the other day. Neither of us can figure it out. He seems to do it whenever he goes in the family room."

"Adam, come here," Arthur called his grandson authoritatively.

Wordlessly, the little boy turned and came to his grandfather, where the older man handed the child a small wooden ornament and pointed at the tree.

"Go ahead," he said. "Put it on."

Adam hung the ornament with a little grin and dug into the box on his grandfather's lap for more. Soon, a section about two feet square was thickly hung with tiny wooden nutcrackers, Santa Clause figures and little wooden snowmen. Marc, with a pained expression, did his best to work around them, still winding the massive tree with strings of twinkling lights.

Julie smiled and shook her head in amazement. It was great how her dad acted on instinct, knowing exactly what to say or do to get Adam's attention. Using only gestures to communicate, the pair retreated to the kitchen for a glass of milk and a well-deserved cookie break.

Hours later, when Adam was finally tucked into bed, and her parents had returned to their cozy suite, Julie and Marc took advantage of a quiet moment to sit together in silence. Holding hands, they sat on the couch together, appreciating their beautiful family Christmas tree. Fully decorated, it sparkled with multiple strands of twinkle lights in the semi darkness. Julie's mind drifted as the rhythmic blinking of the lights began to lull her tired mind. Soon she'd be ready for bed, and grateful more than ever that her husband was home again. The bangs, clanks and otherwise strange noises didn't seem to happen as much when he was home, and her practical husband was always quick with a plausible explanation.

Julie smiled. Now, the challenge was to keep him in town til Christmas. There was still so much to do before the big day. Mentally, she ran through the items on her to-do list. It was their turn to host Christmas that year, and everyone was excited to have the festivities in Julie and Marc's new home. It was going to be a lot of work, and with the pregnancy, she tired easily, but Julie was determined to make it the most memorable Christmas ever!

~~~~

Christmas had finally come, so why was she still so nervous?

Because I live in a haunted house and no one is allowed to know it! Julie answered her own question.

Somehow, she had to keep up the fiction that everything was fine. Bangs and thuds weren't supposed to happen in rooms with no one in them. That was just ridiculous. And yet, this had become her life. What would happen next, she wondered? And would she be fortunate enough to have it happen without her sister noticing? Julie's big sister Laura was a perceptive person in many ways. Their maternal grandmother had done Tarot Card readings in her youth, and while Anne was vehemently opposed to discussing this part of their family heritage, Julie knew her sister saw and sensed things that others did not. She'd never been able to fool her big sister for long about anything, so as the countdown to Christmas entered its last hours, Julie found herself re-doing chores she'd already completed, not really paying attention to her surroundings but only to the clock on the wall and the feeling of the air around her.

Laura and Dean had two children. Rachelle, a dark-haired, olive-skinned child with large exotic eyes was the same age as Adam. Since birth, they'd developed a bond similar to that of twins, seeming to understand each other perfectly without the need for words. Rachelle was shy and quiet, but her eyes held a mystery that made Julie wonder whether their grandmother's gift had been passed on to Laura's eldest. Her sister's youngest child was a ten-month-old
~~~~

baby girl they'd named Arianna. The first time Julie saw the baby, with her golden curls gently framing the cherubic face, she gazed into the sky-blue eyes and knew that this baby was Rachelle's complete opposite. As she grew, Arianna explored her world to the best of her ability, always wanting more, never satisfied with routine.

The sisters brought their children together as often as they could, understanding how valuable the relationship was between them, especially considering Adam's diagnosis. And now, there would be another child to introduce to the group. Julie placed a loving hand on her swollen abdomen. "Soon little one," she crooned. "Soon you'll meet your cousins."

Julie put her energy into making everything as visually perfect and inviting as possible, trying to remember her own advice not to worry about things she couldn't change.

The tree was magnificent. Every light glowed, every ornament sparkled. The table was set to perfection with good china and crystal glasses. Each person was dressed in their Christmas Day finest.

It looked perfect.

"Laura! Dean! Come on in," she called as her sister's family appeared at the top of the stairs. "Rachelle, come see Auntie!" she gathered her little niece in a quick hug, then embraced her sister and brother-in-law in turn. "And how is Auntie's little one?" Julie's voice, filled with excitement and nervous energy, came out a bit too loud. The baby in her sister's arms pulled back against her mother's shoulder and buried her tiny face against the folds of fabric in Laura's festive scarf.

"Oh, I'm sorry sweet thing," she apologized, wincing.

"Um," Dean muttered, looking around as he took the baby from his wife. "I think she needs a change. She's been cranky for awhile. Long ride, you know. Where could we …?"

"The master bedroom," Marc suggested, leading the way quickly down the hall.

Arianna's cries seemed to bounce from one wall to the other, echoing through the otherwise quiet house.

Julie watched them go, feeling guilty.

"Poor little baby, I didn't mean to scare her," she said to her sister, who was fumbling through an enormous diaper bag at her feet.

"That's ok. She's sensitive to everything these days, I should have warned you. You okay with Rachelle? Dean's gonna need this stuff."

"Absolutely," Julie replied, winking at her niece. "We're good, right?"

Rachelle simply shrugged and grinned a little. She had watched the whole dramatic process with a bored expression.

Before Julie could take two steps, Grandma and Grandpa opened their own front door and came rapidly up the steps.

"Rachelle!" Anne called out in surprise as she reached the top. Rachelle smiled shyly at her grandmother as she allowed herself to be hugged. She was so reserved, Julie thought. I wonder how long it will be before she comes out of that shell?

"Mom! Dad!" Julie's sister Laura was just coming back down the hallway, her newly changed daughter held securely over one shoulder. "We were just gonna come find you." She rushed forward to greet her parents.

"Rachelle," Laura called to the little girl who had started inching away down the hall in search of her cousin. "Come here and say Merry Christmas to Grandma and Grandpa!"

The child stopped and retraced her steps, a somber look on her face.

"Merry Christmas," she repeated dutifully.

"It's okay mommy," Anne winked at her granddaughter. "We already had a big Christmas hug, didn't we? But I haven't told you how beautiful you look in your new dress. Just like a princess!"

Rachelle beamed as the compliment seemed to throw some sort of inner social switch.

"Iss my party dress Gramma!" Obviously pleased with her new outfit, Rachelle twirled, her skirt spinning out in a circle. "See Gramma?" She pointed at the embroidered snowflakes on her skirt proudly.

"Oh yes. Very pretty. Doesn't she look like a Princess Grandpa?"

Julie's father smiled and nodded. "Oh yes."

Rachelle grinned, but her determination soon returned, and she edged away down the hallway once more.

"Ad-am," she called. "Where you at?"

"Rachelle, her father called from the living room. "Did you see the tree!"

"Ine busy daddy," she retorted disappearing quickly through the doorway into Adam's room. A moment later, Julie heard her son's distinctive voice calling out "Ra-chelle!" With his garbled pronunciation, he softened the L in her name, making it sound like Ra-chew.

"Hey you two," Marc interjected, poking his head into his son's room. "Come check it out! Presents!"

Rachelle squealed with excitement, rushing past her uncle. Adam, clearly not understanding but eager to follow his cousin, rushed after her.

When both children reached the tree, they stopped short, gazing at the overflowing mound of presents beneath the enormous tree.

A moment later, Adam took off in the opposite direction, heading for the family room. Rachelle followed, squealing in delight. She too, followed her cousin without question. As soon as Adam reached the threshold of the next room, however, he stopped and delivered an ear-piercing shriek, as he'd been doing for weeks.

Laura and Dean spun around in their seats, wincing while the rest of the adults looked on apologetically. Arianna, held securely in her mother's arms looked around, her eyes wide.

"What the heck was that?" Dean asked.

"Sorry," Julie replied.

"What the heck is going on?" Laura gasped, holding the baby closer to her chest.

"Not sure. It's a new game, I guess. We can't figure it out."

A moment later, Rachelle decided to join in the fun, following Adam as he circled from the family room, through the kitchen, past the tree and all the adults in the living room and back to the family room in an endless loop. It wouldn't have been a bad game, except that every time Adam re-entered the family room, he gave a short shriek, and this time his willing accomplice added hers as well!

Adam seemed enormously pleased with her efforts, but the adults universally groaned.

"Can't he stop?" Dean complained. "My head is gonna split open."

"Okay you two," Julie intervened, hurrying to the family room to catch them before they left it again. Taking both children by the hand, she led them to the toy chest and pointed. "Play time is in here. No more screaming."

Adam and Rachelle were soon embroiled in a game of 'empty the toy box', their gazes firmly fixed on each other.

Adam loved his cousin his all his heart. Despite the constant therapy sessions and the two years of developmental preschool, he avoided playing with other children. He didn't seem to understand how to play with them.

But with Rachelle, his disability seemed to melt away, as the tiny girl instinctively included him, patiently waiting while he figured out his role in the games she created.

Watching from the doorway, the two sisters exchanged a long look over the heads of their children, then headed into the kitchen, busy hands beginning to set out the Christmas brunch, but speaking urgently to each other in private whispers to catch up. Since she and Marc had moved to another city, the two had seen little of each other.

"You look different," her sister ventured, emptying the contents of the shopping bag she'd brought with her. A box of brightly wrapped Christmas crackers in one hand, she leaned casually on the kitchen counter with the other and looked carefully at Julie.

"Well yeah, I'm fatter," Julie laughed, affectionately running a hand over her expanded middle.

"Very funny," her sister quipped. "I don't mean that. There's something else. What's going on? Level with me, I know you."

"Um, I-I don't know what you mean," Julie stammered.

"Oh yes you do. You've never been able to lie to me little sis, so don't start now. Something's bothering you. Is it Marc? He's been out of town a lot lately."

Julie smiled ruefully. "It sounds stupid when I say it out loud."

"Say it anyways, it's probably good for you to get it out. And we already went through the 'you're a stupid-head' phase when we were kids, so you're safe."

Julie laughed and smacked her sister in the arm with mock reprisal.

"How can you take one look at me and know something's wrong?"

"Experience," Laura replied. "So, is it Marc? I know he leaves you alone a lot, but that's his job, right?"

"Oh absolutely!" Julie reassured her sister. "It's not his choice to go. He's just so damn qualified and they always seem to need him, instead of the other guys. I'm proud of him, but I miss him. He's not here to deal with ... things."

"I know how you feel," Laura responded. "I used to feel scared to be in the house by myself. Silly hey? I'm a grown woman, but when there's a thunder storm and the lights go out, oh boy! You'd better believe I'm scared when Dean isn't around."

Julie felt her body sag a little. So, her sister did understand what she was going through?

"Yeah," she admitted, surprised that tears had begun to roll down her cheeks. "To be here. By myself. Without him." Julie's words were chopped up. She felt so awkward! Darting sideways looks at her sister, she waited to see what her big sister would say.

"You know, every house is a bit spooky, especially at night. And this one is …well it's brand new, but it has sort of a …" Laura trailed off in thought, while Julie tried hard to keep her expression neutral. "Don't forget," Laura reached for Julie's hand and held it gently. "You're pregnant, so that's gonna affect things too. Your hormones are all over the place!"

Laura made a large circular gesture with her arm in the air over Julie's head to illustrate what she meant.

Although Julie wanted to laugh, she simply nodded and hoped her expression wasn't giving anything away.

"And let's not forget," Laura continued, warming to the subject. "A bigger house means more things to clean, more space to get used to and plenty of what dad likes to call 'settling noises', right?"

"Sure," Julie conceded. "That's dad's favourite explanation for everything. He used to say that a lot when we were kids, growing up in that creepy old farmhouse. You remember that?" Julie watched her sister intently.

This was the moment, she thought. I wonder if she'll guess? Julie almost wanted her sister to guess. She hated having secrets between them, but if she did guess, then what? Would they ever visit them again? Julie was pretty sure the answer would be no.

"Yeah, that's right," she recalled. "He did say that, didn't he?" Laura smiled and tossed her long red hair over one shoulder as she sifted back through her memories. "Dad doesn't like to talk about things that go bump in the night. Makes him uncomfortable."

Julie tried to smile but inside she was convinced her sister knew the truth. A horrible, sick feeling began in the pit of her stomach as she waited for her sister to speak again.

"But you don't have to worry about that here, this place is brand new!" Laura grinned suddenly at her little sister, as she grabbed a package of napkins from the counter and bustled to the table, setting an extra one at each place. "You can never have too many serviettes," she said. "We've got a messy family! You want to get the food from the oven? I think it's time we ate."

Julie pulled on her oven mitts with a sigh of relief. The moment was over.

"You know," Laura continued. "Maybe that's why you miss Marc so much. I mean, our dad was away a lot when you were little. And he did the same type of work as Marc does now. It's probably buried in your subconscious mind. You're worried he won't come home. You used to cry and say daddy wasn't coming home. I remember you worried about him a lot. You used to have a lot of trouble sleeping."

"I did?" Julie replied. "I don't remember that."

"I think there's a lot of things you don't remember. But that's okay, maybe you don't need to. That's why you have me!" She poked Julie good-naturedly in the arm and grinned affectionately. She waited until her sister placed the large tray of scrambled eggs on the table, then enfolded her in a warm hug. "I've missed you, little sis." Laura flicked her long hair away from her face and picked up the package of napkins. "Now let's get this show on the road," she said, going to the oven for the rest of the feast.

Chapter Thirteen

Breakfast passed in a multi-hued blur. A buzz of conversation filled the air; good food was eaten while Adam happily quoted Christmas movie lines to all who would listen. All the while, the lights on Marc's perfect tree twinkled happily. Julie and Marc's startled gazes met several times a thump or bang came from the empty foyer below, and although a few frowns creased the foreheads of the other adults, the moment soon passed and the concern of the moment, opening the brightly colored gifts before them, reasserted itself.

Julie noted happily that Laura and Dean seemed at ease as long as their children were within arm's reach.

Marc was quick to pick up his camera, capturing the moments he hoped they could look back on for years to come. Things were going so well he didn't want to jinx it by thinking this way, but he found himself wondering nonetheless, whether the photos he took that day would show more than the faces of his happy family.

The prints from the roll of film Julie dropped off for developing a couple of weeks ago, were still tucked safely in the pocket of his work coat, downstairs. He didn't want to show them to his wife and yet he was reluctant to throw them out. They were photos taken in the early days of their move. There were snapshots of Adam playing in the mud the first time it rained, and several photos of the rooms with things finally unpacked and arranged to Julie's specifications. Of course, Adam's first Halloween and Pirate Jack O'lantern figured prominently in the mix as well, but it wasn't the content of the photos that bothered Marc. Rather it was the blurry, faded-out patches in several of them that had him worried. He remembered the photos they'd gotten from the realtor and how those same aberrations were present in most of these too. He'd shrugged it off as a fluke then, but it couldn't be shrugged off anymore.

The sound of tearing paper brought Marc back to reality as his niece shredded the wrapping from a huge gift.

"Atta girl, rip it, rip it!" Dean chanted to his daughter.

Her proud grandparents waited breathlessly, their hands clasped as they sat on the couch together.

Rachelle pressed both palms to her cheeks and squealed in delight as the final piece fell away, revealing a full-size doll's carriage. Adam, thinking the game was back on, squealed right back at his cousin and waited for her to repeat the sound.

Rachelle instantly followed her cousin's lead, and the game resumed. Both grandparents covered their ears while Laura and Dean finished uncrating the toy from the huge box. It was big enough to load with every stuffed toy Rachelle owned, and they were quick to redirect their daughter's attention to it, eager to stifle the screaming game once and for all.

Dean and Marc worked quickly to attach the wheels, while Laura and Julie tried unsuccessfully to divert the children's attention from their bizarre game.

Eventually, Rachelle's attention was recaptured by her new and wondrous toy, and Adam was left to squeal on his own.

"Mom and Dad, you outdid yourselves," Laura sighed, wincing at the sound of her nephew's excited noises.

Rachelle was in the process of tucking in the doll she'd been carrying. Without a backward glance, she pushed the carriage out of the room and down the hall.

"Awe, she's so cute," Marc whispered.

"Ah, just a moment miss," Laura admonished the child. "Where are the hugs?"

Hurriedly, Rachelle ran to her grandparents with open arms, obviously not concerned with the quality of the hug, she simply ran at them, leaned in and then quickly ran away to grab the handle of her new toy and disappear with it.

"I don't think she likes it, mother," Julie's dad commented sarcastically. "Better take it back."

"Thanks mom and dad. It's perfect." Laura said, smiling after her daughter.

Marc reached out with one long arm and hooked it around Adam's waist as he prepared to charge away after his cousin.

"Not so fast young man, it's your turn," he told him, sliding another equally large present along the carpet toward his son. Rachelle was happily driving her new buggy up and down the hallway, singing a discordant rendition of 'Jingle Bells' as she went.

Adam shredded the paper with a single movement. The picture on the box inside now revealed a happy child playing with a railroad set. Adam didn't seem to notice, as he stood up to leave once more.

Marc grabbed his son again and together they worked at the flaps on the box.

Adam seemed frustrated by all the tape securing it closed, but with a quick jerk of his powerful hands, Marc circumvented the tape and ripped open the box for his son, saying "See Adam, say O-pen!"

"O-pen," Adam copied. At the sound of his son's clear voice, Marc grinned and dumped out the contents on the rug.

Adam's eyes flew open wider as pieces of brightly colored track and little trains cascaded onto the floor.

"Oh my!" Ann cried out excitedly, clapping her hands. "Oh grandpa, well done!" she said to her husband.

"EEE!" Adam shrieked happily. Trains? To their son, this was the jackpot!

Adam took hold of the flaps on the box and tore it the rest of the way open, looking for more inside, and surprising all with this unusual show of strength.

"I'd say he likes it," Julie told her parents, receiving answering nods and smiles. "Thank you. It's perfect."

With a serious frown and still not uttering a word, Adam took some of the fallen pieces and ran to the next room. This was the gift he'd obviously been waiting for, and to his mind, there was no more point in opening anything else! Christmas was done for Adam.

Adam continued to ferry each piece of the toy back and forth to the family room, a huge grin on his face. Knowing their son well, Julie shot a quick look at her husband and Marc quickly rose from the floor where he'd been sitting.

"We'll let the kids play for awhile, while we open gifts, okay?' Julie said as her husband walked quickly from the room.

Marc picked up the remains of Adam's gift and brought it to the family room on the other side of the house. The small boy was already connecting pieces of track and ripping open the plastic bags containing the smaller items.

"There you go buddy," he said. "You can take it all apart here."

He was on his way back to the living room, before realizing that although Adam had run back and forth to the family room several times, he hadn't screamed even once!

"Huh!" He mumbled. "Hopefully we've seen the last of that little habit. Not a moment too soon." Marc caught sight of Rachelle as he crossed the hallway. She stood at the far end of the hallway, and seemed to be staring at something in the doorway of the master bedroom.

"Rachelle," he called. "Whatcha doin'? Come see what Adam got!"

Rachelle, still gripping the handle of her new carriage, didn't respond, but continued to stare at the doorway.

Marc walked toward the child, his curiosity building. As he approached, his eyes went wide, and he stopped. Rachelle was staring, but not through the doorway, as he'd first thought. To Marc, it seemed there was something *in* the doorway. His body turned to ice and he gulped. This was impossible! A large, dense shadow in the shape of a fully-grown man filled the doorway. His indistinct head reached almost to the top of the doorframe, the shape of its enormous shoulders and shadowy torso silhouetted against the light coming from the French doors beyond. Although Marc sensed this was a man, he couldn't make out any features. Marc's chest constricted as he fought to stay calm.

"Hi," Rachelle said calmly.

Marc was startled to realize his niece was speaking to the shadow-man!

Marc tried to speak, but his throat constricted and no sound would come.

"Who are you?" the little girl asked, narrowing her eyes and leaning forward for a better look. "You look funny."

Marc stifled a gasp and felt tears spring to his eyes. Fascinated, he continued to watch, his hands frozen inches from his unsuspecting niece.

"No." Rachelle said her tone matter-of-fact. She seemed to be answering a question Marc couldn't hear. As his niece stood there waiting for a reply only she could hear, Marc's heart nearly jumped through his skin.

"No, that's silly," the child responded again, with a small smile.

It was clear this shadow was communicating with the child, although the only voice Marc heard was Rachelle's.

"Okay," the child replied, disappointment in her voice. "Bye-bye." With that, the child waved one hand cheerily and spun on her heel. Whipping the carriage around with her, she crashed straight into her white-faced uncle.

"Ow!" he yelped, dodging aside.

Looking up quickly, Marc saw at once the shadow was gone.

Although he was shaking head to toe, Rachelle's only emotion was that of pure annoyance.

"Unca Marc," she complained. "Get outta my way."

"Are you okay Rachelle?" he asked her, finding his voice at last.

"Yeah," she answered as though his question was the dumbest thing she'd ever heard. "You gotta move, 'kay? I'm playin' here."

"Okay, I'm moving, but who were you talking to just now?"

The child pursed her lips, clearly annoyed by the intrusion. "Juss' a man," she replied in a matter of fact tone. "He's grumpy."

Marc gulped. "A grumpy man?"

"Uh-huh," she replied.

What did he want?"

"Nothin'," she said. "He din't wanna play 'if us."

"Is he there now?"

Rachelle looked at her uncle with confusion. "Course not!" she replied, leaning forward to peer at his face. "You okay?"

Marc had to smile at her innocence. "Yeah, I'm okay. I just didn't see the man like you did."

"Oh. Okay," she said, her previous concern completely erased as her thoughts returned to her new toy.

Carefully, Rachelle navigated around her uncle and continued back down the hall without a backward glance.

What the hell was that? He wondered. Obviously, this was no big deal to his niece. If anything, Marc's irritating questions was the weirdest thing about that encounter.

That she wasn't afraid was a saving grace. Marc only hoped that his niece's nonchalant attitude would prevent her from mentioning the incident to her overly protective parents.

As he looked through the archways into the living room, he saw his wife sitting calmly beside her sister, while they watched their dad meticulously pick the tape off his present.

Marc took a deep steadying breath and went to splash some water on his super-heated face, so he could continue to pretend all was normal.

As he entered the master bath, he felt the temperature plummet. What the hell? Were the windows open in here?

Marc turned around quickly. They were all secure.

"Oh I see," he muttered. "So you're still here huh?"

As he entered the master ensuite and flicked on the light, Marc raised his eyes slowly to the mirror, afraid of what he might see. His shoulders sagged with relief as the only thing reflected in the large mirror was his own face, devoid of color, except two spots of red, high on his cheekbones.

Splashing his super-heated cheeks with cool water, he breathed deeply, trying to ignore the sensation that crept up his back and over the top of his scalp like electricity. "This is friggin' nuts."

As he towelled his face dry, Marc heard his wife calling him.

"Marc? Where are you? Mom's opening our gift."

"I'm coming," he called. "Be right there!"

No one will believe this, he thought darkly. Not even Julie. As he returned to the living room, all he kept thinking about was that somehow, he had to keep this a secret. Even from his wife.

He wondered again if Rachelle would tell her parents about the grumpy man she encountered in the doorway. He hoped not. That would just open the door to all sorts of awkward questions and drive a wedge between the two sisters.

~~~~~

"Nothing there in the dark that isn't there in the light," she reminded herself, as she tried to ignore her son's cries while feeling her way forward in the dark.
~~~~~

"I hate power failures," she said to herself as she walked forward carefully, arms outstretched. It was pitch black, and with Marc working late, Julie hadn't even considered getting a flashlight or candles prepared.

Marc was always the one who thought of that stuff.

"Don't worry Adam, mommy's getting a flashlight, don't worry!" She called to her distraught son. Adam hated power failures even more than Julie.

Her reassurance didn't seem to help, as Adam kept right on crying, his voice more hysterical with every breath.

"Adam!" she shouted. "Calm down. It's okay!"

I wish someone would tell me everything is okay, she thought, her heart racing.

Julie's hands groping along the walls, and it seemed the kitchen was farther away than it should have been.

Julie tried not to relive her childhood memories, but they flashed through her mind nonetheless.

"Let's all sing a silly song!" she announced to the darkness, hoping the unexpected phrase would grab her son's attention. All that screaming was ramping up her anxiety and making things ten times worse. She had to try and stop it.

"Silly song!" she heard him say. Like a magnet, he ran for his mother and even without any light, he managed to find her and cling to her legs.

In the total darkness, the rushing, unexpected impact made Julie scream.

Adam screamed in return, and jammed his fist into his own mouth, biting down hard as he cried bitter tears.

Julie wanted to cry too, but she knew that would set him off worse.

"Why do these weird things happen to me?" she muttered.

"What I'd like to know," came a familiar baritone from the stairwell. "Is why you didn't think to get a flashlight ready when you saw there was a storm coming?" The sight of her father coming up the stairs with two flashlights in hand was an instant relief.

"Dad!" she breathed, rushing forward.

"What's all the chaos?" he asked.

"You're right, I didn't get a flashlight ready when I should have," she said. "And oh Adam, No!"

Julie lurched forward to stop her son as he tried to climb over the gate. Clearly, he wanted his grandfather.

The older man chuckled. "Whoah, hold on there, partner. Just a minute." With a few deft movements, Arthur unlocked the gate and swung it towards himself so his grandson could join him. Handing Julie the second flashlight, he waited until his daughter's ready smile returned before allowing Adam to lead his grandpa back down the stairs.

"Where we goin' pal" he asked Adam as they descended the steps.

"Ga-ma," Adam said.

"Oh, are we going to check on Grandma?"

"Ga-ma!" Adam insisted.

"Alrighty then," her dad replied. Over his shoulder, Arthur tossed out a quick "See you later!"

Julie clung to the flashlight with its narrow beam of comfort and ransacked drawers and cabinets in search of candles and more flashlights.

Soon, her house was aglow with candles and every table held an unlit flashlight, just in case. In the comfort of all that light, the young mother felt like she could breathe again. Pausing in the living room, she took a moment to enjoy the beauty of the room, bathed as it was in gentle candlelight.

Julie couldn't help feeling foolish at her over-reaction, but she was happy for her dad's timely intervention. Somehow, he'd known the power failure would send his daughter into a blind panic and he'd wasted no time coming to her aid. She was ashamed to admit she was still afraid of the dark.

Angry at herself, Julie frowned at the nearest candle.

"When am I gonna grow out of this? Fear of the dark is for children!"

As she spoke the words, an errant draft wafted through the room, making the flames on every candle dance erratically, threatening to douse them.

"Oh no you don't!" she shouted, dashing towards the kitchen to retrieve the butane-powered lighter. She was determined to be ready this time.

As she rushed past the stairwell, something caught the hem of her sweater. Pulling free with a frightened lurch, Julie whirled around. Was she caught on the gate somehow?

But as she returned to the stairwell, candles aglow, Julie could find nothing to account for it. The gate was closed and latched, just as it should be.

All around her, candle-light was glowing, but still she needed more. Grabbing every flashlight, she switched them all on, aiming them in every direction. She didn't stop until every corner of the house was fully lit.

"And as for you," she shook her finger at the gate barring the top of the stairs. "Hands to yourself. No more grabbing."

Downstairs, the distinctive sound of the front door banging closed meant Marc was finally home. "Hi honey," she called with relief. "I'm up here. Adam's down with mom and dad."

Realizing she hadn't finished preparing dinner, Julie went to the kitchen and aimed a flashlight into the darkened fridge.

Good thing Marc was home, she thought. We'll have to barbecue this chicken now. Pulling some uncooked chicken from the fridge to prepare it, she called out, "How's barbecued chicken?"

Marc didn't answer, but Julie knew he was probably still hanging up his jacket downstairs via candle-light. He'd be up in a few minutes.

With the safety of at least a dozen lit candles surrounding her, and her husband home at last, Julie finally felt brave enough to switch off the flashlight.

Humming to herself, she waited for Marc to make his appearance, but when the minutes ticked by and still he didn't arrive, Julie reasoned that he must have gone down to see if her parents were alright.

"That's the kind of guy he is," she said, grabbing her flashlight and returning to the stairs. "I should have thought of that. I'm a terrible daughter."

Julie pushed the gate open and watched it swing wide. She was half-way down the stairs when the door at the bottom burst open and Adam raced through it, with grandpa hot on his heels.

Julie grabbed the railing as her son shot past. "Hey! Not so fast, young man! In the dark we slow down."

She looked down at her dad with grateful eyes. "It's okay dad, I've got it from here. Thank you for your help with Adam and for the uh …"

"Light?" Arthur finished. "You're welcome. I just know my daughter," he replied, his voice low. "You've always been frightened of the dark. Even as a baby."

"Yeah, how weird is that, right? I'm an adult for crying out loud." Julie's wry smile showed how embarrassed she felt. "How's mom doing? I guess she's talking to Marc?"

Her dad looked at her, his expression puzzled. "Marc? Is he home?"

"Yeah," Julie started to say more and then pressed her lips together. "You haven't seen him?"

"Not tonight," her dad answered.

The silence lengthened between then as Julie worked to process that.

"That's so weird, I thought I heard the door," she said at last.

"Well," her dad replied. "You want the barbecue on for supper? I'm pretty sure the ovens won't work."

"Oh dad, could you? I pulled out some chicken earlier, but I don't know how that thing works. Likely as not I'd blow it up trying."

Her dad chuckled at that. "Well we can't have that."

The wind howled that night. So many street lights were out that traffic was a mess. It took Marc an extra hour to get home. When dinner was over and it was time for Adam to go to bed, the frightened child refused to stay in his own bed.

Eventually, as the storm continued to howl, Adam curled up between his parents.

Julie was grateful that Marc wasn't making a big deal out of their fears. He seemed content to have his family close in the darkened house.

No matter how childish it seemed, her fear of the dark was very real.

With Adam curled against her shoulder and his breathing regular, Julie closed her eyes, willing herself to calm down so she could fall asleep. "Ghosts can't hurt you," she whispered to herself in the darkness.

It was a phrase Julie's mother taught her as a child when she'd come to her parents' bed, too afraid to sleep in her own bed. As she grew, Julie used the phrase herself to try and relax whenever the fear threatened to take over.

Now an adult but no less afraid, Julie repeated it under her breath, as she tried to fall asleep.

Was it happening all over again?

The thought brought tears to her eyes. Somehow, she had to be wrong. It's the pregnancy, she thought. It has to be. Things like that don't happen to people like us …

To something made only of shadow, the darkness was a comforting place.

He watched her as she tossed and turned, trying in vain to shake off the sense of his presence.

The woman rolled onto her side, her back to the door. *With a single touch, he could wake her from a deep sleep, invade her dreams or make her hear things that weren't there. He was good at this, he thought, a self-satisfied smile playing across his thin lips.*

From the safety of darkness, he leaned against the wall by the doorway and folded long arms against a body that had been used to hard work, before.

He was glad he'd taken the time to perfect his skills. He could now touch and move things at will. Once, he'd been worried that this tortured existence would be an empty, unending Hell, but slowly, he had adapted. He had learned.

The woman in the bed rolled over again, her breathing becoming deeper, even as lightning lit up the night sky and threw the bedroom into full illumination.

He drifted closer, laying a ghostly hand against the pale strands of hair that splayed out across the pillow. Now we will see, he thought. Oh yes, we will see.

Chapter Fourteen

It was clear they needed a communication tool that was easy to use.

Adam had awakened that morning with red cheeks and a foul temper. Julie's temper wasn't much better, having tossed and turned most of the night.

"We've got to get inside Adam's head, somehow," Julie reasoned. "All this speech therapy is great, but he doesn't use normal words. Just movie quotes, and that isn't telling us anything."

Marc nodded his head in agreement. "Let's have a talk with his therapist. Maybe she can help. I saw something in the paper last week about facilitated communication. Maybe we could explore that?"

"Yes!" Julie agreed vehemently. It had taken Julie a long time to relax the night before. She was unable to shake the feeling that someone invisible watched her as she lay shivering beneath the covers. And now Adam's behaviour was pushing her over the edge. She needed something positive to latch onto. Maybe this facilitated communication thing would be the answer they craved.

~~~~
~~~~

"Why is Adam crying?" Julie wrote on the fresh page in the spiral bound note book. She faced her son and smiled gently. The change that came over him when he saw someone take up a pen or pencil, was remarkable. His body stopped rocking, his eyes, brimming with tears, opened wide and he bent his body toward the page, intent on the words forming there. Once she was finished writing, she pointed to the question, then each answer written out in multiple choice format as she read them aloud. When she was done, she handed her son the fat marker she'd used to write the words.

Adam is crying. Will you tell Mommy why?

Yes or No.

Adam carefully circled yes, and handed back the marker expectantly.

Julie wrote:

Adam feels:

A) Hurt

B) Sad

C) Mad

D)scared

 Or E) something else."

The child confidently circled 'scared' then looked at her expectantly, still sniffling.

"Oh, my boy," she crooned, reaching for him instinctively. The child hunched further over the page.

"Okay, we'll do it your way," she agreed. On the page, Julie wrote: Adam is scared. Thank you for telling mommy. Why is Adam scared? As she wrote, she wracked her brain for the right guesses to populate the list.

A) I don't know

B) My toys/movies scared me

C) A sound scared me

D) A person scared me

E) Something else scared me

"That ought to cover the bases well enough." Julie commented under her breath, handing the paper back to her son.

Adam read through the choices quickly, then circled E leaving Julie to scratch her head. He'd been playing happily in the family room only moments before and there hadn't been anything happening that she saw. The TV wasn't even on and neither was the radio.

What could possibly have scared this child when he had been playing a scant two feet from her?

In a sudden inspiration, Julie wrote:

Is it something only Adam can see?

Adam grabbed the marker excitedly and wrote YES

Adam's printing was over-sized, the letters imperfect. His word took up a big chunk of the page, but the message was clear.

Can Mommy see it too?

After only a moment's hesitation, Adam wrote NO.

Julie's eyes filled with tears. This wasn't what she wanted to hear. Dear God, she didn't want this to be happening!

Dashing the tears from her eyes, Julie wrote:

Thank you for telling mommy. Is Adam still scared now?

She handed the marker to her son, but the child refused to take it.

Julie tried to push it back into her son's hand a second time, but Adam stood up abruptly and with his face now beet red, he shouted, "NO!"

"Okay," she replied. "No more."

Placing the marker on top of the page, she deliberately moved paper and pen to the kitchen table. Adam watched her carefully, his lips pressed together in a thin line. His posture was tense, but that was normal for Adam. Julie hoped she wasn't reading more into this than he'd already disclosed.

She needed time to think, but with Adam watching her every move, Julie forced a smile onto her face and grabbed the remote control from the coffee table.

"How about a movie? Movies make mommy feel better."

His answering grin was a welcome relief, and within seconds, Adam inserted a video tape into the player and was sitting cross-legged on the floor, waiting with excitement for the story to begin. It was one he must have seen a hundred times, but to him, every time was like the first.

Julie walked quickly to the table and looked at the words on the page again. With a shudder, she closed the notebook.

"Now what am I supposed to do?" She mumbled. "How do I protect my son from something I can't see?"

~~~~~

As Julie dragged her eyes open, she looked at the clock on her night table and sighed. 6:00 AM.

"Alright, alright," she muttered, reaching sleepily to shut off her alarm, only to realize that the insistent sound wasn't coming from her side of the bed, but from the clock radio on her husband's side.

The insistent clicking and beeping didn't sound like a regular alarm, and the sound set her teeth on edge as she rolled across the bed, to try and stop it.

"Stupid thing," Julie muttered. Reaching over, she picked up the attached phone from its cradle and re-seated it firmly. Another electronic beep and click accompanied the action. "Aha!" she said. "Good! No more Morse Code." Julie watched the device for a moment longer, as though daring it to make a noise. She wagged her finger at it in mock seriousness. "Now you stay quiet. I've got stuff to do and I've no time to talk to you."

~~~~~

Julie's days were busy. As soon as one mess was cleaned up, another materialized. Her little mess-maker was always about five steps ahead of her.

The Behaviour Consultant was due to arrive in another hour. The goal that day was to develop some useful strategies for Adam's strange new behaviours, while moving ahead with the usual topics of improved communication and staying calm.

The last time Ariel called, she'd heard Adam's doorway-screaming through the phone and now she was hoping to witness it herself.

Aside from one brief respite on Christmas Day, their son's new-found habit of screaming before entering the family room continued. With the new baby coming soon, this would quickly become intolerable, but no matter what his frenzied parents tried, Adam was not about to give up the nerve-wracking behaviour.

Ariel said this was filling a need for Adam somehow, and we needed to put our detective hats on to figure out what that need was.

Sure, she always made things sound so easy, like this was no problem at all and would soon be solved. All they had to do was think this through.

Yeah, right.

Julie loved Ariel, but sometimes the woman's eternal optimism made her want to scream.

Within the last few days, Adam had started jamming the side of his fist into his mouth and biting down hard when he screamed, leaving imprints of his own teeth on his skin.

This escalation was worrisome to everyone, but they all agreed a unified approach was best.

She was grateful that Adam was at kindergarten until lunchtime. She and Ariel had planned to meet late morning, so they could make the walk to the school together to pick him up. Julie had no doubt he would repeat the disturbing behaviour for Ariel and she wasn't looking forward to it.

Julie frowned as she leafed through the bundle of papers, re-reading the notes from Ariel's last visit. She liked being informed, but why did there have to be so much paper? It seemed every time there was a new meeting, the stack of papers grew, ten-fold. And these pages, she noted with disapproval, were becoming dog-eared.

Leaving them for a moment, Julie filled the kettle and got out the teapot and a selection of teas. Tea was always a good place to start. Placing some of her mother's baked goods on a small plate, she started humming softly to herself.

"Good thing for mom," she muttered. Without her mother's 'care packages' there wouldn't be any sweets available for guests, as it was always the last item on her shopping list and the first to be consumed by her husband and son. Julie jokingly referred to the cookie jar in the corner of her kitchen as the crumb- catcher, as usually those were the only things left inside.

Julie plucked her son's visual schedule from the fridge door and placed it on the counter, directly behind the chair Ariel always used when she came to visit. The Behaviour Consultant would want to see that it was being used, and with residue of dry-erase marker still clinging to the page, there would be no doubt how often this was used as part of Adam's day.

Suddenly, from the end of the hall, the sound of breaking glass interrupted her thoughts.

"Now what?"

Julie knew she was alone in the house. Already blaming the cat, she ran from room to room, looking for something breakable and within reach of a cat's paw.

But after checking all the rooms, she was no closer to figuring it out.

Everything in that end of the house was as she'd left it only a few minutes earlier.

No broken glass.

Did she imagine it, or was she hearing her neighbours again? She thought back to the mystery surrounding the uncooperative doorbell and frowned.

"C'mon in Ariel," Julie welcomed the smiling woman at the front door a few minutes later.

Ariel's smile was warm and engaging as she came inside, smiling at Julie enthusiastically. "How are you doing?" she asked, as she bent to carefully remove her dress shoes and place the delicately pointed black heels on the mat by the door. Julie took the elegantly styled overcoat as Ariel shrugged out of it and hung it in the mirrored closet.

"Let's go on up, Ariel. You can go first, it takes me ages these days."

Ariel started up the stairs. "You're due any day now, aren't you?"

"Yeah, pretty close," Julie replied, hauling herself slowly up the steps behind her guest.

The two women sat down at the kitchen table and Ariel opened her briefcase, drawing out several sheets of lined paper with long, elegant fingers.

More paper, Julie sighed inwardly.

"How is Adam doing with his visual schedule?" Ariel asked, tucking an errant lock of wavy blonde hair back around one ear as she picked up her pen and smiled encouragingly at Julie. "I brought another one with the new changes, if you want to give it a try?" She looked around briefly, her blue eyes questioning. "Where do you usually keep it?"

"Usually it's on the fridge, but I knew you'd be bringing a replacement, so I put it right over there, behind you on the counter," Julie replied, pointing.

Ariel stood up. "Okay, that's great," she said, leafing through the stack of papers on the counter. "Where is it? I must be looking right at it, but …"

"What?" Julie came over to look herself. "Should be right on top, that's weird, I know I put it there …" Julie trailed off as she went to another counter, beside the telephone and rifled through some more paper. "Maybe I put it here my mistake?" Frowning in consternation, she turned to Ariel and shrugged apologetically. "I don't get it. It was right here a few minutes ago. I am so sorry. This is stupid."

"It's okay, don't stress. Kids move things. I know nothing is ever where I leave it at my house. My kids are constantly moving my stuff. Is Adam using the system okay though?"

"Uh, yeah. Yeah he is." Julie seemed distracted as she returned to the table. "I don't get it. I put that thing on the kitchen counter just before you got here."

Ariel did not comment, but merely took a sheet of laminated paper from her briefcase and pushed it across the table to Julie. "Don't sweat the small stuff mom," she said. "Come and look at this. The way it works is just like the last one, but with this system, we're encouraging more language, so instead of just pointing to the picture of what comes next, he's gonna –."

BRRRINGG!

"Oh geez!" Julie jumped in her chair at the sound of the phone. "I'm sorry Ariel. Do you mind if I get that? It might be the school again."

Ariel's delicate eyebrows lifted at that, but she smiled disarmingly. "Of course. Go ahead."

After only a few moments, it was clear that the caller was Adam's school, and once again, they were reporting another misdemeanor.

Red-faced with anger, Julie hung up the phone and reported the situation to Ariel.

"Keep your emotions in check, mom. We'll tackle this together, like we always do."

Ariel was always so calm, Julie thought, as she watched her retrieve a notepad from the briefcase at her side. Nothing seemed to faze her!

"Now," Ariel said, her pen poised above the blank page. "First things first, tell me exactly what they said to you on the phone…"

<center>~~~~</center>

Julie raked her fingers through her hair and stared at her reflection in the mirror. She'd washed her face three times without even noticing. What was wrong with her? It felt like she was coming apart. And now, to top it all off, she was somehow supposed to put Ariel's advice into action and ignore a behaviour that killed her every time she saw it.

How can I keep going? She wondered.

As if on cue, the sound that she hated most in the world came again.

Adam, screaming at full volume.

Running from the room like she'd been shot from a cannon, Julie deliberately slowed to walk before reaching him.

Slowly, slowly, don't react, she told herself.

But as she reached his open doorway, she found a curious scene. Adam was standing on his bed, with tears rolling down his cheeks as he stared at the window with wide eyes. The blinds had been pulled all the way to the top, exposing the two large panes of glass.

"Adam, Mommy's here. Look at me. I'm here," she said, her voice calm and soothing.

Adam continued to stare at the darkness outside his window, the after-effect of his screams coloring his cheeks.

Julie moved her hands in the sign language movement meaning 'all done' as she worked the strings that allowed the blinds to settle down against the sash. Gathering him in her arms, she helped him to sit down. She could feel the resistance in his muscles as he sat there, rigid.

Afraid.

But what was he afraid of? Julie had looked through that same window just now, and seen nothing unusual.

Sitting beside him, she stroked his hair while continuing to sing one of his favourite songs. Music always seemed to bring back his focus no matter what was happening. Inch by inch, she felt his muscles relax, as he settled down into the crook of his mother's arms.

Finally, he stopped crying and with a loud sniffle, he looked up at her. The tear-filled eyes were so incredibly blue. Her heart broke for him, he was so trusting, so innocent and she had no answers.

"I wish I knew what scared you," she whispered. "I feel so helpless!"

Adam's posture stiffened again, and he whined as he brushed clumsily at his arm with one hand. She knew what that meant: more music. Sign language had been a part of his world since he was two, but he wasn't very good at using it himself, unless he was very motivated.

Oh well. Whatever works, she thought, continuing the song.

Wondering if she was doing the right thing, Julie backtracked to her own bedroom, one arm holding Adam awkwardly against her hip as they shuffled together across the hall. Adam stayed quiet, wrapped up with his mother in her own bed, as she continued to sing softly.

The solution lasted only as long as her song repertoire held out.

As soon as the last song finished, Adam looked up at her face without changing expression, and wiggled out of the warm cocoon of bed covers.

Without a backward glance, he calmly returned to his own room.

She could hear his footsteps as he walked back across the hall.

"Good for you kiddo," she whispered. "Nothing stops you for long."

As soon as the words had left her lips, however, an ear-piercing scream ripped through the quiet household.

"Shit!" she exploded, half falling from her bed in surprise. As she scrambled around the corner, she saw Adam, standing in his open doorway, fist buried deep in his mouth.

His head swung from side to side as he looked around the room, carefully.

Julie stopped, and pressed her lips together hard. What's going on? He usually only did that when he entered the family room!

Ariel's advice played in the back of her mind:

"Let it happen," Ariel had cautioned. "Stay calm."

While Julie hung back, her son peeked quickly behind the half-open door. Just as quickly, he moved farther into the room and hauled open the recently-replaced closet door. He looked carefully inside that too, still not saying a word.

All the while, Adam bit down on his fist, as though it gave him strength, but once he peeked into the empty closet, he stood up straighter, his hand dropping to his side.

Poor little guy, she thought. He's looking for the monsters that only he can see.

Satisfied at last, Adam crawled under his covers, where he let out a deep, contented sigh. Within minutes, Adam's breathing relaxed into a rhythm that meant he was on the verge of sleep.

"Now that was weirder than usual," Julie muttered, still trying to process what she'd seen. Gently, she closed his door and shook her head.

Despite her weariness, she knew what she had to do. Going to the kitchen, she snatched a piece of paper from its place on the fridge. It was the tracking sheet Ariel left behind so she could record Adam's behaviours.

"So where do I write this down?" she mumbled. "Where's the section for totally strange?"

~~~~

"Shut up, dammit! He's not here," she mumbled irritably into her pillow.

She'd come to regard the noises coming from her husband's bedside clock radio as some sort of absurd language, and had even started interacting with it.

"He'll be back Friday," she muttered angrily. "You'll have to wait until then."

The clicking that had been occurring on and off over the last several days, suddenly stopped.

"Is that all you wanted to know? You should learn to speak English. It's more effective as a language." Julie's sarcasm was her only defence and she used it liberally.

Punching her pillow with more ferocity than usual, she laid her head back down and tried to relax.

The silence should have been a welcome change, but her eyes kept snapping open on their own.

A quick glance at the clock on her side table showed it was 4 A.M.

Thanks a lot," she muttered. "Can't a person get some sleep in this house? Why do you always have to do this? What did I do to you?"

As though in answer, another set of beeps marred the silence. "That's it!"

It was awkward, but in the end, she'd managed to unplug the offending machine. Julie debated throwing it into the garbage can
~~~~

outside for good measure, but that would mean going downstairs in the dark and outside too. In the end, Julie simply rolled over and tried to go back to sleep.

Beep … beep …beep.

"Shut up," she muttered sleepily.

I've heard that damn noise so often, it's gotten stuck in my head, she thought.

The thing *was* unplugged, after all.

~~~~

The first night that Marc arrived home, the insistent clicking began anew.

Hands on hips, Julie stood there watching as her husband unpacked his suitcase.

"Don't you hear that?" she demanded.

"You mean that clicking noise? Sure, I was gonna ask you about it when I was done unpacking. Is that the clock radio again?"

"Apparently."

"How long has it been doing that?"

"Since you left."

Marc's eyebrows climbed in surprise. "You mean the whole time?"

"On and off. Mostly at night," she said.

"Did you try unplugging it?"

Julie stared at her husband, only just then remembering her actions of the night before.

"Ummmm."

Marc frowned at her. "Um what" he asked.

"Yeah, I did. In fact …." Julie crossed the room and reached down beside her husband's night table. "See?" she asked, holding up the unplugged power cord and phone line in one hand.

"What the –" Marc wondered aloud. "Maybe, because it's a phone too, it has to have a battery back-up," he suggested.

Julie's shoulders sagged. "Screen's dark," she said. "I thought that meant no power, but somehow it must. Either that, or this damn thing's got a mind of its own."

"Oka-ay," he replied dubiously.

Julie chewed her lip and rubbed her fingers nervously over the gold cross she always wore at her neck. Why did it always sound so paranoid when she said these things out loud?
~~~~

Marc's eyes narrowed as he watched his wife, nervously tugging at her necklace. He recognised the new-found habit.

Click, click… click-click. Beep.

Both husband and wife stared. First at the machine with its dark display, and then at each other.

With long strides, Marc left the room. Julie heard his quick footsteps descending the stairs and the loud bang as the garage door closed behind him. He was back a few minutes later with a small box and a roll of packing tape.

Without another word, Marc wrapped both cords around the offending machine and plunged it into the box.

Julie's eyebrows rose as she watched her husband package up the machine.

"This one's obviously faulty," he commented as he carried the box from the bedroom. "I'll get a new one tomorrow," he said, jogging down the staircase and tossing the box through the hastily-opened garage door where it landed with a thud on the concrete floor. "For now, this thing stays in here. When's garbage day again?"

"Um, yesterday," Julie answered, puzzled at how Marc's hasty reaction made her feel so much better.

"Humph, remind me to toss that thing out next week then," he said.

"Don't worry," she replied. "I don't want it hanging around either."

Chapter Fifteen

Adam was finally in bed, his tears dry and his favourite train quilt tucked in around him. This time, Julie was out of answers. She simply had no idea what had caused her son to suddenly freak out. He'd been happily playing in his room, lying calmly on the carpet, assembling train track with extreme care. A scant few minutes later he'd come out of his room screaming, face beet red and eyes wide in terror. He ran straight to his mother and pressed his face against her. Julie smoothed back her son's hair and tried to comfort him, but the screams went on and on. Marc hovered in the doorway, his face concerned. All either of them could do was wait it out.

Finally, it seemed the child was too exhausted to continue and mercifully, the screams died to weak crying, then faded to hiccups.

Finally, the worried parents were able to tuck their child back into his bed and breathe a sigh of relief. Adam was fast asleep in seconds, and Julie, emotionally and physically exhausted, turned to her husband.

"What's going on with him?" she asked. "He doesn't seem sick."

"I wish I knew," he answered. "Is this the Autism making him act like this?"

"I don't think so. Marc, he said something to me weeks ago, but in all the hoopla that goes on around here, I forgot to tell you."

"What is it?"

"Adam told me that he sees things that scare him sometimes."

"Okay, like what?"

"I have absolutely no idea. He told me that mommy can't see them. Only him."

"Umm," Marc hesitated, unsure of what to say.

"I know, right?" Julie answered, feeling helpless. "What do we do?

"Well, maybe we should take him to the doctor again," Marc suggested.

"Oh no, the doctor Marc? Why?" Julie's shoulders slumped as she thought about what that would entail. Adam hated the doctor, and how could a doctor's visit help something like this?

"Well, we have to be sure it isn't another ear infection or something, don't we? We don't want to jump at shadows."

"It's not that," she disagreed. "He doesn't have a fever, he's not rubbing his ears, he's eating and drinking normally and since he still hasn't learned to flush the toilet, I know all that's okay too."

Marc made a face. "Okay, okay too much information. I get it. He's not sick. So why the screaming then?"

"If I had to make a wild guess I'd say he was terrified."

"Of what?"

"If we knew that it wouldn't be a mystery anymore," Julie replied dryly.

~~~~

Church. It was supposed to be a time of joyous singing and praise. It was a time to re-connect with family and recharge your spiritual batteries. It was a time to put things into perspective.

So how come Julie dreaded it each week?

She wished she didn't feel that way, but to her, attending Mass was like running a marathon. Adam fidgeted, squirmed, said inappropriate things and couldn't be kept still.

Julie spent the entire time worried what other people thought, But if she didn't attend, she literally felt drained, like she wasn't strong enough to face the challenges of the week ahead.

Adam, for his part seemed to enjoy the repetitive phrases of the Mass, with their almost hypnotic effect. And to her delight, he danced around in the aisle beside his parents during some of the songs, while people smiled at him fondly. But each time the Priest spoke more than three sentences in a row, Adam was a different
~~~~

child and this was the part that made his mother cringe as Sunday drew near.

The more intensely she and Marc scolded him, the louder he recited his movie scripts or cried.

Well-meaning parishioners smiled indulgently as Julie and Marc took turns towing their son towards the back of the church, humming Disney tunes under their breath.

Often, Adam spent the majority of Mass outside on the church lawn with one of his parents, waiting for the part of the Mass when there was more singing and they could be together as a family for Holy Communion.

Holy Communion was the only reassuring constant. It became their lifeline and although their attendance at Mass was purchased at great emotional cost, they tried not to miss.

"You guys are great," one woman, a silver-haired senior with a kindly smile said to the couple, after one particularly difficult Sunday Mass. She reached out with one trembling hand to touch Julie's arm as the young family joined others in a long shuffling line to the back of the church.

"Thank you," Julie mumbled, looking at her husband with a wan smile.

"Just keep moving," Marc mumbled, while still smiling politely. "Let's get this boy outside before he blows up again."

~~~~

Julie counted the days, hours and minutes until her due date, circled in red on the calendar. It was so close now. Every day, she looked around her house with fatigue, hoping that last phase of pregnancy would arrive. The "nesting" phase that often prefaced labour was one she eagerly looked forward to. During this phase, many women reported extra energy that they used to clean their houses and get ready for the new baby.

Everything was such an effort now, and the chores kept stacking up.

~~~~

"I'm sorry, you remember what the doctor said. No more walks, not in this weather. You're too close." Marc admonished her.

Julie, her coordination significantly impaired, was strongly advised by doctor and family members alike, to avoid those long walks she loved, and now craved for her own mental health. The icy weather conditions made it dangerous. She knew they were right but with no end to the frigid weather in sight, and still so sign of labour, her mood rapidly worsened.

"It's a good thing that last fall didn't hurt either of you worse than it did," Marc said as he embraced his wife. His trip this time was thankfully short, and both were grateful he would be home again in just a few short days.

"Doctor said the baby is nice and insulated in here," Julie rubbed her belly and smiled. "She didn't feel a thing. I wish I could say in the same for myself, though." The bruise on her hip was still a painful reminder of her latest tumble down the staircase.

"Honey, I'm concerned about you going up and down the stairs. Are you sure you're going to be okay?"

"Marc, there isn't much I can do about that. I can't very well be confined to the upstairs of our house! What happens when Adam comes down here? Am I just supposed to tell him to be good, cuz mommy's not allowed to go down there anymore? Don't be silly, I'll be just fine. Remember, I promise to wear rubber-soled slippers. See?" She grinned at her husband and pointed to her feet. "You'd better get going, you have a long drive ahead of you."

~~~~

The line rang and rang. Why didn't they answer? Julie hung up in frustration as once again the answering machine at the rectory picked up. How was she supposed to leave a message about this?

She'd made light of the fall she'd taken down the staircase, but she hadn't wanted to start that conversation with Marc. No matter how many times she said it to herself, it sounded crazy.

No, it was better to just get this taken care of before the baby was born. How they'd simply forgotten to have their house blessed, Julie still didn't know, but with life about to get even more chaotic, she didn't want to forget this important detail. That fall had been a pretty hefty scare, especially because she had no memory of how she'd gotten there! One moment she was fast asleep, and the next, she was tumbling down the staircase in the middle of the night!
~~~~

Julie flipped through her personal address book until she came to her mother-in-law's number.

"Hi Mom? It's Julie. Hey, can I ask you for a favour? I was just calling the rectory and can't seem to get anyone."

"Well sometimes Father visits the hospitals right after Mass. What were you calling about? Is there something I can help with?"

"Well maybe. Marc and I need to have the house blessed. Um, it seems in all the chaos, we totally forgot."

Julie held her breath, wondering what would come next.

"That's no problem, dear. When would you like to do it?"

"Um, maybe a few months after the baby is born?"

Julie was smiling as she concluded the call. Things would be alright now, she thought. The house Blessing would take care of the problem, she was sure of it.

Julie thought about all the bizarre things that had plagued them since moving into the house. Would the priest understand their concerns? Should they tell him before-hand what was really going on?

A small headache began to form behind Julie's right eye as she thought about how that conversation was likely to go.

Pressing her fingertips to her temple, she put it out of her mind and grabbed pen and paper instead. She would make a list of all the cleaning that would be required before she headed for the hospital.

No doubt she would lack the energy to do all that when she came home with a new baby, so best to get it done now.

Later, as Julie rubbed a paper towel over the smudges on her ensuite mirror, her thoughts returned to the House Blessing. What would the priest feel when he walked into her house? Would he be able to tell the minute he got there, that something wasn't right? Would he even come inside? All Julie had to go on was some vague misinformation gathered from movies and books. He was a man of the cloth, close to God. He was plugged into the source, right? So certainly, he would be able to tell what was going on. And more importantly, he'd be able to help them so they could live in peace with their growing family in their beautiful dream home.

That wasn't so much to ask, was it?

She would talk to Marc about what to say to the Priest. Marc always seemed to know what to do. He would have the right answer.

Nodding emphatically, she began whistling, as she put away toys, wiped down surfaces and arranged her belongings with care, checking off items as she finished each task. She didn't stop to wonder where all this extra energy was coming from.

With a whimsical smile, she propped up her beloved doll in the center of the living room sofa. The doll been a gift from her parents during a family trip when Julie was a child, and those memories were as dear to her as the timeless face of the hand-made doll. She'd only recently unpacked the treasured keepsake and wanted a prominent place for it in her new home. It was a symbol, Julie thought, as she arranged the ragdoll carefully. A symbol that this place was *her* home.

"You're lookin' mighty cute there," she commented, giggling.

It felt good to giggle. There didn't seem to be enough of that in her life, lately.

With the dusting and vacuuming now finished, she took a moment to look around. Such a pretty house. They'd done a lot to it already, so why hadn't they thought to have it blessed before now? They were good Catholics, weren't they? It bothered her that it had completely slipped their minds.

Well, none of that mattered now. The priest would come; he would bless the home and sprinkle it with Holy Water. Everyone present would immediately feel the difference, like a veil lifting, and the darkness would go away forever. It would finally be the home they hoped for. It would be *theirs*.

Julie wasn't aware that she stroked the small, gold cross that hung at her neck, but the gesture repeated as she moved from room to room.

~~~~

"I don't think it works like that hon," Marc answered that evening. "Just because he's a Priest doesn't mean he's also a Sensitive."

"Oh," Julie felt deflated.

"But you know what?" Marc countered. "Maybe he will. Who knows? I'm certainly no expert. Let's just wait and see."

"But do we tell him what's been going on here?" she asked.

"I don't think so," Marc replied. "It's a Blessing, not a ghost-hunt. Besides, I'm not sure how he'd react. He's still human after all,
~~~~

and people have some strange ideas about this sort of stuff. I'd rather our Priest didn't have strange ideas about us, too. "

Julie felt annoyed by Marc's flippant remarks, but if she were honest with herself, his logic made sense.

~~~~

Julie walked briskly to the end of the hallway and the linen closet, a stack of folded towels balanced in her arms. The scent of fabric softener filled her nose. To her right, the staircase creaked, as though someone had just paused there in the middle for a moment. Automatically, she darted a glance in that direction as she walked, but saw no one.

Julie frowned and shook her head. "Playing games?" she asked casually. But as she turned back to the hallway, an icy patch of air engulfed her head and shoulders! With a sharp scream, Julie dropped the carefully folded towels over the edge of the railing.

Reaching into her pocket for the small flashlight she always kept with her now, Julie switched on the beam and flashed it back and forth, cutting through the shadows, and exposing the rooms beyond.

Dropping the flashlight back into her pocket, Julie backtracked angrily to the staircase, so she could retrieve the towels. "Alright that's it!" she shouted. Her voice echoed off the walls. "You cut that out now! You are such an asshole!"

Retrieving the towels and re-folding them, Julie stuffed them hastily into the closet and turned away. She knew he was still there. She could feel his energy.

The thing made of shadows allowed himself a quiet chuckle. All things considered, this was going well. Not too much, just enough ...

"Damn this house and its ridiculous noises," she commented loudly. "I have better things to do than listen to you. And keep your damn hands off my clean laundry!"

~~~~

"Oof, that's nasty!" Julie sat down abruptly on the bottom step of the staircase and rubbed her abdomen.

"Honey, are you okay?" her mother asked, emerging from her suite at the unexpected sound.

"I'm fine," she said, frowning. "I just don't feel right. Maybe dinner didn't sit too well."

"Hmm, I think not," her mother vetoed confidently. "Is it pain or nausea? Or both?"

"Um, both I think."

"Labour?"

"I don't think so," she scoffed. "It's hard to tell."

"Marc!" Julie's mother shouted over the top of her daughter's head. "It's time! Get your keys!"

"Oh nonsense," Julie argued. "It's just indigestion."

"And your due date has already passed," her mom pointed out. "Listen to your mother, and get to the hospital, would you? For once in your life, don't argue."

Chapter Sixteen

"We're home!" Julie called out as she walked through the front door. Crossing to the bottom of the staircase, she arrived just in time to find her son, his face pressed into the bars of the gate, looking down at her from the top of the staircase.

"Hi sweetie!" Julie called, smiling up at him. "How's my boy?"

Adam, of course said nothing. Instead, he started to swing his leg up, as though he would climb over the gate to get to her. Grandma quickly dissuaded him with gentle hands.

"I'll be up there in a minute," Julie called to him. "Daddy and I have a surprise for you!"

Adam seemed to do a double-take. Taking his hands off the gate, he let them fall to his side, and spoke in a serious tone.

"Where were you?" he demanded.

Julie, already weary from the drive home and the dramatic events of the past several days, almost fell over in shock.

"What did you say?" she asked her eyes wide. "Marc!" she called to her husband. "Did you hear that? Adam just asked where we've been!"

"That was him asking?" Marc answered in disbelief. "Well, you'd better tell him!"

"Daddy and I went to the hospital," Julie explained carefully as she climbed the staircase. Marc trailed after her, carrying the car seat with the tiny infant nestled securely inside. "We went to get your baby sister."

As Julie reached the top, she unlatched the gate and held it open for her husband and new baby daughter. With gentle hands, she touched her son's face and smiled at him.

"I've missed you," she said. Tears sprang to her eyes as she gathered him into her arms for a fast, hard hug, the way he liked. It might have been her imagination, but the little boy seemed to cling to her a little longer than usual.

"Wanna see your sister?" she asked, leading him to the living room where Marc was setting down the car seat and unbuckling the harness. As he lifted the baby from the seat, Julie reached over and turned back the corner of the receiving blanket to reveal a little, pink face and a tuft of strawberry blonde hair.

"Look Adam," called his father softly. Marc's eyes glistened as he spoke. It was an emotional moment for both of them. "This is your sister. Her name is Amélie."

Adam darted a quick glance at the baby, then seemingly unconcerned, turned around and walked back into the family room.

Everyone agreed that baby Amélie was beautiful in all the right ways and although her brother was still uncertain, Julie and Marc were happy as they manoeuvred themselves and all their newfound baby accessories into the nursery.

They were home, and that was all that mattered.

~~~~

Snow drifted from the sky like the feathers from a giant pillow. The soft flakes fell deeply, putting a hush over the normally frantic cul-de-sac. School had been cancelled, and giggling children were being pulled along on small sleds, the sounds muted by the swirling vortex of white. Dogs materialized through the gloom, the ends of their leashes still hidden, as though they were walking themselves.

Julie smiled a sad little smile and turned around to face her beautiful prison.

From the carpet on her floors, to the paint on her walls and now the sky outside her window, everything was grey.
~~~~

It matched her mood. The tiny little baby who'd seemed so quiet and sweet in the hospital had screamed herself to sleep every night since.

They'd only been back from the hospital for a week, but to Julie it seemed much longer. She wasn't getting much rest, but the harder she tried to sleep the more elusive it proved to be.

The nurse's advice still rang in her ears. "Remember, sleep when the baby sleeps," she'd said, waving to Julie as she got into the car for the ride home.

"Sure," she had said to Marc as soon as they were underway. "Sleep when the baby sleeps, huh? That's easy for them to say. I'll bet none of them have nightmares like I do."

Marc faced straight ahead, his eyes on the road, but Julie had seen the muscles along his jaw tighten.

"And what about those mommies who have more than one child? Are these mommies simply putting themselves to bed while their older children have free reign of the house? Not if they're like Adam, they're not." Julie had folded her arms in annoyance as she stared out the windshield.

"Hell no," Marc agreed. "With Adam on the loose, we wouldn't *have* a house."

They'd both laughed half-heartedly at that, realizing the truth of those words.

With stubborn determination, Adam refused to look at his baby sister, going to great lengths to pretend the baby simply did not exist. He attempted to carry on as he had before, demanding all his parent's and grandparent's attention.

Was this sibling rivalry? Was this the jealousness the doctor had warned them about? With all those books she'd read on Autism, there was no mention of what to do about this.

Willfully, Adam turned away from his mother's hugs. He hissed like a cornered cat when she tried to draw his attention to the newborn, hoping to make him understand that this tiny little girl would look up to him one day and he needed to be a good big brother.

The gifts they'd purchased on the advice of their doctor were meant to introduce an air of celebration of pride in their son, as Amélie's big brother. But the gifts and special attention were of no interest to him. Adam ignored the gifts, choosing to take the baby's toys instead, stashing them away under his bed. When Julie laid down for a much-needed nap, Adam escaped his grandfather's supervision to creep into the nursery and dump out a whole bottle of baby powder on the carpet, before he was apprehended.

Julie's mother, not yet retired, worried that she wasn't able to help her daughter as much as she wanted to.

"Your father's just not that great with babies," she explained. "Give him Adam instead. He should be able to manage a six-year-old til I get home."

Julie was grateful for her parent's help. It broke her heart to think Adam could be a danger to the baby, but his jealousy seemed to know no bounds.

Despite all her son's antics, Julie and Marc both kept their expressions neutral and pretended nothing was wrong.

The young woman let out a deep sigh full of fatigue and sadness as she stared out the window, lost in her own thoughts. Had it only been a week? It seemed so much longer!

And now not even the weather was cooperating!

Snow was usually an exciting change, but the storm outside didn't feel exciting. It felt just like the mood inside the house: oppressive and heavy.

Everything outside her window was turning to ice, forcing children and pet walkers back inside as they hunkered down, riding out the storm. She was grateful Marc wouldn't be struggling home in this but what about her mom?

Julie glanced at the clock and blew stray locks of hair out of her eyes as she watched the cars outside adjusting for the worsening weather. The swirling snowflakes were mesmerizing, hypnotic … *Wake up*, she thought fiercely. *Why can't I just wake up?*

It felt like she was in the grip of some sort of trance.

"And suddenly, it hit!"

"Adam!" she yelped in surprise, whirling around.

The little boy, demanding his mother's attention, had approached on silent feet and now stood, grinning as he waited for her to provide the next line to the movie he was quoting. "It was the storm of storms," he said, prompting his mother further.

His smile was akin to a beautiful sunny day and although she'd been angry and startled at first, tears welled up and slipped from the corners of her eyes as realization dawned.

Adam didn't understand any of this. He just wanted his mommy back.

Play with me, mommy, he seemed to be saying. *Just play with me.*

~~~~~

Julie slept only sporadically now, her time taken up with a million new chores, while still having to deal with Adam's night terrors and the reality that comes from living with Autism.

Adam was finally calm again, comforted back to sleep after the most recent nightmare that jolted the household awake. The baby was awake but not crying, Julie noted with satisfaction as she automatically crawled back into bed.

If it wasn't for the fact that Adam was such a complex person, his idiosyncrasies so numerous, her parents would have been able to help much more than this, Julie thought ruefully. She shook her head and tried not to blame herself for that. Was she simply too permissive with him? Should she and Marc be stricter with their son, knowing it would lead to a battle but sticking to their guns nonetheless?

Maybe if she had more energy, that would be a thing, she thought irritably. The truth was that Adam's schedule was filled with a thousand tiny details that only Julie fully understood. When someone else stepped in to care for him, even Marc, they did so knowing that Adam would soon seek out his mother, the person who knew him best.

She was his world, and he was hers. That was obvious to her now, but it was too late to change it. She loved her son, but what she wouldn't give to share some of the responsibility! Adam was simply used to a certain way, and when that way was interrupted, that's when the screaming started.

As a result, Julie found herself shuffling through the halls of a house she no longer loved, in a constant state of chaos, unsure whether it was morning, noon or night.

When sleep came, it was the sleep of near-unconsciousness, but each time she rose, she did so with stiff, sore muscles and her eyes were still red with a fatigue she couldn't shake, no matter how many times her husband or parents tried to help.
~~~~~

Eventually it became clear that the baby was easier to care for than their six-year-old!

Patiently, her parents did what they could to help their daughter, but concern for her well-being was evident.

Arthur and Anne frowned with concern but didn't say anything, understanding that Julie's temper hovered on a very thin line and even an expression of sympathy might set her off.

When the baby was about three months old, however Anne could stand it no longer. She knocked three times on the foyer wall before climbing the stairs to the main floor. Assuming a determined but loving expression, she faced her daughter across the kitchen table. She was pleased to see Julie had at least gotten dressed today.

"Julie," she began. "I don't like this, you're spreading yourself too thin," her mother remarked. "It's a beautiful sunny afternoon, and here you are, cooped up in the dark. Anne crossed to the glass doors and opened the blinds to reveal the bright sunshine.

Julie saw at once that the snow had melted. When did that happen, she wondered?

"You've got to get out and enjoy life a little," Anne continued. "Dad and I have been patient knowing you had to work this out, but this is ridiculous! It's time to do *something*."

Two spots of color covered Anne's delicate cheekbones and her green eyes flashed with an inner fire that Julie knew well.

This wasn't going to be easy, Julie thought. I know that look.

Slowly, the weary young mother rose from the table, her infant daughter nestled within the crook of one arm. Wordlessly, she stood at the sliding glass doors and felt the welcoming sunshine warm her face and neck. For the first time in months, she felt a little more like her old self, and she knew what she had to do. With a wan smile, she turned to face her mom.

"You're right," she said simply.

Anne blinked in surprise.

"I think it's time I took my children to the park."

It was a bold, brave statement considering the fact that Adam still wasn't acknowledging the existence of his little sister and he tantrummed daily but everything inside of Julie was screaming at her to get out of the house.

Get out and you'll feel better, she thought. Get out so you can think.

Forcing a look of happiness onto her face that she didn't yet feel Julie went in search of her son.

"I'll go with you," Anne promised her daughter, instantly relieved. "When do you want to go?"

"No time like the present," Julie replied. Peeking into her son's room, she came back to the kitchen, a small frown furrowing her forehead. "Uh, mom? What day is it?"

Anne laughed. "It's Friday, Adam's in school. We'll need to go pick him up in about …" Anne paused and glanced at the clock on the wall. "Half an hour or so. You want to bundle up the baby and come with me?"

"Oh, sure!" Julie's cheeks reddened. "That's why it's so quiet. How far gone am I not to notice something so obvious?"

"It's alright sweetie, you just need to get out of the house, and you'll feel better."

Half an hour later, Julie and Anne walked briskly to Adam's school, Amélie tucked into her stroller, already fast asleep.

The air was cool against her face, and she was glad for the windbreaker she wore and the extra blankets surrounding her daughter. The sunshine was weak but it offered a small measure of warmth. The farther they got from the house, the more Julie felt more like her old self. Before the two women had gone a full block, Julie's steps had gotten so light that she felt almost like she could jog the rest of the way.

"Oh wow," she remarked, on the way back home again. "Mom, you were right, this is what's been missing. I'm gonna do this every day!"

He mother grinned. "It sure is good to see you smiling again," her mom replied. "When you're ready to do this on your own, your dad said he wants to hook up the trailer and take another quick holiday, but I told him we have to make sure you're okay first."

"Oh, I think I'm gonna be fine," she said, automatically gripping her son's hand, while her mom pushed the stroller. "I'm feeling much stronger now. Thank you."

Her mother's eyes widened and she grinned. "You're welcome," she said, pushing the stroller a little faster to keep up with her suddenly energetic family.

That visit to the park heralded in a new reality for Julie, and while Amélie still refused to sleep in her own bed for more than an hour at a time, and Adam's night terrors continued, forcing Julie to be up most nights, she took comfort in the fact that every day, rain or shine, she got out of the house and walked. The thrill she experienced every time the front door banged closed behind her became so enticing it was almost like a drug.

As for the sleepless nights, she wasn't sure how, but Julie simply grew used to it, remarking to her husband that it was amazing how little sleep she actually *needed*. Marc looked sideways at his seemingly happy wife with suspicion, wondering how long she could keep up such an act.

Part of Marc's job was working with high voltage power circuits, and sleep deprivation wasn't something he could cope with on the job. Marc felt a little guilty anyhow, knowing his wife sat up with their children most nights. He often awoke to find her sound asleep in the nursery rocking chair, Julie's arms locked around their infant daughter as they slumbered together.

~~~~

She yawned, rubbing at eyes that felt filled with sand as the memories of her dream lingered.

She was surprised to be dreaming at all, considering the amount of time she slept each night was measured in minutes, instead of hours.

In the dream, she followed a stranger whose face she could not see, as he stalked the hallways of her home. He walked as though he owned the place, and Julie trailed after him, unable to make him leave.

It was always the same; she'd had this dream many times. In her dream-state, she accepted the stranger's presence without question, and although she didn't *want* him there, she did anything he asked of her. Things she would never do while awake made perfect sense to her in the dream. Julie followed the shadow-draped stranger from room to room, where he pointed with imperious gestures at objects, waiting until she moved them to a location of his choosing. Upon waking, she complained to Marc that she'd been 'ordered around all night' by someone she didn't know.

Marc reasoned that it was due to the frustration she felt at their son's diagnosis.
~~~~

"Aren't we always being ordered around by some professional or another?" he'd said, shrugging.

She had to admit, it was a workable theory.

And so, the strange repetitive dreams were chalked up to sleepless nights and frustration.

Over time however, Marc began to notice something was wrong.

"Julie," he asked, acting on impulse one morning soon after they awoke. "Did you have the dream again?"

"Of course," she muttered irritably.

"What room were you in this time?" He asked.

"What difference does it make? I thought you weren't interested."

"I never said I wasn't interested, I just said maybe it's your reaction to stress, that's all." Marc replied defensively. "Still, just humour me okay? What room? Do you remember?"

"Living room and kitchen," she mumbled, swinging her legs out of bed.

"Did you move anything?"

"Oh sure. Umm, a newspaper from the coffee table, and something else from the kitchen," she said, squinting her eyes as she tried to remember. "I can't quite recall, but it was something small and dark, like a wallet, maybe. Why?"

Marc turned away quickly, realizing his expression registered the shock he felt. He'd gone to the kitchen just a few minutes ago, to retrieve his wallet only to discover that it wasn't where he'd left it the night before.

Was this really happening?

~~~~

"No!" she shouted, sitting bolt upright, yet again, her heart thudding.

"Wha-!" Marc reacted, sitting up as well and rubbing his eyes.

"I'm sorry," she replied automatically, one hand pressed to her chest as she willed the details to fade.

Julie reached for the glass of water she'd placed there earlier that evening, but groped across the night table in vain. Her throat went dry as she searched.

Finally, Marc rolled over. "What are you looking for?" he asked sleepily.
~~~~

"I'm sorry," she whispered. "My water glass is missing. Did you take it?"

"Not me," he said wearily. "Did you have one?"

"Nevermind," she muttered. "It doesn't matter."

There was a hidden agenda here, and Marc knew it. He dared not put that thought into words however.

Julie called it out, even argued with it, and now look at her! He wanted nothing more than to leave this place, but with the market at an all-time low, they would lose everything. House prices had fallen, dragging their equity down with it.

This house was supposed to be their leg-up, not their undoing, he thought angrily. Somehow, they had to weather this storm.

Marc watched his wife sleep, relieved to see her relaxed expression. She was truly resting, something she didn't do often, anymore. New babies were rough on sleep patterns, but Amélie was several months old now and still not sleeping properly. Adding to that, his wife had the nightmares to contend with. There were far too many nightmares.

Eventually, the clock on his bedside table read 6 AM and Marc rolled out of bed, careful not to wake his wife. His thoughts were still whirling as he started the shower and stepped inside.

Were they becoming its possessions?

"No!" the sound of Julie's voice reached him, even inside the shower with water pounding down around him. "We won't!"

"Jules?" He called out. "What's going on? Are you okay?"

Marc stopped the shower and got out as quickly as he dared.

"Julie?" he called again. "Is the baby up?"

Hurrying back into the bedroom, he shivered as his still-wet body met the suddenly icy air of the bedroom.

"It's okay honey," Julie whispered hoarsely, as she rolled towards him and offered a weak smile. "Everything's fine. It's just another dream."

Marc stood there, dripping on the laminate and looking around, his heart still hammering in his chest.

"It's not okay," he whispered. "But we can fix it. We have to."

Marc resolved to call his mom as soon as possible. She would know what to do, but he'd have to be careful how much he divulged. His mom knew everyone and the last thing he needed was for this secret to get out.

~~~~

"Now where did I put that –oh Adam!" Julie exclaimed, noting the open tin of diaper rash ointment that lay on the floor, and the long white smears that striped the carpet.

Amélie kicked on the change table as if to say 'hurry up mommy'. Julie practiced deep breathing as she re-diapered her daughter and held the baby to one shoulder.

Adam was liberally smeared with the stuff himself, clumps of white goo in his hair, and streaks of it along his arms and clothing.

"It would have to be the expensive cream you dug into, wouldn't it?" she muttered, picking up the empty tin with one hand and dropping it into the trash.

Julie chewed her lip in consternation as she settled Amélie in a cuddle seat and slid another movie into the VCR. Julie was aware that she over-used this technique but not able to think of another that made him sit still. At least this way she'd be able to clean Adam up without having to chase him all over the house.

Maybe they should put off the house-warming until their son adjusted to his new baby sister with a bit less destruction. Then, she reasoned, the weather might be warmer too and everyone would feel more like celebrating.

What was she thinking trying to arrange it so soon after Amélie's birth, anyways?

"I'm not a super-woman," she chuckled to herself. "Too bad I can't seem to remember that."

The more Julie thought about postponing the party, the better she liked the idea.

Weird things didn't seem to happen too often outside, she reasoned.

It was perfect!

With Amélie cooing happily as she sat in her swing, and Adam clapping his newly cleaned hands along to a familiar theme-song, Julie made her way quickly downstairs for a short chat with her mother.

"Hello?" Julie heard the snick-snick-snick of her mom's slippers as she walked rapidly down the hall to answer Julie's knock. "Hi sweetie," she greeted Julie, opening the door. "What's on your mind?"
~~~~

"Do you think it's too late to post-pone the House-warming?"

"Um, yes," her mom answered, obviously baffled by the question.

"Really?" she replied, her voice plaintive.

"Julie, it's in two days. Why do you want to postpone?" her mother asked.

"There's too much to do mom. And Adam keeps undoing everything right behind me. You know that tin of five-dollar diaper rash cream I just bought? Well Adam got into it, and now I have to go buy more! I don't even know yet if it'll come out of the carpet and the bedding. That kid! He's so jealous, it drives me nuts!" She sighed. "And unlike Adam, this baby doesn't sleep mom! My household is a zoo. Come upstairs and see if you don't believe me."

Anne held up her hands in defeat. "Okay, okay, I get it. Do you want help tidying up?"

Julie cocked her head to the side incredulously. "It's not a case of simply tidying up mom, it's everything!"

"Oh Julie," Anne replied. "Let's just go upstairs and I'll give you a hand for a few minutes. You'll see, a bit of order in that sea of chaos and you'll feel better." She backed her daughter up with a wave of her hands. "Move! Let's go! No time like the present!"

Julie climbed the stairs wearily.

"What the heck?" Anne wondered aloud, climbing up behind her.

"What is it?" she said.

"What's this doing here?" Anne asked. "Are you letting Adam play with your special doll? I don't think that's a very good idea, Julie. Not with him wrecking things left and right."

"What? I didn't give this to him!" Julie said, snatching the doll from the edge of the hand rail atop the stairs. "That's so weird; he's never even shown any interest in it before."

The last time she'd seen the hand-made rag doll was days ago, when she'd lovingly placed it the living room sofa.

"How am I supposed to keep up with him?" she commented, exasperation in her voice. "Look how fast he is! I was barely gone two minutes! I'm sure this wasn't here when I came downstairs."

"Hmm," Anne replied uncertainly as she walked into the living room and looked around. "Oh dear, I'm afraid there's more to this story. Look over here."

The wall that separated the living room from the staircase featured two finished arches cut into the drywall, allowing a wide view into the next room.

It was the sill of one these, the one farthest from the top of the stairs that her mother now pointed at.

"What?" she asked, hurrying to have a look. A child's sized hand-print shone brightly against the eggshell finish.

"Clearly, Adam's been up here," Anne said seriously. "If he fell from here, it's a six foot drop to the stairs, and then another tumble to the bottom."

Julie covered her face with both hands, feeling overwhelmed.

Anne darted a quick, disapproving glance at her daughter. "Well, we can't just ignore this; we've got to figure out some way of keeping him off these ledges.

"I'm not ignoring it mother, but what *can* we do?"

"House plants," her mom answered confidently.

"Plants? What good will plants do?"

"Give you a very loud warning if he climbs up there again, that's what. Look at these ledges. There's barely enough room for a houseplant, never mind a squirmy little boy. If he gets up there, he'll knock everything down, and voila! You'll know about it." The older woman nodded decisively. "I have two pots of ivy that'll do nicely in this first one, and I'll pick something up this afternoon for the others, but you have to promise to water them."

"Wow," Julie muttered. "You know, that's actually a really good idea."

"You're too kind," Anne replied dryly. "Now you just leave the house-warming details to me," she continued. "Everything will go as planned."

Julie resisted the urge to groan, and just pasted a weary smile on her face instead.

Good luck, she wanted to say.

Chapter Seventeen

"I'm sorry, but I'm not able to come," the priest's voice was raspy. "I know it's very short notice, but I'm too sick to come."

"That's alright Father," Julie reassured him. "Just get better and we'll re-arrange it for another time."

"Thank you," he croaked. As he hung up the phone, Julie heard a fit of hoarse coughing before the connection went dead.

"Poor guy," she muttered, wondering why she felt relieved instead of concerned at the sudden cancellation. Since the house blessing was on hold, it made sense to cancel the whole thing. Anne didn't like it, but for once she agreed with her daughter.

~~~

In the weeks that followed, Julie struggled just to take care of herself and the baby.

The houseplants were placed, and Julie was given strict instructions on how to care for them, so they would flourish.

Julie continued her commitment of taking the baby out for a walk on most days, which helped with her mood, but sleep continued to be the enemy.

The cards and gifts they'd received from friends and family when the baby was born had been shifted from the kitchen counter,
~~~

to the table and back again, as they adapted to life with a sleepless child.

As Julie padded down the hall to give her husband a groggy kiss before work, he waved his hand at the items strewn across the table.

"Do you think you could clear this off today?" he asked. "It would be nice to use our table again."

Marc had been careful not to ask for much since they'd discovered the tiny baby hated to sleep in her own room. He knew his wife was functioning on barely any sleep.

Still, Julie knew this was something that irritated her husband and had done for months.

"I'll work on it," she promised, rising on tip-toes to kiss his cheek and offer him a smile.

Marc grinned at her. It was good to see her humour returning. Maybe things were looking up after all.

~~~~

"Pee-yu," Adam said as he followed his mother into the nursery. Julie looked at her son in surprise. He was holding his nose as he looked at his baby sister, who now lay wiggling, on the change table. Julie had to admit the aroma was strong, but it was funny to hear appropriate words from Adam that weren't derived from a movie.

"Yeah, stink-y, " she agreed, smiling. Adam grimaced as his mother quickly changed the diaper.

"Take it back," he said.

"What?" Julie replied, astonished.

"Take it back!" Adam insisted.

"The diaper?"

"No! Take it ba-ack!" With a slight smile on his lips, he waited for his mother to respond.

Julie cocked her head to one side. She knew this game. Adam was playing 'what's the next line'? It was the only way he knew to interact. Not being able to form sentences on his own, he frequently borrowed them from movies and TV. He liked it best when he could engage others to fill in the blanks for him.

"Take ... your sister back?" The young mother queried in disbelief, pointing at the infant.

Adam grinned. It was obvious he wanted Julie to 'say her line'. It was a line she knew well, having watched the same movie with her son a hundred times or more, but she didn't always do the expected.
~~~~

Maybe this time, she thought, it would be more than just a quote. Maybe this time, it would be communication. He'd started strong, maybe if she pushed it just a little, they would make some real progress.

"Take what back?" she asked again, securing the last tab on the diaper and picking her daughter up again to hold her close. The baby craned her body around to watch her big brother, a big smile on her face.

Adam pointed at his sister. "Take … it … back!"

There was no mistaking that, but Julie was still shocked. "Your sister? Take your sister back?"

Could he really mean that?

Amélie kicked her legs and giggled.

Good thing she didn't understand, Julie thought.

"Okay smart guy, where do I take her?" Julie knew there would be no answer, but she was enjoying this divergence from his usual quoting marathon.

"Aisle 9," came the unexpected answer.

Her blue eyes wide, she stared at her son. This was more than the usual departure from the movie quotes for sure. Julie almost wanted to pinch herself. Was this really happening?

"Aisle 9?" she demanded, incredulously. "Why aisle 9?"

But as Julie waited for an answer, Adam narrowed his eyes at the infant, then turned and walked calmly from the room, as though there was nothing left to say.

Perhaps in his mind, there wasn't.

Later, when Marc got home, the strange conversation was related in full detail. As the story ended, Marc began laughing.

"Jules, didn't you realize that in the store we always go, aisle 9 is where all the baby stuff is? The diapers, formula, baby food, all that stuff's in aisle 9! He must think that's where she came from too! What a smart kid! Who says he isn't paying attention?" Shaking his head, he walked over to his son and bent to ruffle the boy's hair affectionately. The small child ducked his head and pushed his dad's hand away in annoyance, still trying to focus on the toys in his hand and the book at his knee.

Julie smiled. Marc needed moments like this. It wasn't lost on her that he was still fighting the depression they both felt over their son's diagnosis. The specialists had all warned them they would feel it; the loss of the child they 'should have had'. It came in waves now, no longer the crushing sadness it had been when they'd first heard the words.

But these moments, when Adam's quirky sense of humour made his parents laugh out loud, helped to remind them that life is never what you expect it to be.

~~~

"Okay, so what are we going to do about it?" Julie asked one hand on her hip. "I need that computer. I have to get that article done before the paper forgets about me. It's been too long already, with the baby and everything. I can't turn down this offer."

"Don't panic, I'll ask Dennis to come over and give me a hand with it, okay? He knows computers. If anyone can fix it, Dennis can."

Julie looked at her husband suspiciously.

"I promise. It'll work. You'll see."

Later that day, the doorbell rang.

"Dennis, come on in," Marc said as he opened the door, Amélie in his arms.

"Hey there little one," Dennis said as he came inside. "Whoah, she's a cutie. Hi Julie!"

He called upstairs as he went to hang up his coat.

"Hiya Dennis," Julie replied from upstairs.

"Well, let's get to it," he announced, as he laid out his tool box on the floor and knelt beside it. "The wife's gonna murder me if I'm not back before dinner," he explained.

His jovial mood was contagious and Julie heard the two men ribbing each other good-naturedly. It was important for Marc to have a friend to talk and laugh with. Life had been far too serious lately, she realized.

All too soon it was time for Dennis to go home.

"Thanks for trying, Dennis." Julie heard her husband's deep voice resonating in the downstairs hallway and she went to the gate, eager for news.

"Any luck Dennis?" she called.

"Sorry Julie, nothing I can do."

Marc came to the bottom of the stairs to stand beside his friend as they looked up at her. "Sorry honey, stupid thing's a mystery."
~~~

Dennis cleared his throat and patted Marc on the back. "A lemon. That's what it is," he corrected. "All the components test fine and the connections are good. I can't find any programming errors, and nothing's overheating. You either bought a lemon, or there's a ghost in this machine, my friend," he chuckled at his own joke. "If you can take it back to the store, I would."

~~~~

The next day, Marc awoke to find Julie, coming slowly up the staircase with the computer tower in her arms.

"What's going on?" he asked.

"The computer is moving upstairs," she explained.

"Now? When did we decide this?"

"You said you didn't know what to do, so I'm doing something."

"It doesn't work, Jules. You heard Dennis."

"Yes, she answered simply. "I did."

"So, what more do you want to do?"

"Move it upstairs. Call it a hunch," she answered.

"Uh-huh," he answered in a monotone, narrowing his eyes at her. "Does this have any basis in fact, or is this another feeling?"

"You know better than to ask that," she replied tartly.

"Okay, okay," Marc replied. "I give up, but does this have to happen now?"

"You forget, I've been up for hours, already. Amélie didn't fall sleep until just a few minutes ago, and now for some reason I'm wide awake and in the mood to write."

"So, we're moving the computer on a hunch, as a last ditch before we return it and get our money back?" Marc paused and watched his wife as she sank gratefully into a nearby chair.

"Yup," she confirmed. "There is a problem with that room," she said. "Nobody's comfortable down there and you know it."

Marc sighed and shook his head.

"Fine," he said. "I suppose you've got everything apart down there?"

"Yup."

"Okay," he mumbled. "Forget I said anything, we'll try it your way."

"I'll help," she volunteered.
~~~~

"Nevermind," Marc replied. "Just open the gate for me when I get to the top, so nobody takes a header down the staircase. That's all we'd need."

"Thanks honey," Julie said smiling. "Now we'll see what's what."

Marc was grateful for the distraction the computer provided that morning. He didn't want to talk about things he couldn't explain. If felt like they just went around in circles. They never seemed to get any closer to a solution. It all came down to this: what were they supposed to do about it?

Truthfully, he was sick of talking about it. What good did it do to argue these things?

Endless wondering seemed to have become his wife's new pastime.

What about holding a séance, or sprinkling Holy Water, or salt, she'd asked? Do those things work? Could they try talking to the priest again? They never did have that Blessing, she reminded him.

Marc needed a break from all the chatter.

He gained the top floor with the last of the components and whistled at Julie, who seemed to have forgotten all about him. The gate was locked, but his hands were full of black wires.

"Jules, a little help here?" he called.

"Oh! Sorry," she replied, hurrying over to open the gate.

She looked at the computer monitor he held in his hands, a confused pile of black wires coiled atop the unit. "Is that everything?" she asked innocently.

"Printer's still downstairs, but we don't need that right now. I'll go and get the keyboard and mouse after breakfast. But Julie," he sighed. "Why didn't you label these wires before you unplugged them?"

"I, uh, didn't think of it," she said. "I was in a hurry."

"Of course you were," Marc replied dryly.

He was treated to a cold stare and icy silence.

"Nevermind," he replied. "So you said Ami's asleep, right?"

Julie nodded. "For now. I checked on Adam ten minutes ago," she added. "He was sleeping then, but he's probably up by now. I think it's your turn to check."

Marc threw her a mock salute and started down the hall before she could say anything else.

"Can you throw on a pot of coffee?" he called to her. "I get the feeling I'm gonna need it."

Marc opened the door to see Adam not only awake, but busy hauling every pair of shorts from his bureau drawer, piling them on his bed.

"Good morning little man, watcha doin'?" Marc said calmly as he opened the door wide. Adam continued to focus on the task in front of him. Already a pile of clothing lay in an untidy heap in the middle of the bed.

"Mommy's gonna love this," Marc commented dryly. "What are we looking for?"

Instead of answering, Adam abandoned the now empty drawer and turned his attention to the one above, picking up handfuls of clean shirts and tossing them over his shoulder and onto the bed.

"Whoah, whoah, munchkin. What are you doing, packing? We're here to stay big guy." Marc quickly closed his hand over one of Adam's, until the child released his grip. "Breakfast time!" Marc quickly scooped his son up into his arms. "Swoosh!" he said, making Adam giggle. Marc used the distraction to full effect as he carried his son from the room.

Julie was just arranging a chair she'd dragged from the kitchen, in front of a collection of TV trays, when her husband came in, carrying their son.

"What's this?" he asked.

"It's a make-shift desk. When you bring up the components they need to go on something right?

"Okay," Marc answered dubiously.

Julie placed her hands on both hips. "As you so kindly pointed out, this is only an experiment, and I happen to need my kitchen table which is probably where you were planning to put everything, right? I would have brought up the desk, but it's kinda big." Her tone held a hint of danger.

"Right," he said, depositing his son onto the couch. "Hey turkey, let's make mommy some breakfast, she's grouchy."

"Turkey," Adam repeated.

"I was thinking more like bacon," his father corrected him, good naturedly.

~~~
~~~

Later that afternoon, Marc began the laborious process of disassembling their sizable desk and setting it up again in the family room.

"I still can't believe that thing works fine up here," he said, as he passed through the gate with the remaining pieces.

"I know," Julie answered, smiling broadly. "I'm just as surprised as you are. But think about it! This means we don't need a new computer after all. And I won't have to deal with that creepy room! I can finally get some writing done."

"I don't know. Adam will be bugging you every second, trying to get into it," he reminded her. "You know what a little hacker he is! We'd better come up with something to keep it safe."

Both parents looked affectionately at their son as he happily bounced on the couch, while watching one of his favourite animated movies on TV. They felt guilty using the TV as a babysitter, but if you couldn't see Adam, you couldn't trust him, and this was just the way it had to be.

Julie chatted happily in a stage whisper as her husband reassembled the desk pieces, and tucked the wires through the strategic cut-outs in the back.

"It's harder than it looks," she commented.

"Yup," Marc grunted, as he slid his body under the desk yet again.

"Do you need any help? I feel bad you having to do all that. Let me in there, I can do that part.

"Julie, I appreciate the offer, but I'm fine."

"I just feel bad," she countered. "What if I just—"

Her sentence was cut off by a child's mournful cries.

"Oh geez, I guess she's up."

"And that would be for you," Marc called, his head and most of his torso still underneath the desk.

Marc was grateful that Amélie was awake and taking her mother's attention. Julie was starting to get on his nerves with all that apologizing.

Plugging in the last few components, Marc sat down at the desk and turned the machine on.

The computer beeped encouragingly.

That was a good sign, Marc thought. Maybe it was okay after all. It certainly seemed to be doing what it should. If only that could extend to the rest of the house, he thought darkly, his mind wandering as he stared at the black screen.

Marc shook his head. Now he was doing it. Everything didn't automatically have to be paranormal, did it? It was just a computer. Get a grip man!

How long, he wondered, would he be able to keep this up? It felt like he was on a friggin' see-saw! He was already doing his best to dodge the real-estate idea, refusing to even consider selling their house and moving away. We aren't quitters, he'd told his wife. We'll see this through.

Despite all that, though, Marc knew it was only a matter of time before he would have to do something. But what, he didn't know. He sensed something different every time he came through the front door, but he knew that giving it a voice would only make it stronger. It was better to deny it, wasn't it?

He thought of his wife and felt a stab of guilt. Maybe he was wrong, maybe ignoring it wasn't the answer, but what was? If he couldn't come up with the right plan, what would happen then?

" ...I'll be divorced," he answered his own question in a low mutter.

He knew what people did when they realized their house was haunted. They got out. No matter what the cost. And Marc knew the cost would be high if they left now. The market was still depressed. If they had to sell, they'd be lucky to break even.

Marc could hear the machine whirring, but the screen in front of him remained dark. Crawling back under the desk, Marc checked the cords snaking away from each component, tightening connections as he went.

"Ah, that's the one," he commented finally, pushing it home with a satisfying click.

As he got to his feet again, he could hear his wife, singing to their children just down the hall. Her voice carried, lilting and sweet as she sang songs from his son's favourite shows.

Marc sat back down and grinned. It was a nice house, in a nice neighbourhood. It was peaceful there, the cul-de-sac offering an insulation they hadn't experienced in their last place. So what if there was a ghost? Couldn't they just learn to co-exist? Nothing bad had happened, right? Even the strange incident with his niece at Christmas had been just that: strange.

Marc clicked the mouse to start a program and then folded his arms across his chest as he thought about that. He knew a thing or two about this stuff, after all. He'd have known if the entity was anything dangerous. It wouldn't be able to hide that from him. No, they would just have to make the best of it and stay until the house prices started climbing again. Everything would be okay. Once the Priest was better, they'd have the house blessed and that would help to settle his wife down.

Eagerly, he clicked the mouse again, opening program after program, determined to put the machine through its paces, to show his wife the computer really was a lemon. Even though he knew that meant taking the machine back to the store and dealing with all of that, he hated to be wrong.

It wasn't that he wanted a fight, but his technical mind just couldn't accept that spirit energy was the culprit here.

Marc listened as the hard drive whirred into life, executing each command with crisp efficiency.

He became aware of the cold air gradually, only rising from his seat to check as his fingers started cramping. Had a window been left open? Rising from his seat, he went to check, but found them all securely closed.

"Honey?" His wife asked, as he passed the nursery doorway. "Everything okay?"

"Yeah," he replied. "Just a bit cold, that's all. You got the window open in here?"

"Nope."

Marc walked to the fireplace and flicked the switch to one side. Almost instantly, blue natural gas flames shot up behind the glass doors.

"That ought to do it," he commented, returning to his seat. He inserted the disk for his newest flight simulator game, determined that if the computer was running anyhow, he would thoroughly test it. This was a complex program. If it could run that, he'd be forced to admit that moving it upstairs was a good idea after all.

As he loaded the program and watched the initial graphics leap to life on the screen, he soon forgot about falling house prices, strange sensations and ghostly apparitions. In fact, he was surprised to find that not only was the computer doing exactly what it should have done, it was doing it faster than he expected!

Marc sat back in the chair and arranged the joystick in front of him. Now, he was going to have to admit that for whatever reason, Julie's hunch was right. Geez, he thought. How long until I live that one down?

The smile was still on his lips when he felt something settle across his hands. Marc felt a rising sense of panic, and he jerked his hands away from the keyboard.

A cold wave of fear raced up his backbone as he witnessed impossibility on the screen in front of him.

Programs began opening and closing in rapid succession, too fast for any human hand. The cursor swept from one corner to the other as though an expert hand guided it.

Marc's eyes went to the computer mouse that sat, immobile on the desk, as more images flashed across the screen so rapidly, it was impossible to tell what they were.

This couldn't be happening.

"Stop it!" he shouted.

The screen in front of him continued to display image after image, flashing fast and faster.

In desperation, Marc hit the button to kill the power and the screen went dead.

"Holy shit," he whispered, sitting back in the chair, he raked his fingers back and forth through his hair, still staring at the darkened screen.

"Is this your sick way of answering my question?" he asked the emptiness.

Marc tried to think of something, anything that might explain this.

"Marc?" his wife called from the next room. "Are you okay? What's wrong?"

"Geez," he muttered. "What the hell am I gonna tell her now?"

Chapter Eighteen

Coats and shoes lay piled in an untidy heap on the foyer floor, as Julie dug through pockets and crawled halfway into the closet, searching in futility for the mailbox key.

"It's got to be here," she muttered. "Dad!" she called.

"Coming," he called back. Emerging quickly from the suite, he came to stand beside his daughter. "What the devil do you have going on here?"

"Dad, have you seen the mailbox key?" she asked.

"It's on the hook," her dad answered. "Where it always is."

Julie hung her head as she sat back on her heels. "No. It's not."

"Well I don't know, honey. Maybe Adam took it?"

Julie groaned. "I've got a list a mile long today, getting Adam ready for school. I don't need this."

"Well, before you go off questioning Adam, you'd better get this mess cleaned up or your mother will have a conniption!"

"Thanks," Julie muttered dryly, watching her dad return to his place, a folded newspaper under one arm.

"And how am I supposed to do that," she mumbled to no one as she re-hung jackets and coats and re-stowed boots into the closet. "Questioning Adam isn't as easy as it sounds."

The key Julie was searching for so frantically had gone missing overnight. A key was issued to each household by the postal service, corresponding to a specific compartment, where mail was deposited each day by the local mail carrier. A large, compartment-style mailbox was located within each neighbourhood, and it was part of Julie's regular routine to take a quick walk there to retrieve the mail.

The key had been securely stored on a single hook by the front door since Julie and Marc moved in.

The notion that Adam had suddenly taken an interest in the mailbox key seemed odd, but odd had become the new normal in their household. As Julie climbed the staircase, she carefully assembled the words she would try with Adam, hoping that this time she'd get a helpful response.

"Adam, come and look at this," she called to him, moments later. She held up a quick sketch of the key she was looking for. "Where is mommy's key?" she asked her son, seriously, pointing at the image. It was unlikely he'd done it, as the hook was well above his reach, but with Adam, she never ruled out a possibility, no matter how slim. And even if he didn't take it, he may have seen it somewhere. He had an amazing memory.

"Adam?" she asked again. "Where is mommy's special key?"

"Mommy spesha key?" Adam repeated, copying her intonation.

Julie wanted to scream. His echolalia was so irritating, sometimes! *How do I get through?*

"Adam, look at me."

"Ad-uh, look-a-me," he copied.

"Mommy needs the key," she said, trying to stay calm and pointing at the drawing again.

Adam reached for her hand, and Julie allowed him to take it. The small child pulled his mother out of her seat, and led her toward the fridge.

Julie's heart leapt. *It was on the fridge? Inside it? How was that possible? Did it matter at this point?*

Placing her hand on the fridge door handle, Adam grinned up at her.

"In here?" she asked.

"Open," he said.

Julie opened the fridge and peered inside, but instead of finding a key as she'd wildly hoped, Adam popped his head under underneath her arm and pushed past her to grab the milk carton.

"Milk," he said happily, hugging it to his body.

"Oh geez, and here I thought you were gonna help mommy!"

"Help mommy," Adam repeated.

"Oh, forget it," she snapped, snatching the milk carton away to pour him a glass.

"Fuh-gettit," he said, looking directly at his mother. His eyes were such an intense shade of blue, his gaze so trusting. Julie had only to look into those eyes a fraction of a second to realize her son had no idea why mommy was mad, especially when he was trying so hard to use his words…

Julie felt her shoulders sag in instant shame and guilt. "And once again, the 'Mother of the Year' award goes to me," she said dryly, handing him his drink. "Is it asking too much to have a day when I *don't* want to cry?"

~~~~

"Oh no you don't," Julie said, striking an action-figure pose, to re-direct her son before he could climb the china cabinet. With a burst of energy and renewed purpose, Julie had started dusting and wiping down surfaces, trying to put her house back in order. She felt guilty that the house still had an air of chaos to it.

She really had to try harder.

Adam tried to sidle past his mother, a silly grin on his face.

Julie hid a smile of her own behind one hand. He was so obvious!

"Back to the rec room young man," she said, steering him back to the kitchen doorway. "You've got oodles of toys in there. You don't need to bug mommy right now."

Adam allowed his mother to turn him by the shoulders and guide him back towards the kitchen, but as soon as his feet touched the kitchen floor, he stopped as though he'd hit a wall.

Without a word, Adam pivoted on one foot, changed direction and ran the other way! Reaching the family room through a different route, he stopped just as suddenly as he had before, and looked back at his startled mother.

"NOOO!" he yelled.

"Fine," she yelled back, holding up her hands in defeat. "Whatever. I don't understand, but fine!"

A familiar wail started up in the other room. Amélie was clearly startled out of her sleep. Julie rolled her eyes skyward.
~~~~

"I only just got her down for a nap," she muttered through clenched teeth. "Here we go again."

~~~~

Adam had woken up early and gone to the family computer before anyone else was up. Still rubbing at her tired eyes, Julie arose to find her son deeply engrossed in a computer game.

The weary mother was forced to use every tactic she'd learned from Ariel and then some, convincing Adam to get ready for school.

She was really looking forward to handing him off for a few hours. With Marc away for the week, she wanted to try and make some headway with that unending list of theirs. Maybe I'll even find that damned key, she thought, grabbing Adam's hand and forcing him to hold onto the stroller, while she locked the front door.

A few minutes later, Julie rolled into the classroom and simply held onto the back of her son's jacket. In one smooth motion, he pulled away and the jacked peeled neatly off his body. She handed the thin coat, now inside-out, to his Special Education Assistant and smiled wearily.

"Tag," she said, in a weak attempt at humour. "You're it."

Mrs. G., as she referred to herself, was a few years older than Julie. She always greeted the young mother and her son with a warm smile, but her no-nonsense attitude meant that Adam was in good hands.

"Anything to report this morning?" she asked.

"Obsession with a video game, I'm afraid," Julie replied. "He was on it before I got up, little turkey!"

"Ah, that's why he's so wired up," she observed, as Adam neatly evaded her automatic attempt to catch him as he ran by. Without hesitation, Adam pressed his nose against the side of the classroom aquarium and stared in wonder at the fish that swam contentedly inside.

Mrs. G soon closed in, and led him away to the cloakroom. "Too much sugar for breakfast?" she quipped, grinning.

"Yes, actually." Julie replied with heavy sarcasm. "But we're trying to cut back, so he only had half a pound this morning."

Although Julie loved Mrs. G, her comments sometimes seemed to have a double edge.

The school staff was always so quick to judge her family, and while she knew Mrs. G understood their situation better than anyone,
~~~~

the constant suggestions were wearing her patience thin. The suggestions themselves spoke of people who didn't understand, but thought they did.

Less sugar, more sleep, cut out wheat, cut out milk, put him on meds, and get rid of the dog … the list seemed endless.

If they only knew, Julie thought. It wasn't that simple. Didn't they think she and Marc were good parents?

The answering grin from Mrs. G however showed that she appreciated Julie's sarcasm. "Great! Anything else I should know for today?"

"It's Monday. Look out!"

"Ah, I see. Well, don't worry mom, we'll have a good day, won't we?" She smiled at Adam, and deftly recaptured his hand.

"Thanks," she said. "Bye sweetie," she called to her son, waving her fingertips. It was gratifying to see him turn around, although she wished he'd wave back like other children. "See you after school."

Amélie began to fuss, and Julie wheeled the carriage back and forth, knowing the rocking motion would put the baby to sleep once more.

"I'd better go, before she starts up again," she said, exiting the school as quickly as she dared, and with the sudden burst of speed, Amélie soon drifted off to sleep once more. Julie always worried some school official would call her back to sign something else, or plan another meeting. No matter how many times they met, the results were the same. They would do their best, but Julie and Marc shouldn't expect too much. After all, their son was complex, and there wasn't much more the school team could do.

It was so frustrating!

By the time Julie guided the stroller back up the driveway, she was already assembling a list of things to get done.

Amélie clung to her mother's neck as they went up the long flight of stairs.

As her gaze fell automatically on the staircase that rose before her, she had to stifle a startled gasp.

Half way up, as though it had been placed there, lay the missing mailbox key!

~~~~~
~~~~~

"It was creepy Marc," she said to her husband that evening on the phone. "The key looked like it was placed there."

"And you're sure it wasn't your parents?"

"They didn't get home until a couple of hours later. There was no one else in the house."

"Oh." Silence stretched between them on the line as each person thought about the implications of that.

Finally, Marc replied. "Well, at least you've got the key."

"I do, and I'm going to think of a better place to keep it from now on."

"Just make sure you tell me," Marc reminded her, chuckling. "You change things around so often, it's like a different house every time I come home."

"You should be used to that," Julie laughed. "I was thinking we could move that small table downstairs and use that for keys and stuff."

 Which one is that?"

"The one with the drawer that sticks" Julie replied.

"Perfect," Marc chuckled. "But hey, wait til I get home okay, and I'll do it for you. I don't want you taking a tumble down those stairs."

~~~~

"I'm not sure if you'll be comfortable enough down here Michelle," Julie waved her hand to indicate the small single bed, heaped with blankets in one corner of the den. The couple had placed bedroom furniture in the front room, turning it into a small guest room.

"It'll be just perfect for babysitters," Marc had enthused.

"You're just saying that because our babysitters are your baby *sisters*," Julie quipped. She was hopeful that the room's negative vibe was only her imagination and with the new décor and the absence of the family computer, it might turn into a functional part of their home once more.

"If it gets too cold for you, there's a space heater. Also, you don't have to stay in here if you'd rather sleep on the sofa upstairs. It's pretty comfy too."

Michelle smiled and dropped her backpack in the center of the bed.
~~~~

"Sounds good," she said, looking around the small room. "I should be fine here once the kids are in bed. You guys fixed it up nice in here. Is there a baby monitor?"

"Yes, I almost forgot!" Julie dashed up the stairs to retrieve it from the master bedroom.

Marc's youngest sister had volunteered to babysit for the evening. It had been a long time since they'd gone out as a couple, and they were anxious to revive 'date night'.

"We can all go to Mass tomorrow morning, and then we'll drive you back home, okay?" Julie heard her husband saying as she returned with the monitor.

"Sure, that's fine."

"I stocked the cupboard with junk food," Julie reminded her. "And Adam is watching a favourite video right now, but we rented a new one in case you want to watch that. Hopefully Amélie won't kick up too much of a fuss."

"We'll have lots of fun, and don't worry about anything," Michelle replied.

But when Marc and Julie got home that evening, instead of their houseguest being in the room they'd prepared for her, they found Michelle curled up on the family room sofa surrounded by blankets and pillows, the baby monitor held tightly in one hand.

"Oh!" She sighed and sat up quickly as they came up the stairs together. "I'm so glad it's really you!"

"What's going on Michelle?" Marc asked her, as Michelle went to him for a hug. "Are the kids settled?"

"Adam's been asleep for hours now," she said. "And Amélie keeps waking up from time to time, but to be honest, it's me who isn't settled."

"Is it too cold downstairs for you?"

"Uh … yeah, something like that." The look she directed at Julie clearly said the teenager had not spoken the truth to her brother, and wasn't about to.

"Do you want me to drive you home tonight or are you still okay to stay?" Julie asked kindly.

"Now that you're home it should be fine. I just got a little freaked out that's all. I wasn't expecting this thing to pick up cross-talk from other houses," she handed the baby monitor back to Marc.

"You could've warned me about that, big brother. Thanks." Her tone was sarcastic and Julie knew she was teasing, but the look in her eyes told a different story. It wasn't lost on the young mother that Michelle said she was so glad to see it was 'really them' coming home.

"Sorry Michelle," Marc muttered. "But if you're okay, then I'm gonna go to bed. I'm beat."

"I'm good here," the teenager readily agreed.

As Marc and Julie got ready for bed, Marc turned to his wife with raised eyebrows.

"What was all that about?" he asked. "What aren't you telling me?"

"Me?" she answered. "What isn't Michelle telling us," she corrected.

"Yeah," her husband replied. "And what was that about the baby monitor picking up cross-talk from other houses? I've never seen it do that before."

"Me neither," Julie agreed.

"Did she tell you why the room downstairs didn't work for her?"

"No, she didn't, but isn't it obvious Marc? *He* doesn't want her there. That's *his* room, remember?"

"We'll just see about that," Marc replied moodily.

~~~~

"You're heavy little one!" she whispered, laying the baby into the crib and rubbing the tiny back with gentle fingers. The baby squirmed, rolled and tried repeatedly to get up. She was clearly not interested in having a nap.

Oh, how I wish you'd just sleep for a few hours, Julie thought, her body slumping forward so she could rest her weary head against the crib rail.

Predictably, within a couple of minutes, the familiar wail began anew, as the tiny child realized where she was and panicked.

"She screams like a goat," her dad noted as he appeared in the doorway. "Did you know that?"

"Oh dad!" She exclaimed. "Yeah, I noticed. Marc and I nick-named her G G. while we were still in the hospital."

"Gee Gee?" her dad wondered aloud.

"Yeah, G G Stands for Goat Girl," Julie laughed. "The first time I heard her cry was when the nurses brought her to me after her first
~~~~

bath. She was coming down the hall from the nursery and I remember thinking, geez, I wonder whose baby that is, screaming like a goat? Imagine my surprise to find out it was mine."

Her dad smiled and went to the crib, reaching out to his tiny grand-daughter. "Do you hear the way your heartless mother talks about you?" he said soothingly. "Goat girl indeed."

The proud grandpa nestled his grand-daughter against one shoulder. To his daughter, he said, "Are you getting enough rest? Your mother's concerned about you. We're still okay to take Adam to school and pick him up, but do you need more help than that?"

Julie smiled weakly. "I truly appreciate the help Dad. It's awesome, but Adam's a handful. You said so yourself."

"Well." Her dad was notorious for understatement.

"Well what?" she asked.

"Get your butt in gear and take advantage of this impromptu visit. If there's stuff you need to do without her in your arms, you'd better snap to it."

"Yes sir," she chuckled, dragging herself from the room. What she really wanted was a nap, but although her body was exhausted, her mind was racing. Instead, she decided to complete a task she'd been putting off for a long time, that of giving the kitchen a thorough cleaning, and stashing away all the cards and baby items.

Eventually the task complete, Julie dragged a cloth across the glass surface of her table, and straightened three placemats on the shiny surface. "Done," she sighed with relief.

Later that evening, with Amélie held tightly against her shoulder, Julie greeted her husband, anxious to hand over the sleeping child.

"Wow! The place looks amazing. But geez hon, you're exhausted." Marc swung his long legs over the staircase gate, and accepted the baby with a warm smile.

"What a wonderful compliment," Julie replied, sarcastically.

"Jules, she's sleeping," Marc replied, taking a closer look at his daughter's face. "Why didn't you just put her in the crib?"

Julie waved her arm. "Ha! Go ahead and try. She might stay asleep for about five minutes, and then she'll holler down the house, but if that'll make you happy go ahead. I'll turn up the volume on Adam's movie so he doesn't melt down again and try to bite her."

"Uh-oh. Sounds like a trying day."

Julie just nodded as she opened the pantry cupboard, getting what she needed to make supper.

Marc retrieved a can of beer from the fridge with one hand while he cradled his daughter in the other. "Feels good to be home," he said gently, looking down at his daughter. "I don't mind holding her. She can sleep in daddy's arms. I'll try a little later. With both of us on the job little mister might mind his manners."

"Here's hoping," Julie answered, stirring the contents of a large silver pot.

Marc settled down gratefully into one of the kitchen chairs. "Man, I'm beat," he said. "It was a tough install today. Good thing it's Friday."

"Mm, hmm," Julie answered, only half listening.

"Uh, Julie?"

"What?" She replied.

"What's up with this ribbon?" he asked suddenly. Julie glanced up. Marc was squinting at the underside of the kitchen table.

Julie frowned. "A ribbon? Where? I just cleaned that whole thing! I didn't see any ribbon under there."

Marc held Amélie in one arm as he pointed to a satin ribbon, caught between the wood frame and the glass.

"Can you pull it out?" she asked.

Marc tugged experimentally at the length of ribbon. "Nope, it's really stuck in there. That's so weird. Where did it come from?"

"I have no idea," Julie replied.

Removing a simple hair ribbon from a kitchen table turned out to be a longer process than either of them anticipated.

It was late the next afternoon when Marc finally laid his tools aside and lifted the glass from its wooden frame. Julie pulled the satin ribbon free.

Running it through her fingers, she shook her head as Marc worked to re-assemble the table.

"You know, I have no idea where this thing came from," she said. "It's not mine."

"Beats me how it got in there too," Marc added. "I had to scrape away the original sealant just to get the glass off. That sucker was tight!"

Julie continued to frown in thought as her husband tightened bolts and ran a fresh bead of silicone around the edge of the glass to re-seal it.

"Well, so much for using our table," he commented. "This has to dry until tomorrow, so it looks like it's either TV dinners or the dining room."

"Not the dining room," Julie vetoed quickly.

"What's wrong with the dining room?" he asked plaintively.

"I don't like it," she said. "It's cold and creepy."

"What?" Marc's incredulous tone prompted an icy stare from his wife. "Aw, come on honey, don't tell me all the rooms are haunted. Besides, what if it's just somebody looking for their missing hair ribbon?"

"That's not very funny Marc."

"Sorry", he said, grinning despite her irritation. "It's all I could come up with on short notice."

~~~~

"Go and haunt somebody else's house! Look outside, there's plenty to choose from." Julie grumbled, as she put the finishing touches on the apple pie she was making for dessert.

Standing up and shaking out both arms, she tried to dispel the cold chill that had settled into her backbone.

It wasn't just that the temperature had fallen outside. Julie had become adept at determining when the 'spirit' was around, and when he wasn't.

Off-hand comments were tossed out by both Julie and Marc, as they went about their lives. Sarcasm seemed to make the intolerable, tolerable.

"Hey, I was watching that," Julie heard Marc say, as the football game he was watching, one Sunday afternoon, randomly switched off. "You've been talking to my wife?"

"Har-de-har-har," Julie retorted snidely from the kitchen. "What happened? Did he turn off the game? And here I thought he never listened to me."

Even Adam, normally caught up in his own thoughts, seemed to think the ghostly visitor could be funny too, as he discovered something waiting for him on the stairs one day after school.

Julie had only just unlocked the front door and wheeled the stroller inside, when Adam ran past her.
~~~~

Her son shouted and raced up the steps with Julie right behind. To her surprise, half-way up, sat one of Adam's toy trains. Balanced carefully on its little plastic wheels, it faced the foyer, as though waiting for her son to get home.

Julie's body felt like ice but Adam giggled, clearly delighted by the gift.

Julie and Marc both felt the spirit was male, but they wanted something more tangible, like maybe a name they could call him by.

"Perhaps," Julie reasoned to her husband one evening, as the couple tried to unwind in front of the TV. "If I have a name, I can appeal to him. Make him see reason."

"I don't know if it works like that," Marc replied, draping one arm around his wife's shoulders. "He doesn't seem like the cooperative type. Remember the grocery fiasco?"

Julie made a face. "Oh yeah, you're right. That was maddening, but at least no one got hurt."

As though on cue, footsteps sounded on the staircase behind them.

Both people turned to look but the staircase was empty.

"I'll never get used to that," Marc said. "I can hear the footsteps getting closer, can you?"

Julie nodded. "Hey!" she called out, the proximity of her husband making her bold. "We can't keep saying 'hey you on the stairs, keep it down', so what's your name?"

As though in answer, the footsteps ceased abruptly.

"Now you've gone and offended him," Marc said, shrugging. "Nice work."

~~~~

Christmas Eve had come at last, but instead of it being the busiest time of the year, it was filled with flannel pajamas, blankets and cold remedies. Adam and Amélie were visibly excited by all the brightly wrapped packages under the tree, while Julie rejoiced at the full packages of cold and flu medication in her cupboard. She was hoping to stave off the worst of it until after the holidays, but it was closing in on her, fast.
~~~~

Marc, with a wry smile, encouraged his wife to open two of her gifts on Christmas Eve, as the full force of the flu-bug arrived.

Trembling with an inner cold she couldn't shake, Julie plucked half-heartedly at the paper, finally inviting Adam to rip it open for her. A pair of warm, flannel pajamas fell out, followed by a new fuzzy bathrobe and slippers.

How did you know I'd need these?" she said, her eyes welling up.

"Okay, okay don't get emotional," Marc chuckled. "I just guessed that's all. You love to be warm."

"Which at the moment, I'm not," she said.

"Go get changed then. I'll make you some tea, and then you get into bed and stay there. Sleep is what you need if you have any hope of enjoying Christmas this year."

"Yes sir," she answered with a mock salute.

Amélie and Adam waited with anticipation of Santa, while their mother lay wrapped in layers of blankets, smelling strongly of wintergreen.

<div align="center">~~~~</div>

"I'm not imagining you," she croaked. Julie wasn't sure how long she'd been asleep, but her throat was on fire, and a careful check of Marc's side of the bed revealed he hadn't come to bed yet.

With her head turned toward the closed bedroom door, she waited for the darkness that was blacker than shadow to fade away. "I know what my doorway is supposed to look like without you there, so why don't you just tell me what you want and then go away?"

The moments ticked past in silence.

Were the children asleep? Why was the house so quiet? Where was Marc?

Was she hallucinating now?

Pulling the covers up around her, she tried covering her head, but soon vetoed that idea. What if it came closer and caught her unawares? Whipping the blankets off again, Julie sighed. In the shadowy evening gloom, she could once again see the door, cloaked in shadow, but still visible.

"At least I know I'm not delirious," she whispered. "Whatever that was, it's over now." Stretching experimentally, she was pleased to note her body wasn't shaking uncontrollably anymore.

Rising from the bed however, proved to be another matter. The room tilted at a ridiculous angle, and she lay quickly back down again.

"Whoah! Okay, Marc's right. I'm staying put. But you," she pointed at the door. "You are going to leave me alone."

Chapter Nineteen

Julie bundled her daughter and the ever-present 'blankie' into the stroller, then manipulated her struggling son into a light windbreaker. Adam hated wearing coats.

Pulling the door closed, she locked it securely behind her. She had to hurry to catch up with her son who was already half-way down the driveway. It would be good to see her mom and dad, she thought. They'd been away in their trailer for a few weeks and were due to arrive that afternoon.

The little girl who often sought Adam out on the playground was there again, her mother not too far away.

Julie raised her hand and waved. The thin, blonde woman she now knew as Jill, returned her wave enthusiastically from across the park. She wheeled her own stroller to meet them. The two women had met accidentally, as they brought their children to and from school and although Jill was painfully shy at first, a tentative friendship had begun. Although it never seemed to go beyond a simple wave or a shy exchange of a few words, Julie was okay with that. Friends were complicated.

A man stood not far off, his back to them. He appeared to be watching both children from a distance.

"Who's that?" Julie asked her friend, concern in her voice.

Recognition washed over her, and she felt her stomach churn. She'd only seen him through wavy glass, in a moment of terror, but Julie knew it was him! The man who'd threatened her family! What was he doing here?

Perhaps feeling her eyes on him he turned, catching Julie mid-stare.

Out of habit, she ducked her head and averted her eyes, but the shock of seeing him brought her feet to an abrupt halt.

Jill, noticing her friend had stopped, looked in the same direction.

"Oh," she said softly. "It's okay, that's my husband."

"Your husband?" Julie echoed in stunned disbelief. She hoped her voice hadn't given anything away. This was too much!

"Adam!" Jill's little girl, already settled onto one of the swings, called out to her silent playmate.

Julie cringed. She didn't want this man knowing her son's name. But if he was Jill's husband, the way she claimed, he probably already did!

Adam, seeing an open swing, made straight for it, oblivious to the fact that his playmate flung her arms wide, attempting to grab him in a hug. Adam nimbly slipped away from her grasp at the last second and settled onto the swing in one fluid movement.

"Hey!" she shouted, momentarily thwarted. Laughing as only a child can, she pumped her legs hard, copying Adam, driving her own swing higher and higher.

Adam darted a quick glance at the girl who was so determined to be his friend.

Julie crouched automatically in front of the stroller to check on Amélie, as her eyes darted between the children and the man Jill claimed as her husband. Why did he just stand there, staring?

It should have been a beautiful moment. Adam was actually playing with someone! If only she could truly enjoy it, without having to worry that this lunatic was watching their every move!

"Want to move closer to the playground?" she asked. *Your weird husband is creeping me out*, she wanted to say.

"Sure, let's go," Jill replied softly, falling into step as they wheeled the strollers forward.

As they walked, Julie noticed Jill kept her eyes downcast. Was it Julie's imagination, or was her new friend on the verge of tears?

"Look how cute they are," Julie said, pointing at the playground. "She's a sweet girl."

"Thanks," Jill answered, sniffling softly. "Yes, she's very fond of him. They're in the same class."

"Oh!" Feeling heat rise to her face, Julie averted her eyes. "I'm sorry, why didn't I didn't realize that? I feel so silly."

"That's okay. It's all we can do to drop them off and get out of there, right?" Jill offered a shy smile. "I'm by myself a lot, so I come here to watch the kids play. My daughter always seeks out your little boy."

Julie smiled. "I wish all the kids were as determined as yours. Adam's hard to play with. Most kids give up."

"Oh, she's determined all right," Jill replied. Her voice seemed a little stronger and Julie took that as a sign that the awkward moment had passed. She wasn't sure what had brought it on, except for the fact that Jill's little boy, although seemingly the same age as Amélie, was content just to watch the other children from the safety of the stroller. He made no sound as Jill pushed the stroller back and forth across the short-cropped grass as they came to a stop to one side of the playground. Julie recognised the strategy. It was a standard tactic used by mothers everywhere for cranky babies who wanted the wheels to keep turning.

Julie wondered why it seemed to work so well with Jill's little boy. That tactic hadn't worked on Adam. He was all about getting up and walking as soon as possible.

But perhaps her son couldn't walk? That might explain the sadness, Julie thought. She knew her own eyes welled with tears when she heard other children Adam's age, talking and socializing with those around them.

We always want what we can't have, she thought sadly.

"You know, she talks about him at home," Jill said suddenly, her eyes on the children.

Julie's face fell as Jill spoke, picturing Jill's husband listening to their daughter, knowing how much he hated them.

"Oh?" she said, trying to sound casual as she tucked the blanket back into the stroller where the baby had kicked it free. "What sorts of things does she say?"

"Oh, just that he's her quiet friend," she smiled. "She tells her daddy and I that he doesn't talk, but he has a special teacher, so it's all right. She's kind of protective I think," Jill replied.

Julie raised her head at that.

Noting the odd expression on Julie's face, she hurried to explain. "Oh, don't misunderstand, she's just such a talker, it's strange for her that your son is so quiet, but obviously, she doesn't mind." Jill waved her delicately boned hand out in front of her at the children, who now seemed to be engaged in a game of follow-the-leader. Julie smiled, if Adam got to be leader, the game would go along fine.

He seemed not to care if anyone followed him, but follow she did, trailing behind as he went from the swing, to the monkey bars, on to the slide and back again.

Jill's daughter checked in with her mother often, but not once did Julie see the child turn to look at her father, even though he stood in plain view, just at the entrance to the field. Something about his body language seemed off, almost as though he was poised to run.

Was he nervous that Julie was friendly with his wife and children?

Emotions raged within her, as she tried to focus on the conversation, but all she kept thinking was how wrong it all seemed. What was this perfectly nice woman doing with someone who hefted a shotgun and threatened people?

Julie was torn. She had so few friends who truly understood her situation and Adam didn't have any! She would be stupid to damage this budding relationship, even if the woman's husband was a raging lunatic! After all, it wasn't like Julie had anything to do with him, and judging from Jill's behaviour, it seemed unlikely that his wife knew what he'd done.

Julie hurried on, eager to fill the awkward silence. "You know what? I don't even think I know your daughter's name."

"Oh!" Jill's cheeks went red. "Sorry, her name is Madison."

"It suits her," Julie remarked. "This is Amélie."

That's a pretty name. Your family is French then?"

Julie nodded. "And who do we have here?" Julie crouched in front of Jill's stroller and smiled at the beautiful child who sat calmly, watching the children play with a happy smile on his sunny face.

"This is Thomas," Jill said. "Say hello, Thomas," she instructed the child, who looked up at Julie for a quick moment, his bright blue eyes piercing hers with their intensity. "Sorry," Jill said. "He doesn't talk much, yet."

"No problem, I know the drill," she smiled. "One day, he'll talk your ear off!" Julie bit her lip and turned away. Now why had she said that? She'd heard the well-meaning phrase a million times as she and Marc waited painfully for their son to speak. It wasn't helpful to them, so why had she repeated the inane phrase to this poor woman?

Jill's tight smile gave evidence to the fact that she didn't much care for it either, but she was obviously too polite to mention it.

"It's, uh, hard for Adam to find friends because of the language thing. Most kids get weirded out when he doesn't talk to them. I keep telling them they should wait, cuz he's slower than they are at talking. But like you said, your daughter doesn't seem to be bothered."

"Well, she has that same problem at home, so I guess she's gotten used to it," Jill replied softly, her lips twitching into an impulsive grin. "As a matter of fact, half the time I don't even think she notices that other people *aren't* talking. She just loves the sound of her own voice!"

The two women exchanged a knowing smile and the awkward moment passed.

Adam, having tired of the game, dashed away and ran full-speed into the field, followed closely by Madison, who laughed in delight. Thomas watched them go, and it seemed to Julie that he did so with longing in his eyes. Julie felt for the woman beside her, whose audible gulp told her she was trying just to enjoy the moment without becoming emotional.

As they ran, Jill's little girl grabbed for Adam's hand, but he deftly avoided her attempts and ran faster, a look of pure delight on his face.

"They are so cute," Jill said, her face brightening into a brave smile. "Madison!" she called out. "He doesn't have to hold your hand! He just wants to run!"

Julie made a show of looking around. Jill's husband was gone.

Why did he bother to come there at all, she wondered? Was he keeping tabs on his wife? She looked at Jill with sadness and hoped her new friend wouldn't have to answer to him for making friends with the enemy.

<p style="text-align:center">~~~~</p>

"Oh Adam," she sighed, looking at the wrecked bedroom. "What possessed you to throw around your toys like this?"

It was a figure of speech, but the moment the words were out of Julie's mouth she regretted them

"I mean," she paused another moment to collect her thoughts. "Holy Moly, what a mess!"

"Holy Moly!" Adam echoed.

"Are you having fun my boy?" she asked.

"Yes!" Adam announced.

Julie smiled. An actual answer? That was cool.

"How does one boy make so much mess?" She commented, bending to pick up his laundry basket as she headed for the door.

"Two," Adam whispered.

The word, spoken under his breath would have gone unnoticed, were it not for Julie's hyper-vigilance. She'd programmed herself to listen more carefully than ever for the faint signs that her child was talking.

The smile fell from her face as she stopped mid-stride, and turned around. Adam spoke random single words from time to time, but no matter what he was offered, he would never repeat them.

"What?" She asked, ever hopeful. "What did you say?"

Adam concentrated on the tower in front of him, stacking the connecting blocks higher and higher.

"Adam?" she asked deciding to try something different. "One boy?"

"Two," he corrected, still not looking at her.

"Adam, listen to mommy."

Adam, recognising the familiar phrase, turned toward his mother, his piercing blue eyes looking into hers with concentration.

"Two …?" she prompted.

"Boy," Adam answered, filling in the gap she'd given him.

"Two boys?"

"Yes."

"Where?" Julie flung both arms out and looked around the otherwise empty room. "Where is the other boy?"

"Ah, he's gone! Gone, gone, all gone, goodbye, see-ya!" Adam answered, accessing a memorized piece of scripting from one of his movies.

She stood back and stared at her son. Was this scripting or something else? Ariel had given her lots of information all about something called echolalia, which many children with Autism exhibited. They often repeated phrases they'd heard on TV, for the sheer comfort of it. But nowhere in the literature had it mentioned that a child might use it to communicate. Was that even possible?

If so, Adam had just told his mother quite clearly that he hadn't been playing by himself after all. Could her son be the next member of their family to have seen a ghost?

"Sweetie," she said to her son. "Look at mommy. Who is this boy? Does he have a name?"

As unconcerned as he had been previously, Adam continued to play, his eyes on the toys in front of him.

"Adam, answer mommy," Julie asked again, her voice rising in frustration. "Tell me the boy's name."

Slowly, the child looked up at her. "Casper," he said confidently.

"Oh geez," Julie replied rolling her eyes in disappointment. "Casper?" She repeated. "Your friend's name is Casper? That's the cat!"

"May, 1995," Adam replied. "Universal Pictures and Amblin Entertainment."

This last phrase was the type of information Adam repeated often. He loved to quote random movie trivia, but in this case, the phrase was offered as a correction.

"Ah, I stand corrected," Julie said, shaking her head. "A movie character, right? Thinking about the movie?"

Without looking at her, Adam cupped his hand to his mouth, as though about to divulge a state secret. "Casper wants the boy," he whispered.

Had she heard that right? Carefully, she sank to her knees in front of her son.

"Casper wants … what?" she whispered.

"Boy," he whispered again. A moment later, his attention returned to the toy in his hands.

"What boy?" She asked. For the first time, Julie was afraid of what her son might say.

"Me," he said, his tone unconcerned.

Julie sat back on her heels, her head pounding.

Throughout the rest of her day, Julie tried to stay a few steps ahead of her children while keeping the house in order. But as she completed each task, in the back of her mind she replayed the brief, seemingly impossible conversation.

She resisted the urge to run back to his room and question him further. There were so many things she wanted to know: Is he nice to you? What did he look like? Where did he go? Is he coming back?

Frustrated, she knew her son couldn't answer these simple questions. But then, he wasn't supposed to be able to have a conversation with her, either.

What did this mean? Would it happen again? Was he afraid? What should she do about it? No matter how long Julie worried at it, the problem kept spinning and spinning.

By the time her husband arrived later that evening, Julie knew what she had to do.

There were no secrets between them and she wasn't going to start keeping them now. Somehow, she would find the words and they would figure this out together, like they always did.

~~~~

Okay, so what have you said to him?" Marc asked his wife as they sat together that evening. "Did he witness anything strange with you?"

"I haven't said anything, but he does live here, Marc. He's bound to have seen things. Remember the footsteps on the staircase? The first time it happened, he heard it too. And let's not forget that he may have had things happening to him that we don't even know about yet. He can't even tell us what he did at school; much less communicate a strange incident that even we have trouble describing."

"Geez," Marc shuddered. "I don't want to think about that."

"Me neither, but Adam has no way of understanding something like this. That's why I wonder whether the reference to the movie is his way of trying to understand. To give it a frame of reference, you know? What do you think?"

"I think you're fishing," her husband answered with a tight grin.

"Oh really?" Julie asked, exasperated. "Remember his arm? That happened right after we moved in. Neither one of us knew how to explain that." She spread her hands in front of her in a gesture of futility.
~~~~

"Right," her husband agreed slowly. "What or who did he see?" Marc replied. "Adam always needs a motivator for his scripting. The quoting is his way of commenting about something he's seen or heard, right? So what gives?"

Julie shrugged, just as puzzled as her husband, but with a growing suspicion she wasn't ready to share yet.

"Maybe this is his way of asking what's going on in our new house?"

Chapter Twenty

"BEEP, BEEP, BEEP, BEEP!" The high-pitched noise rattled her eyelids open.

Surely she'd only been asleep for minutes instead of hours, right?

"Rise and shine," Marc called.

"You gotta be kidding," she muttered, glancing at the clock radio as she hit the snooze button and rolled over.

"Nope, time for a new day. Adam's already up," Marc replied, gently turning Julie by the shoulders. "Come on, we've got lots to do. Are you getting up or what?"

"Do I have a choice?" she muttered grumpily.

"Ha-ha," he replied. "Very funny. Coffee's on in the kitchen. I already started breakfast. Didn't you sleep last night? What time did you get to bed?"

"I don't know," she moaned, rolling over. "Amélie had another bad night. I saw two, three and four o'clock this morning, that much I know." Julie lay there for a moment longer. Despite Marc's enthusiasm, she wanted to just roll over and sleep, but with the thoughts now churning in her suddenly active brain, there was no possibility of that now.

Just then, the tell-tale noises of an unhappy child filled the air.

"That's the reality alarm," Marc muttered, rising quickly from the side of the bed, his eyebrows raised. "I'll go get her, if you can keep an eye on breakfast," Marc checked his watch as he spoke. "Remember we were gonna go to that Home Show today, so we've got to get a move-on."

Marc held out his hand and pulled Julie out of the bed. Wriggling her feet into slippers, she peered sideways at her husband as he disappeared out the door. How was he so awake and cheerful? It wasn't fair.

"Because he wasn't up half the night with the midnight wailer," she answered herself with heavy sarcasm.

"There's Daddy's princess," she heard him remark from the next room. Julie felt like a sleepwalker as she shuffled down the hall in search of coffee.

"The forecast is for more sun today," Marc called to her.

Clutching her coffee mug, Julie poured herself a steaming mug of energy and picked up the egg flipper, with one eye on her son as he played. He was lying on the floor in the family room with his tiny toy cars. He loved to line them up, and did so endlessly. Seeing her husband jog down the hall to the kitchen, rumpled daughter in his arms, she shook her head and poked at the pan full of sizzling bacon.

Although she was still groggy, the coffee and the smell of bacon did help. Julie smiled at her husband's enthusiasm as he held their daughter securely over his head, zooming her down the hallway like she was a jet plane, with all the proper sound effects. Some people just loved mornings, she thought.

Julie's smile quickly faded, however as another familiar high-pitched shriek filled the air. The sound raced up her spine like an electric shock. One glance told her Adam was no longer playing, but running from room to room, screaming at the top of his lungs!

The latest mystery of 'what's bugging Adam' had already begun. She turned the sizzling pieces of bacon over in the pan, aware that there wasn't anything she could do until the storm inside her son had run its course. Taking another sip of coffee, she massaged her temples and waited.

It was going to be another long day.

She only hoped the folks at the Home Show were an understanding bunch.

<center>~~~~</center>

Julie watched her father get to the top of the stairs and start to head down. To her surprise, he stopped mid-way and turned around, looking back at his daughter with sad eyes.

"Dad? Is something wrong?"

"Well," he said. "I'm not sure. How about you tell me?"

Julie couldn't help flashing a quick smile. He knew her so well.

"Dad?" She turned away and raked her fingers through her long hair. "Am I going crazy?"

Her father snorted derisively. "I don't think so. You seem sane enough to me."

Julie smiled wryly. "Thanks, but sometimes I wonder, with all this going on."

"You know, sometimes answers just lead to more questions, Julie. Is it so important that you 'figure it out?" He asked.

Julie shrugged.

"I might've known," he sighed. "Do you remember the house we used to live in, the one with the pool in the backyard?"

Remember it? It was engraved in her memory! Where was he going with this? Julie simply nodded, as she waited for her father to continue.

"We lived there for quite a few years, and we never figured anything out. It simply was. Do you understand?"

Julie stared. This was the first time her dad had ever acknowledged the paranormal events that took place in her childhood home. Even though as adults both Julie and her sister tried to draw their parents into discussions, they'd remained steadfastly quiet on the subject, seemingly content to remain safely in denial, until now.

"Dad, you've never said a word before ..." she began.

"People are quick to judge," her father explained. "We didn't need any of that, and neither do you."

"I know. But to just deal with it day after day and not know what's going on? How did you and mom do that?"

"There wasn't another choice," he said with finality. Turning around, he continued down the stairs.

Julie heaved a deep sigh. Her dad was a man of very few words.

~~~~
~~~~

The dream started out the same. The tall figure stepped forward, his form a part of the shadows that draped every corner of her home. As he did every night, he reached out with one hand and beckoned to her with silent gestures. Julie arose from her bed and followed him down the hallway. She passed family photos, and wondered briefly who these people were, as she passed indifferent to her own surroundings. But as dream-Julie arrived in her own living room, the detachment left her abruptly. Her heart thudded uncomfortably as she stood, waiting in bare feet on the top step of the long staircase.

But what was she waiting for? Dream Julie clutched the railing and tried to call out, but no sound left her lips. In wonder, she turned to see the shadow man deliberately pluck her beloved rag doll from atop a piano. He half-turned, meeting Julie's eyes for a split second.

His thin lips curved into a self-important smile and with a negligent toss, he sent the ragdoll sailing end over end past Julie, where it bumped and bounced down the hard wood steps into the darkened foyer below.

Even deep in a dream, Julie winced each time the doll bounced. His smile grew wider as he watched her reaction.

All Julie could do was to watch, her limbs frozen.

She looked imploringly at the man who now leaned casually against the kitchen doorframe, his features still mostly cloaked in shadow.

"Won't you let me go?" She asked plaintively.

He threw his head back and laughed.

The sound was chilling. Slow and deliberate. It wavered from masculine to feminine and back again.

Who was he?

The sound of his indifferent laughter chilled her heart, and she awoke with a gasp.

The clock at her bedside read 4:15AM.

"You okay?" Her husband mumbled sleepily. "Is the baby up?"

"No. Just a nightmare," she replied in a whisper. "It's okay now."

Julie watched as her husband rolled over and went back to sleep. A burning sensation in the back of her throat made her peel back the covers and creep quietly from the bedroom in search of a glass of water. She'd given up trying to keep one her night stand.

Throwing on the kitchen lights, she was immediately comforted by the bright light that bathed the kitchen. With cup of water in hand, Julie walked to the doorway and reached for the lights, wishing she wouldn't have to douse them again.

Maybe I should just stay up, she thought. Amélie would be up soon anyhow.

As she debated, Julie ran her hand over the smooth wood of the railing that separated the hallway from the staircase. It was early and shadows still clung to everything, turning it all a somber shade of grey. As she often did, Julie leant on the railing, and stared down its length into her darkened foyer below. It was an absent gesture, something she did to gather her thoughts, but that morning, something different caught her eye.

A patch of early morning sunlight had begun to creep along the foyer, through the glass inserts in the front doors. The warm yellow light chased away the grey and threw its illumination onto something that made Julie gasp.

Her childhood doll, it's limbs splayed, lay face down at the bottom of the staircase.

The doll from her dreams lay crumpled, human-like as though she'd taken a bad fall ...

"So, the dreams are real after all," she mumbled, wrapping both arms around her, Julie hugged herself hard and tried to concentrate on just standing. She could feel her knees giving way.

He was inside her head!

But how? And why? Why show her this?

On shaking legs, Julie swayed unsteadily and wiped away the tears that fell from her stinging eyes.

"Why are you doing this to me?" she whispered.

You really think you're in control?

The hoarsely whispered words brushed against her left ear. With a whimper, she shied away, clutching at her ear. Had she really just heard that, or was that her tired mind trying to make sense of the things she saw?

It was like a horrible game of cat and mouse.

Worst of all was the uncertainty. If this vile entity tortured her without relief, what would it do to her children? Was it already doing it?

Julie thought about her son's unrelenting night terrors and her daughter's sleep habits. Things like that don't happen to people like us, do they?

This last thought whirling around and around in her mind, she wasn't even aware that she'd moved to the top step of the staircase, until a sleepy voice interrupted her thoughts.

"Julie?" Marc called. He was standing in the bedroom doorway, shielding his eyes against the light. "What are you doing? It's not even five yet."

Julie looked at her husband, and then down at her feet.

"I– I don't know," she muttered.

"Well get back up here. I don't want you to fall."

"Neither do I," she replied.

Marc walked down the short hallway and peeked into Amélie's room.

"She's fine for now, come on," he called to her as he headed back to the bedroom.

"This house belongs to him Marc," she mumbled, descending the stairs with jerky movements.

"What?" Marc stopped and leaned wearily onto the banister. "What did you say?"

"The house, the land, everything. It all belongs to him. Even us."

"Julie, stop it!" Marc's whispered rebuke was loud in the silent house. "Get back up here. You're not yourself."

Julie turned incurious eyes toward her husband. "But I have to get my dolly," she replied, her voice suddenly child-like.

"Julie, leave it. We'll get it later," he said, walking towards his wife, arms outstretched.

But Julie neither heard nor cared.

"At least hold the railing," Marc asked, but Julie, her arms swinging freely at her sides, just ignored him.

Marc watched her go. This was bizarre! She was a grown woman, certainly capable of walking down a flight of steps without difficulty, so why was he was holding his breath as she took each step. Marc understood with growing clarity, that whoever or whatever haunted them had a hidden agenda and his wife was at the center of it.

As Marc waited, Julie remounted the stairs, the beloved rag doll held tenderly in her arms, as though it was a real child!

With gentle hands, Julie looked down at the doll in her arms and smiled as she carefully smoothed back the red, yarn hair from the carefully embroidered face, and straightened the rumpled dress and pinafore.

Not sure what else to do, Marc guided her back towards the bedroom and helped his wife to bed. She held the rag doll firmly to her chest.

"You just rest," he told her, pulling the blankets up securely. "You need sleep."

"Uh-huh," she murmured, rolling over onto one shoulder, still carefully embracing the doll.

Although his wife was soon sleeping, Marc was wide awake. He was forced to admit that the actions of this unseen entity, far from being harmless, as he'd once thought, were growing more sinister. Since moving day, it had become increasingly obvious that whatever this thing was, it wasn't going to stop at just possessing a house.

~~~~

Wow, looks like you had a rough night," her dad remarked as he came upstairs for his usual morning coffee.

"Thanks," Julie replied dryly, pouring another steaming mug for herself and a fresh one for her dad. Just then, a piercing scream could be heard from down the hallway. "That would be your grand-daughter," Julie said, her eyes narrowed. "Care to do the honors?"

"Sure," he replied, already moving off down the hall.

Julie spooned sugar into her cup and stirred.

A few minutes later, her dad reappeared, a distraught-looking Amélie in his arms. The child's cheeks were bright red and her hair tousled.

She buried her face in her grandfather's shoulder as they arrived in the kitchen. Automatically Julie's dad rubbed the child's back in small circles as he held her close.

"Somebody's been having trouble sleeping, lately," Julie said, reaching a hand out to smooth down the rampant curls on the top of her daughter's head.

"Hmm," her father commented dryly. "I can't imagine who that would be."

"Yeah, right," Julie replied. "You get three guesses and the first two don't count."

Father and daughter exchanged a grin.
~~~~

"Dad," Julie asked. "Do you remember when I used to come into your bedroom in the middle of the night, and just stand there, waiting for you and mom to wake up?"

The corner of her father's mouth tweaked into a smile. "Sure. How can I forget?"

"Even though I didn't say anything, you and mom woke up anyway. You knew I was there."

"Of course we did," he said. "It's parent intuition. Parents always know what their kids are doing, even if they can't see them."

"Yes, exactly," Julie agreed. Tilting her head to one side, she indicated the steaming cups on the table. "I have the same thing happening almost every night."

"Welcome to parenthood," her dad quipped."

"It's not Amélie or Adam waking me, Dad."

Julie watched the smile fade from her father's face.

"What do you mean?" her father asked, his tone wary. He set his granddaughter, feet-first on the floor beside him and grinned as she ran off to the next room to dig noisily through the toy box.

"She seems none the worse for wear," he said.

"I'm sure she isn't, but I can't take much more of this dad."

"What's going on?" Julie's father leaned forward, and picked up his coffee cup.

Julie took a deep breath. "Okay, here goes," she began. "It's the same thing, almost every night. I'm sound asleep in my bed, and I can tell I'm being pulled deep into a dream. I'm not worried, cuz dreams are nice, right? Suddenly though, my dream changes, and all I can see is a man's face, close-up. His face is angry, intense. He's staring at me like he wants something but I don't know what, and he won't stop it, no matter what I say."

"Is it someone you know?"

"No. I've never seen this man before," she answered. Julie looked away awkwardly and stared at the floor. "His stare is threatening, and then he starts coming closer, so I back up. I feel like if I don't move, he's going to hurt me."

"Sounds scary."

"It is. I just keep backing up and he keeps coming closer. And then, just like that, I'm falling! I reach out for something to grab that will slow me down, but there's nothing there." Julie put down the cup she'd been clutching. "So that's why I look like this all the time," she said, making a sweeping motion in front of her face. What do you make of it?"

"Sounds pretty powerful, but it's still just a bad dream, honey. Dreams can't really hurt you. Likely it's just a sign you're getting too worked up over something. We all know you've got plenty of stress, with the children and everything. Maybe that's it."

"Maybe," Julie agreed doubtfully. "But you know what? It doesn't feel like a dream. It's such a powerful feeling that I think it's really happening! When I do wake up, I sit bolt upright and gasp. Marc ends up waking up in a panic, just like me, so neither one of us are getting much rest these days."

Instead of speaking, Julie's dad settled back into his chair and raised his eyebrows slightly.

"Of course, the first thing I think of when I wake up like that is the safety of my kids," she continued. "Thankfully Adam's usually still asleep, but when I get to Amélie's room, she's wide awake. I can hear her whimpering in the dark. When she sees me, she starts this high-pitched screaming and won't let go of my neck. I know she's terrified. But terrified of what? I never see anything."

"Do you maybe cry out in your sleep?" Her dad asked. "Maybe she hears that."

"I don't know how she could, there's two rooms between us, and apparently, all Marc ever hears me do is gasp when I wake up. How could she hear that?"

"It's certainly strange," her dad admitted.

"What's strange is how she's waking up terrified at the exact moment I am. I keep wondering if maybe we're having the same nightmare? It doesn't make any sense, dad."

"You're right about that," her dad muttered.

Julie nodded and took a long swallow of her coffee, still avoiding her dad's eyes. She didn't want to see the judgment she was sure to find.

"Hmm," he said, as the silence lengthened. He glanced up and drew in a deep breath as though he would say something, and then returned his eyes to the mug in his hand.

"I don't know what to say," he admitted finally. "That's quite a tale."

"A tale?" Julie asked, incredulous. "You think I'm making this up?"

"Now, now, that's not what I said. Don't go and put words in my mouth. But you have to agree this is quite an unusual thing you've got going on here."

"Well I didn't make it happen," she snapped, rising abruptly, she took her own mug and poured the rest of her coffee down the drain. "Look, I don't expect you to have any answers dad, I just thought you'd like to know why I'm so jumpy all the time."

"Okay, okay just calm down," her dad replied noncommittally.

While Julie waited for him to say more, her father drained the last sip from his mug, and carried it to the kitchen counter, placing it on the shiny surface with a sharp click.

"If you want my advice," he began slowly, his gaze level. "I think you and Marc need to get away for a few days. Take the kids and go to the cabin. We'll manage things around here."

"Dad," Julie objected. "That's not what I —"

"Julie, just go and don't argue," her father interrupted. "I know the stress you're under. I see it building every day and now you've become over-wrought by it. I watched this happen to your mother, so you need to listen to me. You need a break, so take one. Get your family out of here for a few days. That's what the cabin is for, remember?"

Julie stared at him.

"Well?" he countered. "Amélie's older now. And you obviously shared this with me because you want my fatherly advice. Yes?" He raised his eyebrows at her. "So, this is the advice, kid. Are you gonna take it?"

Julie sighed, unsure what to say. "We still have so much to do here, and won't it be too hot to go during summer?"

"Hmm, could be yes." Her father shrugged. "Go in September, then. It'll be cooler."

"So, you think going to the cabin is going to sort all this out?" Of all the things she'd expected her father to say, this wasn't even close!

"No, likely it won't solve anything, but it will help you calm down. You can't do anything if you're this reactive. It's what your mother and I always did when times were tough, and it always helped." Her dad stood, his usual jaunty grin reappearing. "Thanks for the coffee, kid. I gotta go."

She gave her dad a quick hug and watched him walk purposefully back down the stairs and disappear into his suite.

Julie let out an explosive sigh, as the door closed behind her father. She realized then that she'd been holding her breath.

Why did her Dad have to be so damned cryptic whenever he gave her advice? Why couldn't he just agree with her that something odd was going on here?

Can you admit it to yourself? The thought raced quickly through her head. Julie sighed and ruefully shook her head. Perhaps that was the first step.

Chapter Twenty-one

Marc shook his head sadly. "I know," he said. "I want to have fun in the sun just as much as you do, but we really need a fence back there. With everything fenced, the dog will be safely contained and maybe then she won't bark so much."

They'd had to save aggressively to afford the expensive project, since they needed to rent heavy equipment as well. It had become clear to the young couple soon after moving in, that not only had their yard been a catch-all for bits and pieces of construction materials, but also, the dirt was so hard-packed and so full of over-sized boulders, it was like digging into the side of a mountain. So, when Marc rented an auger to dig the post holes for the new fence, Julie half-expected it to unearth old rusted cars and trucks, but the only thing the auger revealed was an excess of rock.

Well there goes that wild theory, she sighed to herself. *If it isn't toxic waste buried beneath the grass, why the heck won't anything grow? Maybe I really do have a black thumb!*

The row of neatly planted pansies had wilted almost immediately, despite the promises from the local nursery, the expensive plant fertilizer they'd bought and the advice gained from Julie's mother, who had a flair for gardening.

Strangely, Julie's mother found the whole situation comical.

I tried, but it died.

The phrase was etched with fancy calligraphy into a stone tablet.

"I thought of you as soon as I saw it," her mom chucked. "So I had to buy it. You try so hard, but nothing seems to work. I thought this might put things into perspective for you. They're just flowers. You shouldn't get so worked up over it."

Julie had to admit the phrase on the tablet would have been funnier if it hadn't been the bald-faced truth.

The grass didn't sprout, the flowers wilted and died, and even the small, expensive sapling trees that she and Marc purchased from the local nursery withered and dropped their leaves instead of growing tall and offering shade and privacy to the small, exposed yard. Julie and Marc were desperate to erect some type of screen between their yard and the three others that looked down on them at close quarters, but nothing they did made any difference.

It was like living in a fish bowl.

When they moved in, the yard had been awful. Uneven, hard-packed soil, patchy crab-grass and skeletons of long-dead Christmas trees, abandoned by the neighbours.

Julie and Marc had a vision of what it could be, with time and patience and of course, money.

They could both see it in their mind's eye, but unfortunately the vision never came to fruition.

Adam had fun playing in the mud, which seemed the only thing they still had plenty of.

Summertime was supposed to be peak growing season, but in their backyard, all that grew well were the things they didn't want.

~~~~

"False advertising," Marc grumbled, tossing away yet another empty bag of 'Premium quality, Kentucky blue-grass seed'. "The only thing growing out there is weeds!"

Marc stood just inside the glass door, hands on his hips as rain continued to fall. The water pooled in one persistent, low area in the center of the yard.

"I mean, how many times did we add soil to that spot? Huh? Julie? How many wheelbarrows? How many?"

Marc was waving his hand in the direction of the yard as he paced around the room.

"I don't know," she replied. "Quite a few."
~~~~

"I just want a yard," he muttered. "One the neighbours don't make fun of, when they think we can't hear them."

"Well, I don't know what else we can do," Julie offered. "We've aerated, raked, watered, planted, tamped and watered again. What's left?"

"It's like the ground itself isn't willing to cooperate with us, you know?"

It was an offhand comment, but in the seconds that followed it, the couple's eyes met and without having to say a word, they understood.

Could the strange things happening inside their home be connected to the land as well?

They both just wanted a home they could be proud of. Was it so much to ask?

~~~~

Julie stared out the windshield of the minivan, half-listening as Adam quoted movie lines from the back seat, while her husband tried to find something other than static to listen to on the radio. Amélie slept peacefully, tucked into her car seat with blankets and stuffed toys. The tiny girl had nodded off before they'd gone five miles.

"Why don't they have any decent radio stations up here?" Marc complained irritably, finally turning the radio off in frustration.

Julie closed her eyes and clamped her lips together. She didn't trust herself to speak. She and Marc had been exchanging nothing but biting comments since the first bag was packed that morning, and all she truthfully wanted to do was hit him; he was being so deliberately antagonistic!

A few more minutes, she told herself. A few more minutes and we'll be there. Whether Marc knew it or not, he was just as affected by the constant negative energy in their home as she was. It hadn't helped of course, that Adam's school days were one big, long challenge. September always brought mountains of paperwork, and new people to be introduced to their defensive, reactive son.

The effect on their already stressed-out household was enormous.

Julie looked out the side window and watched the landscape change, becoming rocky as they climbed into the mountains.
~~~~

Julie's thoughts raced. Even in the quiet moments she and Marc managed to spend alone together, he still wasn't himself. It was like he couldn't bring himself to relax, even for a moment.

Even those rare intimate moments were interrupted by unexpected bangs that sent Marc rushing through the house, looking in vain for the source and effectively killing the mood.

That tight, on-edge feeling never left them, now. Julie blamed the house, while Marc blamed Adam's diagnosis and all that went with it.

As the minivan brought them all closer to their destination, Julie assembled a checklist in her head to pass the time. There was going to be a lot of cleaning up before they could move in and unpack. No one had been to the cottage in a long time and here they were, coming up with a baby!

She would need to ensure Adam was busy and not wading in the creek while she swept and aired out the house. Marc could help with that. Maybe Ami would stay asleep.

Fingers crossed, she thought hopefully.

At last, the minivan made the final turn into a narrow driveway, mowing down the small shrubs and plants that had sprouted up in the middle of the winding path that was only just wide enough for a car.

Marc navigated the barely visible dirt tracks that wound through the woods.

Soon, a rustic A-frame cabin came into view and a smile broke out across Julie's face.

She sighed happily and was surprised to hear the exact same sound from Marc as he guided the vehicle up the last few hundred feet.

Marc was smiling as the vehicle came to a stop. "We're home," he said.

"Look Adam," she said, turning around to catch her son's attention. "We're here!"

The toddler looked excitedly out the windows at the place his mother had been in love with since her childhood.

"It sure feels like home, doesn't it?" she asked her husband as they swung open the doors and Marc released the dog who went bounding up the front steps to the wide porch, now covered with pine needles and stray branches.

"Yayyy!" Adam shouted. Both parents winced and covered their ears, laughing.

Amélie's eyes popped open in alarm, but surprisingly as though she were echoing the sentiments of her relieved family, the infant merely looked around with wide eyes.

The couple soon realized that Julie's dad had been right. The cabin was exactly what they needed.

The wooden floorboards needed sweeping, and cobwebs festooned the corners, but sunlight shone through every dusty window and warmed Julie's face. Walking out onto the front porch, she looked fondly out over the expanse of fir trees. Amélie snuggled in her car seat that Marc had removed from the vehicle and brought up to the sun-drenched porch. Adam was lying calmly on his back, amidst the pine needles, his eyes riveted on the swaying canopy of fir boughs overhead.

Julie giggled as she heard Adam humming a theme song from one of his favourite movies.

It was right decision to celebrate his birthday up here. This was proof! As she watched her son, she felt lighter and happier. No one would be staring at her awkward child as he ran with wild abandon up here. Here, they could all be themselves.

Julie stretched her arms over her head and tipped her head back to receive the warmth of the sunshine on her face. A cool breeze rippled through the trees.

Was it her imagination, or could she actually feel the stress leaving her body?

"Hey Jules, help me with the cooler?" Marc called from the van.

"Yup," she answered quickly, her sneakered feet almost bouncing down each step as she ran to help. It felt good to be back. "I'm sorry I've been away," she whispered to the trees as she jogged happily toward her husband.

Julie spent much of her time indoors with the baby, but Adam and his dad followed the game trails that criss-crossed the property and for the most part, their unpredictable little son was happy.

The young boy tipped over every rock he could, fascinated with the scurrying insects he discovered beneath. Just as quickly as the thought came to him, he ran in another direction, pulling experimentally at moss that hung from the old-growth trees that surrounded them.

Seizing each opportunity that presented itself, Marc took delight in the simplest of tasks. He chopped wood for the wood-burning stove and fireplace, cleared brush with an old machete he found, and cooled their drinks in the icy waters of the creek that ran at angle behind the cabin.

There were no modern conveniences, not even electricity, but Julie didn't care. It was the break she'd been looking for; a break from things that defied logic.

Every noise they heard was explainable and nothing moved on its own. Even their dog seemed more relaxed, spending long periods of time simply sleeping on the sun-warmed wooden planks of the front deck after a rousing game of fetch with Adam or Marc. There were no mysteries here, Julie thought. Best of all, the disturbing dreams, an exhausting constant in their cul-de-sac home, were mysteriously absent. What a relief!

The next morning, Amélie awoke with a sharp cry and Julie was jolted awake, expecting the worst.

Marc was at his daughter's side instantly, his joyful tone soothing away all Julie's fears.

"Hello sleepyhead!" He greeted the baby, scooping her up into his arms. Julie didn't have to look to know Marc was grinning ear to ear. His behaviour had changed so completely, that Julie couldn't help grinning too. He was once again the fun-loving husband and father she knew and loved so well, quick to tell a joke or tease his wife.

"I never want to leave," she whispered into her pillow as she rolled over, drifting easily back to sleep.

Later, with both hands wrapped around the chunky green ceramic coffee mug, she took a satisfying swallow and repeated the same phrase. "I never want to leave."

Gazing out over the property she knew so well, Julie tried to drink it in. Maybe, she thought, if I just stand here long enough, I can imprint this on my mind.

It's worth a try, she thought, closing her eyes. She knew that all too soon they would have to leave again. Her heart raced at the idea. A long weekend wasn't nearly long enough.

Her dad was right, this was the right place for them, especially now. Looking around, she saw many half-done projects and places where the cabin needed repair. It was clear the place needed them as much as they needed it.

Julie realized with a pang of sadness that neither she nor Marc had been this relaxed since the move to their new house.

She made a promise to herself in that moment, that she would work hard to make sure they came back to their 'decompression chamber' as often as possible.

If this was the place that restored them, then this was where they'd come.

~~~

"I can't believe they both conked out like that," Marc said, his tone low as he fed the cast-iron fireplace in the rustic living room. Light snoring could be heard from the adjacent room where their son slept. "Adam had a busy day with his new birthday presents, but he's never asleep that early. And Amélie … well that kid just doesn't sleep, period."

"Tell me about it. It's wonderful being here isn't it?" Julie agreed. "Dad's right. This place is a decompression chamber for all of us."

"Yeah," Marc smiled at his wife, poking each log in turn, to stir up the flames and generate heat for his family. "Why did we stay away so long?"

"Hmm," Julie replied. "Just busy I guess. Too much technology and chasing the almighty dollar."

Marc made a face and poked harder at the fire.

"I wonder if pioneers appreciated the peace and tranquility of a gently burning fire?" Julie's tone was hushed as she stared into the flames.

"Probably not," Marc said. "They were too busy making a life for themselves, and keeping the wood-box full so they didn't freeze to death."

"Maybe so," she replied. "But I'd like to think they had some enjoyment."

"Oh, I'm sure they did," he said, grinning suggestively and raising his eyebrows.

Julie grinned.

"Some of our modern technology is pretty good though," Marc added, nodding at the battery-operated baby monitor that sat beside them on a low table. "This sure beats having to hold her while she sleeps. She's getting heavy!"
~~~

Julie chuckled and nodded her agreement. After a few moments, her expression grew pensive. "Hey Marc?"

"Uh-huh?"

"Do you ever wonder what our neighbourhood looked like back then? After all, up until a couple of years ago, it was mostly just bush and farmland. The realtor said the big house on the hill has been there a long time, but I was thinking about the hired hands who worked the land. I mean, they had to live somewhere too right? People didn't commute the way they do now."

"Sure, I guess. Like a guest cabin or something?"

"More likely it was just a shack," Julie disagreed, frowning. "Maybe a log cabin, but it wasn't anything grand."

Marc nodded, wondering why she seemed so specific. Where was she going with this?

"And for all we know, it could have been built on the same spot where our house sits now, right?"

"Yeah, I guess it's possible."

Julie was staring into the fire. She didn't see the strange look her husband directed at her.

"Well, we live there now," he said with finality. "That's what matters."

"Uh-huh," she replied absently, poking at the dying embers with a long stick. "We sure do."

~~~~

Dandelions and buttercups proliferated in the soft mud, and spongy moss filled the space in-between.

"If you squint, it's generally the right color, so I think I'm gonna leave it," Julie told her well-meaning neighbour, after he suggested that she rent a 'de-thatcher' to remove all the moss. "Besides if we rip out all the moss, I'll have no yard at all, and then it'll be just mud. With winter on its way, I think that would be worse, don't you?"

He'd pursed his lips at that. Julie knew he was suspicious the rampant weeds in her yard would creep through the fence and infect his meticulously groomed lawn.

Looking at it through the chain-link fence, she had to agree this was a definite possibility. No wonder he was so touchy.

The bright red blooms on her mother's roses stood out in stark contrast to Julie's somber mood.
~~~~

"How is it possible," she muttered, absently reaching out to touch the soft, velvety petals of the nearest rose. "That you bloom so beautifully in a clay pot, but not in the ground?"

Despite her well-intentioned teasing, Julie's mother didn't seem to trust the quality of the soil either, claiming it was better for roses to be potted rather than have them wither to nothing in such 'deadly soil'.

It was a strange comment, especially from a woman so completely opposed to the idea of anything unusual.

Chapter Twenty-two

"But Marc, it just doesn't feel like home yet," she complained to her husband. He was scrutinizing the pile of magazine articles and hardware store flyers that covered the telephone table in the kitchen.

"I realize you want to make-over the house Jules, and it looks really good," Marc replied patiently. "But we really can't afford this. It's gonna be Christmas soon and that'll be wickedly expensive. Remember, we just paid for a very expensive fence not that long ago."

Julie averted her eyes and folded her arms in a mute expression of anger.

"Has that newspaper you're writing for decided to pay you now?"

"Well, no. Not exactly," she replied, not looking up.

"That's what I thought."

"Look, you know it doesn't work like that, Marc," she replied, turning to pace in tiny circles. "When you've been out of the field for as long as I have, you need an up-to-date portfolio. No one wants a profile writer who hasn't been published in five years. Submitting free copy is the only way I know to get back in the game. I give them free, printable copy and they give me a by-line."

"Okay, but what does that have to do with all this?" he muttered, gesturing at the décor magazines that littered the table.

Julie waved an impatient hand and walked back to the stove top, angrily stirring the spaghetti sauce she was cooking.

"No, I mean it. Look, I realize you want this place to feel like home and in our last house, that meant painting and renovating but honey, we just can't," Marc implored his wife.

Julie pursed her lips and frowned in mute response.

"I know, I know," her husband held up his hands in surrender. "We did say we were gonna spruce up the place, but this stuff looks expensive!" Marc picked up the nearest newspaper flyer where several items were circled in red pen. "This is a lot more than sprucing."

"I'm trying, Marc, but it's not easy. It so …different here," she said, her voice small.

Marc sighed. "The nightmares? Are they still coming?"

Julie looked away.

"Oh geez hon, I'm sorry. I know this is tough on you, you stay here all day with the kids and look at the same walls over and over, but we have to consider the budget, okay? This house is costing a lot more in upkeep than the last one. We just don't have the extra budget for renovations right now."

Julie's mind was whirling. He said he understood, but did he really? How could he? He barely spent any time in the house. When he was working in town, he left for work so early. Often, he came to kiss her goodbye where she'd fallen asleep, still sitting in the bentwood rocker, arms locked in place around the body of their sleeping daughter. When he got home, he was just in time for dinner and the marathon of Adam and Amélie's lengthy night time routines.

They both lived each day in wonder that they could still function, amazed how little sleep they now needed in order to keep going. It was weird how the human body adjusted. With age, Amélie's sleep patterns had not smoothed out as the doctor had predicted.

"I'll tell you what," Marc said, interrupting her thoughts. "If you'll hold off on all this, we can go to the cabin this next weekend. I've got some banked time coming to me and we could both use a break. What do you say?"

"Oh Marc!" Julie responded excitedly. "Yes! That's a great idea!"

"Okay, it's a deal then." He grinned at her. A second later his expression changed as he looked around. "Uh-oh, where's Adam?"

"Probably where he shouldn't be," Julie replied, watching her husband go in search of their son, who was suddenly nowhere in sight. "Check the backyard," she called. Out of sight meant trouble when it came to Adam and Julie was grateful to have her husband home again for tag-team parenting.

Julie watched the steam rise from the pan in front of her. It was their dream house, it really was, but when the opportunity came to leave, even for a few days, they jumped at the chance.

Julie felt like an unwanted guest in her own house and she knew Marc shared that sentiment. Paint and wallpaper wasn't likely to change all that, but it was all she knew how to do.

~~~~

Julie, her arms full of groceries, was startled as she opened the door to find her mom, ashen faced, staring with frightened eyes up the staircase.

"Hey mom," Julie said. "Is everything okay?"

"Oh!" Her mother answered, turning sharply to face her daughter. "You're only just coming home now?"

"Yeah, I'm finally done. You know how it is when you're planning a trip. There's always a lot more to buy than you think, but I should be all done now." Julie narrowed her eyes. "Mom? What's wrong? Where are the kids?"

"What? Um … they're good. They're fine. I– I'm fine. The kids are watching TV with grandpa," she replied, her eyes returning to the top of the stairs.

"Mom?" Julie asked in wonder.

"I didn't know Marc was coming home early?" the older woman asked, a hopeful gleam in her eyes. "That was him, right?"

"What? No, it shouldn't be … at least I don't think so," she replied. "I didn't see his work van outside. Why? Is Adam being a pain? I'll just put this stuff away and then I can come get him."

"No, no it's not that," the older woman had dropped her gaze to the floor and seemed to be thinking fast. "I'm sure it's nothing. Nothing to worry about."

"Oh, ok-a-ay," Julie replied dubiously. "If you're sure."

"Of course I'm sure," her mother replied, taking a deep breath and squaring her shoulders. Julie recognized the movement as her mom's 'I can take on anything' stance.
~~~~

"Mom? Did something just happen? Are you okay?" Julie set down the bags in her arms and reached out to clasp her mom's hands, demanding her full attention. Her hands felt like ice in Julie's warm grasp.

"Oh Julie, don't be so dramatic. I'm fine. You go ahead and put away the groceries." Taking her hands from her daughter's, she waved one of them in the direction of the stairs and tilted her chin in a show of strength. "Shoo, off you go. There's nothing to worry about, just a few noises. Shocked me a little. I guess I'm still not used to living in a cul-de-sac. The houses are so close, here."

With furrowed brow, Julie continued to unload the groceries and put them away, but her mom's casual comment stayed with her. Still not used to living in a cul-de-sac? How much longer was it gonna take? And what about the home Julie had grown up in? Didn't that count as a cul-de-sac house?

The answer didn't make sense, but she wasn't going to get anywhere by arguing the point.

Her parents felt strongly that if no one could find an explanation for something, then perhaps it didn't need one and was best ignored.

~~~~~

"Mom, I just don't know what's wrong with her," Julie wrung her hands in anguish as the two women looked down at the tiny child. She was tucked securely into bed, blankets pulled up to her chin. Her pasty white skin, in stark contrast to the bright colors of the quilt, only served to heighten the young mother's concern.

"She can't keep anything down and I gave her medicine but her fever won't budge."

Anne laid a professional hand on her granddaughter's forehead and frowned. "Grab her coat and blanket. I'll go get your dad. He can stay with Adam. She needs to see a doctor. Now."

"Oh mom, you think so?"

"Don't worry, I'm going with you."

~~~~~

"Tonsillitis?" Marc repeated. "Are you sure?"

"Mom and I took her to the doctor today," Julie confirmed. "There's no way we can go to the cabin now."

"Well, at least you got her to the doctor before she got worse," Marc answered. "Good thing your mom is here."

"True," Julie looked away, suddenly ashamed. "What's wrong with me, Marc? I should have known it was something serious. I should have been able to make that decision. I'm her mother, after all. Instead, I just stood there in her bedroom, watching her suffer, and all I kept thinking was 'what do I do?'"

Marc looked down at his hands, folded on the tabletop between them.

"You've been through a lot lately. Don't be so hard on yourself."

"Easy for you to say," she retorted. "You weren't there. Again."

Marc's jaw stiffened and he looked away.

~~~~~

Marc would be home again soon, but even that thought didn't fill her with the excitement it once had. With his return, there would be so many things he didn't understand, and didn't really seem interested in learning. Julie made a face as she continued to fold, the rhythmic motions somehow comforting as her thoughts turned to the unerring fact that she and Marc didn't seem to know each other anymore. How could that have happened? They'd been so in love before Amélie was born.

Could it have been the arrival of their beautiful baby daughter that drove a wedge between them? Julie shook her head as the thought formed.

No way, Marc loved that kid! And so did she.

As though the answer was somehow stamped on the wall, Julie stared at it while her hands performed the simple tasks that kept their household running.

~~~~~

Christmas was over for another year. While the family usually looked forward to it with excitement, this year's celebration had been more like a pageant of color, lights, music and food. They'd begun to decorate on November 1st, making sure to skip Halloween, considering Adam's fears. His aversion somehow affected all holidays, not just Halloween, forcing the family to dial down the excitement, while desperately searching for answers.

Julie's eyes filled with water as she thought about Adam's last speech therapy appointment. Adam had swept away the Christmas books his therapist Ruby prepared, and grabbed a piece of lined paper from her desk, instead, handing her a marker, eagerly.

Using the system they'd developed together, Adam was telling Ruby with his specific actions, that he wanted to talk. But what he wanted to say shocked everyone.

Adam wrote confidently on the page in big block letters, using the fat marker he preferred from Ruby's collection.

VAMPIRE.

Ruby quickly wrote a sentence under it.

What is a vampire?

As Ruby wrote several options for Adam to choose from he watched carefully.

A)A character from a movie

B)Someone bad

C) Make believe

D)Someone who looks scary

E) Someone who scares children

F) Something else

Adam very quickly circled B and E. Someone bad, and someone who scares children.

Ruby took the pen. Adam fixed his gaze excitedly on the page, watching her form each letter with rapt attention.

Did Adam get hurt or scared by this person?

 A) No

B) Yes

C) I am scared to tell

D) I don't know how to tell

E) Something else

With a heavy heart, Julie watched her son circle 'yes.

Will you tell Ruby now? The therapist asked, as she wrote the phrase out on the page.

Adam took the pen and carefully spelled out 'not now'.

Julie and Marc looked at each other, unsure of what to say, as they gathered their things and said goodbye to Ruby for another week.

"I know what you said about vampires, son," Marc told his son, as the two sat down at the breakfast table the next morning. "But it isn't true. Whoever told you that, they were lying." Marc wrote the words on a blank piece of paper he had placed on the table. He wrote each word as he spoke it, taking his cue from their therapist.

Adam read each word as quickly as Marc could write them. As soon as the last letter was formed, Adam looked away.

"No!" he shouted, a fierce frown on his face.

"Sometimes, bad people lie. Vampires are NOT real. They are make-believe. The end."

Adam, his cheeks red with suppressed emotion, studied the words on the page.

Suddenly, Adam slid from his chair and snatched up the paper in one fluid movement. A second later, he'd hauled open the fireplace door and hurled the paper into the blue flames of the gas fireplace, where it caught immediately and turned to ash.

Although Marc knew that an ornamental gas fireplace wasn't really suited for burning paper, he had to admit his son's actions were a strong statement.

~~~~

Amélie's first birthday had come and gone without incident.

After much discussion, Marc and Julie had opted for a 'package' birthday at one of the local fast food restaurants. After all, they reasoned, they'd been doing this for Adam successfully and happily, for the past several years. And it would be nice to celebrate their daughter's birthday like a normal family.

"With that grand house of yours, I'm surprised you're having the party here," one of Julie's sisters-in-law commented.

She and Marc exchanged knowing looks over the tops of the children's heads.

"Too much work," Julie answered, smiling. "Just too much work."
~~~~

Chapter Twenty-three

"You've got to be kidding me? I thought we had the computer problems fixed?" Marc asked irritably.

"We did, but this isn't the same as before," Julie explained.

"Shit," he complained. "Could it be a tech issue?"

"No …it's hard to explain, so just listen and don't say I'm paranoid, okay?"

Marc nodded and folded his arms.

"You know when you're typing an email? You sort of say the words to yourself in your head before you type them, right?"

"Yeah," Marc agreed. "So?"

"Well, lately, when I go to type those words, that's not what comes out on the screen."

"I don't understand," Marc answered, shaking his head.

"Neither do I," Julie replied, looking away. "Instead of finishing the articles for the paper, all I'm doing is overworking the delete key! And then, inevitably the whole thing just locks up!"

"You mean the screen freezes?" He asked. "Did you do a hard re-set?"

"Yeah, I turned it off and then back on again. As you know, it takes awhile to completely re-boot, so I went downstairs to put the wash into the dryer, and when I came back, there he was, sitting in my chair. I nearly fainted."

Marc went cold and goose bumps stood out on his forearms. "Sitting in your chair?" he repeated, dumbfounded. "What did he look like?"

"Just like he did the night you came home late," she replied. "Shadowy. No details."

Marc paused in the act of opening the fridge. They'd been talking in the family room, grateful that the kids were out with Julie's parents, and they had a few minutes to themselves.

"But it was light enough," he argued. "Surely you could see some detail?" Grabbing a can from the shelf, he popped the top automatically and took a long swallow. He'd only just come home from a long, gruelling day and this was the last thing he wanted to talk about.

Things were ramping up, exactly as he'd feared and this entity was taking steps to show himself.

"It wasn't just an outline, Marc. He was actually *there*," Julie said, pointing at the chair in front of the computer. "He just sat there," she added, wringing her hands as she relived the memory. "It was only for a second, but I didn't imagine it Marc. I know I didn't."

"Okay," he replied, his tone neutral.

"I've been trying to convince myself ever since that I couldn't have really seen that. But if I didn't really see it, then that means I'm losing my mind. I don't know which is worse! Sometimes I wish we'd never left our little house. Things were better there."

Marc had no answer for that. Instead, he shook his head soberly, and turned away. There was an odd sensation in the room that he was only just beginning to pick up on. As Julie described her encounter, Marc became increasingly aware of its presence. So far, she wasn't reacting to it, but he wasn't about to tell her. He didn't want to scare his wife any more than she already was.

There was no doubt in his mind that the thing Julie saw down there was real, but why was it there? Was he right in thinking it had somehow attached itself to her? It showed itself only to his wife, while it seemed to hide from him.

Julie watched her husband's back stiffen as he looked around the room. She knew he didn't believe her story, but who else could she possibly tell? She wanted to pound on his broad back and make him understand, but her arms fell limply to her sides.

How long was he going to stand there, she wondered?

Tears spilled from her eyes as she went silently back down the hall.

~~~

Clomp ... Clomp ... Clomp ... Clomp ...
Someone was on the stairs again.
The sound was louder than it had ever been, and Julie awoke with a start. She'd just been drifting off when the first bang sounded.
Marc lay by her side, sound asleep as Julie wondered whether she had really heard the noise, or if she'd been dreaming? As she lay there, debating what to do, another sound sent panic shooting through her body.
CRASH!!
It was the unmistakable sound of something heavy smashing to pieces. In her mind's eye, she could see the plant that used to be on the ledge by the stairs, smashed to pieces at the bottom. Which could only mean –
Adam! Throwing off her blankets she bolted from her bed.
Two plants, still in place on both ledges caught her eye as soon as she gained the hallway. The moonlight spilling in through the massive living room windows gave enough light to see where she was going, but the effect was disconcerting.
Ducking her head around the corner of her son's room, she breathed a sigh of relief. He was wrapped snugly under the covers, snoring softly.
Before she could check Amélie's room, she felt the air change.
It settled over her like a shroud.
Julie tried to swallow the lump in her throat.
No one was awake, and yet she could feel eyes on her staring her down.
CREAK.
Her eyes flew open wider, heart pounding uncomfortably in her chest. Someone just walked past the doorway, right in front of her! She knew exactly which spot gave off a sound like that. It was three feet from where she stood, just inside the doorway to the family room. With legs that shook of their own accord she inched forward.
There was safety in not seeing anything, she told herself. She just had to make sure.
~~~

The empty room was lit in part by the glow from the staircase chandelier, and by the almost-full moon that shone brightly through the glass doors.

Julie stepped forward again, and the floorboards creaked under her feet.

CREAK. It was the same noise from a few moments ago.

The room looked like it always did, except for one curious patch of dense shadow in one corner that drew her attention. Moonlight poured in through the open blinds just beside it, enough to fully illuminate the room, but the corner impossibly dark.

Julie took a deep breath. "Oh boy," she whispered. "Is someone here or am I losing it?" Her heart leapt into her throat as the shadow in front of her shifted. Julie blinked rapidly and concentrated on her breathing. In and out like the waves of the ocean, she thought desperately. Don't pass out *now*. Her stomach fluttered so violently, she felt sick.

It was her imagination, right? She really wanted it to be. How could she keep going if it wasn't? With one foot on either side of the proverbial fence, this was getting ridiculous!

Swish. The distinctive sound of fabric against fabric brought her fear to a fever pitch.

"Oh no, no, no." she stammered. "You just stay where you are. I don't need any more proof." Backing away, she retracing her steps down the hall and prayed that whatever this was, it wouldn't follow her.

She didn't dare take her eyes away for even a moment. Just blinking was risky enough.

Her eyes burned as she stood outside her bedroom door, grateful for the blazing light of the chandelier overhead. She didn't care what Marc thought. She was leaving that sucker on!

Whatever this was, it lurked in the shadows. Therefore, it stood to reason it would avoid the light. Julie hoped her reasoning was sound. It was all she had to go on.

Licking her suddenly dry lips, she went through her home bravely, throwing every switch she could find, until the house glowed with artificial light.

Julie sagged against the wall with relief, knowing every corner was lit, and nothing could sneak up on her.

Let her husband try and say something, she fumed. Their safety was more important than the cost of electricity. If this kept the shadows away, then that's what she'd do.

Julie didn't chance turning on her kid's bedroom lights, lest she wake them. Amélie's sleep was rare and precious.

Needing to believe that the light from the hallway was warding enough, she went back to her own room, and crawled back into bed, switching on the bedside lamp.

~~~~

Marc hadn't liked it, but he knew it was futile to argue. Settling on a compromise they could afford, he went to the hardware store and bought powerful nightlights for every room in their home.

Julie had argued fiercely, saying nightlights weren't enough, but in the end logic and the price of electricity won out.

Marc shook his head as he recalled how upset she'd been. He knew it was only because their argument took place in the comforting light of day. Had they been discussing this at night, he would have easily lost.

~~~~

"Adam!" Julie called out, her voice a harsh whisper. A sound like the rustling of dry leaves stopped her in mid step and she looked towards it source.

"Oh, for goodness' sake," she whispered again. "Would you get up here? It's the middle of the night!"

Hands on her hips in a show of motherly anger, she turned to face the empty stairwell. The light from the hallway night light only reached so far. Beyond that, the darkness was impenetrable. Marc had logically argued that the front foyer didn't need to be lit at night when they were all upstairs.

"Adam Marcus," she whispered sternly. "Get back to bed young man. I mean now!"

The rustling sound stopped, and Julie waited for her son to appear.

Although Julie expected to see a chagrined little boy mounting the stairs, the seconds ticked by, and still nothing happened. Julie headed for the gate, her movements quick despite her fatigue.

Here we go again, she thought, passing a weary hand over her forehead.

"Man, I hate Autism," she whispered angrily. "Why do things always happen when I don't have the energy for it?"

"Adam?" she whispered again.

Silence was her only answer.

The stairs were carpeted, but as her bare foot came down on the top step, it gave forth a loud creak. Julie winced.

"New house, my foot!" she whispered angrily.

Halfway down the staircase, Julie tiptoed onto another protesting step.

Creak.

Reaching the bottom, Julie flipped on lights and pushed open doors, checking rooms as she went.

There was no sign of her son.

Bewildered, but with her mind racing to alternatives she wasn't ready to think about, Julie retraced her steps.

A quick glance at the front door revealed the gleaming metal deadbolt, still firmly in place. The door to her parent's suite was tightly closed and securely locked. For good measure, Julie tried it anyhow.

The longer she stood there, the sillier she felt.

What the hell am I doing? She thought. I'm a pretty picture, aren't I? Standing here in pajamas, at three in the morning, chasing shadows ... Wild goose chase.

Julie resisted the urge to turn around as she headed back up the stairs.

Now that powerful little night-lights glowed in every room, her eyes could see no one was there, but the feeling that someone watched her was again, very strong.

"Can't you just leave us alone?" she whimpered. "Just go away!"

Julie poked her index finger into one ear and wiggled, trying to alleviate the pressure she felt there.

Still at a loss where to find her son, Julie peeked inside his room a second time. The room was bathed in a soft glow by the night light Marc had placed there.

Just as before, his bed was empty, but this time, Julie noticed something she hadn't before.

Feet.

Julie discovered, to her intense relief, that Adam had put himself to bed underneath it! One of his favourite blankets was in there with him, as well as his pillow, but he was quite definitely asleep, under his bed.

And the sounds she'd heard?

"My imagination," she whispered firmly. "I'm not doing this to myself again."

Closing her son's door, she returned to her own room, still confident that light was the answer. The light would keep them all safe.

But what about those footsteps?

Julie frowned. They happened too often to be dismissed. Could it be the cat?

She and Marc often teased each other that their cat wore army boots, and it was he who stomped around, making so much noise. It was the type of humour that got them through each bizarre day, but when darkness returned, Julie didn't find much comfort in it.

The more she thought about it, the less sense it made. A cat wouldn't climb the staircase like that. Step by deliberate step …

Stop it! Julie admonished herself, folding her arms tight across her body. This wasn't healthy. She was talking herself out of her own logical, rational explanation!

The muscles in her legs trembled with fatigue as she crawled back into bed, careful not to make a sound, lest she wake her sleeping husband or their soon-to-be awake infant.

It was the cat. It had to be. Julie lay there in the semi darkness, convincing herself. By sheer force of will, she would make the explanation fit! Besides, to believe anything else just made her paranoid. She still had to function. No one was going to suddenly swoop in and save her from motherhood. She just had to keep going. And to do that, she needed to rest. All of this would have to wait, or take a back seat, or ...something!

As Julie snuggled down under the covers, her legs encountered a warm lump and her heart sank.

The cat was already in bed with them.

This wasn't happening. It couldn't be happening. Can people honestly live like this?

Pressed up against her husband, she shivered.

"Honey, what's wrong? You're like ice." Her husband whispered, his words slurred by fatigue. "Is the baby up?"

"No," she replied, secretly relieved she'd awakened him.

"Why are you so cold?"

"You wouldn't believe it if I told you," she whispered back, taking a deep breath to steady her shaking voice. "I heard someone stomping around in the house. It wasn't Adam and it wasn't the cat."

"Okay," he mumbled. "You stay here, I'll go check it out." He sat up and blinked rapidly, trying in vain to shake off his exhaustion.

"No need," she said. "I already did. There's nothing there."

"What? No one there?" Marc yawned and lay back down. "Where's Adam?"

"Sleeping. Under his bed."

"Huh? Sleeping? Oh, good," he yawned again. "Neighbours?"

"No, I don't think so. It's okay. Just sleep. It's fine now."

In truth, Julie wanted to speak with him, to hear his reassurance that everything would be okay, instead of having to do that task herself, but his breathing deepened almost instantly. A quick glance told her Marc was already asleep.

Julie hugged her knees, the covers twisted securely around her body. She tried to tell herself it was okay to close her eyes. It was okay to sleep.

But even with the reassurance of the night lights scattered through her home, sleep took a long time to come.

That night marked the first of many that Julie would lay awake, staring at shadows, and willing them not to move.

~~~~

It seemed to Julie that she blinked twice and it was already time for Halloween again!

The endless preparations the school went through were exhausting. Field trips to prepare for, special lunches to pack and of course, a costume! What would her high-maintenance little son allow her to do this year?

Any time there was change, Adam hated it. The usual pumpkin carving event at school prompted him to come home early. He hated getting his hands dirty and apparently, he 'drew the line at touching pumpkin guts'. Or at least that was the opinion voiced by his teachers, and captured in his communication book. The red duotang travelled between home and school, keeping both parties up to date on the daily happenings at home and school.
~~~~

Despite all that, however Adam chose his costume readily and seemed excited for the big day, although he wavered between excitement and fear, not sure which one to settle on, as the big day drew closer. Marc and Julie had opted for less of a display this year, worrying they'd overdone it the previous year, although they still couldn't figure out how.

Nevertheless, they didn't enjoy having a reputation as the 'creepy house' in the neighbourhood, so this time they were going to play it safe.

There were no special sound effects, and no fake cobwebs. The only things they'd compromised on were: a black light, in place of the normal porch light, a jack o'lantern with a cheerful grin, that same ridiculous doormat, with its tinny automated laughter, and a crepe paper spider that would hang above the door.

For the costumes, following Adam's excited lead Julie transformed her children into two iconic children's favourites.

"They're raggedy Anne and Andy!" she announced, as her parents came out of their suite in time to snap a photo before the grand adventure. This would be Amélie's first experience, and she was bundled up with blankets against the chilly evening, and securely buckled into her stroller. The hand-made red yarn wig that sat atop the child's head, combined with the dress and pinafore she wore, created an amazing look, when paired with her brother's blue sailor outfit. Except for the fact that he kept tugging on his wig, and Amélie snatched hers off completely every three seconds, the effect was perfect.

"Brilliant! Oh Julie, they're wonderful!" Anne congratulated her daughter.

"Well, I guess we'd better go!" Marc said, as Adam grabbed onto the stroller and started pushing it towards the door. Marc grinned happily, while Julie, shrugging into a coat and following her family, adjusted the costumes as they made their way out into the night.

Little did Julie and Marc know that their son's Halloween experience that evening would prove to be his last.

Adam came home a scant twenty minutes later, his eyes wide and terrified.

<div style="text-align:center">~~~~</div>

But why is Adam so scared? Julie wrote on the sketch pad in front of her.

Adam had been inconsolable since his aborted Halloween excursion the previous night, and while she knew he was scared, she didn't know why.

A) I saw something
B) I heard something
C) I thought of something
D) Something scary happened
E) Something else

These were the choices, and as she turned the page to her son, she saw him read through the list, faster than he usually did.

Grabbing the pen from her hand, he drew a hasty circle around D, before turning around and throwing the pen with all his might into the family room, sliding down off the chair at the same time.

"Oh!" Julie exclaimed. "Is that it for now?"

Adam, his face serious, looked at his mother. Was he waiting for a reaction?

"It's okay," she said softly. "We can be done."

Adam turned and ran from the room. A moment later, she heard the slam of his door.

Julie let out an explosive breath and sat back in her chair. What now?

~~~~

"Julie," the speech therapist called over the intercom in her office, where she sat with Adam. He was having one of his usual sessions, and it was typical for Julie to be out in the waiting area, where she could watch her son through one-way glass, but he couldn't see her.

Julie picked up the phone in the outer office and spoke into it. "What is it?" she asked.

"I think you need to see this," the therapist said, her tone serious.

As Julie came slowly into the room, she could see that the woman was writing down something on the paper in front of her, while Adam waited patiently, watching as she formed each letter.

"Is it okay for us to tell mom?" she wrote. As she wrote, she spoke each word.
~~~~

Adam eagerly grabbed the marker his therapist was using and in large, childish script, he wrote YES.

"Can I show mom our talk-write?" she said, writing down the same words on paper.

Again, Adam wrote YES.

To say the therapist was practiced at keeping a poker-face would have been an understatement. She maintained an exceedingly calm demeanor. But Julie, despite the training she'd received under Ariel's guidance, had a hard time controlling her emotions that day.

VAMPIRES ARE REAL.

The letters were spelled out in Adam's childish, over-sized printing and they covered one whole page.

"What? Oh my God!" Julie whispered to the therapist. "What's going on?"

"There's more," the therapist informed her, handing over another page. Adam watched his mother carefully, as he'd done the day before.

CRY BABY. SCARED. HOUSE.

The words seemed to jump off the page at her. "What did he see?" Julie asked, returning the pages to the other woman. "He went out trick-or-treating with us, that's all. Marc and I never left him! He was in our sight the whole time. How is this possible?"

"This is just the first step," she reassured. "We'll get him to tell us more as time goes on. It may be as simple as a nightmare, but it could be a lot more serious than either of us would like to think. But please know that I'm obligated as a professional to investigate this and take it seriously. I'll keep you and Marc informed, as it develops, not to worry."

Trembling, all Julie could do was nod.

The news didn't sit well with Marc, but Julie hadn't thought it would.

Vampires? Are you kidding me? You were there, Jules. All we saw on our walk was a bunch of movie characters, and superheroes in department store costumes. There were plenty of witches, but they were all about three feet tall!"

"I know, I know," she soothed. "I can't figure it out either. About the only different costumes I remember were those couple of dads, dressed like giant pumpkins. But absolutely nothing resembling a vampire! I would have remembered that.

"Exactly!" Marc agreed. "And this year, he didn't try to go inside anyone's house, so there's no way he could have accidentally seen something on a random TV screen."

"I know, and we're so careful what he watched on TV, too!" Julie added, looking over at her son.

"The only other place he goes is school," Marc said. "Maybe someone there said something or showed him something? You know what he's like. He could have misinterpreted it. Did his teacher say anything in the communication book?"

"Not a word," Julie replied. "I can't for the life of me figure out how or even why someone would tell a child that vampires are real, though."

"Well I'm gonna go over to that school and ask some pointed questions," Marc said heatedly. "I want to know who is filling our boy's head with this crap! And I want to know right now! Not waiting another week for his next speech therapy session so he discloses something else!"

"So do I Marc," Julie replied. "And believe me I said much the same thing when Ruby told me this, but storming into the school when we don't have any clear answers isn't fair either."

"So we do nothing?"

"I didn't say that. I made another appointment for early next week. Maybe he'll tell us more then. If we ask too much, too soon Ruby says he'll probably just clam up."

"I hate to admit, but she's probably right. If we keep at him, he might not tell us anything. But it just makes me so mad! I want answers."

Chapter Twenty-four

Amélie was in an awkward phase. The tiny little girl was growing like crazy now, exploring her world. She should have been exhausted by all that, so why didn't she sleep? In the arms of her parents, grandparents or Godparents, she slept soundly, even snoring slightly, her little nose wrinkling with the effort. Even in the car seat, or lying on the couch or the floor, beside her brother or parents, she nodded off without issue. But as soon as she lay in her own bed, the eyelids would flutter open almost immediately. At best, they got thirty minutes, before the tell-tale crying would begin again. The sounds pierced their ears even over the baby monitor.

Instead of it getting better as she aged, it was getting worse.

What were they doing wrong?

The young parents were truly puzzled. Their son, even with his disability, had never done this. Sure, babies had to be taught to self-soothe, but she was well-past that stage. No matter what book they read, or what technique they tried, the little girl rejected every effort. She simply couldn't stand to be alone in her room.

It was a grey day outside, and the rain fell softly. The weather seemed to match Julie's mood. Amélie, in her high chair, dropped cereal on the floor while banging her tray with a small spoon. Julie was too exhausted to care.

"I didn't know it was possible to live without sleep," she mumbled to her mother, who was just coming up the stairs.

"Oh no. Another bad night?" the older woman asked.

Julie nodded. "She went to sleep okay, but she was so restless all night. I had to stay in her room, rubbing her back. As soon as I stopped, like because I was falling asleep standing up, she woke herself up again and we were back to square one. I don't know what to do about this, mom. Adam wasn't like this at all."

"Is Adam at school?"

"Yeah," Julie answered, checking the clock on the wall behind her. "For another hour at least. Geez, I feel like a zombie, but look at her, she's fresh as a daisy." Julie shook her head. "I don't get it."

"Oh no," Julie's mom disagreed. "She's tired all right she's just a champion fighter. Look at those bright red cheeks! Are you ready to let me have a try? That little one has to learn to sleep in her own bed. You just have to be firm and not coddle her, that's all."

Julie's eyebrows arched. "Coddle?" she asked. "So we're back to that tired, old argument?"

Despite the danger in the young mother's voice, her comment was lost on Grandma. Julie's mom was suddenly all business.

"Now you take yourself off to bed. I took the day off today, so I can help you. I'm taking over. Shoo!"

"Okay." She didn't have to be told twice. She couldn't remember the last time she'd had a good sleep. Maybe with her mother there, the staircase would even be quiet. For some reason Julie couldn't fathom, the entity didn't show itself to her mom.

Too tired to form cohesive thoughts anymore, she crawled into bed. It felt like heaven, and soon Julie was on the edge of sleep. So complete was her exhaustion that when she felt the covers inexplicably tightening around her body, all she could muster was an admonishing whisper of "not now". She already knew what it was. She'd felt the chill even through the thick blankets.

She knew what he wanted. It was always the same.

He wanted to scare her, manipulate her moods, control her and deprive her of the one thing she needed now more than ever: sleep.

"Piss off asshole," she mumbled. He was going to have to wait his turn, like everyone else. All around her, sunlight glinted and sparkled through the multifaceted window panes but Julie saw none of it.

<center>~~~~</center>

Grandma's dedication was impressive, but even she could not convince the child to sleep like other babies her age. Amélie, now almost fifteen months old, would go from peaceful sleep to a wild tantrum in mere seconds. Anne was at a loss to explain it.

Her behaviour upset everyone, especially Adam.

The two were having daily conflicts, and her interruption of his sleep only made things worse. Amélie had reached the age where none of Adam's toys were safe. Adam frequently left his toys lying around on the floors, and they were the first things she took, running off to her room with the newfound treasure.

"Adam it's not nice to bite," Julie wrote on the paper in front of her. Handing it with a serious expression to her son, she watched him scan the words, his expression unreadable.

"Amélie is just a baby. She doesn't understand. Special toys get put away so sisters can't get them. Always gentle please. There is no biting. Understand?"

A) I don't like it!

B) No, I don't understand

C) No. She is a bad baby!

D) Yes, I understand

E) Something else.

Hoping she wasn't grasping at straws, Julie slid the paper over to her son. Adam quickly circled B at first, frowning intently, but before putting the pen down again, he sighed dramatically and drew a big red circle around D. So, he did understand?

Julie heaved a sigh herself and reached out to hug her son. "That's my boy," she said aloud.

"Amélie will grow and learn. When she's bigger you can play together." Julie wrote each word as she spoke it, hoping to improve her son's understanding. He seemed to do much better with spoken words when they were also written out for him.

But Adam, instead of mellowing his behaviour, grabbed the pen from Julie and shouted: "NOO!!" following the same process as his mother, and writing out the long, drawn out word across the page in letters that were over an inch tall! As he completed the last of five exclamation marks, he threw pen in the family room. "No mom, no!"

"Whoah, dude!" Julie responded, holding up her hands in shock. "What's that about?"

As she went to retrieve the pen, Adam jumped up from the table and ran to his room, where a second later, his bedroom door slammed shut. The sound resonated through the house, followed by the unmistakable wail of a startled little girl.

"Crap!" Julie muttered, following her son. "He knows he can't slam doors. And I only just got her settled. Here we go again."

"Adam, fifty times," she said, upon opening the door. "Let's go."

With one eye on his mother, Adam opened and closed the door gently, fifty times, while counting aloud. He knew this drill. The only outward sign he was still upset came through in the counting, which was done in a falsetto voice, through clenched teeth.

"Mommy!" Amélie cried, as though her heart was breaking. "Mommy, mommy, mommy!" The child's cries had become a chant, interspersed with melodramatic breathless sobs in between each word.

"Just a moment Ami," Julie called. "Settle down, I'm coming."

As Julie crouched down to look her son in the eye, hoping she was handling this right, she tried to stay in the moment with her son. These moments were all they had together, and she was keenly aware of how important they were. If he was ever to figure things out, she had to spend the time.

"How about a big squeezer hug to get the mad out?" she asked her son. "That's better than slamming doors." Adam came to her immediately and hugged her with all his might, while his baby sister hiccupped and sobbed in the background. These 'squeezer hugs' were a coping skill they'd learned early on, to help him feel better and not stay stuck, being angry or sad. In times like this, Julie realized her son's 'squeezers' worked for both of them.

"I know you feel mad son," she told him, drawing him back by the shoulders and looking him in the eye. "But hurting your baby sister is not okay. Understand?"

"Yes mom," Adam answered contritely, hugging her again.

Julie had to smile at that. It was a phrase he'd just learned, and she loved hearing it but she wondered whether he actually meant it, or did he simply know that each time he said those words, mommy backed off? Probably the latter, she thought with a sheepish grin. But then again, he wasn't the only kid who told his parents what they wanted to hear.

~~~~

"I don't understand it," Julie's mother sighed in frustration. "She fell asleep okay, even in the crib, only to wake up screaming half an hour later. It's almost like she's being pinched in her sleep."

Julie's head snapped up at her mom's casual comment.

"Don't even say that mom!"

"Oh Julie, relax, it's just an analogy. After all, she's in there by herself. You really are jumpy."

But Julie wasn't listening anymore. Her brain leapt to conclusions, but she deliberately shut them out.

Not everything had to be paranormal. It was almost as though she could hear Marc saying it. It was a familiar phrase in their home.

Could it be Adam? He had been aggressive towards his sister already. Was he sneaking into the baby's room at night to torture her when no one could stop him?

That night, Julie looked with chagrin at the baby monitor, already turned up to its highest level.

"A lot of good that does," she muttered. "Just gives me a headache when it goes off. If only I could hear something else just before she cries. Maybe then I'd know how to fight this."

"Too bad it doesn't have video," Marc replied. "Then we might see something."

Oh geez, you're right," Julie said, her tone weary. "Do they make that?"

"I'm sure they will one day, but right now we just have audio. I could maybe ask your dad if we can borrow his camcorder," Marc said, yawning. "We could set it up in there on the tripod and just hit record."

"That's a great idea Marc, let's ask my dad. It's either that or I just stay up and watch her."

"All night?" her husband asked with incredulity. "That's ridiculous!"

"Well, we've got to get to the bottom of this. Especially as we're already suspicious the culprit is Adam."

"Oh wait," Marc said. Julie noticed he looked a bit sad.

"What?"

"You know how Adam is with electronics, right?"

"Sure, yeah," she replied.
~~~~

"What if he does go into the nursery while we're asleep? He'll have it all taken apart by morning and then we're on the hook for a new camera."

"Oh no," Julie groaned, remembering the stereo he'd mysteriously disassembled. "I still can't figure out how he took that stereo apart so completely, so I think you're right, we can't chance it."

"I hate to say this, but we don't have the money to replace your dad's camera if something goes wrong. Santa just doesn't have that in his budget this year."

Julie sighed. "Oh well, something told me it'd come to this. What's one more sleepless night?"

~~~~

Her body protested as she tried to make herself comfortable in the bentwood rocker, a tall glass of ice-water at her side. She checked her watch and opened the book in her hand. A lamp at her elbow cast a wan circle of light over the page.

Amélie had been asleep for only a few minutes. A soft smile touched her lips as she watched the baby, wisps of golden blonde hair curling damply against the crisp white bedsheet.

"Just stay like that, baby girl," she whispered. "Mommy's here."

The soft glow of the lamp, with its pink lampshade bathed the room in a rosy glow. Julie looked around and sighed. Was this really going to work? As the minutes ticked by, she rocked silently in the corner, vigilant for the slightest sign that something was amiss.

Amélie mumbled and sighed as she slept, causing the hyper vigilant mother to look up in surprise, her pulse quickening, but each time, the child settled back into the rhythmic breathing pattern of a baby completely at rest.

Sure, this was probably the only night she would sleep all the way through, she thought sarcastically. How poetic.

A sardonic smile on her face, Julie set the paperback in her hand onto the table at her side. There was no point trying to read anyhow, she thought. My mind is whirling!

Maybe she would just grow out of it. Maybe mommy was being paranoid and over-protective. This was probably just another baby phase, right? Wasn't that what all the experts said? Yes, Julie nodded
~~~~

her head emphatically. That had to be it. True, Adam had never gone through this, but Adam was a totally different person.

Julie began to wonder how she was ever going to make it through the night without getting some sleep herself.

This was a stupid idea, she thought, checking her watch. *I didn't think this through. I have to be functional for Adam.*

Blinking to sharpen her vision, Julie realized it was 3 AM! She felt like crowing with delight! Amélie never slept this long, except at the cabin! She couldn't count how many times she'd walked the hallway with her daughter, as one, two and three o'clock passed. But here it was, three o'clock in the morning, and Amélie was still sleeping peacefully!

Her eyes stayed riveted on the child, a glow of pleasure filling her. The soothing rhythm of Amélie's relaxed breathing had a lulling effect, and before she could stop it, Julie's chin tilted to her chest and both eyelids slid closed.

So complete was her exhaustion that she didn't notice the closet door as it inched its way open. She wasn't aware of the darkness that seemed to spill out of the narrow opening and creep past the very chair where she sat, oblivious.

The shadows pressed in around mother and child, but Julie slept on, believing that the night-terrors were behind them at last.

Positive energy poured off her like nectar.

He needed that energy. He fed on it. There was nothing he wouldn't do to keep the supply fresh.

Eventually, she stirred realizing she'd fallen asleep. Dragging open weary eyes, she scanned the room.

Had the closet been open before?

As soon as the thought formed in her foggy brain, the baby's eyes popped open, and a sharp wail pierced the silence.

Julie nearly fell out of her chair in surprise. Amélie was sitting up, her mouth wide in an ear-splitting scream, her feet furiously kicking away her covers. The baby looked around, her eyes wide with terror. Seeing her mother, she began pulling herself up at the crib rails and reaching out.

"Mama!" she screamed.

Julie was quick to pick up and comfort her screaming daughter, but inside she was crushed with disappointment. Despite camping out for half the night, she was no closer to figuring out this mystery.

The child's body shook as she clung to her mother. "Ma-ma," she sobbed.

"Ssh, it's okay now," Julie murmured. It was obvious her daughter was afraid, but of what?

"What is it?" Julie breathed against her daughter's cheek. "A bad dream? What's in your dreams that makes you so afraid little one?"

Amélie, her blue eyes streaming tears, pressed her face into Julie's shoulder and cried harder. The words she mumbled were too garbled to make out, but it was clear the little girl was deeply affected.

~~~

The evidence kept mounting, day after day, but the couple who had no choice in the matter just kept putting one foot in front of the other, shying away from shadows, turning inward, confiding only in each other, unknowingly immersing themselves in the darkness that surrounded them.

Each night, as they got ready for bed, Julie would turn to her husband, and Marc's eyebrows would rise in an unspoken question. In other households, the meaning of that look would have been clear, but not for Julie and Marc.

Neither one wanted to be the last person to turn off the light. The darkness, once soothing to her husband, if not to her, had become their enemy.

And although they had a million things to say, the words simply wouldn't come.

The toddler became stronger and steadier until she could stand on her own. Inside the crib! Whoops! Like any good mother, Julie snapped a photo first, then plucked the baby from her bed, and set her up in the nearby 'exer-saucer', hopefully preventing any unauthorized exploring, while she worked quickly to lower the mechanism in the crib. They couldn't have her tumbling out of bed in the middle of the night, after all. Just in case she ever decided to *sleep* in there.

That night, the ritual Julie knew so well began again. Low whimpering emitted from her daughter's room. Julie crept down the hall for a peek through the slit in the door.
~~~

She could just see the end of the crib and the side rail that faced into the room. Amélie was still lying down.

Well at least that's good, Julie thought.

Moving carefully, the young mother retraced her steps back to the kitchen where she was finishing up the day's dishes.

Adam was already sleeping, and the rhythmic sound of his snores was comforting in the otherwise eerie silence.

Again, Julie heard her daughter whimpering.

Julie stiffened, the dish cloth poised above the soapy dish, listening intently.

Was this the prelude to her full-on cry? Or would she finally stay asleep in her own bed tonight? Julie and Marc had been careful to follow the experts' advice for the past several months. They were no stranger to professional consultants and following a "written plan" was something they understood well. And while the techniques seemed to be working for her daytime naps - she slept in the crib for a full two hours, rising with tousled curls and a cheerful smile - night was a whole new ballgame.

Julie winced as the whimper became a loud moan that quickly dissolved into the heart-rending sobs that only a child can create.

The dish clanked onto the countertop as Julie's shoulders sagged in defeat. "What am I doing wrong?" she wondered aloud. "What more can I do?"

But as she moved off down the hall, the sounds coming from her daughter's room seemed to change.

Was she …giggling?

Puzzled, Julie slowed her stealthy advance.

Peeking through the narrow opening, she saw Amélie standing up in her bed, both hands gripping the crib rail as she faced forward.

Oh, I'm glad I lowered that today, Julie thought. If she didn't have to intervene, she wouldn't. Hoping she could just tip-toe back down the hall, she stood there a moment longer, watching to see what happened next.

But as she watched, Julie's eyes narrowed, then widened again in alarm.

Amélie, her gaze fixed on the opposite side of the room, leaned forward, her arms reaching the way she did when her parents came in.

"Up," Amélie said, stretching her arms wide.

At that, Julie burst through the door, as she took in the otherwise empty room.

Amélie, startled by her mother's sudden entrance, fell back against her blankets. "Mama!"

"Yes baby, Mama's here," Julie soothed, going to the crib immediately, she grasped the crib rail and tried to stop her hands from shaking.

"Dat?" Amélie asked, her index finger pointed questioningly at something behind her mother.

Julie's eyes went wide. Afraid to look, but knowing she had to, she turned slowly, her heart hammering in her chest.

A moment later, her shoulders sagged in relief. No sinister shadows, and certainly no menacing figure, as she'd been half-expecting.

The night-light shone bravely in one corner, but Julie shuddered anyways. The meagre light was enough to see by, but it didn't chase away all the shadows, especially those that gathered inside the open closet. Julie wasted no time closing the closet door, wondering as she did, why it didn't seem to stay closed.

Frowning in thought, she turned back to her daughter. The look of wonder she'd seen on Amélie's face was still there, and the child appeared to be looking at something that was just past Julie's right shoulder. Julie turned again, but she saw nothing.

As though she was trying to see something more clearly, Amélie tilted her head from side to side, and let out a small giggle.

The happy sound chilled the young mother. Clearly, Amélie saw something her mother could not.

Julie gathered her daughter in her arms and held her close.

"Keep it together," she muttered to herself. "Just keep it together."

Julie held her daughter for a long time, staring blankly at the wall behind the crib. There were no tears left to cry.

Chapter Twenty-five

Rolling up the sleeves of her shirt, Julie picked up her glass of water and stepped out onto the back deck. The sunshine was glorious, and she finally had a plan.0.

"Honey!" she called to her husband. "Do you want a drink of water?"

"No, but I'd appreciate a beer!" he replied, poking his head out from underneath the deck. "Adam could use a drink, too."

"Okay, two orders coming up," she replied, disappearing back into the house. Reappearing minutes later, she set the drinks on the outdoor table. "C'mon you two."

Adam's sun-bleached hair bounced as he took the steps at a run. Grinning, Marc watched his son and shook his weary head. "Whew! Where does that kid get his energy?"

"I wish I knew," she said. "Are you all done?"

"Yeah, but I still think this is a bit extreme," he said, taking a long swallow from the can she handed him. "You're really convinced this is going to work, huh?"

"Yes," she said, narrowing her eyes as she spoke. "I really do."

"Okay, " he replied doubtfully. "If flowers are so important to you, then have at it. I'll bring the dog inside with me and Adam. Amélie's down for a nap?"

"Yeah, such as it is. No guarantees how long she'll stay down."

"Don't I know it," he answered.

"This shouldn't take too long, and then I'll start supper."

"Ri-ight," he answered. "You're the queen of understatement. If we want to eat, I think I'd better cook."

"What a wonderful suggestion," she quipped. "I'm so glad you thought of it."

Marc shook his head good-naturedly. Adam shot through the door, past his father, plunging both mud encrusted arms deep into his toy box.

Julie narrowed her eyes.

Marc grinned and quickly kissed his wife on the forehead. "That's my cue. Master disaster is hard at work!"

"You look exhausted," she told him.

"Of course I am," he agreed. "But so do you. We're a matched set."

Marc ducked through the open door after his son. Moments later, as Julie carried a tray of pansies down the back steps, she heard Adam's protesting screams.

This was the way Adam registered a complaint. Unfortunately, as their son grew, the demands of school and home did too. It seemed like every day there was a new challenge; something else he or they had to learn, a new problem to face, and a new change to accept. And the weary family had to do it all without the ability to get a full night's sleep.

Funny how sleep affected everything, but sleep was the one thing they couldn't seem to get enough of. Julie narrowed her eyes in thought.

How long had they been functioning on just a few hours? Since the new baby, for sure, but hadn't it all started when they moved into the house?

Adam was loud, to be sure and unpredictable, and Julie had often been physically worn out from all the things Adam had done in their old house, but one thing she could always count on was his sleep schedule. Down by 9, up at 5.

But now?

Now, it was anyone's guess. Adam's sleep schedule had become as erratic as his baby sister's.

Was it coincidence or something else?

"The baby will get used to the noises in her house soon enough," the doctor had said. "Every sibling develops the ability to cope. She will too. Give it time."

Sure, Julie thought, as the familiar sound of her daughter's cry filled the air. How much time was this going to take? She was already a year and a half! Driving the small spade hilt-deep into the earth before her, Julie peeled off her gloves and ran up the stairs.

These situations often called for two parents.

~~~~

It was odd but sort of soothing, working outdoors when the moon was out. The houses that surrounded theirs were full of people getting ready for bed.

Marc had scoffed at the idea of working by moonlight, but Julie was determined to get her project done. In the back of her mind, she doubted whether her experiment would work, but she wasn't going to tell Marc that.

"Just a little bit of normal, that's all I ask," she muttered, as she carefully planted the delicate row of flowers, grateful that it stayed light so late in the night.

Looking back at her work, she stood and stretched her aching back.

The moon had just begun to mute the colors of the pansies that now lined the edge of her yard. Framed as they were against their new fence, the effect was peaceful. The dark earth looked even blacker in the fading sunlight, but the delicate looking flowers, so vital and healthy, gave her hope.

"Please stay that way," she muttered, watering them all liberally. "So far, so good."

Her husband appeared on the deck just then, their daughter nestled against his neck and shoulder.

"She settled now?" she whispered, as she reached the top of the stairs.

"Yeah, fast asleep. I just turned on the juice, and she conked." Marc stroked his daughter's back as he spoke. The 'juice' he referred to was their private joke. Ever since Adam was born, all Marc had to do, to calm his children was simply to hold them. It was like magic, and with Amélie, they needed all the help they could get.

The problem with Amélie was, the magic ended shortly after she was laid back into her own bed. They knew it was likely adding
~~~~

to the chaos in their household that Amélie's sleep patterns were all over the place. They tried to encourage regular sleeping times, even ditching the idea of naps altogether, but all that seemed to do was make things worse.

As a result, Marc often held his daughter for hours on end, often walking the halls of their home, or sitting on the couch, watching TV with the tiny girl held securely in his arms.

"It's time to come inside. We should have a full 30 minutes before she wakes up again," he called, a sarcastic grin on his face. "Are you done yet?"

"Yeah, I've done all I can," she admitted.

"Honey, don't get your hopes up, okay? They're just flowers," Marc commented as they both walked back inside. "They look nice, though."

Julie turned to the sink, and lathered up her hands. "You think it's stupid, don't you?" she asked. "After all, who in their right mind would plant living flowers on top of plastic? Erecting a barrier for a garden against the earth it grows in?"

Julie let the warm water run over her hands, washing away the remnants of black earth she'd purchased especially for this project. She couldn't help but notice that Marc had gone quiet again.

Let him think what he wants, she thought. Time will tell.

~~~~

"Oh, you've got to be kidding!" She spluttered, rushing once more down the stairs to the incessant banging of the washer. "Off balance again?"

Half way down, however, Julie's slippered feet hit the edge of the step, and she slid down the next five or six steps like she was on skis, before finally managing to grab the railing.

A shaken Julie descended the rest of the way in careful silence. Her husband's earlier warning echoed in her head.

"Slow down on those stairs," he'd warned as he left for work that day. "Did you know that a large percent of serious accidents occur in the home? You shouldn't wear those floppy things on your feet. Get yourself some shoes with grip. You don't want to fall."

A heartbeat later, another memory flooded her mind, replacing the chagrin she felt with cold dread.
~~~~

Her childhood doll, its limbs splayed, lying face down at the bottom of the staircase.

Was it a warning? *That could have been me, just now.*

Just one push would have sent her flying with no chance at recovery.

Julie gulped and looked back up the staircase. The sound of Amélie's favourite TV program played on in the family room.

With Marc at work and her parents out of town, she had only her children to help if she took a bad fall. And as much as she loved Adam, would he know how to call for help? Amélie was simply too young.

It didn't bear thinking about. It simply could not happen.

"I won't let it," she muttered. Julie straightened her shoulders and tossed her head in defiance, as though she could manage to stay injury-free through sheer force of will.

Eerie laughter sounded in her head as she stepped down the remaining few stairs.

That's why they're called accidents, the male voice she knew to be his, seemed to echo in her head as she crossed the foyer and flung open the laundry room door.

"Shut up you jerk," Julie muttered. "This stupid thing is gonna shake itself to pieces."

But what she saw as she stood in the doorway didn't make sense.

The washer was empty. Its lid open, it waited for the next load.

Her response was so automatic; she hadn't even stopped to consider that laundry day had been yesterday.

"Well, at least my washer's not broken," she sighed.

What her tired brain needed was fresh air and exercise. No more impossible scenarios and confusing circumstances. It wasn't good for a person to live with stuff like this! A person could go crazy trying to make sense out of it, she thought, marching resolutely back up the stairs.

As soon as her feet touched the top step, Julie caught sight of several sheets of paper strewn across the table. In a flash, she remembered what she'd been doing when the sound that couldn't possibly have been the washing machine sent her literally flying down the stairs.

Julie's eyes flitted to her children, still exactly where she'd left them, mesmerized by the story unfolding on the TV screen, despite the beautiful sunshine streaming in through the glass doors.

"Best mom ever," she quipped, feeling a stab of guilt as she reached for a pen.

That night, she stood at the bathroom counter, washing her face and listening intently for the sounds that would tell her Marc was finally home. He was working late, but at least he was working in town.

As Julie stared at her reflection, she wondered how long she could go on like this.

She did everything she could to pretend life was normal. She planned birthday parties for her kids, and made phone calls to their friends, mindful that if they didn't keep up appearances, their lives would be empty.

It was hard to make light-hearted comments, and offer a sympathetic ear as their friends dealt with stress of a different variety. Mundane matters like injustices at work and shortened holidays filled their lives. Julie felt like a terrible friend for thinking these things, but all she wanted to do when they called, was to share the awful secret that *somehow*, they'd purchased a haunted house and now, they hadn't the faintest clue how to get themselves out of this big, fat mess. Help!

"Who are you, anyhow?" Julie asked her reflection. "I don't know you anymore."

The dark circles under her eyes spoke of too many sleepless nights. Fine lines radiated across her forehead in premature wrinkles.

She slammed the wet facecloth onto the counter. "I'm not even thirty, but look at me."

A moment later, the front door banged and heavy footsteps mounted the stairs.

Marc was home.

In relief, Julie walked back out to the hallway, to wait for her husband. Everything was still dark downstairs.

"Sorry I forgot to leave the lights on for you," she called out in a stage whisper.

Thud … thud …. thud …. slow and heavy, her husband's footsteps continued to climb the staircase.

"Honey," she hissed into the darkness. "Take off your boots first, you'll wake the children."

Julie waited, her hands on the railing as she listened to the slow, measured footfalls.

"Marc!" she admonished. "Did you hear me?" The lights in the foyer were off, and the only source of illumination came from the bedroom behind her. It cast a muted glow halfway down the staircase. She could just barely see the outline of his shoulders, his head bowed with obvious fatigue as he paused on the lowest steps.

"Whatever," she whispered. "Just get up here then, I'll fix you some supper. We've got leftovers."

Thud … thud …. thud …. thud.

Unconsciously Julie counted the steps as she busied herself in the kitchen, flipping lights on as she went. A backwards glance at the staircase showed it was empty.

Where had that man gone now? He moves like a ghost!

Julie rolled her eyes at her own bad joke as she set a place at the kitchen table for Marc. She knew he'd be tired and hungry after his long shift.

The top step gave a loud creak, and the metal latch on the gate rattled, announcing his arrival at last.

"Chicken and potatoes sound good, or do you want something lighter?" She asked, rounding the corner.

Julie frowned at the empty space before her. "Marc? Where did you go?"

Had he been so exhausted, he'd simply gone straight to bed? What was that about? Why wouldn't he even respond? Was he sick?

"Marc?" she hissed, down the empty hallway. "Honey, did you go to bed?"

Julie walked quickly to the bedroom, but there was no sign of her husband there either.

"What's going on?" She asked, hands on her hips. Irritation brought her instantly alert. "I'm not gonna chase you, ya know." She could only assume Marc had forgotten something and gone back down to the foyer to grab it. His footsteps would make little or no sound if he'd already removed his boots, but …

Julie looked around the room. No boots! It was unusual enough for her husband to climb the stairs with his boots on, but what was up with all this silent treatment? Had she done something *else* to piss him off? This was just plain ridiculous!

A low growl issued from the dog's kennel in the far corner of the family room and Julie turned towards her with a sharp reprimand. "Keisha! Hush! It's just daddy."

Julie stood deliberately at the top of the staircase in a pose she knew Marc would recognise. He had a fantastic sense of humour, but her nerves were raw and he had to learn not to play games!

"Marc," she called again, her voice a little louder as she started down the stairs. "Look, it might feel like five o'clock in the afternoon to you, but I'm tired and *not* in the mood for games, so just get up here and have your dinner."

"Marc?" She called again. Worried he might be sick or hurt, she descended the steps and flipped on the foyer lights. Julie realized then, with a cold wave of fear, that despite what she thought she'd seen and heard, her husband was not yet home.

There was no sign of the work boots and enormous tool box that would have rested just inside the door.

"This can't be happening," she whispered, as she peeked through the inset window in the front door. Her husband's work truck was nowhere in sight. Julie's hands shook as she gripped the railing and re-mounted the stairs. "I know I saw him. I saw him, right *here*." Her eyes watered as she replayed the last few minutes in her head.

"Why are you doing this?" She asked, her voice low and warbling with emotion. "I – I'm not playing your stupid games. It's not funny!"

She turned, and keeping the foyer in full view, she began backing up the staircase.

Suddenly, the deadbolt turned of its own accord and the front door swung open.

It sent a shock through Julie's body like a bolt of lightning and she yelped in surprise.

"Honey?" Marc stepped through the open door and only just managed to set his toolbox on the floor before his terrified wife launched herself into his arms.

"Whoah! That's quite a welcome," he said, laughing.

A moment later, the smile fell from his face as he realized Julie wasn't letting go, and her body trembled against him. She was crying! But why?

Marc had no choice but to hold his wife as her tears soaked the collar of his shirt.

"What's going on?" he asked gently, automatically rubbing her back.

Julie raised her head briefly, her expression serious as she dashed away the tears and shook her head. Marc was puzzled and worried, but he'd only just gotten home from an unexpected night shift and he was tired. If she didn't want to tell him what happened, maybe that was a good thing. He wasn't sure he was ready to hear it.

~~~~

"I'm sorry I launched into you last night," Julie said, her head down as she prepared the coffee next morning.

"That's okay, you seemed pretty scared."

"Yeah, I was, but feel kinda silly for nearly knocking you over."

"I'm tough, I can take it," he quipped, smiling. "What happened?"

Marc saw his wife's expression change, and her eyes took on a frightened cast. "I, uh … I don't really know how to explain it," she began, swallowing nervously. "It's just … last night, I heard the front door bang, and then I saw you … or what I thought was you, at the bottom of the stairs." Julie folded her arms tight across her chest and shuddered. "And then it wasn't you … and then all of sudden you really *were* there, and I, I guess I just fell apart."

"Oka-ay," Marc replied slowly, trying to piece together the disjointed information. "Wait, you saw me *before* I was home?" he asked.

"Well, I *thought* it was you," she clarified. "There was *someone* standing at the bottom of the stairs. The lights were off, so I couldn't see clearly."

"Are you sure? What did it look like?"

"It looked like you. A man with big shoulders, about your height," she described, her voice starting to shake. "I could have sworn it was you Marc."

"This place is full of shadows," he replied calmly. "Especially at night, and with your parents away, it's easy to get freaked out. Did you have the dog with you? Are you sure you didn't just imagine it?"

"I didn't imagine it," she retorted hotly. "I heard his footsteps on the stairs, Marc. And so did Keisha. She was in her crate, growling! I thought she was being silly, but I guess she knew better."
~~~~

Julie turned around and got two coffee mugs from the cupboard. The cups rattled together as the young woman's hands started to shake uncontrollably.

"Hey, come on calm down. It's okay now," Marc soothed. "Come sit down, I'll get the coffee."

Julie sat down at the table and pressed her palms to the cool glass surface to try and stop them from shaking. "Someone is here Marc. He watches us. We need to cut the bullshit and just admit it, okay?"

Marc filled both cups with coffee careful to keep his expression neutral. "Okay, what do you want me to say?"

"I don't know," she retorted, looking around in frustration. "There've been too many unexplained incidents. First you agree with me, and then you don't. You seem to be constantly on the fence about whether there's a ghost or it's just my imagination."

Marc turned away to look in the fridge.

"Marc, I'm serious," she said, irritated.

"I hear you," he said. "I'm not deaf, but it's breakfast time, and I'm hungry. Keep talking, you don't think this is your imagination, I got that."

"Look, while it doesn't seem to have bothered you too much, this thing is torturing me on a daily basis!" Tears sprang once more to her eyes. "I can't live like this Marc. We've already got an overdose of drama with our son. Do we have to live in a haunted house too?"

"I know, I know," he soothed. "You want me to call the church rectory after breakfast?"

Julie nodded.

"Okay, but let's not say anything weird to the Priest. He doesn't need to know what's been going on here."

Julie blinked and stared at her husband. "Just like that?"

Marc threw up his hands in frustration. "What do you want me to say? Did you want to fight some more, is that it?"

Sheepishly, Julie shook her head.

"Drink your coffee," Marc said, handing her the steaming mug. "Be careful it's hot."

~~~~

"One o clock and all's well!" Adam hollered.
~~~~

Julie winced. She recognized the quote, but knew Adam also had one eye on the clock.

"I know, I know," she said. "We're late!"

Of course, she thought, grabbing his hand. I'm always late. What's new?

Struggling into her own jacket, she let go of Adam's hand long enough to grab her keys and then ran to catch up with her son, who'd taken off through the front door. He was bolting for the van, still hollering at full volume.

In Adam's world, there was a quote for every occasion.

"Why do I bother taking him to speech therapy?" she muttered, faking a smile for the few neighbours who'd come outside to see what all the fuss was about.

"Aw let's just forget it!" Adam said. His words sailed easily through the partially open window beside him.

Julie had to laugh. She knew he didn't really understand the meaning of the words he quoted but for once they rang true. She didn't want to go either.

"Hang on partner," she called out, trying to get his attention by affecting a southern twang as she accentuated each word.

"Yee-ha!" Adam crowed, already fidgeting around in his booster seat.

Julie smiled and silently thanked her parents again for keeping Amélie at home. They'd only just arrived back from their latest trip and were anxious to spend Christmas with their grandchildren.

She thought back to Adam's last speech session and winced. It hadn't gone well at all with Amélie loudly protesting each time her brother chose a toy from the therapists' cupboard.

Adam had screamed at his baby sister, full volume while prying her little fingers from the toy, only making her yell louder.

Julie found herself apologizing over and over.

Everything with Adam was such a production, and one day Julie hoped her daughter would get used to it, and maybe dial down the drama herself, but today was not that day. Amélie had awoken with a dangerous look in her eyes and Julie just knew it was going to be a day full of willful battles.

With Amélie in her arms, Anne came out on the top deck and waved goodbye to her daughter and grandson as the van backed down the driveway.

"Look Adam!" she said, pointing through the windshield. "Say goodbye to Grandma."

"Say goodbye to Grandma," Adam repeated, looking out the wrong window.

Chapter Twenty-six

Instinctively, she grasped her son's hand and pulled him away firmly as she unlocked the front door.

"Hold on there young man," she said. "Let me take your backpack first."

Julie slid her son's backpack off his shoulders with one hand, while opening the door with the other.

A moment later, she dropped the bag and her hand shot out again to snatch her son back from the glittering piles of broken glass that littered her foyer.

"What the hell!" she spluttered, staring at the glittering mess.

Adam, oblivious to the danger, strained against his mother's grip.

"Hold on, hold on," she told him, her brain whirling to figure this out.

He tugged at her hand insistently, whining loudly. Why are you just standing there? He seemed to say. We're home, let's go in!

As she stepped inside gingerly, glass crunching and popping beneath her sneakered feet, she was grateful both had shoes on. Guiding him past the mess he didn't even notice, she sent him upstairs still wearing his shoes while her eyes swept the area.

Julie quickly retrieved a broom and dustpan, eager to clean up the mess before anyone else came home, but frustrated and angry at yet another wildly unexplainable event.

As she squatted to sweep up the broken pieces that littered her foyer, her heart sank.

In the shards at her feet lay the remains of a delicately-crafted miniature elephant. Her eyes darted to the empty shelf where the lone surviving piece of her collection had rested.

Julie couldn't help shivering as she realized the implications.

She closed her eyes tight, grateful that her parents were away and she wouldn't have to try and explain this. There wasn't any rational explanation she could offer! Not even the cat could have managed this. The doors to the den were still closed, as they'd been when she left the house, only a half hour ago.

Somehow, this tiny little ornament moved itself through a closed door, and smashed itself to pieces in the exact center of the foyer.

Someone wanted her attention, obviously. It was the only explanation that made any kind of sense.

Julie realized with dread that Adam would have stepped right into the whole mess had she not held him back. The shards of glass weren't huge, but they were razor-sharp and that was enough to cause injury to an energetic child.

"What the hell is going on here?" she whispered. "Why do you hate us so much?"

~~~~

Marc didn't understand, but how could he? He wasn't experiencing these things.

Julie tried to explain, but after stammering through sentences that didn't make sense, and searching for the right words only to have them leave her head, she gave up. Her arms dropped like lead weights and she turned away, leaving Marc to stare after his wife with a furrowed brow.

How could she put this into words he would understand, without thinking she was blaming him?

It was like the old adage: 'you had to be there'.

Life in this house was complicated. All she wanted to do was get out and never come back.
~~~~

<center>~~~~</center>

"Look," she began. "Obviously, you like this place, but we live here now. This is *our* house. I don't know what it used to be for you, but that's over now. All you're doing is messing up our lives, and scaring our children. That has to stop."

Julie couldn't be sure if her well-meaning attempt would really do anything, but she had to try. They still had to live there, and it was obvious this dead guy wasn't going to leave.

It was easier to be brave in the daylight, she thought with a rueful smile.

After all the drama that came with Adam starting another year of school, she craved predictability.

She and Marc both realized that the haunting of their home and Adam's obsession with vampires probably wasn't a coincidence, but try though they might, they couldn't seem to solve the puzzle.

"Tell you what?" she spoke to the air around her. "If I give you the downstairs den, which I'm prepared to do, will you agree to leave us alone?"

Silence was her only answer. For once, Julie wished something would happen, even just to acknowledge her offer had been accepted.

Why was any of this happening? She wondered. Whoever this was, he wanted complete control.

With inexplicable noises, and nightmares plaguing the whole family, he was even able to control when and how deeply they slept each night. The strain of it was wearing on Julie and Marc, who snapped at each other over practically nothing.

"Why are you here?" she called out to the silence, stamping her own foot hard on the linoleum. "See? I can stomp too," she said, stomping again and again, as though she were having a temper tantrum. "But here's the difference: I have a right to do whatever I want here. This is *my* house."

She grabbed Amélie's jacket and manoeuvred the squirming child into it. "We're going shopping!" she said, looking into her daughter's face, and forcing a big smile. "Mommy's got lots on the list today." Snatching her handbag and keys, Julie took Amélie and headed down the stairs.

"Julie?" Anne asked, coming out of her own front door as her daughter gained the foyer. "What's all the banging about?"

"Sorry mom," Julie apologized. "Just trying to make a point, that's all." She smiled wryly and pulled the front door closed.

~~~~

CRASH!

Julie was still in the act of pushing open the heavy front door, when she heard it.

Instantly alarmed, she set down the bag of groceries she carried and picked up her daughter who had wandered inside on her own sturdy legs. Amélie struggled in her mother's arms, preferring to walk everywhere now, but Julie held her tighter as she rushed upstairs, arriving to a scene of chaos.

Anne emerged from the basement suite and called up to her daughter. "What's going on? I heard something fall! Are you okay?"

"Yeah, we're fine," she answered. "Amélie and I only just got home."

"What made all that racket?"

"Uh, looks like everything fell out of my cupboards," Julie called to her mom in disbelief, shifting her daughter to the other hip as she surveyed the damage.

"Everything did what?"

"Come and see," she called.

As mother and daughter stood together in the doorway of the kitchen, neither could believe their eyes.

The kitchen floor was littered with granulated sugar, pasta noodles and several kinds of cereal. Several cans of soup and vegetables lay on their sides, some dented, as though they'd been thrown with great force. On the table, lay half-emptied boxes of cereal, the contents strewn liberally across the table and onto the floor.

Julie shook her head at the mess and set her daughter down in the nearby family room, where Anne hurriedly grabbed the first toy she could find and handed it to her curious granddaughter.

Carefully, Julie began to pick up boxes and cans, wondering how the heck something like this could have happened? Another earthquake?

"Mom, did you feel any tremors? I didn't feel anything in the car, but maybe…" Julie trailed off, at a loss for what else to say.
~~~~

"No, I didn't feel anything," Anne replied, curiosity creasing her brow.

Julie shied away from the obvious answer. She didn't want to think that the entity they shared their home with had this kind of power. The implications of that were staggering.

A moment later, Julie sat back on her heels and pressed shaking hands to her cheeks. Into the middle of the jumbled mess of groceries lay several bouillon cubes, stripped of their foil-packaging and crushed flat, as though something heavy had fallen on them. The resulting mess was spread across the white linoleum, but what took Julie's breath away was the fact that in the middle of that mess was a pattern that looked a lot like the partial imprint of a man's work boot.

"Was Adam with you the whole time?" Julie asked her tone even.

"Yes honey. I'm sorry to say he was. I can't imagine how …" her mother's sentence petered out as she shook her head in wonder.

Julie wasn't sure whether Anne saw the mark on the floor or not, but she said no more about it, as mother and daughter worked side by side to clean up the mess.

She had to get ready for what was coming next. There was always a part two to these things.

As she stowed away the last of her fresh groceries, Julie thought about what she'd said that afternoon, how she'd tried to connect with this unwanted house-guest and help him see reason.

"Stomping," she muttered wearily. "I shouldn't have mentioned stomping."

~~~~

As Christmas approached, Julie's limited interaction with the neighbours dwindled farther. The worsening weather forced many people to stay inside, and while Julie still walked the two blocks every morning to her son's school, pushing Amélie in her stroller, she noticed that the little girl who'd befriended her son with such dedication was no longer in class. A sign on the lawn proclaimed the house was for sale, and quickly after that, a red 'sold' sticker slanted
~~~~

boldly across the sign. The thin blonde woman and the only friend her son had, were suddenly and mysteriously gone.

It was Marc's opinion that the abrupt departure of their neighbours had something to do with the woman's husband.

"You said it yourself, Jules," Marc said one evening as they hurriedly wrapped Christmas presents in the master bedroom. "He's a weirdo. It was probably him that night with the shotgun at our front door."

Julie nodded, as she wrote out a gift tag and stuck it to the colorful present. "Yeah, but last time we talked, she didn't mention anything about moving. It seems weird to me."

"We both think it *was* him at our door that night," Marc said. "But you still want to be friends with this guy's wife? That's messed up."

"I didn't know she was married to him when we first met," Julie replied defensively.

"Do you know what he told me when we were doing the lawn de-thatching thing?" Marc asked.

"What?"

"We were all hanging out in Steve's garage having a beer after we finished with the de-thatcher. Buddy came over and helped himself to a brew as well. He wasn't there five minutes, before he started bragging about being a great carpenter," Marc told her. "Claims he built a hidden closet underneath his stairs. According to him you can't see it at all, unless you know it's there. Steve teased him about using it for his secret stash, but I notice he didn't get corrected."

"He has a secret stash?" His wife wondered aloud.

"You bet he does. He invited all of us over to have a joint, and that's when I suddenly remembered I had to go home." Marc grinned. "So that's why I can't figure out why you'd be so desperate for friends that you'd want to associate with that creep's wife. It's obvious he has no respect for women."

"I'm not desperate!" she replied hotly. "I just wish I had someone I could really talk to."

"Look, I know you're finding it hard. Everyone's busy with their own lives."

"Do you really think that's it, Marc?" she asked. "It feels like since Adam's diagnosis, we've lost all our friends. They just don't come around anymore."

"Maybe it's time to throw a party?" Marc suggested.

"Ha!" Julie interrupted. "And who would we invite to this party? All those people who used to be our friends?"

"Well, you can't sit here moping. It's not good for you. Lately it seems like you just hide out in this house. And we both know that's not doing you any favours." Marc raised his eyebrows suggestively.

"I know," she replied. "But when I spend time at home and I keep my temper, things are okay. He doesn't like it when I go out too much, but as long as I tell him where I'm going, and when I'll be back he seems okay with it."

"Are you serious?" her husband asked incredulously. He held a roll of wrapping paper in one hand and he waved it at her for dramatic emphasis. "Do you realize what you're saying? Reporting your every movement? That's messed up! What do we owe this guy? God knows we didn't invite him, and so far we can't seem to get rid of him, but geez hon, you can't give in to him like this. You can't let him control you."

"That's easy to say Marc. Not so easy to do," Julie shook her head. "I know it's like a game of cat and mouse, but what else can I do? It's not like we can just move out."

"No, you're right, we can't do that. Not until the market comes up a bit. But this game of cat and mouse you're referring to can't be played very well if there's no mouse in the house, right?"

Her husband was right, even though Julie was loath to admit that.

It was important to have friends in her life. She talked to her best friend often on the phone, but the two women lived over an hour's drive apart, and since both had small children, long-distance travelling wasn't a regular event. She needed friends close by.

~~~~

Most mornings, several young moms could be found either in the schoolyard with their younger children or in the front foyer of the school. Wearing her friendliest smile, Julie made a point of heading towards the largest group of women, gathered near the fake Christmas tree in the foyer of the school.

Before she could reach them however, a woman Julie's age, with dark shoulder-length hair and glasses, called out to her, wearing a friendly smile.
~~~~

"Hey, hi there, are you Julie?" she asked. "I hope you don't mind, but my son's teacher said you might be able to help me."

"Sure," Julie replied automatically. "What can I do for you?"

"I understand your son has Autism?"

"Ye-es." She answered hesitantly.

"Sorry," the woman apologized hastily. "I don't mean to be so forward, it's just that I don't know anything about Autism, but I'm told you do."

"Well," Julie chuckled wryly. "I know a thing or two, I suppose since I live with it. What kind of information are you looking for?"

"Direction, mainly," the woman answered. "You see, I don't have a clue what to do next. I'm quite overwhelmed by all the information out there. Do you have time to meet for coffee?" She looked nervously at the group by the tree whose attention they seemed to have attracted.

The woman smiled again, and Julie realized she instinctively liked her.

"I have time now," Julie offered. "If you want to, we can go to my house for that coffee. It's just a short walk."

"Perfect!" the woman answered. "I'm Brenda by the way. My youngest is in Mrs. Smith's room, just down that short hall." She pointed at a hallway to their right. "I'll just leave my van here." Brenda smiled good-naturedly as she followed Julie out the doors of the school. "You're sure you don't mind? I practically accosted you."

"Nevermind," Julie answered, smiling pleasantly. "I'm happy you did."

The two women set off through the school playground, and made their way through the usual short-cut toward the house.

Julie couldn't help but wonder at the timing of this chance meeting. Julie had begun to wonder whether she gave off an air of negativity to those around her, or was Marc right, and she'd simply given up on friendship?

Well, none of that mattered anymore, she told herself firmly as she unlocked the front door and invited Brenda inside.

Please don't freak out the guest, she thought fiercely.

The two women were soon seated at Julie's kitchen table sipping hot coffee while Amélie played quietly in the family room.

Over the course of the next two hours, Julie and Brenda discovered they had much in common. Not only did they both have a fascination for Autism but they also seemed to enjoy a lot of the same things. When Brenda stood up and announced she had to go, Julie felt an automatic pang of sadness. Would she see this woman again? A desire for information had brought them together, and they'd seemed to hit it off so well, but Julie knew by now that people weren't always as comfortable with things as they first appeared to be.

"Hey," Brenda said as she was leaving. "Let's have coffee at my place next time. What do you say? I'd like a chance to get to know you better. We have a lot in common."

"Indeed we do," Julie chuckled, secretly thrilled. "I would love that."

"Great!" Brenda waved cheerily, as she walked briskly back down the driveway.

"Wow!" Julie mumbled as she closed the door. "I think I just made a new friend."

In the days that followed, Brenda and Julie met often and their friendship grew. Brenda introduced Julie to a friend of hers, whose children attended the same school. Julie was surprised to learn that Brenda's friend lived in the house directly behind Marc and Julie's!

Content in the knowledge that she would not have to spend her days alone anymore, Julie happily made plans with her new friends and tried not to worry about the secret that lurked in her home.

~~~~~

The trio of women had been visiting for about a half hour in Julie's kitchen, hands wrapped around mugs of coffee as they talked about their Christmas plans. The children played happily in the next room, a scant six feet away. Adam was happiest when he created things, and he piled cushions and blankets atop the growing fort with glee.

"Oh yeah, well," Jenna said doubtfully, leaning back in her chair. "You know what guys are like. You can ask, but I doubt he would *really* let on–"

Jenna stopped suddenly and twisted in her seat to face the stairway. A hush fell over them, as distinct footsteps were heard climbing the stairs toward them.
~~~~~

"Who is it?" Brenda asked, twisting in her seat. "I can't quite see."

Jenna continued to stare with wide eyes. She had a direct view of the staircase from her seat at the table. "Um, no, I don't uh … I don't think there's anyone. It's… uh, no."

"What?" Brenda replied incredulously. "Very decisive, Jenna," she teased.

Jenna said nothing but continued to stare.

Julie felt her face get hot.

"Jenna?" Brenda asked. "Say something, you're being creepy!" She reached across the table and poked her friend in the arm good-naturedly.

Jenna turned slowly back to the table, her face white as she looked at Julie.

Julie's throat tightened and she looked away.

Of course, she thought with heavy sarcasm. *Of all people, you had to show yourself to Jenna.*

"Jenna?" Brenda prompted her. "What's the matter?"

Julie bit her lower lip as she waited to see what Jenna would say.

She was one of the most direct people Julie had ever met. If she decided to play twenty questions with her hostess, there would be no getting out of it.

Practically leaping to her feet, Julie grabbed the coffee carafe from the counter.

"More coffee anyone?"

"No," Jenna replied, her voice deadly calm. "I think we're gonna get going. We've got stuff to do before school's out."

Without another word to her hostess, she stood, gathered her purse and called to her daughter. "C'mon Kasey," she said, beckoning to the small child as she turned towards the stairs. "We're going."

Within minutes, Jenna was gone, leaving Brenda and Julie still at the table with matching expressions of confusion.

"Well, I'll take that coffee, if you're still pourin'," she said, removing her glasses, she rubbed her eyes. "Jenna took off like she saw something she didn't like, hey?"

Julie heaved a deep sigh. "Really?" she replied, wincing at the sound of her own voice. It sounded small and afraid and she silently chastised herself for getting so worked up.

"Yup she did. You didn't notice?"

"I don't know her as well as you do."

"Yeah, that's true," Brenda agreed. "I guess you don't." Brenda narrowed her eyes. "And I suppose it's equally true that you don't wanna talk about this right now, huh?"

"Uh, I don't, um, I really don't think I, uh …" Julie stammered.

"Nevermind!" Brenda replied. "Jenna can be funny like that sometimes, but you shouldn't worry about it. When you get to know her better you'll see. How about we have dinner and drinks at my place? We can swap gardening stories, okay?" The joke was intended to poke fun at Julie's unhealthy-looking yard, Julie wasn't laughing.

A look of concern immediately replaced the smile on Brenda's face. "Hey, are you okay?"

"Who me?" Julie smiled weakly. "Yeah, sorry, my mind was drifting there for a sec."

"I know," she replied, her tone matter-of-fact. "It's one thing to read a ghost story, but it's another thing to live it! Poor Jenna, she took it pretty hard."

Julie nodded, wondering how safe their secret was *now*.

Chapter Twenty-seven

"WHAT THE HELL?" she yelled.

Hands on hips, the angry young mother stood there, staring at her ruined laundry and wishing there was someone else to blame.

An open bottle of bleach was on its side atop the washer, its contents spilled all over the laundry basket full of jeans and dark shirts that sat just beneath it.

Wracking her brain, Julie still couldn't remember even taking out the bleach.

"I'm cracking up," she muttered. "Either that, or someone is having a huge joke at my expense."

Although the statement came pouring out of her in frustration, Julie had to admit it was closer to the truth than thinking she'd just somehow forgotten about the bleach, and that magically, it had tipped over, inexplicably taking off its own lid, and pouring out all over the basket full of clothing below.

With shaking hands, Julie began sorting, hoping to salvage whatever she could.

The words played over and over in her head.

Somehow, magically, inexplicably. Who was she kidding?

"Fantastic," she muttered sarcastically, pulling out shirts, sweaters and jeans from the sodden pile, the stench of bleach filling her nostrils.

Hastily throwing open the window made her think of the cat.

Where was he? Somewhere in the house, no doubt. Julie continued to clean up the mess, wondering why she hadn't yet seen him. Casper always appeared within seconds of the window being opened. Marc liked to joke that the sound of 'freedom' awoke the feline from even the deepest sleep.

Later, once the ruined clothing was safely outside in the garbage bin, her thoughts returned to the missing cat. Despite a cursory search, he was nowhere to be found. Maybe Marc let him out that morning?

Suddenly her eyes narrowed. Could he have been the one who tipped over the bleach?

Julie called out half-heartedly "Kitty, kitty, kitty, c'mon Casper. Where are you?"

A faint response made her freeze in her tracks. She felt certain it was a cat's long, drawn out meow, and it was coming from the garage!

Hauling open the heavy connecting door, she was surprised to find their young Siamese, his eyes wide and frightened, crouched atop a pile of cardboard boxes. His back arched at her approach the normally smooth fur standing up in a ridge along his back.

"Casper! What are you doing in here?" Julie was relieved to see him unharmed, but confused by his obvious fear. How long had he been in there?

With one eye on the clock, she coaxed the cat down from his perch. But as soon as the animal's feet touched the floor, Casper flashed through the open window in the laundry room, and was gone.

"I didn't do it," Marc replied angrily, when she asked him about it later. "Must've been you. Sometimes you don't remember what you do when you're on the phone."

"What's that supposed to mean?" She retorted.

"Just that when you have the phone to your ear, nothing else seems to compute," Marc said unkindly.

"Don't be nasty, mister Marc," Julie reminded him. "Maybe I'm concentrating on the conversation."

"Uh-huh," Marc replied dubiously.

~~~~
~~~~

"Now what?" Marc fumed.

Pulling the couch away from the living room wall, he reached behind it and grasped the top edge of the large oil painting that lay resting against the back of the couch. The piece of art was the length of the couch and half as wide. Marc frowned as he slid it from behind the couch and felt around the edges of the ornate frame, looking for damage.

Why hadn't he heard it when it hit the floor? Something of this size would have made one hell of a racket, he thought. How long had it been like this?

Finding no damage, Marc turned his attention to the picture hook on the wall.

But instead of finding it bent and damaged by a piece of art that was too heavy, Marc was stunned to find the hook was completely undamaged.

"What?" he wondered aloud. As if he needed another mystery! What was Julie going to say about this?

A few minutes later, Marc had taken out a small step stool, so he could re-hang the large piece. Marc adjusted it carefully, hoping it was straight enough to escape Julie's notice. The thought of telling his wife about another curious incident was the last thing either of them needed. Things were tense enough already.

With a backward glance at the newly re-hung painting, he wondered how long it would stay there.

~~~~

Who's in Ami's room?

Although Amélie was already well past the baby monitor stage, they kept using it anyhow. Somehow neither of them could bring themselves to simply trust things were fine, without another source of proof.

The monitor itself was located so anything that happened in either of their kids' rooms would be captured.

The receiver sat propped up on Julie's dresser.

In addition to sound, the unit was equipped with an LED display that indicated volume.

When Amélie was younger, her cries illuminated every bar, filling the screen with red lights, and her exhausted parents made countless trips across the hall to investigate the problem.
~~~~

Marc sat up, his eyes wide. Red LED bars filled the screen again. But instead of Amélie or Adam crying out, as had been the norm of late, he heard musical chords like the notes of a nursery rhyme.

He knew these tones by heart, but as to why they were playing now, was beyond him! They were the introductory bars of his daughter's crib mobile, although it hadn't been used in ages! It wasn't even attached to the crib anymore, but to a high shelf, out of the way from curious fingers. Julie and Marc had finally disassembled the crib, and their proud daughter now had a 'big girl' bed. The toddler bed looked like a smaller version of Adam's, with a blue painted finish and a decorative quilt. While Amélie was out of her bed more often than she was in it, the little girl was thoroughly enjoying her newfound freedom.

But why was the crib mobile going off now? It wasn't battery operated, it had a hand crank mechanism on one side, and neither he nor his wife had wound it since the day it was re-mounted to that shelf.

Marc glanced at the clock. His daughter had been asleep for just over three hours, which wasn't bad, given her usual track-record, but having her up and messing around with an old baby mobile wasn't acceptable. Marc folded back his covers, and sat up slowly.

The sounds came again, lighting up every bar on the display. This was more than a few random notes. The familiar tune played on, as though it were fully wound. The bewildered father stared at the display as he rammed his feet into slippers.

"There's no way," he mumbled.

"Wha-?" Julie muttered, rolling over towards her husband. "Wuz wrong? Who's up?" Her speech was slurred with fatigue.

Marc pulled the blankets up around his wife and whispered, "Everything's okay. Go back to sleep."

The crib mobile played on as Marc tip-toed across the room.

How was she even reaching the damn thing? It was impossible.

That thought had only just formed when the music suddenly stopped.

Quickly Marc entered his daughter's room, surprised to find her still sound asleep, the colorful mobile still and quiet. Everything was exactly as it should be, but that fact was little comfort. Tiny toy clowns in their colorful silk outfits seemed to mock him from their place in the corner of the room. All six of them were suspended from strings attached to the apparatus of the mobile. Each toy clown was hung by its enormous clown feet, as though swinging from a permanent trapeze. The effect was supposed to be bright and cheery, but Marc squinted at the mobile in the half-light of early morning with a deep frown on his face.

Clowns in a haunted house? Maybe they *were* nuts.

But why had it gone off now? It had been hours since Amélie had gone to bed, and against all odds, the little girl was still fast asleep, something they hadn't been able to count on since her birth.

Watching the child calmly sucking her thumb as she slept, he knew that curiosity or not, he wasn't about to risk waking her by removing the mobile now. It would have to wait until morning.

Back in the master bedroom, Marc held the monitor up to his ear, but the only noises coming through were those he expected. The gentle snores of his son, with a soft counterpoint of thumb-sucking from his sleeping daughter.

Relieved at last, Marc climbed back into bed and drifted off to sleep at once.

After only a few moments, however his eyes snapped open again. Automatically he rolled his head to the side to check the digital readout on the clock.

Red LED's once again filled the screen on the device, and the irritating nursery tune blared forth. He'd only been asleep another hour! This was going to be a long night.

"What the hell?" he muttered. Throwing off the covers, Marc's feet had only just touched the floor, when the music stopped as suddenly as it started and the sound of his daughter's anguished cries pierced the silence.

This time, both mother and father responded to the sound. Marc reached her first and lifted her easily from the crib.

"It sounded like she was hurt," Julie whispered, taking the child from her husband's strong arms and holding her close. "It woke me up out of a sound sleep."

"I know," Marc answered distractedly.

"Marc, what are you doing?"

Her husband stood beside the mobile on the far side of the room, poking at it experimentally and examining the crank mechanism. Was it possible to coax any sound from the spent device without cranking it again?

"Marc? What's wrong? What are you doing?" Julie's hands moved quickly, despite her fatigue, as she re-wrapped the child in warm blankets and knelt beside her daughter's bed, encouraging Amélie to lie back down.

"Just a sec," he replied, his hands busy at the mounting screws on the back. He still had no answers. "She doesn't need this anymore. It's going."

"Whatever you want, dear," she replied sleepily, rubbing her eyes. "I think she'll be okay now," she muttered, massaging her daughter's back in circles as she hummed soothingly.

It was a familiar routine, but Marc couldn't help noticing the tune his wife hummed so automatically was the same song from the mobile.

~~~~

Amélie's third birthday was only days away, and everywhere she looked, the place was a mess! With a determined grimace, Julie got out the vacuum cleaner and switched it on. As it roared to life, Adam ran out into the hallway, a look of annoyance on his young face. With hands pressed tightly against both ears, he screamed at full volume, tears springing to his eyes.

A moment later, Amélie joined in and the two of them screamed, while she calmly ignored both of them and kept vacuuming.

She was 'monkey see, monkey do' with her big brother.

Although his screams had died down while she vacuumed other rooms, they grew to a fever pitch as soon as he saw the vacuum enter his own room.

"Adam, you need to settle down right now." Julie, tired of fighting with him was stern as she looked him in the eye and pointed furiously to his bed. Adam red faced, stepped aside for his mother, and climbed up on the bed even though he continued to yell. Julie noted with suspicion that he wasn't exactly crying though. His eyes were dry.

"Little monster," she muttered, moving as quickly as possible.

She was determined not to let this child run her life. Ariel was always saying that she should keep challenging him. He was a child and she was the adult.
~~~~

Out of the corner of her eye, she watched Adam's demeanor change. Mercifully he'd stopped yelling and Julie allowed herself a small sigh of relief.

"That's better," she congratulated her son is as she switched off the machine and went to unplug it from the hallway. She'd only just started to wind up the vacuum cleaner cord, when a new sound intruded, making her jump in surprise.

It sounded like breaking pottery.

"What's going on now?" she moaned.

"Mommy will be right back," she said to her son, who was still eyeing the vacuum cleaner from his perch atop his bed. "I think Casper just ditched grandma's plant."

Peeking into Amélie's room she saw that the child was happily engaged with her new Christmas toys and seemed oblivious to the new sound. Julie dashed to the stairway to have a look at what fell. It sounded like the plant on the ledge but she'd been fooled before.

"Damn," she grumbled, noting the mess of broken pottery and plant matter on the foyer floor at the bottom of the staircase. "Well, it lasted longer than I thought, but Grandma's not gonna be happy about this."

Strangely, although there had been two plants on the nearest ledge, only one lay in pieces at the bottom. The other plant still sat where her mother had placed it so long ago, to keep Adam from climbing the walls. There were two more in the other windowsill, and those didn't appear to have been moved either.

Wanting to believe it was just feline hijinks, Julie ran a hand through her hair as she grabbed the whisk broom and began the process of sweeping up.

The air thickened as she worked, and the odd sensation she'd felt in her ears returned.

Julie stood up, and wiggled her forefinger in one ear, trying to clear it. She'd been experiencing the strange sounds more and more lately, and she suspected it was either an oncoming ear infection, or maybe just the by-product of all that screaming she endured day after day.

As she went to the front door to dump the plant matter and dirt into the garden, Julie took a moment to lift her face to the warm sunshine. Although snow still covered the rest of the yard, she could almost smell the promise of spring.

Coming back inside, the young mother did a double take. The last three steps at the bottom of the staircase, where she'd crouched moments before, were almost obscured with a shadow so deep, she couldn't seem to see through it.

"What's going on here?"

It made no sense ... but then again plant pots that threw themselves down the stairs weren't exactly normal either, she thought.

With a flick of a switch, the chandelier overhead banished all shadow, real or otherwise, and Julie breathed a sigh of relief.

"Nuts to you!" she said, stomping with purpose back up the stairs. "Quit trying to scare me, you can be such an asshole sometimes!"

~~~~

At the first hint of an impending storm, Adam's anxiety would start to build, finally exploding in a fury of temper, during which he would verbally express everything except that which bothered him! Ordinary tasks, like setting the table, getting dressed or bedtimes turned into willful battles, filled with shouting, stomping and slamming doors.

It was almost a relief to the weary parents when the storm finally broke. As thunder and lightning raged outside, Adam's behaviour would change from angry to fearful. Strangely, that was easier to deal with, even knowing it might mean another power failure. Although it was a new subdivision, the power grid in their neighbourhood seemed temperamental. Most wind storms meant the power failed. When that happened, Adam's panicked screaming could be heard throughout the house, and likely down the block.

"Marc, this is ridiculous," Julie complained as they stood side by side looking through the glass doors at the back of the house. "Another one? I can't take much more of this. There's been so many this season."

They had a clear view of the darkening sky, with its angry bluish-grey clouds swirling overhead.

Later that evening, Marc installed his new purchases throughout the house. Emergency lights that came on when the power went out. It seemed like such a small thing, but Julie insisted what they needed was light. Lots and lots of light!
~~~~

He was too tired to disagree, but he drew the line at keeping all the lights on throughout the house.

It's my job to keep them safe, he thought as he twisted the screwdriver. But what kind of security am I giving them by installing a few night lights? Who am I kidding? We should just move.

Packing up his tool box with deliberate force, Marc drove these thoughts from his head. It wasn't practical to think this way. He simply would not allow himself to do it.

~~~~

Rain beat hard against the windows, the wind pushing relentlessly against the house with booming gusts. Julie and Marc went from room to room, lighting candles and placing them above their children's reach, a flashlight in each hand.

Adam followed his parents as they went from room to room with candles and flashlights, making their hasty preparations.

His quoting had risen to a fever pitch, and every negative, angry scene from every movie he'd ever seen, spilled forth in an endless tirade.

"I know Adam, I know. You don't like it," Julie told him, trying to insert the words between the phrases, so he would be able to hear her. "It's okay, it's gonna be okay."

Amidst this flurry of frantic activity and unending noise, Amélie sat calmly, chatting to herself in the center of a circle of stuffed toys.

Adam went to the doorway of his sister's room still quoting loudly. Amélie, looked up from her play and looked at her brother in silent contemplation, before returning to her imaginary meeting.

Julie shook her head and turned to Marc.

"If I were someone else, I would think that was weird," she said.

Marc directed a hasty look down the hall at their children and laughed. "Our whole life is weird. You have to be more specific."

"Amélie's toys. Why would she group them like that? Have I dragged her to too many support-group meetings? Now she's having her own?"

Marc looked around with alarm as the lights dimmed and came back quickly, ignoring her question. "We have enough stuff to worry about without borrowing more. At least she's happy for now, and not glued to our hip."
~~~~

A second later, the lights dimmed, then came back full strength as the power struggled to stay on.

"Whoah! That was another power bump. Did you see that? Power's going out soon. Let's make sure those candles stay lit!"

Chapter Twenty-eight

So, I have a question for you," Julie asked her husband, when he arrived home from work that evening. He was clutching several plastic shopping bags in his hands as he tried in vain to work the mechanism on the staircase gate.

Irritated, he glanced up at his wife. "I'm not exactly in the mood for guessing games," he snapped, wondering why she just sat there at the kitchen table, watching him struggle. "I could use a hand with this you know."

"I would if I could," she replied sadly.

"What? What are you talking about?"

"What kind of an idiot falls down her own stairs?" Julie asked her husband, rising painfully from her seat. She grabbed something from just beyond his line of sight. Marc was startled to see it was a wooden cane.

As his wife moved closer, his puzzled gaze slid quickly to the thick bandage wrapped around her ankle, and it all became clear.

"Oh no," he moaned. Lifting the bags up and over the gate he set them down gratefully and flexed his fingers. "What happened?"

"Do you want the highlights?" she asked. "Or the whole story?"

"Well," he said. "I'm going to want the whole story, but give me a few minutes to get the rest of these groceries upstairs first." Marc grinned sheepishly. "And stay out of the way, okay? They weigh a ton."

Once Marc had brought all the shopping bags upstairs to the kitchen, Julie manoeuvred painfully out of her seat and stood on one foot as she opened the pantry. Marc watched, his expression disapproving.

"What are you doing?" He asked.

"Helping," she replied, with one hand on the seat of the chair beside her, Julie lowered herself to the floor and began to put away the cans of food, still sitting in bags around her.

"So, what did the doctor say?" Marc asked, as he sorted through the remaining bags on the opposite counter.

"I didn't go yet, but I think it's probably a sprained ankle."

Marc's eyebrows rose, an unspoken question on his lips.

"I tried to, okay? But I couldn't drive. You were at work and my parents were out til about a half hour ago."

"Oh my God!" He said, shaking his head slowly. "You could have called an ambulance."

"For this?" She scoffed. "I hardly think that's necessary, Marc. It's just an ankle. The way I fell, I really must have twisted it. It's still pretty painful."

"You need to get to the doctor," Marc replied, obvious concern knitting his brow.

"If it's still painful and swollen tomorrow, I'll go. Mom said she'd take me."

Marc nodded his eyes distant. "How did this happen?"

"I took a nasty fall." Julie shrugged, her gaze riveted to the cupboard in front of her.

"Fall?" Marc's eyes were wide and questioning. "Not down the _"

"I'm afraid so," she answered sadly. "It's okay, though. I'll be fine. I wrapped it up, see?" Julie pointed at the tensor bandage wrapped around her ankle and foot. "And Dad gave me this to use," She pointed to the wooden cane still leaning against the chair behind her. "Good thing he had it in the back of his closet. It's not perfect but it helps."

Marc stood at the counter, hands resting on its polished surface. He nodded for a moment, processing the information, then stood up straighter and looked around, his expression troubled. "Where are the kids?"

"Downstairs with mom and dad," she answered. "I can't exactly chase them right now."

Marc seemed relieved at that, and he gave a single nod, and then frowned again. "So, if those are just the highlights, what's the whole story?"

Julie took a deep breath and let it out slowly. "I was dashing around getting Adam off to school," she began. "He went back upstairs and I followed him."

Marc nodded encouragingly.

"I was on my way back down again when I felt this weird pressure in the middle of my back."

"A pressure? What do you mean?"

"Like I was … almost like someone …pushed me." Julie shut her eyes tight and shook her head slowly, trying to banish the memory. "Marc, I know I didn't trip."

"What?" He asked incredulously.

"Well, obviously, I've tripped before. I know how it's *supposed* to work, so you can believe me when I tell you I *didn't* trip," she said, shaking her head. "I know this doesn't make much sense."

"And," he urged.

"I'm … well I'm not really sure *how* to describe this, but for a moment it felt like I was flying."

"What? Flying?"

"I know," Julie replied. "It sounds ridiculous when I say it out loud, but that's the best I can do. I felt both of my feet get knocked out from under me, and I couldn't even grab the railing. I was too far above it."

"Above?" Marc asked incredulously. "That's intense."

"Tell me about it," she replied defensively.

"Sorry," he replied. "You have to admit, it's an incredible story."

"Story?" Julie asked suspiciously.

"You know what I mean," Marc answered, placing several groceries on the counter. He got out a cutting board from the cupboard at his knee, and began chopping vegetables. "So, you must have landed pretty hard by the look of you. How did you get back up here?" he asked, putting a chunk of frozen ground beef in the microwave to thaw. "Your parents weren't home today, you said. How did you manage?"

"Crawling mostly," Julie replied.

Marc's eyes opened wider.

"Well, you do what you have to do, right?"

"Uh huh, I guess so," he answered. "What about Adam though? How did he get home from school?"

"He didn't go," Julie replied.

"So, this happened before school?" he asked.

"Yeah, just before we were gonna leave," she said. "Amélie was already in her stroller, but at the last second Adam must have forgotten something and he dashed back upstairs. Of course, I had to follow him."

"Too bad you didn't just wait," Marc muttered, as he transferred the chopped vegetables into a large skillet on the stove.

Julie turned to her husband and her eyes were haunted. "If I didn't follow him, it could have attacked our son. He's just a little boy. He doesn't understand any of this."

In that instant Marc realized that it didn't matter whether he believed his wife's story. She believed enough for both of them.

Marc's heart was in his throat as he stirred the contents of the pan mechanically. What the hell was going on? Was this thing stepping things up?

Just then the microwave beeped and both adults jumped at the unexpected sound.

Guilty smiles flashed across both their faces and Julie got to her feet reflexively, but pain shot though her injured leg so viciously she gasped and sat back with a thump.

Marc looked up sharply. "What do you think you're doing? I've got this. It's not hard, I'm making my specialty okay? You just sit."

She smiled weakly at her husband. He's a good man, she thought warmly. Too bad he's stuck with me.

"How bad is it?" Marc asked, wincing at the sight, as she pulled up on the hem of her jeans. Julie's lower leg and foot were already twice their normal size, and angry red flesh showed both above and below the hastily wrapped bandage. "That looks pretty bad. Maybe I should take you to 'Emerg tonight."

"It feels pretty bad," she said. "But I can manage til tomorrow. What's the doc going to do in an Emergency room? Wrap it and send me home, right?"

"Well yeah, I guess. But make sure you go okay? I want x-rays of that." He turned his attention back to the stove and added a pot of water, then grabbed the thawed meat and added it to the sizzling pan. "You should be propping it up and icing it though, " he said.

Grabbing a bag of frozen peas from the fridge freezer, he hurriedly wrapped it in a tea towel and handed it to her.

Julie propped her leg up on a kitchen chair and pressed the compress to her swollen ankle, grimacing. It was both wonderful and painful, and with each passing minute, she was more convinced than ever that the ankle was sprained at least, and maybe even broken. How was she going to look after two kids in a big house with only one functioning leg?

"Well, I'm glad you weren't hurt worse," he said. "And the kids are obviously fine. "Are they eating with your mom and dad?"

Julie nodded. "Yeah, I should have told you. Sorry."

"That's okay, more for me. And that way I don't have to make a special sauce for mister, minus the veg!" Marc grinned a little, as he darted a quick glance at his pensive wife.

"Wanna hear some good news for a change?" He asked.

"Sure," she said. "Can you pass me some pain killers and a glass of water first though? This thing is throbbing again, so I guess it's time."

Marc got a bottle from the cupboard and handed her glass of water.

"What's the news?" she prompted.

"I'm in town for at least the next two weeks," he announced.

"Oh Marc, that's awesome!" Julie enthused, gulping down the last of her water. "Good timing."

"Yeah, little did we know, hey? Doesn't usually work out that way, but I'm glad it did this time. You're in bad shape."

There wasn't anything she could say to that, so Julie just waited.

Her husband shook his head. "I keep telling you to hold onto the railing as you go down," he said, unwilling to let it rest just yet.

"I know that," she replied heatedly. "I was *already* holding onto the railing." Her eyebrows shot up again as she carefully enunciated each word. "Do you see now?"

Turning away, Marc grabbed a package of spaghetti noodles from the pantry and dumped them into the boiling pot of water. He darted another look at his injured wife. "And you're certain you didn't trip, right?"

"No," Julie shook her head for emphasis. "I mean yes. I mean … I just … oh I don't know. It doesn't matter now." She ran both hands through her hair with a frustrated, raking motion. The effect made her bangs stand up on end and Marc turned away, lest she see the automatic smile on his lips.

"So now what?" he asked, stirring the noodles as they cooked.

"I wish I knew," she muttered. "How am I supposed to run around after two kids with only one good leg?" Julie's words had taken on a sharp, sarcastic edge. "Any ideas?"

"Let's see what the doctor says tomorrow," Marc replied. "Maybe it's not as bad as we think."

Julie rolled her eyes to the ceiling. Inside she was counting to ten.

~~~~~

"Okay my dear," Anne coached, as she opened the gate for her daughter and helped her achieve the last step. "Here we are. Now let's get you settled, and I'll put these things away. Marc's home late tonight, isn't he? Maybe you should have supper with us."

As Julie dropped into a nearby chair, she nodded, and laid the newly acquired set of crutches by her side.

"He said he'd be back around seven." Propping her re-bandaged foot on another chair, she breathed a sigh of relief. "Thanks mom, I didn't know going to the doctor could be this exhausting. I'm beat."

Anne went to the freezer and prepared a cold compress, then took a small bottle from the cupboard to shake two elongated pills into her palm.

"Remember what the doctor said, okay?" Anne spoke gently as she handed over the pills and glass of water. This is a very bad sprain, and you have to stay off of it. Take more of this every 4 hours, drink plenty of water and use ice to keep the swelling down. The children can stay with us for now."

Anne pulled open the fridge. "Do you have any leftovers you want used up?" she asked, pushing aside several items. I can't see anything in here."

"What do you mean?" Julie replied defensively.

"When was the last time you cleaned this out?"

Julie's sigh was long and drawn out.

Anne straightened up quickly. "Nevermind, I'll make supper in my kitchen."

"Thanks," Julie mumbled her expression slightly sour.

"I'm just grateful you didn't hurt yourself worse, and that you weren't carrying one of the kids when you tripped."
~~~~~

Julie ground her teeth at the word 'tripped'.

"When supper's ready," Anne continued. "I'll bring it up and we can all eat together. Then, we'll get everything sorted for the weekend. We're gonna have to alter things a bit, in light of this, but I still think we can make a go of it."

"The week–oh no! The party!" Julie gasped. "With all of this, I totally forgot!" Her face went red as reality set in. "We're gonna have to cancel," she whispered fiercely, banging a fist against her open palm. "This is terrible mom. How could I have forgotten about our first-ever cocktail party?"

"Now, just hold on a second, don't get all dramatic. That's why you have a mother." Anne smiled comfortingly. "You've been working hard, doing all that painting and decorating. The house looks so nice and I know this is important to you. You need friends now more than ever."

Julie looked askance at her mom. What did she mean by *that*?

"Who says we have to cancel?" Anne continued, shrugging. "We've already done up the menu, and you did the party shopping the other day, right?"

Julie nodded.

"Well then. We're ahead of the game! No need to ruin everyone else's plans, is there?"

Julie frowned but inside she was elated. Her mom was right, this party was important for more reasons than she could even say, but the thought of pulling it all off on crutches was worrying. Her mother made it sound so easy.

"Oh mom, really? Do you really think we can do it?"

"We'll make do," she said. "Besides, it's not until tomorrow. And let's not forget this is my party too. My friends would be just as disappointed if we canceled it."

Julie smiled, and blew out a long breath, consciously lowering her automatically hunched shoulders. "What would I do without you, mom?"

"I hope you don't have to find out for a long, long time," Anne answered, reaching out to squeeze her daughter's hand. "Now I gotta get supper going. You should probably get in some practice with those," she said, nodding at the crutches. "You're gonna be using them awhile. And Julie, please listen to me on this. Stay off of that foot. Marc knows how to vacuum."

~~~~
~~~~

"The doctor said it's a bad sprain. It would have been better if I'd have broken it. He said ten to twelve weeks on crutches," she reported later that evening, as Marc sat at the kitchen table with her. He was gratefully digging into the leftovers his mother-in-law had provided. With his mouth full, Marc merely nodded.

"The way I fell," she continued. "He said it was a miracle I didn't break anything important."

Her husband's eyes bulged at that as he swallowed hard. "So, tell me again why you and your mom didn't call everyone and cancel the party?"

"Because we need this, Marc! And cancelling the day before is just …rude."

Marc's eyebrows shot up.

"Our friends have been looking forward to this for a long time. I can't disappoint them."

"Uh-huh," Marc answered dubiously. "Mom took over, didn't she?"

Julie blushed and looked away. "Maybe."

Marc smiled at his wife. "You two make quite a pair. So, where's the list?"

Julie frowned. "What list?"

"I assume there's a list," Marc replied, settling back in his chair. "Of all the things you want *me* to do before the party?"

"Well …"

Marc just smiled and shook his head. "Here we go."

Chapter Twenty-nine

The Party guests arrived one after another, each of them exclaiming over Julie's injury, and in the next breath, wondering aloud why she hadn't just cancelled the party.

Julie grinned and employed the good manners she'd been raised with to dodge the repetitive question of 'how did it happen?'.

"Oh, you know how it is with stairs," she replied lightly. "I couldn't let a little sprain cancel our first-ever cocktail party. Besides, I'll be fine in a few weeks."

As the party progressed, however, Julie's ankle throbbed harder and harder, to the point where pain killers weren't cutting it anymore. Clearly, she was overdoing it. She sank gratefully to the rocking chair in the corner of the room, and propped her leg up on the matching footstool.

"Julie, it's fabulous!" Brianna grinned as she approached. "So fancy!"

Her husband Luke leaned in and whispered: "She's jealous."

Brianna tried to smack her husband but he dodged quickly and went to the table to fill his plate again.

"What?" he said when he heard the laughter behind him. "The girls said to eat. C'mon Marc! Don't be rude. What are you waiting for?" Marc shook his head and grabbed a plate.

"Leave some for me," he teased good-naturedly.

Luke and Marc had grown up together and kidded around as though they were still in school.

Taking note of his wife's drawn expression Marc put down his overflowing plate and brought her another cold compress. "How are you holding up?" he asked.

"I'm fine. No problem," she lied.

"Uh-huh," her husband replied. "Save that for the guests. You look tired."

"Nice," Julie muttered sarcastically. "You mean I look ugly."

"What?"

"Tired is code for ugly."

"Don't be dumb," he teased. "You're not ugly, you're exhausted. You've been pushing too hard. This isn't the Olympics you know. It's just a party."

Just then Brianna, Luke's quiet, gentle wife came to sit on a chair to one side of her hostess. "Want to talk about something other than your ankle?" she asked with a wink.

"Do I ever!" Julie replied with relief.

"Good! As soon as the newest guest is settled, we'll go sit into the family room and catch up, okay?"

Julie tilted her head in wonder. "Newest guest?" she asked nervously.

"Abby's here," she said simply.

Julie breathed a sigh of relief, and trained her eyes on the staircase as she heard someone coming up.

At the sight of her best friend, she felt some of the tension leave her. Now the evening was complete! She needed the emotional support of her best friends now, more than ever, but would she be able to confide in them? Not likely, she realized with chagrin.

Abby sat down heavily on the couch next to Brianna. She was past her due date and had taken a chance driving herself out to Julie's party alone, but their friendship was strong and both women seized every chance to be together.

Awkward hugs were exchanged as the two women assisted their friend in relocating to the quieter atmosphere of the family room.

The three petite women got along so well that they often completed each other's sentences, following trains of thought that baffled others. Julie straightened her shoulders, realizing she'd have to make a conscious effort not to let down her guard. If anything strange happened tonight, she'd just follow the script she and Marc had agreed upon, playing the part of the bewildered hostess.

Above all, she had to be careful to show no fear.

The women soon drifted into casual conversation.

One of her mom's friends, an older woman with graying hair drawn back into a bun poked her head through the family room doorway, addressing the woman crowded on the couch together.

"If you still want the bathroom, it's free now," she said pleasantly.

"Pardon?" Julie replied, tilting her head in wonder.

"Someone was knocking on the door just now, wasn't it you?"

"Oh, yes, thank you," she replied, smiling automatically as the guest retreated.

As Julie returned her attention to her friends, she saw they were both frowning.

"What was that about?" Abby asked. "You were here with us. Why did you say that?"

"Oh, I don't know," Julie replied, waving her hand in dismissal. She hoped her comment would steer the conversation back into safer territory.

Brianna giggled just then, elegant fingers covering her mouth as she tried to stifle the sound. "Poor lady, someone was knocking on the door while she was actually *in there*? How embarrassing!"

Julie chewed at her lip and tried to rise awkwardly from the couch.

"Let's go join the rest of the party before they come looking for us."

"Good idea," Abby replied. "You make sure you're sitting down though okay? How are you managing, I mean especially with Amélie? Can you still pick her up?"

"I'm managing okay. She's walking now, so it's much better." she said "And mom helps a lot too."

"Nothing keeps you down," Abby agreed with a sly wink. "I honestly thought you were going to cancel the party. I mean, you should have. Everyone would have understood."

"Why does everyone have to say that?" Julie replied, exasperated. "Besides, did you ever try to stop a ship from sailing? Once mom gets going, there's no stopping her."

The comment hung in the air as both women exchanged glances behind Julie's back.

Julie moved slowly toward the living room.

"There she is," Anne announced, smiling at the sight of her daughter, rejoining the party.

As soon as the words were spoken, a large bang shook the floorboards under their feet and Julie grabbed for the wall.

"What was that?" Abby asked, shock and surprise on her face.

Brianna, her hazel eyes wide, was staring at the empty stairwell. "It came from down there," she said.

"Whew! I don't know, basement door maybe." Julie replied automatically, hoping her casual comment would head off further questions. She already knew there was no one else downstairs.

"Who's downstairs? I thought everyone was up here?"

"Well, obviously somebody's down there. It can't slam by itself," a middle-aged man Julie knew as a friend of her dad's replied, sagely.

Abby and Brianna exchanged a wary look and Julie flicked a glance at the man, silently cursing his quick tongue.

"Well, houses do bang from time to time," Anne interjected.

Her dad nodded at Julie, his expression serious as she manoeuvred into an empty chair beside him.

With their plates and glassed re-filled, the exhausted host and hostess sat amongst their guests, and tried to enjoy themselves. It was hard work pretending everything was perfect, but they had little choice.

Julie's nerves were raw. Would they make it all the way through the evening without anything else happening?

Suddenly, a wave of crackling energy raced through the room, and from the startled looks on the guests' faces, the curious sensation was felt by all.

Before anyone could comment, however an odd, booming sound encompassed the whole house, and a moment later, a gradual rumbling built in intensity until the vibration shook the whole house!

Julie's eyes registered shock as she clung to the chair underneath her. An earthquake? Here?

The whole house undulated, like it was being battered by the waves of an angry sea.

Anne scrambled to her feet, only to freeze in disbelief as she and many others stared at the giant chandelier that hung over the staircase. The light fixture could be seen rocking back and forth, as its smaller counter-part that hung over the dining room table also reacted to the violently shaking house.

A hush fell over the room. Guests quickly grabbed their drink glasses before they could topple from the fiercely wobbling TV trays.

Julie watched it all through wide eyes. Could this really be happening?

Whimpers and nervous glances came from all sides of the room as people tried their best to be brave in the face of such a shock.

As suddenly as it started, the shaking stopped.

The light fixtures continued to sway with the after-effects of the big quake, but a glance around the room revealed that apart from a few things that were knocked from the countertop and table, everything was okay. Their guests appeared stunned, but unhurt.

Nervous laughter was followed by low muttering as the party-goers struggled to process what had just happened.

Earthquakes were not unheard of, but in that part of the world, they were rare. The type normally charted by weather gurus went largely unnoticed, reported as a side-line on the six o'clock news when there was nothing better to report.

It was safe to say none of them had much experience with a quake of this magnitude.

After a few moments, Luke interjected. "Whoah Marc! Is this your idea of a party game?"

Julie and Marc exchanged a startled glance, while Julie's mother drained the contents of her wine glass in a single swallow.

"That was weird," Marc admitted his voice low. A moment later however he seemed to realize that his wife's party, the one she'd sacrificed so much to have, was in danger of coming to an abrupt and curious end.

Forcing a smile onto his handsome face, he turned back to his guests, and spread his arms wide. "Now that our heart rates are up, who wants to play Twister? Julie, you go first ..."

"Very funny." Julie, quickly realizing her husband was trying to save the party, rose to the challenge and lifted one of her crutches threateningly. The unexpected comedy routine seemed to have the desired effect, and a murmur of conversation began, as people compared reactions to the unexpected event.

Half an hour later, the party was over. Guests made their excuses one by one and collected their things, remarking that this was one night they'd never forget.

~~~

"I can't believe how quickly they all left!" Marc commented, as the weary couple got ready for bed that night. "But you," he paused and picked up his startled wife, sweeping her around in a circle. "You were amazing! Crutches and all!"

"Marc!" she protested, laughing. "You've been drinking. Put me down, silly."

"Guilty as charged," he said, settling her gently back on the edge of the bed. "But seriously, an earthquake? Who has an earthquake in the middle of a party? That's messed up!"

"We'll be the talk of the town, for sure," she replied. "But at least this is a natural phenomenon."

"True. I wonder how big it was?" Marc wondered aloud.

"I don't know, but you can bet it'll be all over the news tomorrow. We'll just have to wait and see."

"Yeah. I'm still really shocked at how much the house shook. Did you see Mildred's face when it happened?" Marc referred to one of the guests who'd been sitting next to the table full of food. "I've never seen her move so fast. She was up and out of her chair as though driven by electricity. "Marc chuckled as he pulled his shirt over his head. "And did you see the walls? No damage, so that's good "

"Yeah, I'll say that's good," Julie agreed wearily, yawning as she turned back the bed covers. "I don't have the energy or the time to re-paint."

"Yeah, that was a lot of work. Good thing you got it all done before that ankle thing happened."

"Yup," Julie replied as she pulled on her pajamas.

"Okay, enough said, I'm bagged too," he said, yawning. "Let's get some sleep. Kids are sleeping, but knowing your daughter, she'll be awake and dancing before we know it."

"Don't remind me," Julie grumbled, as she watched Marc crawl quickly into bed and lay back against his pillow.

Julie's mood was somber as she climbed into bed and tried to concentrate on melting her tired muscles into the softness of the mattress beneath her. As sleep claimed her, a manic giggle bubbled
~~~

forth. Good thing for that earthquake, she thought. Now their guests would be talking about that, and no one would think to dwell on anything else.

Maybe the next party would go more smoothly. Earthquakes in that area were so rare, the odds were ridiculous that it would ever happen again.

Tomorrow was another day, and it would be there soon enough. In time, she fell mercifully into an exhausted, dreamless sleep.

The shadow that filled her doorway shifted, outlining the form of a man for just an instant before blending back into the darkness.

Julie's soft snores were testament to the fact that at least for now, she was immune to his presence.

He felt himself fade a little more. It cost him a lot to use that much of his energy, but the effect was satisfying. And besides, he would re-build his energy in no time. There was plenty available here, especially now ... and there was time. He smiled as he thought about that.

Things made only of shadow have nothing but time.

~~~~

"Hi mom!" The young woman at the door cried out exuberantly.

A welcoming smile instantly spread across Anne's face as she opened the door wider.

"Abby!" She cried out excitedly. "Oh sweetheart, do come in!" She stepped back to welcome the young woman who'd become like another daughter to her.

Abby came through the front door, a huge grin on her face. "I was in the neighbourhood and had to stop in. Where's that good-for-nothing best friend of mine," she teased.

"Up here waiting for you to use your two good legs and climb the stairs," Julie called out, a grin of equal size covering her own face, as she stood at the railing. It hadn't taken long for Julie to recognize the distinctive voice of her best friend. It carried easily upstairs and Julie patted the wooden railing under her hands in anticipation, crutches balanced expertly under each arm.

"Did you bring him?" Julie called.

"Sure did," her friend answered. "I wasn't going to deprive you of seeing my little boy."
~~~~

Abby arrived upstairs, carrying her infant son still strapped into his car seat. Cradled gently by the form-fitting foam, he snored contentedly.

'Here you are dear," Anne said, as she followed a step behind. She set down Abby's diaper bag at the entrance to the kitchen and turned to regard the infant.

"Oh, he's so tiny!" she commented, her voice deliberately low.

"Adorable," Julie chimed in, as she looked at the baby, swaddled in layers of blankets. Dark eyelashes lay thickly against his flushed, round cheeks. His delicate skin was the color of a new peach and Julie couldn't help marvelling how much he already resembled his mother.

Abby gratefully set her precious package on the floor and gathered her friend in a warm hug.

"I've missed you so much! And Nathan wanted to see his cousin of course," she grinned.

The two women smiled and held each other's hands fondly. They'd been best friends since junior high, and with the arrival of Abby's new baby boy, they were determined to introduce their children as early as possible, dubbing them unofficial 'cousins' in the hopes that they too would enjoy a life-long friendship.

"I just put Amélie down for a nap," Julie replied with disappointment.

Abby covered her mouth and cringed. "Oh no," she dropped her voice to a whisper. "I'm sorry, I made such an entrance, I probably woke her up."

"That's okay," Julie giggled. "That kid never sleeps for long anyhow, and she will be thrilled to see her new cousin."

"Well he's still sleeping, so maybe we could just peek and see if she's up?" Abby wrinkled her freckled nose mischievously.

Anne moved in. "Let me just go and check," she said. "Julie, go and sit. Remember what the doctor said, you've still got a few more weeks with those things." She nodded at the crutches and gestured toward the family room.

"If she's up I'll bring her in here. You girls have a lot of catching up to do, and I'm in the middle of baking a pie."

"Thanks mom," Julie replied gratefully.

Abby moved her son, still in his carrier to the family room and removed one of the many blankets covering his tiny body, so the child wouldn't overheat.

Julie lowered herself to a kitchen chair and silently cursed her stupid ankle. It was taking forever to heal, still painful and swollen if she tried to put any weight on it. It had been several weeks, and despite a hopeful visit to her doctor, she was advised to stay off of it, as no substantial progress had been made. How long would it be before she'd be able to walk again?

Anne reappeared and lay a finger to her lips to indicate the fact that her granddaughter was still asleep. She drew the pocket door in front of her closed and jerked a thumb over one shoulder, to say she was heading back downstairs.

Abby grinned and waved happily at her 'adoptive-mom'.

"Okay," she said, sitting down opposite her best friend. "Spill it."

"Spill what?" Julie asked in surprise.

"You know what," Abby demanded. "I still can't figure out why you were so weird at the party."

"Well it was weird, you have to admit. I'm not allowed to think it's odd that an earthquake happened in the middle of my party?" She asked defensively, her eyebrows raised.

"That's typical," Abby replied. "Your idea of a good defense is a strong offense." She smiled and rose from her chair. "You want tea? I feel like having tea."

Julie sighed deeply.

"I heard that," quipped Abby. "Listen, you were acting like somehow, that earthquake happened deliberately, like it was out to get you! And don't bother denying it. I've never seen you act so strange. It was like you and Marc were running on pure adrenaline that night. I know you were in pain with the ankle and all, but there's obviously more to this story."

She finished filling the kettle and plugged it in, then settled back against the counter and folded her arms.

"Don't you want tea first?" Julie asked.

"Nice try. I'll make the tea, and you'll do some talking. Am I still your best friend?"

"Of course," Julie replied, her face growing hot.

"And you trust me, right?"

"Yes, I do trust you."

Abby pursed her full lips and waited expectantly.

"Okay, okay you win. But you aren't gonna like it."

"Just have a little faith in me," she soothed.

"Okay," Julie's tone was dubious. "Just for the record, I'm not crazy."

A frown creased Abby's delicate forehead. "That's an auspicious beginning."

Julie tried to smile but inside her stomach was in knots.

"Turns out we're living with a ghost, Abby."

Her friend's expression instantly changed, and she dropped her arms to her sides. "For real?" She asked.

"Yeah, I'm afraid so. Neither of us wants to admit it, but there've been too many things happen here for us to ignore it any longer."

"Like?" Abby asked suggestively.

"We-ell," Julie hedged, wondering whether she should go into detail, especially considering her fears of isolation, once word got out. Would Abby make her excuses and leave too? She couldn't bear the thought of it, and yet it was a real possibility. They were mothers after all, and a mother's top instinct was to protect her child. If she knew the truth, would she view it as a threat?

"Well what?" Abby prompted. "Are you gonna tell me or do you think I'm gonna run away if you do?"

Julie's eyebrows shot up in surprise.

"Ah, seems I guessed correctly," Abby said with a self-satisfied smirk. "You shouldn't be so surprised. We've known each other too long. I can read you like a book."

"True," Julie replied. "Marc thinks we shouldn't tell anyone, but I can't stand to do this alone anymore. If you promise not to run away, I'll tell you."

Abby smiled and came to sit beside her friend, the unmade tea forgotten. She took Julie's hand in hers and locked eyes. "I promise I won't leave you."

Julie's eyes began to tear, and she looked quickly around the room, embarrassed by the flood of emotion. "Great, now I need some Kleenex and I haven't even started," she laughed weakly.

Abby smiled and got up. "I saw a box in the living room when I got here. I'll just grab it."

As she went to retrieve it, another sound reached their ears.

"Uh oh," she said, quickly handing over the box. "I think somebody's awake. I'll go get her okay?"

"Of course," Julie replied. "Amélie loves you, it shouldn't be a problem. Just tell her who it is before you open the door, okay? She gets startled easily these days."

Abby grinned and disappeared down the hallway.

The tiny baby in the carrier was still sound asleep.

Amélie instantly recognized her Auntie Abby and she giggled in delight at the sight of her.

"Hi there little darling!" Abby greeted the child as she lifted her easily from the crib where the child stood, her arms eagerly reaching. "My you're a big girl now!"

Abby and Amélie arrived in the kitchen doorway, smiles on both of their faces

Amélie touched Abby's cheek fondly and snuggled into her shoulder.

Abby giggled. "Ooh, what a cutie!"

She's walking really well now," Julie announced proudly, looking at her daughter with a critical eye. "Good thing, hey?"

"I'll say," Abby agreed. "Especially with you on the injured list."

In between the myriad of motherhood tasks that come with non-napping babies, the two friends spoke in hushed tones over the course of the afternoon. Julie was grateful for Abby's unwavering support as she tried hard to explain the events in her life that had no rational explanation. As she spoke, Abby nodded seriously and patted her son's tiny back as she held him against one shoulder. Julie hoped she didn't sound as irrational as she felt.

"And to top it off," she said, as her narrative finally reached its completion. "The so-called earthquake we had at the party wasn't reported on the news, and none of the neighbours felt it either, which is certainly odd."

Abby frowned. "That's totally ridiculous, it wasn't our imagination. We all felt it."

"I know, it doesn't make any sense. You know Marc, he went straight to the source and looked up every contact he could find. He couldn't find a mention of it anywhere. So where does that leave us?" Julie sat back, feeling breathless.

"Wow," Abby commented, heaving a long, drawn out sigh of her own. "So, for starters, I don't think you're crazy. And I do believe you."

"Just like that?" Julie asked. "Don't get me wrong, I'm grateful, but you're usually a bit more skeptical. Why the sudden shift?"

"Well, I too have a confession to make."

"Uh-oh, what do you mean a confession?"

Abby looked down at the floor as she composed her thoughts. "I've been living with a secret as well. And I've been just as worried about sharing it as you and Marc are."

Julie leaned forward eagerly. "Tell me," she urged, automatically glancing at Amélie as she played on the floor beside them.

"You've been in my basement laundry room, right?" Abby asked, chewing nervously at her lip as she rocked her suddenly restless son.

"Sure, on the lower level, at the bottom of the staircase?"

Abby nodded. "I've been having some …stuff happening there." She explained hesitantly. "I guess you'd call them experiences."

Julie eyes widened. It was the last thing she expected to hear. Abby had always declared herself a skeptic of such things.

"A full basket of blue-jeans weighs a bit, as I'm sure you know," Abby told her quietly. "I'd just taken the jeans out of the dryer and placed the basket on that long, low table I have in there so I could fold them all before bringing them upstairs."

"Uh-huh."

"Next thing I know, the whole thing, basket and all, slides off the end of the table and dumps out upside down on the floor!"

It was Julie's turn to frown as she listened carefully. She'd been in Abby's house and she could see the spacious laundry room in her mind's eye. The walls of the room were unfinished, the floor a dull grey concrete. The table she mentioned sat to one side of the washer and dryer. It was an old elementary school table, low and narrow. Her dad bought it for her at a garage sale when Abby and her husband moved into their new place just a few months ago.

"Shortly after that, I started hearing footsteps on the stairs right behind me," she continued. " There was no one there." Abby laid her son on the blanket she'd placed on the floor. He seemed content to simply look around, his large hazel eyes taking in everything. "I'm tellin' ya, I can totally understand how you must be feeling here. This stuff is unnerving! It doesn't happen every day, but when things fall off a shelf and you know there's no reason for it, you can't help but be creeped out."

Julie tilted her head to one side as she let Abby's words sink in. "Have you told Jake?"

"I tried to, but he's such a drama king, everything's always gotta be about him, so I don't think he took me seriously."

"I wish I had some answers for you Abby," she said. "Unfortunately, we seem to be in the same boat here. The only saving grace is that Marc has seen things too so he can't deny it. Still, neither one of us knows what to do." She looked apologetically at her friend. "How are you holding up?"

"I'm coping, just like you guys. So you see, many of the things you've just told me sound quite familiar."

Julie hugged her friend spontaneously, wishing she could do more.

Abby and Julie heaved equal sighs of relief, then noticing the mirrored reaction, the two women burst out laughing.

"Jinx," Abby mumbled with a smile.

It was as though all the years fell away and they were just two little girls sharing secrets.

Abby's visit recharged Julie in a way she had not thought possible. With renewed vigor, she dialed the church rectory almost as soon as the door closed behind her best friend. She was determined to get some answers for herself as well as Abby.

Once their house had been properly Blessed, all of this would go away. Then she would waste no time arranging one for Abby's house.

"Why don't they answer?" She muttered into the phone as it rang and rang.

Eventually the answering machine at the church rectory kicked in, but Julie hung up with a frown. She barely knew what to say to a living person, never mind telling a machine!

Chapter Thirty

One step forward and two steps back, she thought irritably. That had been the pattern of her life over the last few months.

She was finally back on two feet again, the sprained ankle now just a bad memory, but life had reasserted itself with a vengeance and with that had come a flurry of details Julie could have cheerfully done without.

In the months that followed, Marc's work continued to call him away, while bills mounted. The more bills that piled up, the more out-of-town work Marc accepted, insisting that the overtime would be good for their bottom line.

Adam's problems at school were ever-present, but lately, his fears of vampires had ramped up again. With those fears, his behaviour worsened to the point where Julie debated with herself every morning whether it was worth sending him to school. Likely she'd have to turn around and go pick him up after only a few hours, spending the rest of the day either coaxing him to talk, or trying to quiet his tantrums.

Amélie had grown used to her brother's tirades and although the tiny girl watched him with fascination, she didn't always feel the need to join Adam in these extreme mood swings.

Adam was once again fearful of almost everything! He'd stopped screaming at the threshold of their family room, which was a blessing, but for some odd reason, their son had chosen to sleep *under* his bed, rather than in it, an illuminated flashlight gripped in one hand.

And now things were escalating once again. It was bad enough that Marc was away, but did her parents have to pull out too? It seemed everything dissolved into crap as soon as the fifth-wheel trailer left the driveway. She rubbed her temples and tried to slow down her thoughts.

Why couldn't people just mind their own business?

A simple act of grocery shopping had turned into an unnecessary nightmare, and with Amélie growing more verbal and more defensive of her big brother all the time, it had taken all of Julie's persuasive powers to get the two of them, plus her groceries loaded back into van.

She half-expected to be pulled over by the local police as she drove home. The ten-minute ride had been punctuated by unrelenting screams from Amélie, as her brother hurled ridiculous insults and took out his anger on everyone within earshot.

Cries of "stupid head!" and "morons!" were hurled into the air as Julie flicked nervous eyes at her rear-view mirror, ensuring both children were still strapped securely into their seatbelts.

Unnerved motorists turned to stare at the van-full of screaming children at every stoplight, and Julie stared silently forward, her jaw set as she counted to ten and concentrated on her driving.

The phrase "some people don't understand" was small comfort, but it was the only thing Julie had at her disposal. She used it to try and explain the bad behaviour of others to her children.

She silently and fervently wished people who had no tolerance for children like Adam would keep their uneducated mouths shut!

Julie balled her fists in fury, replaying the memory.

"What an asshole that guy was," she muttered, gritting her teeth as she spoke. She stormed quickly down the hall toward the master bedroom, vengeful thoughts in her head. "What business did he have, talking to my son like that? I'd like to punch that guy square in the face!"

A moment later, her footsteps faltered.

To her absolute amazement, the shadows that draped the doorway in front of her seemed to grow thicker and darker as she approached. Was something wrong with her eyes?

Julie glanced behind her, frowning at the contrast. The end of the hallway where she'd just come from was adequately lit by the overhead fixtures. With the help of the staircase chandelier, everything behind her stood out in sharp detail, and yet here, the doorway to her room was so completely dark.

Inside of her, a switch flipped and with it, a boiling anger made her grit her teeth again.

"Get out of my way!" She muttered irritably at the darkness, pushing ahead. "You picked the wrong day to mess with me!"

Julie shivered as the sudden change in temperature slid over the flesh of her bare arms. Light from the streetlamp outside shone through the narrow slats of the venetian blinds, casting an eerie glow over everything, but a quick glance behind her revealed that the shadow she'd just walked through seemed to be gone. Was it just a trick of the light, she wondered? Maybe I was looking at it from a strange angle?

She picked up a nearby basket full of clean laundry and turned on her bedside lamp. Anger still fuelling her muscles, Julie slammed the laundry basket onto the bed, her thoughts churning. Why was that Priest taking his time calling her back? What was that about? And what was going on with the world today anyhow? This was all such bullshit!

With unnecessary force, Julie began shoving items carelessly into dresser drawers. The air around her thickened and a feeling of dread raced up her backbone.

"What's your problem?" she fumed. "You aren't even man enough to talk to me!" The words were whispered fiercely as she paused, anger seething inside of her.

In the ensuite bathroom, something heavy fell to the floor and she jumped at the unexpected sound.

"No!" she yelped, instantly regretting her last statement. "No, I – I didn't mean it. It's bad enough I can see you, I don't need to hear you too."

The circle of light that her bedside lamp cast wasn't strong enough to meld with the light coming from the hallway. The resulting area of shadow that lingered in the doorway was completely natural. Wasn't it? Julie blinked rapidly. It looked as though it was …moving?

As she blinked again, the shadow coalesced. It was taunting her, daring her to speculate. In her tired mind, she saw a man. His shoulders were well-developed from years of hard work, his torso lean and strong. He worked this land, she thought in a sudden flash of inspiration. She could almost smell the stalks of waist-high grass, baking under the hot sun; the image was so crisp in her mind's eye.

But why? All she saw now were shadows. Where had this come from?

She couldn't decide if the shadow she *might* be seeing was real or imagined. Her eyes watered as she watched the shadow turn, as a man would, to face her. Although she could not see his features, she knew it was a man. She could almost *feel* the self-satisfied smirk.

Julie sucked in a sharp breath, but instead of fear, all she felt was anger building to a fever pitch.

"You're such a coward, you know that?" she mocked the figure in her doorway. "You can't even show yourself properly, so how much power do you have? Not much! You're a bully that's what you are! Well look pal, you're not in control here, we are! We're alive and you're not, so you can just quit with all this shitty manipulation. I won't be your possession, and I won't let you control my family either! You just LEAVE US ALONE!"

Julie hadn't realized her voice was escalating, until she'd finished her tirade and heard the echoes of her panicked voice bouncing off the walls. Julie's hands flew to her mouth, realizing her children were supposed to be sleeping.

Why was she always so damned impulsive?

In silence, she waited to see what would happen next. Would it be a cry from her son or daughter as they awoke, confused at all the noise?

Bad things always happened when she lost her temper. Why couldn't she just learn?

Walking on tip toes to the door, Julie peeked ahead, expecting to see Adam or Amélie standing in the hallway. With Amélie recently graduated to a toddler bed, the tiny girl was often found wandering the halls.

But as Julie approached her open doorway, the man-sized shadow that filled the empty space held firm.

She was no longer sure of what lay ahead.

She should have been able to see through it. It was only a shadow, right? But no matter how she squinted or stared at the unrelenting darkness it refused to fade.

Her imagination started giving it more definition. She started to see shoulders, a strong torso and the suggestion of two powerful legs planted firmly in her way.

"Oh no you don't," she said, her voice shaking. "Get out of my way!"

Despite her brave words, Julie felt small and vulnerable.

"What now?" she whispered. "Who are you?"

Her breath caught in her throat and she coughed; gasping for breath. This fear was constricting her chest! It ached with every breath.

Fear is robbing me of the air in my lungs? That can't be! Shit like this doesn't happen.

"Leave me alone, she said, her laboured breathing making the words come out choppy and hoarse. "Leave my kids alone. Leave … us … be."

"Mama?" Amélie's voice cut through the air like a knife. She sounded scared and Julie called out to her daughter the best she could. "Ami, it's okay ... Stay there. … Mama's coming."

"Mama?" Ami called again. Julie could sense the fear in her daughter's voice.

"I'm here baby girl," she gasped. "Mama's here."

"No! Bad! Go Home!" Adam suddenly shouted. "NAAAH!"

Julie backed away in surprise. Why couldn't she see her son? The hallway reverberated with the after-effects of his scream but all she saw was darkness. Was he talking to the shadow that separated them? What did he see?

"Adam?" she called out. "Stay there, I'm coming."

Julie blamed herself. Just snap out of it, she thought. I'm giving this thing power with my own imagination. My children are scared and this is all my fault!

"For God's sake, snap out of it!" she whispered hoarsely, suddenly consumed by a fit of coughing as she felt the invisible pressure on her chest tighten its hold.

It was her dad's favourite phrase. Yes, she'd heard it often, growing up. Think of dad! Always un-rattled, always calm.

Dad wouldn't allow this type of thing. Dad would simply deny it, and it would have no choice but to go away.

Julie focused all her energy on that one thought, and whether it was her imagination or not, the pressure in her chest eased up a fraction.

Could it be as simple as that?

"It's not simple at all," she whispered, wiping perspiration from her forehead. It took a tremendous effort for her to focus with such intent. Random thoughts tried to intrude, but Julie locked them out, determined to win this battle.

It's just a shadow, she told herself. It has no power over me.

Marc was always telling her not to assume things were paranormal. Here was a perfect example.

"Don't believe in it, and it'll go away," she muttered. The grip on her chest loosened a little more and she took a deep, shuddering breath. Closing her eyes firmly, Julie plunged ahead into the wall of darkness, her hands outstretched.

The air was ice-cold, like stepping inside a freezer ... *or an old barn, smelling of mildew and decay.*

Goose bumps stood out on her arms as she recognised the feeling for what it was.

Now engulfed, Julie knew with certainty that this had all happened before.

"NO!"

Her thoughts strayed farther. A child, terrified in the darkness, listening with dread to the sounds all around her that should not be there …

But as her detached mind travelled back to that moment, twenty years ago, she reeled at the implications and shuddered violently. Snapping her eyes open, she panicked at the darkness that enfolded her body.

No longer conscious, the young woman's limp form made almost no noise as it slid down the wall to the floor.

"Mama?" The child called to her mother, not knowing the adult she trusted could not hear. The blackness that was always there, seemed to hover for a moment, as though pleased at what it had done.

Amélie watched with curious eyes. She knew this shadow should not be there. And although it frightened her when the man who hid inside the shadow looked through her window, or stood at the foot of her bed, the tiny girl simply watched him. What would he do now?

Amélie, already possessing an iron will, instinctively projected a defense that the shadow man could not break through.

He hadn't counted on this. Especially considering how much strength this woman possessed. Had he gone too far this time? That was how the last one left, he reminded himself. Shaking his ghostly head, his soulless eyes caught sight of the child. She intrigued him. Devoid of expression, she simply stared at him. He could sense no fear, only curiosity. Somehow, and he was convinced it happened purely by accident, this child had discovered a way to keep him out of her head.

Glancing down once more at the unconscious figure at his feet, he took his leave.

I can come back any time, he told himself. I'm in control here.

The first thing Julie heard was her own heartbeat. Lifting arms that felt like they were made of wood, she pushed against the hard surface under her cheek and slowly sat up. Opening both eyes, she blinked rapidly, her vision slowly sharpening. Her head hurt where she'd connected with the hard laminate, but otherwise she seemed okay. Julie looked around her and the first things she saw were the frightened eyes of her children.

Adam stood just a few feet from his mother, inside the doorway of his room, while Amélie stood similarly in hers.

Both children were silent. Their faces said they'd just witnessed a nightmare.

Automatically, Julie got to her feet and brushed ineffectively at her clothing.

How far did imagination go? Was this the extreme side of sleep deprivation, coupled with paranoia?

The stares of her children said otherwise.

Random strands of hair fell in her face, but as she brushed them away, she was startled anew by her son. He came to stand in front of her, his gaze clear, deep concern reflected in the pucker between his brows and the set of his down-turned mouth.

"Oh no," he said, shaking his head. "Oh no."

Julie wanted to laugh and cry at the same time, but she simply gathered him in her arms and held on.

"It's okay," she told him, hoping she was telling him the truth. "Mommy's fine now. Everything's fine."

Adam shook his head sadly and without another word, walked down the hall to the family room. Julie heard the tell-tale click that told her he'd turned on the TV.

It was his comfort after all. She should have expected that.

Pasting on a comforting smile for her daughter, she gathered Amélie in her arms, and followed her son down to the TV room. She sank gratefully onto the couch beside Adam, the eerily silent toddler held securely in her arms. Her son's eyes, so frightened a moment ago, were now fixated on the images dancing across the TV screen.

Amélie snuggled against Julie's side.

For once, she was glad for Adam's obsession. She still wasn't sure what had just happened, but it was intense. Julie wondered if she would ever discover what, if anything, her children had witnessed in those few terrifying moments.

Drawing a nearby blanket around them all, she was too tired to care and too tired to fight. Glancing at the clock, she saw it was already well past the children's bedtimes, but none of that mattered now. Her body felt as though she'd just finished running a long-distance marathon.

How long could she keep doing this?

Her training as a journalist told her the experience she'd just had was very subjective and most people, if she had the courage to share it, would simply point a finger at her and say the fault lay with her. Somehow, this was the product of a deranged mind.

Or maybe, as her mother would say, she was 'simply over-wrought and over-tired'.

Julie was fairly certain she wasn't insane, but tired? Hell yeah.

After all, hadn't she read somewhere that if you're rational enough to think you might be cracking up, you're obviously okay?

~~~~

Hours later, Julie awoke, a pain in her neck and the muscles in her arms stiff from staying locked in place around her still slumbering child. As she carried Amélie back to her own room, it only took a moment to discover that Adam was fast asleep too, tucked securely *beneath* his bed.

Half-closing her children's doors, she couldn't but help wonder what would happen next? Would her children be safe? The supposed
~~~~

guard dog who slept in a dog crate in the corner of the family room hadn't uttered a sound through this whole thing! The thought was disconcerting to say the least.

Glancing up at the crucifix that hung in each of their bedrooms, she breathed a silent prayer of protection.

Together. The word stood out in her head like it was written in big bold letters. If they stayed together and prayed together, they would make it.

As she lay down in her own bed, Julie pulled up the sheets and blankets to her chin, puzzling it through as much as she dared.

In the end, the realization she came to, was a sobering one.

The stress she and Marc lived with daily was taking its toll on both in ways no one could have anticipated. Whether these things were real or imagined, whether Julie was sane or crazy, none of that mattered anymore. The reality she lived in was the one she had to deal with.

Household chores had to get done and there was only her to do them. She had two children to care for, often with only one parent in the house. She had a part to play, and as long as she played it, things would continue as they had until they could get the hell out of this beautiful prison.

It was only when she tried to seize control that things got nasty.

Like it or not, they had become the *possessions* of a deranged entity.

Chapter Thirty-one

"Mom, I think we really need to do the right thing and have the house blessed," Julie tried to keep her voice neutral, as she spoke to her mother-in-law on the phone. "We meant to do it shortly after the move, but then Father got sick. I've been trying the rectory, to re-book it, but I can't get through.

"That's strange," Marc's mother replied. "Did you leave a message?"

"No, I uh …" Julie trailed off, unsure what to say.

"Are you alright?" her mother-in-law asked. "You sound a bit shaken up."

"I'm just tired, that's all," Julie replied. It was the truth. She was tired.

Tired and terrified, she thought.

"I'll try and give him a call," she promised. "Leave it with me."

The reassuring response lifted a heavy weight from Julie's shoulders. As the call ended, she slumped back in her chair and heaved a deep sigh.

A blessing! This had to be the answer!

~~~~

A flurry of house cleaning preceded the Blessing, but finally all was in readiness. The house had never looked more beautiful, and
~~~~

although Julie and Marc were equally exhausted, they were both secretly delighted this day had come at last.

The warm sunshine slanted down through patchy clouds overhead. With streams of sunshine pouring through the large windows, it showed off the interior of the house to its full potential.

"Please come in Father," she said, watching the small-statured man carefully for any signs of concern or alarm as he entered the house. Despite what Marc thought, Julie was certain this man would be able to tell *something* was amiss.

"Lovely home you have," he said, his brown eyes looking around appreciatively.

"Thank you," Marc replied, coming up behind his wife, he reached around her and shook the weathered hand. "I'm glad you could make it."

"Yes, I'm so sorry that I had to call it off before," he said, his voice was so soft Julie found it difficult to distinguish every word. "I was quite ill, you see. It took a long time to recover … I completely forgot to call you. I'm so sorry."

"Oh no, it's us who got busy and forgot," Julie replied quickly, wincing as she realized how loud her own words seemed in the stillness of the foyer. "You've got enough on your plate without worrying about us. It's totally fine." Her attempt at being casual just seemed awkward, and she clamped her lips together as Marc shot her a worried look behind the Priest's back.

Father Joseph climbed the stairs quickly, his movements sharp and efficient. When he got to the top, he looked around, selecting the end of the living room coffee table to lay out the things he'd brought. Julie watched with bated breath as the priest drew a purple sash and a worn-looking brown leather bible from the deep pockets of the shapeless grey cardigan he wore. He ran a hand over his short-cropped dark hair and adjusted the white cleric's collar at his neck, where it contrasted sharply with his black shirt and pants. As though keenly aware of being watched, Father Joseph adjusted his collar once more before tossing a wide, reassuring smile over his shoulder at the nervous couple. Julie couldn't help feeling excited. She had high hopes for this.

He murmured a prayer, then touched the purple stole to his lips before draping it around his neck with gentle hands. Julie's hands twisted together, the fingers lacing and unlacing as Father Joseph opened the bible and leafed through the pages. The priest looked up fleetingly catching sight of Julie's nervous hands. His eyes were questioning, but a reassuring smile hovered on his lips.

Marc noticed the movement too and moved close to his wife, taking her hand in his.

"Shall we begin here?" Father Joseph asked smiling again as the home-owners nodded eagerly.

The Priest lifted both hands to his waist, and read from the open bible balanced in the palm of one hand.

"Let us pray," he began. Julie and Marc bent their heads reverently as Father Joseph evoked a Blessing over the home and all who resided within. He walked from the living room through to the dining room, ancient words of prayer and protection on his lips, as he shook several drops of holy water from a tiny vial. Julie watched them fall like tiny raindrops on the antique oak table top, where they mingled with the brilliant sunshine in a dazzling display of color.

Marc squeezed his wife's hand encouragingly.

The Priest walked through the doorway into the kitchen.

"The kids are playing in the next room," Marc offered. "Should they join us?"

The Priest considered that, a small frown creasing his unlined brow, before he waved the suggestion aside. "No, they're fine where they are," he replied, continuing his tour of the upstairs.

Julie and Marc trailed after him through the abnormally still house, and it soon became clear that, for the priest, the only unusual thing about this House Blessing was the nervousness of the home-owners.

Julie felt a stab of disappointment as the rite concluded and Father Joseph made the sign of the cross in front of them, prompting her and Marc to cross themselves in the same way.

When would she feel the change, Julie wondered? Would it feel different now?

They had kept the House-Blessing as low-key as possible, inviting no one. Julie, Marc and their two children were the only participants.

Marc's mom and dad had insisted on giving them gifts to commemorate the occasion, and so had Julie's parents. Two giant wooden crosses, one decorated with a simple silver cross on top of the wood, and the other adorned with a bronze figure of Jesus, now lay across Father Joseph's open palms, as he murmured a special Blessing over the religious objects.

"And now it is complete," the Priest murmured, grinning at them as he packing away his things and headed for the stairs.

At the front door, Julie leaned forward eagerly as Father Joseph turned to them one last time.

Surely this was the time when he would give them the straight goods?

"Thank you for inviting me into your lovely home, and for giving me the opportunity to Bless it," he said. Julie couldn't help feeling crestfallen. Was that it?

"Is everything alright?" Father Joseph asked, his dark eyebrows rose as his eyes strayed to Julie.

"Yes, everything's fine," Marc answered, taking the Priest's hand in a hearty handshake. "We're glad you could come. Thank you very much. We both feel much better knowing this important task is done."

The Priest's ready smile held a hint of question, but he did not ask it.

The door had only just closed again, when Marc headed straight for the garage, retrieving his ladder, a hammer and some nails so he could hang the crosses in places of significance.

Julie and Marc caught each other's eye frequently over the next several days, exchanging a look that clearly said: 'Well? We had the Blessing. What now?'

It was what they'd been waiting for, so why didn't their home feel any lighter?

Maybe it was a delayed reaction? Maybe, like the gradual warming that was happening outside, their house would start to feel lighter as time went on?

Although they'd lived in the house almost three years, Father Joseph hadn't said a word about the delay.

He hadn't said a word about anything else, either.

Several nights later, Julie expressed these sentiments to her husband as they prepared for bed.

"What did you expect him to do?" Marc asked, truly puzzled by Julie's statement. "I told you it doesn't work like that. Just because he's a priest, doesn't mean–"

"I know, I know, it doesn't mean he's a Sensitive," Julie interrupted. "I get all that, but I was still hoping he would notice *something*. I guess I was just expecting ... well it doesn't matter, he didn't, so that's the end of it."

"We probably should have told him," Marc said, after a thoughtful pause.

"Maybe," she replied, frowning.

"It's not too late," he offered. "We could call him up?"

"Oh sure. You go right ahead."

"Why me?"

"It was your idea."

"Technically this was all started by you," he countered. "You never told me why it was suddenly so important to get the Blessing done, just that we had to hurry."

"I know," she admitted. "Does it matter though?"

"Well, no. I just wondered."

"Let's just say that I realized we hadn't followed through, and I wanted to get it done. Okay?"

Marc eyes his wife, knowing there was more to the story, but frankly too tired to delve into it. "Well, I'm glad it's done. It doesn't feel any different in here though. Does it to you?"

"No," she admitted. "That's why I think you need to tell the Priest what's been going on."

Marc sighed. "I was hoping you'd forget about that."

Julie made a face at him.

"What am I supposed to say anyways?"

"How should I know? That's why you get to do it. I haven't the faintest idea how I'd start *that* conversation."

"Great. Thanks." Marc replied with heavy sarcasm. "What do you think he would do if we did tell him? Do you think he would call someone, do an extra Blessing maybe... would he even believe us?"

"He'll probably call your mother and ask if her son is taking medication," Julie quipped.

"Be serious," Marc retorted.

"I'm sorry," Julie said, turning towards her husband so he could see the worry in her eyes. "I guess that's why we haven't said anything before. We can't control people's reactions."

The couple fell silent, as they turned down the covers on their bed.

From the other room, a faint sound, like the rustling of fabric could be heard.

Julie and Marc looked a question at each other.

"Adam?" Julie wondered, her voice low.

"Last time I checked on him, he was out like a light," Marc whispered.

"Ami?" she whispered, as Marc swept back the covers and got to his feet.

Both parents faced the doorway, as they listened to the sound of footsteps making their way along the hall, through the squeaking gate at the top the stairs and going rapidly down the steps.

"Oh that kid," Marc muttered. "He must have heard us talking in here."

Julie frowned.

"He's the only one who knows how to open the gate," Marc said. "I'll go get him."

"What the heck is he doing? It's far too late for running around," Julie whispered urgently to her husband as he donned his house robe and left the room.

A moment later, Marc returned, a strange look on his face. "I don't know what we heard, but it wasn't our kids," he whispered, his face looked paler than usual and there were two bright spots on his cheeks as he spoke. "Both of them are fast asleep, I just checked."

Julie's eyebrows shot up.

"So I guess that's our answer," she said, her voice small.

"I guess so," Marc agreed as he sat down heavily on the edge of the bed, his hands resting loosely against the comforter as his shoulders slouched in defeat. "We gotta talk to that Priest. We don't have any choice."

~~~~

"Holy Water," Marc's mother said, pulling the non-descript plastic bottle from her purse and plunking it with a soft thud on the kitchen counter.

Julie and Marc didn't trust themselves to speak. Her visit came out of left field, only minutes after they'd left a somewhat disjointed phone message for Father Joseph.

"Just sprinkle a few drops of this in each room. Be mindful that you only keep positive thoughts in your mind, and recite this
~~~~

prayer." She handed them a small slip of paper that looked as if it'd been clipped from a magazine.

"I thought that Father Joseph would be doing this," Julie said, her voice small.

"There's no need for that, you can do it quite easily," she responded confidently. "People do it all the time."

Marc, obviously more familiar with his parent and her thought processes, stepped forward and hugged his mom.

"Thanks mom, we really appreciate it," he said. "It's just for peace-of-mind, you understand."

"Of course," she replied with a wink and a knowing smile.

Julie shot Marc a look, but he was obviously just as floored by his mother's response.

Spontaneously, Julie hugged her mother-in-law. She had no idea what had prompted the visit, but she now had a thread of hope, no matter how slender and she was grateful.

"We'll do it right away," she promised.

"The sooner the better," the older woman answered. "You both need some rest. It's obvious you're exhausted. Now you just let me know if you want more. I can get as much as you need."

~~~~

"You wanna build what?" Julie asked. "Now? I thought we were gonna try and sell this place? Why do you want to build something?"

Marc grinned at his wife, hoping he could distract her with the new project. He didn't really want to tell her that he'd already stopped by to chat with a realtor, and been given the disappointing news that although prices had risen some, they weren't yet high enough for the couple to make the type of move they needed.

"It's gonna be perfect for the kids," Marc replied. "And it'll increase our property value too. Can't you just see it out there?" Marc led his wife to the back porch and leaned on the railing beside her. "I've got it all worked out. I got two weeks' holidays coming to me, and Dad said he's gonna help too."

"How much?" Julie asked, eyeing him suspiciously.

"Payment plan," Marc answered.

"Done deal?" Her eyebrows rose in question.

"Not yet. Told the guy I had to convince my wife first."
~~~~

Julie sighed in defeat. Marc knew how much she loved home improvement projects.

"When do we start?" She asked.

~~~~

The structure went up quickly, which was a good thing, as Adam had to be physically restrained so he didn't try it out before it was ready. Julie and her mom mostly watched the men's progress and plied them with cold drinks and food.

"Keeps 'em moving," Anne quipped, winking at her daughter as she placed a tray of sandwiches on her patio table.

It was clear Marc needed the diversion and so did Julie, but she continued to wonder at the timing of the monolithic structure as it rose out of the back yard.

"Marc, are you serious?" she asked when it was finally done. "Are you sure it's not too tall?"

"Dad and I did everything exactly according to the plans they gave me," he replied defensively.

"Okay," she replied dubiously. "You'd better try it out then, I guess."

Marc climbed the cargo net happily and stood at the top with a huge, boyish grin before whooshing down the slide with alarming speed. As his feet touched the ground, his body pitched forward with left-over momentum and he had to take several steps forward so he wouldn't crash straight into the fence.

"Wow!" he said, laughing. "It might be a bit too high at the top. I might have to shorten it down a bit before Adam tries it."

Julie shook her head and smiled, but then her expression changed as a blonde-haired blur shot past her and down the stairs. Faster than thought, Adam climbed straight to the top of the new structure, and before either of them could stop him, he careened down the slide and literally flew off the end of it, straight into his father's waiting arms!

Adam squealed with delight and squirmed away to do it all over again.

Marc beamed at his son's seal of approval, but Julie shook her head sternly. "Tomorrow, Marc," she called to her husband. "Tomorrow you lower that thing. I don't want to be peeling our son off the new fence."
~~~~

Marc issued a mock salute, and then turned to receive his son like a high-speed football, as the young boy rocketed down the slide, a huge grin on his face.

~~~~

"I don't know where it went," Julie replied, clearly irritated. "I thought you took it!"

"I haven't seen it since my mom brought it over," Marc insisted. "Maybe Adam took it? Maybe he thought it was bubble solution?"

"I've gone over his whole room, twice. I even emptied the toy bin, just in case. There's no sign of it. I couldn't even find the empty bottle!"

Frantically, the young woman pulled the cushions from her sofa and dug her hands into the crevices. She came out with handfuls of cereal and cookie crumbs, but no bottle. "Are you sure you didn't put it somewhere for safe keeping?" she asked her husband, her voice muted as she got down on the floor to look under the edges of the furniture.

"That's your usual go-to, not mine," Marc snapped.

"Well, don't just stand there staring at me, keep looking! It's got to be somewhere," she sighed, standing up and throwing her arms into the air with exasperation. "It's not like it grew legs and walked away."

"We could always ask my mom for more," Marc suggested, as he turned away, his eyes searching.

"Oh great," Julie replied with heavy sarcasm. "And what'll that lead to? Questions we can't answer, at the very least. But how did she find out about, you know… this *situation*? I thought Priests had to keep things secret when people told them stuff?"

"That only applies to the confessional," her husband, a Catholic since birth, corrected his wife. "And aside from that phone message asking him to call us, I didn't say anything to him."

"Oh? Then how did she –"

"Marc? Julie? You home?" the sound of her dad's voice interrupted the conversation, and prompted an instant change in Julie's demeanor.

"Yes dad?" she answered sweetly, smiling as she met him at the top of the stairs. How much had he heard? She wondered, chewing at her lip.
~~~~

"When was the last time you two got out and had any fun?" Arthur asked the couple.

Marc and Julie hung their heads, not looking at each other.

Her dad grunted. "That's what I thought. Listen, your mother and I will watch the kids tonight so you can go out together. What do you say?"

He was right. After the House Blessing, the energy in their home had seemed almost normal, but it hadn't taken long for the air to thicken, like a brewing thunder storm. The atmosphere was taking its toll on both of them. They hardly saw family anymore, and even their close friends didn't come around much.

Julie and Marc smiled weakly at each other. What they really wanted was to find that vial of Holy Water and get a good night's sleep, but at this point, they would take whatever they could get.

Maybe being out of the house for a few hours together would bring some clarity. If nothing else, it might improve both their moods. After all, Marc was due to leave again Monday morning for a new project, and that meant they would be apart for weeks.

Chapter Thirty-two

Julie chatted away to her husband as she got ready for bed, aware that he was already under the covers and would likely be asleep before she finished her narrative, but she needed someone to talk to. Spending her days with just Adam and Amélie for company made her crave adult conversation.

"So, I've been thinking," she continued. "Maybe we should ask your mom for some more of that Holy Water. It can't hurt, and frankly I don't know what else to try."

Julie turned to her husband, waiting for an answer, but Marc simply stared at the ceiling.

"Marc?" Julie prompted.

Receiving no reply, she crossed to the side of the bed and looked down at her husband. "What wrong with you? Why are you just ignoring me?"

"Somebody's here," Marc replied.

Julie frowned in confusion for a moment, until realization dawned and her eyes widened in surprise and alarm.

"Where do you feel it?" she asked.

"Right here," Marc tapped his chest.

Her logical mind screamed at her. It wasn't possible! How could this be happening? The bumps, shadows and random noises, none of them were really explainable, but this? There was no way to rationalize an experience like this.

Something invisible was pinning Marc to the bed and the powerful man seemed unable to shake it off.

She thought suddenly of the clock radio. Unplugged and yet working. Was this another example of the random energy that now seemed to have her husband in its grip?

Her mother's words came back to her in that instant.

Ghosts can't hurt you, she'd told her young daughter. Things like that only happen in movies. You have the power to take control. No one controls you unless you let it happen.

But the advice given to her as a little girl was small comfort now.

Julie's tears collected in pools on the edges of her ears as she lay beside her husband, praying for this to be over.

"Are you okay?" she asked. "Is it hurting you?"

"No, not hurting exactly, it's just so *heavy*."

"Do you think I could feel it?" she queried.

"I don't know," he answered. "Put your hand here." Marc pointed to the center of his chest.

With an almost casual movement, Julie laid her left arm gently across her husband's chest, her palm facing up.

At first, she felt nothing, but then, unexpectedly, small shocks of electricity seemed to dance across her fingertips and open palm! The sensation was so strong, Julie jerked her hand back with a yelp of surprise and sat up.

"What the hell!?" she gasped, her eyes wide.

"You felt it?" Marc asked, his eyes questioning as he turned to look at her.

She nodded, wondering how long it would take for her heart to stop racing.

Slowly, Marc dragged himself upright and drew his shoulders back, stretching. A look of relief replaced the grimace he'd worn moments ago. He heaved a sigh and "Thanks hon. Whatever you did chased him off." He looked at his wife, her eyes wide and staring.

"I actually felt that," she said, her voice coming out in a whisper.

The experience had frightened her so badly that she was at a loss for words.

"Whoever he is, he's gone for now. It's okay," Marc reassured her.

As she pulled the sheets back up over her bare legs, the smooth texture felt like sandpaper. Every inch of her body seemed to still be electrified by the strange phenomenon. She sat up again, unable to settle.

"I need a drink of water. You want one?"

Marc laughed weakly. "Sure," he said. "What I really need is something a little stronger but I'll settle for water."

"One order of water, on the rocks," she replied, grateful for the diversion.

"Jules?" Marc called to her as she turned to go.

"Yeah?"

"I don't think we should mention this to anyone, do you?"

"I was just thinking the same thing," she agreed. "No one would ever believe us."

"Exactly."

"Marc, do you think this thing, whatever it is, will come back and do that again?"

"Probably."

"Then what do we do?"

"I don't know.

Julie felt her childhood memories stirring. The feeling terrified her.

"Let's have that drink of water and get some rest. It's late," he answered, lying back down.

"Yeah, but Marc, we've got to have a plan," she countered. "We can't keep trying to do this on our own, this is crazy!" She climbed back onto her side of bed to look closely at her husband, the intensity of what they'd just experienced sharp in her mind.

Marc didn't answer.

"Marc?" she whispered, peering into his face, worried she would see him in the grip of another attack, but this time, her husband lay calmly on his back, already asleep.

How did he do that? Not five minutes ago, he struggled with a powerful entity, as it pinned him down in his own bed, and now he's out like a light!

The sheer ridiculousness of it made Julie want to laugh out loud.

As tired as she was, Julie knew she'd still be up for hours. The electricity she'd felt coursing through her finger tips as she touched her husband's chest seemed to flicker and dance inside her as she walked slowly to the kitchen in search of water.

"Whoever you are," she whispered into the darkness. "Just leave us alone. We don't belong to you."

~~~~

The shadow who had once been human scoffed at her statement.
He sneered at the tiny lights and their little pools of light.
What a pathetic attempt to keep me away.
That little display was just to let you know I'm still here.
His lips parted in a cruel smile.
You really think you're in control?
All of you are mine. I will take you when it suits me.

~~~~

The next morning, Julie noticed the light had been left on over their kitchen table. It was early, and the morning light hadn't yet chased away all the shadows. The lamp over the table cast a yellow glow over half the kitchen. As she approached, she realized Marc was seated at the table, where several tools and electronic components were laid out on its surface.

"What are you doing here?" She asked.

Marc looked up briefly from the item he was working on. Julie recognized it at once.

"What's that thing still doing here?" she demanded, one hand on her hip as she stared at the small alarm clock from their bedroom.

"I thought I'd take another look at it," Marc answered, gesturing with his screwdriver as he talked.

"Oh geez, hon," she said, going to the counter to start the morning coffee. "You swore you were gonna throw it out a long time ago."

"Yeah, I know, I was looking for something else in the garage, and there it was. I couldn't resist giving it a quick look. No one else was up, so I thought I'd have time."

"Of course," she replied with heavy sarcasm. Her husband loved to tinker with anything electronic. "But I already bought you a new one. Why bother with it?"

Receiving no answer, Julie tried again, aware that Marc probably wanted her to drop the subject. "Are you making much progress?"

"I haven't figured it out yet, but I will. I mean, look at it," he said, gesturing at the device with its face-plates still lying on the table. "There's no damage, I've checked." He turned the small machine over and over in his hands. "I've tested it over and over, and it's just an ordinary clock-radio, with a phone attached. It works fine, see? And you know, it's been plugged in for over an hour and I haven't heard that clicking sound even once."

"Meaning?" Julie's tone was dangerous.

"Meaning we didn't really need a new one." Marc reassembled the pieces quickly, a grin on his handsome face.

Julie's gaze fell absently on the power cord as Marc picked up the unit to reset the time.

"That's weird," he said. "The display's gone out."

"Unless it's magical too," she noted with a smirk. "You'd better try plugging it in."

"What?" Marc ducked his head and looked under the table. "What the heck? I don't get it," he said. "It was plugged in just a second ago."

Julie yawned and folded her arms. A small buzzing began in her right ear, and an unexplained tightness developed across her chest. "Just being near that thing makes me feel sick," she muttered. "Marc, I really don't like that machine. You and I both know why."

Her breathing was heavy and she leaned against the counter for support. Julie felt her heart racing as she stared at the offending machine.

Marc looked at his wife questioningly for a long moment.

Can't I have anything? He wanted to say, but the look on her face stopped him. Whatever the reason, she was looking at the clock radio like it was a live snake.

"Yes dear," he answered contritely. Wrapping the cord quickly around the machine, he plunged it back into the box. "I'll just put this back in the garage."

"Thank you," she said simply, watching as he tucked the flaps of the box together and went to the stairs.

"I'm bagged. I'm gonna go back to bed for awhile." Julie went back along the hallway, her feet shuffling as she yawned again. "Maybe if I'm lucky, I'll get a bit of sleep before the kids wake up."

Julie crawled into her bed willing her heart rate to slow down. Night-time was always the worst for her, and last night had been one of the most uncomfortable she'd had in a long while. Sleep had not come easily, and she was paying the price now.

"Well, at least that creepy machine is gone," she muttered, closing her eyes.

~~~~

"Mommy?"

"Oh! Sweetie, I thought you were in your room."

"Wuz a matter wiv Adam?" she asked.

"I don't know," she answered distractedly. "Why?"

"He's cryin'," she stated simply, pointing at her brother's closed bedroom door.

Julie dashed to her son's door and threw it open before remembering he was still at school.

The room, of course was empty and there were no sounds within that she could discern.

So, who was crying? Amélie was far too young to be making it up. Was her daughter overhearing one of their neighbors again?

But as Julie went to the window in her son's room to ensure it was closed, a giant crash behind her, made Julie jump.

"What the heck?" She spluttered. Rushing to the hallway, and leaning over the railing for a better look, she saw plant matter, soil and broken pottery scattered all over.

"Dammit, that cat!" Julie fumed, turning to her daughter, who stood a few feet from her mother, hands over her mouth in surprise.

"Mommy, you said a bad word," the child admonished.

"Ami," Julie said sternly, ignoring the remark. "What happened? Did the kitty do that?"

"Nope," she answered simply. Turning quickly, she slipped past her mother and back into her room.

Julie watched her go with annoyance. "Ami," she began.

"–lookit mommy!" the little girl interrupted. Proudly, she gestured through the open doorway. Stuffed animals sat on the carpet in a circle, facing a plastic tea set, all laid out on an old receiving blanket. "A tea party!"

"Oh, yes very nice," Julie complimented her daughter. "Ami, who did that?" she indicated the stairwell with a quick jerk of her thumb.

"I don't know mommy," Amélie answered sweetly.

Julie sighed.
~~~~

A heartbeat later, the tiny girl seemed to have forgotten all about it, although Julie continued to fume over the mess. "Can we have real tea mommy?" she asked. "Casper wants real tea."

"What?" Julie replied distractedly. "Tea? No sweetie, no tea. Mommy's got enough to deal with here. And besides, cats don't drink tea."

Amélie stuck out her bottom lip in a dramatic pout and went back to her room. As she was closing the door, Julie heard a high-pitched cat's meow.

"Just a second." Julie said, pushing the door open all the way. "The cat's in here with you?"

"Let him stay mommy," her daughter pleaded. "He wants tea with me an' Dessie."

The cat looked up at Julie with hooded eyes and blinked lazily. He was curled up in the rocking chair and seemed oblivious to anything, including the prospect of tea.

"You and Jessie huh," she asked, resting a hand on her hip as she shook her head.

"Mommy don't be mad. Dessie's sorry she broke the plant. She was mad with you 'afore mom but she's sorry now. Can we have tea ple-ease?"

Julie felt her shoulders slump. Was Amélie really suggesting Jessie pushed the plant off the ledge?

"No, I told you. Cat's don't drink tea." Julie pulled the door closed quickly, so her daughter wouldn't see the tears that she was unable to stop.

~~~~

"Adam," Julie began, using the method they'd come to rely on, with pens and paper.

"Please stop screaming. Mommy has a headache."

Adam paused to carefully read the words in front of him, and then promptly clamped his lips together with a meaningful look.

Whew! If only that worked every time, she thought, hastily picking up the pen again.

"Why are you so upset today?" she wrote, while she spoke.

Adam started to reach for the pen before she'd finished writing out some possible choices. Hastily he circled the choice labeled 'something else'.
~~~~

Julie sighed deeply. She hated that choice. It meant she was on the wrong track and would have to search creatively for where to go next. Often, in the interest of accuracy, she tried to entice key words from him.

Drawing out phrases with long lines intended as blanks, she wrote: I feel ______________ today.

Adam wrote MAD in the blank and gave the pen calmly to his mother.

Julie sat back. Okay, here we go, she thought.

She wrote: I feel MAD today, because

a) a person did something

b) something happened

c) I thought of something

d) there is a change

e) something else

Feeling at least somewhat proud of herself for being so thorough, Julie pushed the paper towards her son, who read the choices over with a serious expression, before circling E: something else.

Julie tried to keep her face neutral, to encourage Adam to keep communicating but inside she was disappointed. Where could she possibly take it from there? Her mind was mush.

"Uh, I'm not sure what to write," she said aloud to the waiting child, who was once more holding out the pen to his mother. "Why don't you write something?" she asked hopefully, pushing the pen back towards him.

But Adam, having said his piece, or at least all he was capable of expressing, threw the pen onto the table and stomped from the room.

Julie heard his heavy footsteps echo down the hall, all the way to his room, where he proceeded to slam his door repeatedly.

Julie cringed as she heard the door contact the frame with brutal force. Again and again he slammed it. Well! If that wasn't communication, then what was? She thought, hurrying from the room. So much for being kind to mommy's headache!

Julie looked with chagrin at the splintered wood and felt defeat wash over her.

"Oh Adam!" she whispered fiercely. "Daddy's not gonna like this."

"Oh Adam," Amélie repeated, emerging from her bedroom at the sound of the slamming door. "Bad boy."

The little girl stood solemnly, her arms folded, frowning in apparent judgment of her big brother. As Amélie got older, she seemed to be growing bossier too.

"That's enough Ami," Julie warned, pointing a finger back at the child's room. "Turn around and march, young lady."

She'd already had her fair share of chaos for the day and didn't welcome the thought of separating those two again.

Chapter Thirty-three

The simple fact that she was reacting to the paranormal, and almost regarded it as commonplace, was not lost on her. It was a strange way to live, but as Marc had so casually quipped the night before, 'the bizarre has become the norm'.

"If I don't talk to someone, I'm gonna really go crazy," she confided to her best friend Abby. The two had finally been able to get together for a much-needed visit. Abby's baby was already learning to walk, and Amélie was racing through the house at top speeds. This meant that if they wanted to visit at all, they'd have to leave the children with their daddies.

Eagerly, they hunched over the small table, their heads close together as they spoke in hushed tones. Disposable coffee cups in hand, they sat in a tiny restaurant and tried to catch up, but each of them was so breathless, it felt like their words tumbled out over each other.

"I don't blame you," Abby said. "I would do the same in your shoes. After all, Adam doesn't talk and Amélie's only just started babbling. Marc's gone all the time and even your parents aren't there as much as you thought they'd be. Noise is noise. To TV or not to TV, that is the question from people who don't have kids! But seriously, are you looking after yourself? I thought you were gonna try some yoga and meditation? Hasn't that been helping?"

Julie made a face.

"Have you tried leaving the radio on?"

"You love to sing, so maybe try it. What have you got to lose?" Abby asked.

"Not much, just my sanity," Julie quipped, laughing.

"I know, I know," Abby replied, chuckling at her friend's sarcasm. "Just try it, okay? I worry about you."

"Okay, I promise."

~~~~~

The sound of popular music following her from room to room did have a soothing effect on Julie. She laughed at the simplicity of it, and if Abby had been there, she would have hugged her.

What an amazing thing this was! It lifted her spirits more than anything had done in a while.

The simple fact that a song, especially a familiar one, also helped keep Adam on an even keel was a newfound joy.

Julie found herself humming along to the familiar songs from her son's movies and often, even when he was away at school, she'd catch herself singing the upbeat tunes as she went about her daily tasks.

Amélie seemed to enjoy the music just as much. The tiny little girl, now speaking clearer with each passing day, copied her mother and brother endlessly. Versions of Adam's favourite songs, often just the one or two lines that she remembered, were sung at full volume. Adam cast dark looks at his sister and covered his ears as she passed by, but Amélie continued to sing, unabashed.

Unfortunately, Adam's tolerance didn't run very deep.

Oh Autism! Julie thought as she intervened yet again, separating her children, and reaching for a favourite video that had the power to calm them both. Amélie had reached the age where she didn't share her brother's love affair with movies, but for some reason, a tape they'd received prior to his diagnosis had the power to quiet both children, and restore calm. It was two children's stories, told both in verbal English and American Sign Language. Julie was always amazed at the power it had over her children, but when times were tough and it seemed like nothing would make them behave, the tired parents fed the worn tape into the VCR and in minutes, the siblings curled up together on the couch, their quarrel forgotten.
~~~~~

~~~~

Anne gripped the railing, her knuckles white. "Julie!" she called out sharply.

When her daughter didn't appear, Anne shouted again. "JULIE!"

"Yes? Yes, mom what is it? Are you okay?" Julie arrived at the gate, looking down with concern at her mother.

"I refuse to keep climbing these stairs," she proclaimed. "I'm simply too tired."

"Oh, okay," Julie answered uncertainly. "Do you need something? I'm just in the middle of –"

"You're always in the middle of something," her mother snapped. "When I need to get your attention, I shouldn't have to yell and scream."

Anne was furious with her, but what had she done? Julie hadn't a clue where this was coming from. She sifted through her memory, looking for some promise she'd forgotten about or an appointment she'd missed.

Coming up empty, she spread her hands out in front of her, and shrugged. "What? She asked. "What's going on? What did I miss?"

"Oh, nothing," her mom retorted. "Just next time I call don't make me wait a million years before answering."

With that, her mom pivoted on one heel and went back inside her suite, banging the door closed with finality.

Julie's shoulders slumped. What now? Her parents had only just come back from another trip in their new trailer. Shouldn't they be happy?

Perhaps the peaceful nature that existed inside their 'home away from home' served as too much of a contrast to everyday life, Julie thought wryly. Living with their daughter and the chaos that surrounded her was no picnic.

~~~~

"This place is driving me crazy!" Julie shouted at her husband. "How can we *not* sell it?"

"I didn't say we wouldn't. I'm just trying to be realistic. I mean, what makes you think *he's* gonna cooperate?" Marc's sarcastic comment only served to infuriate Julie further. "So, you're just gonna give up and let him win?"

"Of course not, don't be ridiculous," Marc answered, his face growing redder.

"I'm gonna thaw something for dinner!" she shouted over her shoulder as she stomped down the stairs, pounding each step with the anger that coursed through her body.

The heavy connecting door banged satisfactorily as it closed behind her with a resounding thud. Julie's anger continued to build as she flung up the lid to the chest freezer. Rummaging around inside, all she saw was disorganization and chaos. Her life was in shambles, and he didn't seem to care! They functioned on auto-pilot in a haunted house. They worked, cooked and cleaned day after day, all the while telling themselves it wouldn't be like this forever. One day things would be alright again.

Julie wondered whether her suspicions were correct after all.

Was Marc having an affair? Was that why he insisted on going out of town so often? He claimed it was for the overtime, and that he had no choice, but was that really true? She had no proof of course, and Marc's paychecks *seemed* to reflect the overtime hours he claimed to be working, but she was no fool. Their relationship was strained and awkward.

Her husband, usually so loving and involved had become emotionally distant, almost selfish. He didn't even involve himself with the children anymore, and it had been a long time since they'd been intimate.

Boxes and bags full of frozen food practically flew from one side of the freezer to the other as she searched for something to make for dinner.

Julie's eyes swam with tears as she pulled a package from the depths of the freezer. Not even bothering to look at the label, she stomped her way back up to the kitchen. With her back to Marc, she counted to ten over and over in her head.

Amélie and Adam were fighting again. She could hear them screeching at each other down the hallway.

Marc ignored it all, calmly watching the news on TV, his arms folded resolutely.

Of course, she thought bitterly. He's more interested in that, than his own family! How typical.

The chunk of frozen meat hit the glass dish inside the microwave with a clatter and she punched buttons angrily to start the defrosting process.

"Hey, watch it," Marc admonished her, darting an irritated glance in her direction. "You're gonna break that thing and then we'll have another bill I can't afford."

Julie rounded on him, her index finger already in the air. "I don't need your sarcastic comments," she said, her voice dangerously low. "If you're gonna keep that up, you might as well leave."

A range of emotions chased each other across Marc's face. His jaw tightened and his normally flushed countenance flamed into a red so deep, it shocked her to see it.

"I, uh …" she began.

"No!" Marc shouted. "For once, I think you're right."

With that, Marc turned on his heel and stormed down the staircase, much as she'd done. A few moments later, the house shook as Marc slammed the front door after him.

Julie continued to stare at the place where her husband had stood only moments before. Had he just left her? Was this the forever break-up she'd been dreading?

Julie's hands shook with suppressed emotion. Automatically, her hand fluttered to the gold crucifix at her neck.

"Please God, please," she whispered. Closing her eyes in heartfelt prayer, she leaned heavily against the kitchen counter, hardly daring to breathe as she waited for the sound that would come next: the whine of an engine as he drove away.

"Don't let him leave us," she prayed. "Please make him see. This house is turning us against each other. Please God, we have to get out of here *together*. Please make him see."

The heat of Marc's anger transferred through his powerful shoulders as he slammed the front door. He was aware that his actions could very well cause damage, but he didn't care. He hesitated outside the driver's door of the minivan, keys jingling in his palm as he tried to slow down and think. Why was she always so head-strong? What the hell was wrong with her, anyways? She acted like she didn't even trust him anymore. I'm a stranger in my own house!

Before he even realized, Marc was striding down the steep driveway, his long legs covering ground quickly, taking him farther and farther from the source of his stress.

The anger in his head and heart faded with each step, but Marc kept going, his arms and legs pumping fiercely in the cool night air.

As the moments passed, his thoughts cleared, and gradually his pace slowed to a steady, soothing rhythm.

It was a beautiful night, he thought, looking up at the stars twinkling overhead. The orange glow from the streetlights obscured portions of the sky, and Marc wondered idly what it would be like when they were finally able to escape subdivision life. At the cabin, the night sky was always so clear, with an unobstructed view of the heavens.

"That's what I want," he whispered as his footsteps brought him around the final curve of their block. "A little solitude."

Marc stood at the base of the driveway and looked up. With all the rooms fully lit, it wasn't hard to see what was going on through the gauzy curtains. He had a clear view of his wife as she moved rapidly from room to room.

She's a whirlwind, he thought, a sardonic smile pulling up on the corners of his mouth. What were we fighting about, anyway? Try though he might, Marc couldn't remember.

If it wasn't so maddening it would be laughable. Just a couple of minutes earlier, he had been ready to leave his wife, his children and this house.

This house.

The more Marc thought about it, the surer he felt that somehow, both of their irrational anger was being fuelled by someone they could not see or hear in their conscious mind. They were all being influenced.

Marc squared his shoulders for a moment before hauling open the heavy front door.

The walk had done him a world of good, and now that he fully realized the implications, he needed to have a plan. He only hoped that Julie, pissed off as she was, would work with him to figure one out. He needed her cooperation.

"Jules?" he called, closing the door after him. "I'm back."

"Good for you!" Her sharp reply from upstairs reached him easily. Apparently, she was still just as angry as she'd been when he left.

Marc wasn't normally an argumentative guy, but lately, he'd taken an almost perverse sense of satisfaction in the creatively snide comments he threw at his wife. He realized now how easily these venomous comments came to his mind. Often, they supplanted earlier more gentle thoughts.

And that simply wasn't him.

~~~~

In the weeks that followed, Julie's mood blackened to the point where anything unusual resulted in tears. Anne came upstairs often, efficiency on her mind and a question on her lips, only to discover a young woman staring into space, tears running unchecked down her cheeks.

It was alarming for her parents to see her this way, but Julie couldn't bring herself to care.

At least no one was yelling at her.

It was a grey day when she and Marc made the long drive in to see the doctor.

The appointment passed by in a blur.

The doctor assured them both that the pills he was prescribing were a temporary tool to help Julie through this rough patch in her life. She was advised to try yoga and meditation, to combat the high anxiety she lived with daily.

"It's stressful raising two children, especially one on the Autism Spectrum," he pointed out kindly as they left his office. "Keep your chin up, things will get better with time."

Marc and Julie had nodded and listened patiently, but inside they were both certain that the unpredictability of their ghostly houseguest also played a huge role in Julie's condition.

"This is so not like me," she said to her husband as they left the doctor's office, prescription in hand.

"I know, I know, but these pills will help. Just be patient, you'll see.

Marc gritted his teeth and tried to smile as Julie shuffled through the room like a sleepwalker, paying no heed to the question he'd already asked her, three times.

"I'm gonna take that as a yes," he commented dryly. Grabbing the phone, he called his best friend Luke, and made last-minute arrangements for a quick camping get-away for the two families. It was a good distraction, and by going on vacation with friends, his wife would be more likely to show her fun-loving side, at least *trying* to be happy for a few days.

~~~~

Since Julie's parents were away too, and taking a cat on a camping trip wasn't a good idea, Marc suggested they call his little sister Mandy to ask if she would house-sit for them.

"Sure! I'm game," she replied. "It'll be a nice change of pace," she laughed.

Marc happily stocked the fridge and the pantry with food for Mandy, then packed up the children, the dog and their camping gear as quickly as he could, whisking them off for their holiday long-weekend.

The short trip did the trick for Marc, who felt energized spending time with his best friend. Luke and Brianna were avid campers and hikers, eager to explore the surrounding countryside whenever the opportunity presented itself.

Julie tried to get into the swing of it, but with the lack of predictability for Adam, it was a lot more work than fun.

Still, the sites they visited were beautiful and wasn't her mom always saying how a change was just as good as a rest? So what if they didn't get much sleep? They could catch up when they got home.

Yeah …sure, she thought dryly. What a loaded statement that was!

Lakes and rivers flashed by the windows of the minivan as they raced along in search of Luke's favourite campsites. Marc loved to tease his friend, and took every opportunity to point out the flaws in his friend's logic.

"Where's this one located?" he'd teased his friend. "Next to a railroad track?"

"Oh, come on! Where's your sense of adventure?" Luke replied, a broad grin on his tanned face.

The camera captured new experiences, as Luke led the way confidently, his powerful legs climbing easily over boulders and brush as the two families explored the surrounding wilderness. But setting up and striking camp in three different locations over as many days was tiring, especially with children! Brianna and Julie hid their weary eyes behind large, oval sunglasses, determined to make the most of their trip and their time together.

Sensing their wives were about to mutiny, Marc and Luke banished the women from the campsite one afternoon, loudly proclaiming they would make dinner with the small camp stove and open fire.

With wary glances at their children, Brianna warned her husband. "You'd better keep an eye on the kids and let Marc do the cooking, you're liable to burn everything and we're gonna be hungry when we get back." Her soft voice held a hint of danger as she locked eyes with her husband.

"Yes dear," Luke answered contritely, with a sly wink in Marc's direction.

"Get out on those paths over there and wander for a bit," Marc suggested. "We saw a beautiful little creek down there. You two deserve a break!"

"Yeah, leave it to your wonderful husbands; it'll be a great surprise," Luke added. The cheesy grin only added to the comedy of the moment, and Julie found herself laughing.

That sound had been missing for so long, she almost didn't recognise it.

"Oh, I'm sure we'll be surprised," Brianna laughed, shaking her head good naturedly as she spoke. "I only hope it's a good surprise."

Julie darted a look back at the tents as the women turned to go. "Adam isn't in a very good mood," she commented, uneasily.

"Just leave him here," Marc answered with a shrug. "He likes the tent, and I'm one half of this parenting team, aren't I? I can handle it. Now will you two just go? Just take the dog and this walkie-talkie." He handed Brianna the small device and waved his hand dismissively.

"Alright," the women agreed in unison.

With a backwards glance at the bright colors of their camp, Julie had to hurry to keep up with Brianna's brisk pace.

She longed to enjoy life again. When would these pills take effect? Why couldn't she just 'snap out of it'?

The trees surrounding her waved their boughs as the two women passed. "Go, go, go!" they seemed to say. Julie forced another smile onto her face and breathed deeply. The mountain air felt good in her lungs.

"You okay?" Brianna asked, her naturally soft voice held a note of concern.

"Yeah, I guess," Julie replied automatically.

"But you're not really, are you?" Brianna, perceptive to the feelings of others was not easily fooled.

"No, not really," Julie admitted. "I really want to be Bri, but I'm just … not."

"Tell you what? Endorphins are what you need. Let's pick up the pace! C'mon, follow me!"

"Okay, c'mon Keisha! Let's run," she challenged the energetic dog at the end of the bright red leash.

The dog leapt into action, running easily over rocks and fallen logs while her human counterparts followed as quickly as they dared. The terrain underfoot was rocky, and mostly uphill. Soon Julie was removing the extra sweater she'd been wrapped in all day and tying it at her waist.

"Wow! This is a workout!" she commented, aware that for the first time all weekend, she was feeling better in her own head.

By the time the trail opened out to the mountain stream Luke had promised, both women were ready for a break.

Settling onto the large boulders at the sides of the rushing stream, Brianna turned to her friend. "You want to talk?" she said. "I'm all ears."

This time Julie didn't have to force a smile. Brianna always knew just what to say!

Hours later, as afternoon faded into evening, the women returned from their mad dash through the forest to find that not only was dinner not burned, but the children were all sitting together at one of the picnic tables, happily gluing, coloring and digging through the ample collection of art supplies Brianna had brought, that now covered the plastic table cloth end to end.

She couldn't help grinning as she walked up and wrapped her arms around her husband. He was right, this trip was just what she needed. She was starting to feel like her old self. "Thanks honey," she whispered, hugging him harder. "That was a great idea! I just have one question."

"Sure!" Marc answered, a wide grin lighting up his handsome face. "What's that?"

Julie pressed both hands together in a pleading gesture. "Do we have to go home?"

Chapter Thirty-four

Marc expected to see his sister at the house, since she had no classes and wasn't scheduled to work that day. He and Julie had talked about making a nice supper for her, to thank her for house-sitting.

But when they arrived, the house was empty. Strangely, the door to her parent's suite sat propped open with a pile of heavy shoes, and a box of laundry soap braced the door to the den.

"That's weird," Marc commented, climbing the stairs.

Julie shrugged and hung up the hastily discarded jackets her children had thrown on the floor as they ran through the foyer and up the stairs.

Marc soon discovered a note left on the kitchen table.

Mandy's distinct handwriting covered the sheet of lined paper, and Julie's heart dropped as she read over her husband's shoulder.

HI!

Sorry I'm not there. I hope you had a good time. Don't worry, nothing's broken, I think. ☺

I left the doors blocked open downstairs, as you can see, For some reason, they made a lot of noise last night. I don't know why. Maybe the wind? Unfortunately, I didn't sleep that well, so I went home early. I'm starting a new class tomorrow and I need a solid night in my own bed.

BTW, Since you said before that it was fine with you, Tom came over Saturday night so I didn't have to be here alone. It's kinda creepy here at night! Ha-ha! Talk to you soon, Mandy

"Oh geez," Marc said, running a hand through his hair in a gesture Julie knew well.

"What did she mean about the doors making noise?" Julie asked. "That doesn't sound good."

"Yeah," Marc admitted. "Obviously, she was a bit spooked being here alone. Good thing I told her we were okay with Tom coming over."

"Your parents would have a cow if they knew that," Julie laughed.

"Yeah, that's true," Marc replied. "But she is in college after all." He was still frowning as he followed Julie back down the stairs to grab the rest of the camping gear.

The couple worked together to bring in the last item, an awkwardly-sized cooler, still heavy with food.

"How come we brought back more food than we packed?" Marc muttered irritably.

Julie rolled her eyes and chose not to answer. As they reached the top step, Julie's heel caught and she lost her footing, dropping her end of the cooler as she sat down hard.

"No!" she shouted.

"Whoah!" Marc added, grabbing for it quickly, as it slid toward him. He caught the full weight of the cooler, and managed not to topple backwards, but as he struggled to hold it, the lid popped open and a squeezable jar of mustard flew out. The top came off as it hit the first step, spraying mustard everywhere as it bounced down the remaining steps, leaving both carpet and walls stained with big yellow blotches of goo.

"Oh NO!" Julie groaned. "Not mustard!"

"What a mess," Marc agreed.

"You have no idea," she said dejectedly. "Mustard never comes out!"

"Gre-eat," Marc groaned, his shoulders slumping. "I feel a renovation project coming on."

<div align="center">~~~~</div>

The medication that Julie took for the depression had an unpleasant side-effect, and the normally petite woman began to gain weight, her mood worsening as she packed on the pounds.

As the weeks passed, Julie became increasingly bitter, instead of more positive as the doctor had promised. Marc suggested a date-night, hoping that might give his wife something to look forward to. Despite repeated attempts to set that up, however his little sister Mandy continued to be unavailable, and her comments strangely cryptic.

"Uh, I could watch them here, if you want," she answered, hesitantly.

"Sorry, but you and I both know mom and dad won't go for that. Last time, Adam hid dad's remote control for the TV, and then the little bugger tried taking apart the VCR, remember? Dad was furious!"

"Oh, right …" Mandy trailed off. "Sorry bro, in that case, no can do. I have to study. I, have a project due um … soon."

Marc hung up the phone with a look of confusion.

"What's going on with her?" He wondered aloud.

~~~~~

Marc was desperate for some inner peace, and tired of dodging Julie's questions about when they were gonna rip up and replace the stained carpet on the stairs, the house-beautiful projects seemed to be the only thing she still cared about.

Julie's answer to the imperfections she saw all around her was to fix them all, immediately. It was no secret that she grew impatient and excited about projects, and she wished Marc shared her enthusiasm, but with their budget so tight, it was a careful game, not unlike tug-of-war.

So, when opportunities came along for Marc to work out of town and make some overtime, he jumped at the chance, thinking that while his wife wouldn't be completely on board, he knew she could never outright prove he was leaving on purpose. If he couldn't find the solitude he craved at home, he'd search for it in his work.

"So, you're going away again?" Julie asked, walking slowly into the bedroom.

Marc looked up, a pair of folded pajamas in his hands, an open suitcase on the bed.
~~~~~

"Uh, yeah, I gotta go swap out some equipment at an office on the island," he said, wincing inside as he wondered how his wife would react. He'd been putting off telling her, unsure of how to broach the subject. "I'll get some good overtime hours, and it'll only be about a week or so."

"Hmm, okay," she said, her voice devoid of emotion. Turning around, Julie left the room. Her rubber-soled slippers scuffed against the carpet with slow repetition.

"Creepy," Marc muttered, watching her go.

~~~~~

Julie threw off the covers and sat up.

Something was different.

A glance at her bedside table showed that it wasn't quite six o'clock, and yet she was wide awake with a list of things she wanted to get done, slowly populating in her mind.

Later that day, with several things already crossed off her list, Julie marvelled at the energy she still had! Making her way down to the garage, she took a deep breath. It was always such a mess in there, she thought. Will I even find what I'm looking for?

The time flew by and soon it was time to pick up the kids from school. Just one more box! She thought to herself, as she spied one that was still sealed with packing tape across the top.

"Eureka!" she cried, ripping it open. A dusty aerobic step and instructional videos, along with skipping ropes and a pair of well-worn runners lay in the bottom of the box. "Just as I remember it," she sighed triumphantly. "Now we'll see!"

Within days, working out had became Julie's new addiction. Mornings, before the children woke up, the young mother plugged in the video and followed along as best she could while laughing at her own clumsiness. Eventually she became more proficient with the 'step aerobics' lessons and looked forward to them like she would a visit with a dear friend. With the added sense of control she felt at dropping the excess pounds, Julie's renovation bug seemed to fade as well.

Marc's arrival from that trip was the happiest reunion either of them had enjoyed in what seemed like years! He was elated that his
~~~~~

wife had finally discovered something to perk up her mood, but even so the Julie he knew was still masked behind the meds.

"Julie, I can't help but notice, you're always on the move, and you're not eating regularly, either." Her mother said as Julie came back in the front door. She's just come from taking Adam to school, with Amélie in the jogging stroller.

"It's all those endorphins mom," Julie explained. "Exercise is the only thing that makes me feel better. Remember the doctors said I have to stay active. It's either that, or I take more meds, and we all know how fat I got doing that!"

Anne frowned at her daughter. "So you're not taking the medication anymore?"

"Nope! And I feel way better, too."

"Alright dear, as long as you don't become obsessed."

"Obsessed? Is that what everyone's saying now? That's hilarious! I dare them to live my life for even one day! They wouldn't be able to take it without some sort of obsession," she replied lightly. "Besides, exercise is good for me. Sometimes, it's like I could keep running forever."

"Well you can't," Anne answered bluntly. "You have responsibilities."

Julie shook her head and grinned at her mom.

"You're under a great deal of stress," her mother noted. "It's good to see you smiling again, but your father and I are still concerned. Are you and Marc okay?"

Anne looked at her daughter uncertainly. It was obvious she didn't know how to put her thoughts into words.

Julie's expression clouded. "We're managing, we're doing okay. Don't worry."

"Worrying is a mother's job," her mom replied, smiling weakly. "And watching you waste away to nothing is gonna make me worry more."

"I'm not wasting away," she argued. "I'm just fit! I feel better than ever."

As Julie undid the straps to release her daughter from the stroller, Ami went to her grandmother with a wide grin. Anne stooped to pick up her granddaughter. As she did so, she glanced hesitantly at her daughter.

Julie turned. "What is it mom?"

"Well, I hate to mention it."

"I'll be more worried if you don't tell me."

"Well, it's just Adam's little trampoline."

"The rebounder?"

"Yes, remember we talked about it before? When Adam jumps on it in the family room, it bangs on our ceiling and makes such a racket."

"Sure, I remember." Julie frowned and looked to her right through the glass doors. "It seemed like such a good idea when we bought it."

"That's alright dear, but we really can't take it anymore. It has to get moved."

"What?" Julie looked once more through the closed doors and into the room beyond as she spoke. "Mom, we did, already."

"No dear, maybe you just thought you did. I know how busy you get." Her mother argued.

"Mom, we took care of it," she reasoned. "Marc and I moved it several days ago. It's -"

"You couldn't have," her mother interrupted. "I heard it again this morning, obviously before you were up."

Julie took a deep breath and let it out slowly. "Mom, c'mere a minute, okay? I want to show you something."

Anne allowed herself to be led, arms still wrapped securely around her granddaughter.

"Look," Julie pointed at the small trampoline in the den. "It's been there since last Sunday."

Her mother went silent as she stared through the glass door. A moment later, she handed the child back to Julie and went silently back through her front door, closing it firmly behind her.

~~~

Julie faced the dancing flames of the campfire and cocked her head to one side.

"I feel so much better here," she sighed.

"Me too," Marc agreed, poking at the embers on his side with a long, crooked stick.

"Yeah, and we didn't have to haul up a tonne of stuff for Ami now that's she's older. Bringing a baby up here isn't great."
~~~

"True," Marc agreed. "Is Adam asleep?"

"Yup, he's out like a light."

"Nice. And Ami?"

"Sleeping like a lamb." Julie produced the battery-powered baby monitor they'd brought with them from her pocket and set it on the bench between them.

"Figures," Marc muttered. "Never sleeps like that at home."

"Can't blame her," Julie muttered. "Neither do I."

They sat together, enjoying the crackling fire and the silence, but both were keenly aware there was so much they needed to talk about.

Finally, Julie turned and looked at her husband, the glow of the campfire lighting up half of his rugged face. "I wish I loved our new house as much as I love this place" she said. "I'm sorry."

"Why sorry?" Marc asked, still poking at the fire.

"Well, we have such a big mortgage now, and I feel like maybe we bought the house because I wanted us to."

"Nah, I was drawn to it too. I wanted that house as much as you did."

"Sounds like you don't want it anymore," she queried.

"I wouldn't say that exactly. But I feel the same as you. I love being here," he waved his hand around at the surrounding darkness. "And I'm not in a hurry to go home. This place feels so calm, so inviting. Even out here in the pitch black. I know exactly where I am. There's no sense of disorientation, no uncertainty. Our house doesn't feel like that."

"You're right." She moved her feet closer to the fire and drained the last drops from her wine glass. "But why couldn't you tell, when we first looked at it? Why didn't you feel anything different then?"

Marc frowned. "I don't know. I've been trying to figure that out too. It's not like this thing is an exact science, after all. But you're right. I should have been able to sense something. I mean now, it hits me in the face as soon as I walk through the front door, but then … I don't know. All I can think, is maybe it was hiding."

"Could it do that?"

"Search me. I don't pretend to understand any of this, or even why it's there in the first place."

"Or what it wants from us," Julie added.

"If it wants anything at all." Marc picked up the can of beer at his side and took a long drink.

"Marc, do you remember when we were looking at houses? There were some you wouldn't go into. You just said they weren't right. What did you mean?"

"Well," Marc stared into the flames for a few moments, searching for a way to put his thoughts into words. "The air felt …heavy. Negative. You know when you're in a bad mood, and everything pisses you off?""

Julie smiled ruefully. "Yup."

"Well, when we got out of the car and went inside, I was instantly angry, only there wasn't any reason for it. You know what I mean?"

"Yeah," Julie chuckled. "I get like that when I'm having PMS. You got PMS symptoms from a house?"

"Very funny. You asked me to describe it, so I'm trying."

"Sorry. Go on."

"So no, not PMS. But places, like people, can retain energy. They soak up stuff that's either positive or negative, you know? And in that house, it felt like someone was barring the door saying 'you can't come in here.' Didn't you feel the pressure change?"

"I didn't feel anything at all, except a bit confused why you weren't following me inside," she confessed, smiling.

"Well, that's the reason I didn't come in. Remember that electricity you felt on your hand?" he asked.

"Oh yeah. I'll never forget."

"Okay, so take that, and add in a strong magnetic pull that feels so negative it almost makes you sick."

"Wow. Okay, well I can understand why you didn't want to go in then. And yet you didn't feel that way when we looked at our house."

"I don't know why," Marc admitted. "Usually when something is as strong as that, I'll feel it right away. I can sure feel it now."

Julie looked askance at her husband.

"Oh, not here," he corrected. "I meant I feel it at our house. The thing is," he continued. "As soon as I know a spirit is there, the spirit knows about me. It's like a mutual recognition. And that's all I need to make me walk away."

"Except now it's too late to walk away," she whispered, twirling the stem of her empty wine glass between her fingers. "And I don't even know how to fight it Marc."

"Neither do I."

~~~~

Life continued for the beleaguered couple as it always had. Bumps in the night were now the norm, and anomalies didn't just happen, they were expected.

When Abby called her best friend excitedly to report that she and Jake were getting a new place, Julie wept for joy. At least Abby would no longer be plagued by unseen forces in her new home. And she wouldn't have to worry about her young son being influenced by something they couldn't see. It was a relief, but Julie couldn't help feeling a pang of jealousy. Abby's solution seemed so simple, and yet it was the only thing she and Marc couldn't do!

They'd tied everything up in this stupid house, she thought irritably. If only they could move and leave this manipulative spirit to his own tricks, that would show him!

~~~~

As she walked, Amélie chatted to herself, often turning to scold her mother for some imagined transgression, wagging her finger at Julie and frowning.

"No, you don't mommy!" she would say.

Amélie talked everywhere she went, regardless of whether there was someone there to talk to.

"She never stops talking," Julie commented to her husband, as she followed their daughter at close range. "I'll be darned if I know who she's talking to, though."

"She's a girl," Marc said, as though this explained everything.

Julie stuck her tongue out at her husband and made a face. "Be nice," she said.

In truth, the little phrases their daughter used began to make more sense, the more times they heard them. Amélie was quickly perfecting her speech.

She talked a lot about fairies and colors to her bewildered parents, as they tried to coax her into eating her lunch or dinner. She also repeated much of what she heard her brother saying.

"Trains goin' …whoosh!" she would say with a quick smile at her brother.

Adam, who often ignored his sister, seemed to suddenly realize these sounds she was making had meaning, and he paid closer attention.

Amélie was thrilled by her brother's sudden interest, and in the months following this strange discovery, the two of them could be found together often, Amélie copying whatever her big brother said.

Adam, for his part was repeating movie phrases, and although his baby sister couldn't articulate that well yet, it didn't seem to matter.

Julie and Marc, thrilled at the interaction, encouraged it.

But when Adam went to school, Amélie, instead of turning to Julie for a playmate, grabbed one of her dolls and toddled off to her room, where she sat on the carpet, talking and laughing to herself.

Concerned that maybe their daughter was feeling abandoned and perhaps this was a sign of loneliness, Julie went down the hall, and stood close by the open doorway, where she could easily listen, without being observed.

"No! Iss mines! No don't …me do … okay …mommy… uhh, and daddy, and Adam!"

The sound of laughter and clapping hands made Julie smile, but a moment later, the smile slipped from her face.

"No!" Amélie's sharp rebuke was startling. "No. Dats mean. You can't do dat. You a bad gull! You gonna' get trouble."

"Ami?" Julie called to her, rounding the corner.

Amélie looked startled, but quickly recovered and returned a fake-looking smile.

"What mommy?"

"Who are you talking to in here?"

"Dessie," she announced, as though this was no big deal.

"Who?"

"Dessie," Amélie repeated.

"Who's Jessie?" Julie asked, looking around the room in wonder.

"A gull," Amélie answered, again in that same matter-of-fact way, as though Julie's questions were ridiculous.

"Oh, okay. Can you see her?"

"Uh-huh," she nodded confidently. "Over dare!" Amélie pointed across from where she sat, a pile of stuffed toys on the carpet in front of her crossed legs. The way the toys were piled, suggested Amélie was sharing with this imaginary child.

"Oh, that's so nice, you're sharing your toys," she said.

"Yes," she replied emphatically. As she said this, Amélie turned to one side and stuck out her tongue as though taunting another child.

Julie stifled her laughter with one hand. Amélie sure told that friend a thing or two!

"Okay, you keep playing then," she said, as she left the room.

But when Julie was half-way down the hall and she knew Ami couldn't see her anymore, she stopped to listen again. She wasn't surprised to hear the one-sided conversation resume.

"Nuh-uh, mommy said no," she heard her daughter say. "Ssh."

Shaking her head, Julie resumed her tasks in the kitchen, confident that this was just another phase that Amélie would soon outgrow. Most children had imaginary friends, didn't they?

~~~~

"Ami," she called to her daughter. "It's snack time! Do you want fishy crackers or something else?"

"Ami?" Julie called again, getting no response, even though the child was sitting only a few feet from her. "Come here please. Mommy's got your snack."

When she still didn't respond, Julie walked over and picked her up.

"Gone, mommy," she said.

Julie heaved a weary sigh. "Ami, we've been over this. Mommy isn't going anywhere. Now come on, you little monkey it's snack time. Aren't you hungry?" Julie fitted the child into the high chair without waiting for an answer.

"No!" Amélie insisted, as Julie worked to get the safety strap done up with the tiny girl kicking her legs in defiance. "Gone! Da gull. She gone!"

"Ami, settle down," Julie replied, exasperated. "What are you on about now? Who's gone?"

Amélie, kicking harder, shouted at her mother. "Da GULL!"

"Ami!" Julie said angrily. "Stop it NOW!"

The child stopped and looked at her mother with wide eyes, surprised by Julie's sudden show of temper.
~~~~

The young mother clicked the highchair tray into place, and pointed to the snack in front of the child. "Here's your snack. If you're hungry, now is the time to eat. You can tell mommy about the birds when you're all done."

"No," Amélie pushed at the tray, obviously still upset. "Not a bud …a gull."

"Well I'm afraid all we have today is fruit and fishy crackers," she said pointing to the tray. "No seagulls. Come on now, you love fishies! At least you did yesterday."

Amélie pushed at the tray again and shook her head at Julie.

"Okay tell you what? Mommy will look for birdie crackers next time we go to the store, but today it's just fishies. Just try it."

Amélie heaved a sigh of her own but began eating the snack in front of her. As she ate, she craned her neck around the edge of the chair to look down the stairs.

"What are you looking for?" Julie said, glancing down the empty staircase. "Somebody here?"

"I wanna see da Gull," Amélie replied.

"Are you saying girl?" Julie asked, smoothing her daughter's hair affectionately.

Amélie immediately smiled, and clapped her hands together. "Yes! Gull!" she replied excitedly, banging her legs against the chair. "Da Gull mommy, da gull!"

"Okay, okay," Julie replied, grinning. "Yay for mommy. I got one! At least now we know you're saying 'girl' but I still don't know why."

Amélie seemed irritated by Julie's statement, and darted a withering glance at her poor, stupid mother.

Chapter Thirty-five

"So apparently, that's how she says 'girl', Marc. I still don't know why she was so adamant about it though. But I'm glad I figured it out. She got so mad at me when I thought she was talking about birds."

Marc laughed and looked affectionately at his children, where they sat curled up together on the couch, watching a movie on TV.

"What girl is she talking about?" Marc asked, looking to his wife.

Julie shrugged. "I don't know. An imaginary friend?" she guessed. "She chats away in her room sometimes like she's playing with another child. Maybe that's this mysterious 'gull'?"

"Hmm, maybe."

"Maybe we should mention this to Ariel," Marc suggested later as they got ready for bed. "Maybe Ami has Autism too."

Julie looked at him sharply. "Don't even say that," she replied, her voice low. It's probably just a phase she's going through. It's imaginative play, right? That's usually a good sign, not a cause for worry. I don't think we need to involve Ariel. Why are you getting so worked up?"

"No one is getting worked up," Marc argued. "But we do have one child with Autism. Remember what the doctors said? There's a chance she might have it too. You've heard how she goes around repeating things. Adam did that too remember?"

Julie started to reply, but Marc cut her off.

"What's the harm in enlisting the advice of a professional? Just humour me, okay?"

Julie, biting her tongue to hold back the retort, stewed in silence.

~~~~

"No," she replied, still clinging to her father's neck, Amélie shook her head vehemently.

"Ami, there's no girl here," her mother ventured, looking around the room. But instead of being mollified by the statement, the little girl lost her temper. Bright red spots flared in both cheeks and she balled her tiny hands into tight fists.

"Dessie!" she shouted, pointing imperiously down the hall. "Right dare!"

"Ummm, Marc? Do you …?"

"I don't see anything either, but I'm not gonna let on and neither are you," he replied, his voice taking on a sing-song lilt as he spoke through his teeth, grinning at the toddler in his arms. He'd begun rocking from one foot to the other, bouncing her the way he did when trying to soothe one of her tantrums. Marc was practiced at this.

Registering the non-verbal cue, she dropped the subject.

"Okay," she said, rubbing her hands together and faking an excited smile. "Over there, of course! I didn't see her before. Hi Jessie." Looking down the hallway, she pointed the way Amélie had, and waved at her daughter's imaginary friend.

If Amélie wanted to play this game, her mother would play; anything to head off another tantrum.

The tiny girl's mood changed like the flip of a switch. A smile replaced the suspicious frown she'd worn only moments before. As soon as her feet touched the floor, her eyes darted to her favourite toy, and moments later, she was merrily pushing a brightly colored toy shopping cart away into the next room. Marc could hear her chattering away as she bumped the toy off walls and furniture.

Husband and wife watched her go, identical expressions of wonder on their faces.
~~~~

The deep sigh they heaved came out at the same time. Suddenly, the nervous laughter Julie had been holding back, threatened to explode and she turned away quickly, pressing one hand against her mouth.

"Julie?" Marc followed, concern in his voice. "Are you okay?"

Safely out of sight, Julie removing her hand and laughed. "What a kid!" she said, in between giggles. "She's so serious."

"I know," Marc replied, allowing a grin to spread across his own face. "Is this parenthood? What next?"

"I'm not sure," Julie replied, shrugging. "We never had this with Adam."

"Are you calling Ariel, or am I?" Marc asked, raising his eyebrows.

"Okay, okay, I'll call her tomorrow."

~~~~~

"Amélie is not Autistic," Ariel's soothing voice came over the phone. "She doesn't show any of the markers, except the verbal copying you've seen. My suggestion is to get her enrolled in a play group as soon as possible. When she meets the other children, and has more people to copy you should see these behaviours go away. Then you and Marc can truly relax about this. Right now, the only person she has to copy is her brother, so it's no wonder you're feeling a bit nervous."

Marc and Julie breathed a collective sigh of relief as their daughter's behaviour changed, becoming less repetitive and solitary. But even though their daughter's social skills improved along with her vocabulary, the most mystifying of her behaviours continued to baffle them.

Amélie continued to have long talks with an invisible little girl

Amélie interrupted the conversation at the dinner table with news of her own.

"Dessie got mad a' me today."

Marc looked at his wife. "This again?" He muttered.

Julie shrugged.

"Oh right, your little friend, Jessie. She's mad at you? Why?"

"She din't come a' school." Amélie replied with a slight shrug of her tiny shoulders. "On a'ly me."

Julie and Marc shook their heads and exchanged puzzled looks.

~~~~~

As spring approached, and Amélie continued to talk about and play with her imaginary friend, Marc and Julie looked forward to their daughter's first preschool experience.

The costs of their complicated life made Marc cringe, wondering how he was going to continue to pay all these bills with one income. Even with the overtime, they lived paycheck to paycheck.

At the same time, Adam's temper was soaring to new heights and his behaviour at school plummeting. The school called almost daily now, demanding that Julie pick him up immediately, making it clear that they didn't have a place for children like him in their midst. Until he could learn to modify his behaviour, he wasn't welcome.

Due to what they labeled as his 'unpredictable behaviour', Adam was deemed unacceptable for participating in class field trips and any special classroom parties unless she or Marc was present, no matter what. The added stress and anger this caused, made everything else ten times worse.

Their home environment was like a pot on the very edge of boiling over. When one crisis was handled, another three popped up in its place.

Although both parents were eager to support him, Adam acted worse when his parents went to the school, effectively sealing the deal and striking his name from the class field trip list.

Neither parent knew what more they could do. All Adam knew was that he was missing out.

Furthermore, he was convinced that the teachers hated him. This was borne out every time Julie and Marc touched pen to paper to converse with their son.

Why is Adam so angry? Julie wrote.

HATE HIM. Adam printed, in large, blocky letters.

Hate who? Julie wrote.

TEACHER.

Whoah! She thought. This is big. Let's slow down a bit.

On the page, Julie wrote: HATE HIM means:

A) Adam hates the teacher

B) Someone else hates the teacher

C) Something else.

Adam took pen in his hand and carefully circled the letter C.

Okay, here I go again," she thought.

Trying a different tactic, she wrote ___________ hates ___________.

The letters her son wrote spilled over each line, but there was no mistaking them. Her son pressed so hard, he almost tore the paper. As soon as he finished the last letter, he got up from the table and ran to his room, slamming the door, hard. Adam's angry, hurt sobs were audible even in the kitchen.

She should have followed, trying to comfort him, but her own eyes were too full of tears.

The letter on the paper in front lost focus as tears clouded her vision.

TEACHER hates ADAM.

~~~~

"Anger and frustration are poor bed-fellows for effective advocacy," Anne warned her daughter. "You've got to try and simmer down before you go in there."

"I know it," Julie muttered, her voice low and dangerous. "But mom, so help me, they've picked on the wrong family!"

One week later, a meeting was called by the school board, and Adam's teacher was firmly invited to take some 'sensitivity' training.

But apart from some vague promises that the teacher would eventually partake of this, and the school administration would 'keep a close eye on the matter' there was nothing more they could do.

And so, the pressure mounted each day, as Julie took her son to school and stood by the door, glaring openly at the classroom teacher.

It was only a matter of a few days before Julie was invited to a meeting in the principal's office, and asked not to do that anymore.

Marc was angry over what he termed 'their fish bowl environment'. He craved space and privacy, two things that they could never have in a neighbourhood where houses stood shoulder to shoulder and the backyards were tiered in such a way that they all looked in on each other.

"I hate it!" he fumed, as Julie handed him a tray of food to be cooked on the barbecue. "Everyone's business is everyone's business."

"I hear ya, but what can we do?" she sympathized.
~~~~

Marc stepped out on the back deck, and lit the barbecue, casting side-long glances at their nearest neighbour.

To his relief, their deck was empty. They got along fine, but Marc was just so done with being on display all the time, both inside their house and out.

So what if you can see me? Do you have to say something every time?

Just as Marc was lowering the lid on the barbecue, a man's voice called out from another adjacent yard. "What's for supper, Marc? That's a lotta smoke you got goin' on there! Maybe I'd better call the fire department."

Instead of laughing along, Marc simply pretended he hadn't heard, and went back inside, banging the glass door so hard it almost jumped off its track.

Julie heard the noise and turned quickly, but seeing Marc's expression, she bit back her comment. Instead, she watched in curiosity as Marc, still muttering curses, took the stairs two at a time. Julie heard the garage door open and close. In another moment, her husband reappeared, the local phone directory in his hands.

"Uh, Marc?" Julie asked. What was the phone directory doing in the garage, and why was he being so intense about it?

Her husband leafed through the thick book, almost tearing the delicate pages in his haste.

"What are you lookin' for hon?" she asked, trying to sound casual. "Can I help?"

Marc simply pressed his lips together and hunched farther over the book. A moment later, he stabbed his index finger at a listing on the page. "Aha! Found it!" Grabbing a nearby notepad, he scribbled some numbers onto it and stuck it to the fridge. "There," he said. "I've had enough. Let's see if we can get out of this place."

"Oh Marc!" she enthused, noting the name on the page bore the terms 'real estate'.

The couples' conversation that night was more hopeful than it had been in a long while, as they imagined properties surrounded by trees, where the nearest neighbour was a phone call away, instead of within shouting distance.

"Oh Marc," Julie sighed happily, snuggling down under the thick duvet. "Do you really think we can do it?"

"I don't know," he answered truthfully. "But it can't hurt to try. We've endured this long enough."

~~~~

"Okay, let's talk about the asking price," the realtor patiently explained the next evening. "The reality is, the market has taken another down-turn and properties like yours are flooding the market. So, although I realize you'd like to get this much," she tapped the paper in front of her where Marc had written some numbers. "That just isn't doable in today's market. Even if you get top dollar for your home, we're still gonna come in way under this."

"What about if we just moved to a different house, but stayed in a subdivision?" Julie asked.

Marc shot her a dark look

"Oh sure, if you want to upgrade to a newer home, that could still be doable. How much equity do you have here?"

"Not enough obviously," Marc replied softly. "But I don't want another subdivision house. We need some privacy and space. Lots of green space."

"Oh. Okay, that's different then. Are we talking about acreage?" the realtor asked, raising her carefully stencilled brows.

Marc sat back, his own brow furrowed in frustration. "Maybe. Even just a bigger lot would be nice. Are you saying it's out of the question?" he asked.

"Certainly not," the woman answered. "All I'm saying is that acreage is a hot ticket item right now. Everyone wants space," she smiled. "Properties come rarely and they go quickly. We'd have to act fast to secure one."

Julie felt tears spring to her eyes, but rose quickly from the couch to hide the fact. "Would anyone like some water?" she asked, walking towards the kitchen.

"No thank you," the woman declined politely. "I need to get going. I'll leave you this information. There's a few facts here about things to do when you're getting ready to sell. That part is just as important as the actual listing, and sometimes it can take a while to get it sale-ready." Carefully, she looked around her. Julie knew she was appraising all the little imperfections and she took deep, steadying breaths.
~~~~

"Remember, this is how the market is today. There's no telling how it's going to be in a few months. Real estate is like that. It ebbs and flows."

~~~

"There's no point trading this house for another one in a similar set-up," Marc reasoned later that evening.

Julie was so disappointed she felt like screaming. "Well that's a cheerful picture," she complained. What she wanted more than anything was to get out of that house and never look back, but going into another subdivision? She had to agree with Marc. Their yard was tiny now, but the houses they'd seen on the market lately had even smaller yards. And what if the same thing happened all over again? Would they be blinded by the beauty of hardwood and new appliances, missing the bigger picture? After all, this thing hid itself from them successfully until they'd already moved in and it was too late!

"So, we can't get away from a subdivision home?" she asked.

"Well, not with a single income, no." Marc explained. "But remember what she said. It might perk up in a few months. That would change the whole conversation."

"You believe that?" she asked dubiously.

"I think I have to," he said.

The couple shared a weary smile. Like it or not, they were in this together.

"So what do we do?" she asked. "Can we afford to tackle some projects? What if we make this house irresistible?"

Marc smiled at his wife's enthusiasm. "Heck," he joined in. "Maybe we can get some trees to grow in our back yard too, and then those nosey neighbours won't be able to see in!"

"I like it," Julie agreed. "Let's do it."

~~~

Laminate flooring was laid, and new paint coated the walls. The mustard stained carpet on the staircase was ripped out and replaced with stylish wooden planks. Even the yard looked less like a project and more like someone was actively caring for it.

Meanwhile, life went on. Julie's parents continued to worry that Amélie was having strange conversations with people who weren't there, and Adam suffered from something they termed 'night terrors'. The weary parents listened to the concerns carefully, but somehow, both Marc and Julie couldn't bring themselves to do anything about them. They'd already been down that road so many times, and knew there was no more that could be done. Neither of them could afford to spend their energy on things they didn't know how to fix.

They had an agenda, and selling this house was at the top of it. Both were convinced that selling and moving was the only way to make life better for all.

Chapter Thirty-six

"When were you going to tell me about you going back to work?" Marc asked his wife as he set about making breakfast for his family that morning.

"Huh?" Julie replied, moving quickly through the kitchen, a pair of Amélie's socks in one hand as she tracked down their youngest child.

"Ami!" she called sharply. "You can't just leave your socks everywhere like this. If your feet are hot, take off your socks in your own room."

"Julie!" he said sharply. The sound resonated louder than he'd intended and his wife whirled around.

"What?"

"About this job of yours. Did you really get an offer?"

"Yeah Marc, I really did. Adam's speech therapist told me about a friend of hers who was looking for part time help, so I asked a few questions, and voila!"

"So, when do you start?"

"Next Wednesday," she replied.

"Part time or full time?" he asked. "What are they paying you?"

"Part time to start. It's just administrative stuff, so we're gonna have to see if it's a good fit. It's a far cry from a newsroom, after all. And of course, we won't know if my mom can handle watching both kids unless we try it out. It's a good plan, Marc." Julie's tone was defensive and Marc knew he should probably drop the twenty questions routine, but he was still annoyed.

It was so unlike his wife to keep things to herself, and this was a pretty big secret to keep. What else was she keeping from him?

"Look honey," Julie explained, deliberately softening her tone. "You've been stressing over money more and more these past few months and while I couldn't help before, Amélie's older now and Adam is finally settling down to a point where I think, maybe, I can work a bit. Besides my mom volunteered to help, since she's fully retired now and Lord knows we need the money, so we can get the heck outta here."

"Yeah, you're right," he conceded. "I just hope it all works out."

"Fingers crossed," she quipped, rising on tip toes to give him a quick kiss. "Time will tell."

~~~~

"So the kids were in your line of sight all day? Every minute?"

"Yes dear. All day, every minute. This isn't my first rodeo, you know. I know what Adam is capable of and his sister is a willing accomplice," Anne replied.

Julie frowned and looked away.

"I have absolutely no idea who broke those figures," her mother continued. "But clearly it wasn't the kids. I don't know what else to tell you! Maybe it was the cat? He's an energetic sort."

Julie frowned, not trusting herself to answer.

When they first moved in, they had received two garden statues for a house warming gift. The statues stood two and half feet tall and resembled Greek cherubs, each balancing a chalice on one shoulder. They were sturdily built, but Marc felt they'd have a better life if they stayed in the living room.

Julie made a face. The statues looked anything but great now.

Both were missing their heads!

Small chips of pottery lay scattered over the rug in a trail of destruction.

Later, Julie related the news to her husband who was quick to investigate for himself.

"Geez! Are you kidding me?" he said, viewing the wreckage. "This is not the work of a cat. These things wouldn't break like this
~~~~

unless they were hit with something heavy, like a metal bar or a baseball bat."

"All my brooms are accounted for," Julie quipped.

"Nah, a broom handle wouldn't do this," Marc disagreed. "Not enough weight to it. Let's check Adam's room for a metal bat."

"Now how would he have one of those? I didn't give him one, did you?"

"Nope, but you know our son, he's resourceful. Maybe he conned his grandparents."

"Oh I hope not," she moaned.

"The thing is, why didn't your mom hear anything when it happened?"

"I dunno, she says neither one of them was out of her sight all day."

"And yet, we have smashed ornaments."

"I know," she said. "I don't understand it either." Crouching beside Adam's bed, she looked underneath. "Okay, we have a pair of pajamas for the wash," she said, pulling out the garments. "Some nasty smelling socks, a couple of books, some race track sections, and …"

"And what?" Marc asked, crowding closer.

"A dried up peanut butter sandwich with a bite out of it," Julie answered, pulling out each item. "Gross!"

"No bat?"

"Nope, no bat."

"Strike one for our team," Marc replied sourly.

The next day, Julie went to work again, wondering what she'd find at the end of the day.

That evening, Julie wearily closed the door behind her. It didn't take long to discover that day's ornament massacre.

Atop the counter in the master bath, lay a creamy white porcelain statue. Elegant except for her missing head. As Julie swept the broken pieces from the counter top, she vowed to have a private chat with her son. Somehow, it had to be him.

"Adam," she began, facing the small boy, her hands resting on his shoulders as she squatted to his height. "Do you know what ornaments are?"

Adam looked seriously at his mother. "Tree," he said. "Christmas."

"Yes," she answered. "Like that, I suppose. These ornaments are bigger. Some of them look like people."

Adam frowned at her, obviously confused.

Julie knew that visuals were always the best way to communicate, so she took him by the hand and led him gently down the hall to the master bath. "Come on, let mommy show you," she said.

The two entered the room and Adam frowned at the broken statue on the counter. Quickly, he grabbed the broken head and matched it to the figure. "Uh-oh," he said, when it wouldn't re-attach. "Fix it."

Julie wasn't sure how to respond as her son handed her the small piece and waited expectantly.

"Adam, did you break this?" she asked.

"Break this?" he repeated.

Running one hand through her hair and sighing heavily, Julie tried another track. "Adam, who broke mommy's ornament?"

"The boy," Adam answered, his tone matter-of-fact.

"Yes, but *which* boy?" she asked, hoping she was onto something.

"Casper," Adam replied, turning quickly to leave the room. "Casper *bad* boy."

Julie watched her son go, uncertain what to say or think.

Over the next two days, three more figurines were relieved of their heads.

And still, although she was on high alert for anything unusual, Anne saw and heard nothing untoward. Despite her best efforts, Julie's treasured items were summarily destroyed.

The placement of these items didn't seem to matter. The destruction happened day by day, first with the large Greek figures in the living room, and then a smaller Southern Belle ceramic in the master ensuite. The day after that, a gold and white Spanish lady her mom made for her in ceramics class. All strategically beheaded. Even a lone cowboy, high atop his horse and displayed proudly way up on top of her kitchen cupboards couldn't escape the massacre.

What was goin on?

The more adamantly Anne defended her grandchildren, the more worried Julie and Marc became.

~~~~

"I think I have to quit my job," she told Marc on the phone later that evening. "Adam is obviously out of control."

"Oh geez. Are you sure it's him?" Marc asked.

"Who else could it be?" Julie replied, exasperated.

"Well, I admit that seems like the logical answer," he said. "But there are some pieces here that just don't fit. Like how did he get to those things without making a sound? And why didn't he *finish* breaking them? You know how he's like with things that are just a *little bit* broken."

"Yeah, all he has to see is one flaw, and the whole thing is toast," Julie agreed. "Do you remember the sock incident?"

Marc nodded as he tried to remember.

"He went to school wearing two perfectly good socks," Julie reminded him. "The only imperfection was a single thread hanging off the toe. He didn't even make it to lunchtime, Marc. He unraveled that sock halfway down his foot by the time his teacher called me, and he'd only been there an hour and a half. That's a typical Adam move."

"Yeah, exactly," he agreed. "So, does it make sense to you that a kid like that would break only one part of each statue and leave the rest for us to find?"

"Unfortunately, you've got a point," she conceded.

"So," Marc continued. "Are you still going to quit your job?"

"Yeah, I think I'd better. If this is a message, there might be worse to come, besides, the commute is killing me."

"We really need the money right now," Marc replied worriedly.

"Not to worry," she said. "I might have another job lined up. One that Adam won't even know I'm at. I can work while he's in school."

"Okay, fill me in?"

"One of the Behaviour Consultants I know asked me if I'd like to work as a Behaviour Intervener."

"What's a Behaviour Intervener?" Marc asked.

"A one-on-one teacher for children with autism," she said.
~~~~

"Sounds like something you're fairly qualified for," Marc agreed, a hint of pride in his voice. "Do you have to take any courses?"

"Nope, apparently I've already been attending the best school there is. The school of Adam." Although the conversation had been heavy up to that point, Julie couldn't resist a small chuckle.

"Well," Marc replied. "Sounds good. Maybe if Adam doesn't know you're at work, it'll save the rest of our house from getting broken."

~~~~

Soon, Julie's days were booked up teaching other people's kids.

While the job began as only school-time hours, it quickly mushroomed as Julie discovered her niche.

Adding one client at a time, she was soon able to work a full day, with no more damages occurring.

Julie proudly pointed out that it must have been Adam breaking all those things, but Marc ever the realist, pointed out to his wife that they didn't have any more statues to break!

The schedule seemed to work for her mother and dad, and Julie was proud of the money she added to their bank account, but Marc wasn't excited about the hours she kept.

Often, she arrived home tired and grouchy, much later than she'd anticipated, to find her husband angrily stirring a pot at the kitchen stove, avoiding any eye contact.

"I'm sorry, it ran late."

The phrase was spoken often but seldom accepted.

"Julie, you have to learn balance," her husband said crossly as they both tumbled into bed each night. "You're exhausted and you're putting your own family second."

"You're just mad because you have to cook sometimes," she shot back irritably.

"Sometimes?" Marc retorted. "Name the last time you made dinner."

"Uhh," Julie rolled her eyes to the ceiling as she thought about it.

"Exactly," Marc interrupted vehemently. "Look, I don't mind cooking but just tell me, okay? Don't keep pretending you can do it all when clearly you can't."
~~~~

Sighing deeply, Julie rolled over towards him, hoping to smooth things over but all she saw was Marc's back.

"When Amélie starts preschool I'm gonna switch to working days, so I can be home earlier, okay?"

Marc was silent.

"I really am sorry," she said. "Not that you believe me, but I really am."

Long deep breaths from Marc's side of the bed were the only answer.

Clearly, he was finished with that conversation.

~~~~

Her screams were piercing. Both Julie and Marc sat up in alarm. The clock read 3:00AM.

"Ssh, Ami, ssh," Julie wrapped both arms around the shaking shoulders, attempting to soothe her tiny daughter.

"Bad man mommy," she sobbed. "Bad man."

"Man? What Man? Where?" Julie asked.

"There's no man, Jules, she's just having a bad dream," her husband replied calmly from the doorway, as the tearful child pointed back into her bedroom.

"Come on Ami," Marc called, holding out his hand. "Come on and tuck in with daddy for a bit. Did you have a nightmare?" The child nodded, and followed Marc to the master bedroom.

"It was just a bad dream, that's all," he said.

Amélie sniffled loudly and wiped her nose with the sleeve of her nightgown as she clambered up onto the bed with her parents.

Julie climbed back under the covers herself, and laid a hand on the child's head, smoothing the rumpled curls. "It's okay now Ami," she told her daughter. "They're gone now."

"No," the child said, her tone adamant. "Dessie got hurt." Her face crumpled and she started crying again. "Make him stop, daddy."

"Ami," Marc scolded her softly. "It's sleep time. Jessie is just remembering the hurt, but she's okay now. I promise. It was a bad dream, but bad dreams can't hurt you. You're safe now. Ssh, just go to sleep. It's okay."

Julie frowned in wonder. Marc's strange explanation seemed to mollify the child, and she allowed herself to be tucked in, held in the comforting circle of her father's powerful arms.
~~~~

I wonder, Julie thought, staring at the ceiling.

~~~~

"Well, this is interesting Ami, what's happening here?" Julie asked. "Are the toys having a campfire?"

"I dunno," the tiny girl answered.

Julie quirked a smile at that. It was a phrase Adam used often, but it seemed strange to hear it from Amélie. "What do you mean you don't know? Weren't you in here?"

"Uh-huh."

"But you didn't do this, I suppose?" Julie asked doubtfully.

"Nope."

Again, a smile twitched at the corner of Julie's mouth. Nope? She really was borrowing phrases. That last one sounded just like her daddy.

"Well then, who did?"

Amélie rolled her eyes theatrically. "Dessie," she said, taking care to enunciate the name. "She always do that."

"Jessie did it?" Julie asked, already regretting the question.

"Yeah." The child sounded bored, as though this happened all the time. Julie took another look around at the toys that ringed her daughter. Outwardly, the young mother was calm, but inside she was trying not to freak out.

Julie had been in the room only moments earlier, picking up these same toys. One by one, she'd tossed them high into a small mesh hammock. It was made specifically for storing stuffed toys, high up and out of reach. The triangle of fabric hung from three hooks, screwed into the ceiling, where Julie had thought they would be safe from Adam's busy fingers, only now, they were back on the floor, arranged in a rough circle as though waiting for something.

The effect was startling, but Amélie continued to play, as though nothing untoward had happened.

So many unexplained things went on each day, that it was odd for something normal to occur. And yet Julie found herself staring, unable to form a cohesive thought.

She took a few seconds to breathe in and out, as calmly and deeply as she could.

Once again, she thought of her own childhood, remembering how her parents had said there were no such things as imaginary friends. They'd done it because they loved her, and they were afraid
~~~~

of what they didn't understand. In fact, their actions mirrored her own.

"Mommy has trouble seeing Jessie," she told her child, as soon as she could find her voice again. "Can you ask if she wants to eat supper with us tonight?"

Amélie brightened at that. "Okay," she said.

Julie backed up a step as Amélie looked around. A moment later, she turned back to her mother.

"She went hiding."

"Oh," Julie replied, trying to sound disappointed but feeling relieved instead. "Where is she hiding?"

"I dunno. Mebbe 'n there," Amélie replied, pointing at the closet with confidence.

"Okay then," Julie replied, still trying to sound calm. "Let's just leave her be okay?"

"Kay," Amélie answered, yawning as she sauntered away down the hall, dragging her favorite doll by one arm.

Chapter Thirty-seven

"We're getting a kitten?"

The tone of Marc's voice spoke volumes, and Julie held the phone out from her ear, as she took a deep breath.

"Honey, mom's friend called to ask for our help. They're adorable! And they need good homes."

"We aren't the local shelter, Julie. And besides, with two active kids to keep track of, and me out of town so much, aren't you worried this might be taking on too much?"

"Marc, don't be like that. This little kitten is an orphan. She needs us."

"Her mother didn't survive?" Marc's tone softened as Julie related the facts.

"Apparently not. She died shortly after giving birth. They've all been fed with an eyedropper since then. If she doesn't find new homes for them now, they probably won't survive. There's too many of them for her to keep up the feeding schedule. She brought them to work at first, but she can't do that now. Without constant care, they'll die."

"What does your mom think of all this?" he asked.

"Mom is all for it. She said she would take them if we don't. Apparently, there were eight at first, but a few have already died. Marc, it's something I want to do."

Marc knew his wife's mind was already made up. "You said 'them'. I thought it was just one?"

"Well," she hedged. "There might be two, but mom said she would take one," Julie amended quickly.

"Alright," he agreed. "I suppose you've already arranged this, so when is it happening? Do you need me to pick stuff up on my way home?" He knew how quickly his wife set things in motion.

"That would be great," Julie replied, grinning. "Saves me a trip. My mom's colleague is coming by tonight after supper. We'll need some essentials. They're quite tiny. Only four weeks old. And Marc, I haven't told you the best part."

"Oh yeah?"

"They're Siamese."

"Hmm," her husband answered.

Julie knew he had a soft spot for this breed.

"I'll stop at the pet store on my way home to pick up some supplies," he assured her. "Let's keep it as a surprise for the kids til then, ok?"

"Good idea."

~~~~

"Well, since they're orphans, how about Oliver and Annie?" Marc suggested, as he and his wife cleared the dinner dishes, with one eye anxiously fixed on the clock. Amélie was kneeling quietly at the coffee table, coloring with flamboyant strokes, while Adam played with his train set in one corner of the family room.

"I think that's perfect," Julie whispered.

~~~~

"Oh! She's so tiny!" Julie exclaimed.

Gently, the woman who stood just inside their foyer placed a tiny, towel wrapped bundle into Marc's hands.

"Where's the little boy?" Julie asked.

The woman's shoulders sagged. "He didn't make it," she said sadly.

"Oh!" Both husband and wife said together.

"She's just four weeks. Too young to go, but I can't keep up with the feeding schedule. They need constant care. Thank you for taking her," the woman said, turning her attention back to the tiny bit of fluff inside the towel. "Oh no, she messed herself on the way over. I'm so sorry. I swear she was clean when we left."

A familiar scent wafted towards Julie and she wrinkled her nose.

"That's okay," she reassured the woman. "That's nothing new in our house. We'll take good care of her."

"Welcome to the family little one," Marc crooned to the tiny creature. "Let's get you cleaned up and see if you'll eat something." He was already walking back towards the staircase, looking with tenderness into the startling blue eyes that stared back at him.

"Thank you for bringing her," Julie said.

"Thank you for giving her a good home," the woman answered, turning back to the door. "I'm sorry but I have to go, I'm delivering the others tonight, too. If they're going to survive, they need more care than I can give them."

~~~~~

Marc carefully bathed the tiny kitten in their ensuite sink while Julie sat on the bed and watched her husband. He used a blow dryer on 'low' and a soft brush to ensure the tiny body was completely dry, before carrying the kitten, now resembling an enormous cotton ball, cupped in both hands. He and Julie headed eagerly back to the family room and their waiting children.

Adam and Amélie sat on the couch side by side, glued to the animated TV show.

"Kids, come here, we have a surprise," Marc called them.

"Come on, Adam," Julie prompted, already behind her son. "Let's see what Daddy has."

While Adam crossed dutifully to his father, a serious look on his face, Amélie remained enthralled with the TV. Incuriously, Adam allowed himself to be propelled toward the small animal still cupped in his father's big hands. He leaned towards the kitten and stared in fascination for just a moment. Julie realized she was holding her breath. Would her son say anything? Would he reach out to pet the soft, downy fur?

A moment later, Adam turned and twisted out of his mother's grasp, dashing back to the couch and his TV show.

"Oh Adam!" Julie remonstrated. Do you know what it is?"

"A kitten," Adam replied calmly, not looking at her. "Is good."
~~~~~

"A kitten?" Amélie squeaked, turning curious eyes towards her brother. "Where?"

Adam flicked a glance over his shoulder where Marc still stood, watching this curious scene unfold.

Squealing with delight, the little girl leapt from her seat and immediately began reaching for the tiny animal.

Marc jerked his hands away instinctively. "Whoah!" he said. "Settle down there young lady."

"Ooh! Daddy!" she squeaked. "You got a kitty for me?"

"Well, uh …"

Marc and Julie's gaze met over the top of their daughter's head. A knowing smile passed between them.

So much for this being a family pet.

"Not so fast!" Marc cautioned, as Amélie began jumping to reach her father's hands.

"I wanna see! I wanna see!" she chanted.

"Not til you're sitting quietly," he said. "You need to be very gentle. She's still a baby."

Although Amélie was only three, she was motivated. In an instant, she dropped to the floor at her father's feet and sat with crossed legs, pulling the nightgown she wore tightly over both knees.

She grinned expectantly up at Marc. "See daddy? I made a nest," she announced proudly.

Annie squeaked with alarm as Marc transferred the kitten to the waiting toddler.

Amélie, showed remarkable restraint for a child her age. She carefully stroked the tiny head and body with only two fingers, announcing with a serious voice that she was being 'so careful'. Annie let out another squeak, before curling herself into a tight furry ball and promptly falling asleep in Amélie's hastily prepared 'nest'.

Although the little kitten was unsure of her surroundings at first, and still too young to be away from her mother, the moment Annie was placed into Amélie's lap marked the beginning of a dedicated love that stretched far into the future.

At first, the kitten had to be fed special 'cat milk' with an eye-dropper, but soon she grew in size and strength, until she could be found scampering after Amélie from room to room as the child played with her new pet.

Annie was still quite tiny, but growing fast. As the weeks passed, Julie would often find her daughter, crouched on the floor in front of the sofa, trying to coax the kitten out from underneath.

"Come on out, mommy will get mad," Amélie said, in a voice so serious, it made her mother laugh.

It felt good to laugh, Julie realized. There hadn't been much reason to do so, lately. Having a kitten in their midst would hopefully lighten things up.

~~~~

"No, you can't!" The tone of Amélie's voice was unmistakable. The three-year-old was having a serious argument, but with whom? Julie had a clear view straight down the hall and into the bedroom at the end. Her daughter was arguing vehemently, but there was no one else in the room. The child appeared to be arguing with herself.

Amélie sat on the floor, cross-legged, her kitten nestled securely in her lap, and Amélie's arms encircled her protectively. "I told you why," she argued. "Quit it!"

"Ami?" Julie called, coming quickly down the hall. "What's going on? Who are you talking to?"

"Dessie," Amélie explained. "She wants to hold d' kitty, but I said no. She's mine."

"Ri-ight," Julie replied slowly, looking around at the stuffed animals, once again arranged in a rough circle around her daughter.

"And what did Jessie think of that?"

"She's mad," Amélie replied, pursing her lips. "But I don't care!" The small child narrowed her eyes and stared across the room as she spoke.

It was clear to Julie that whether this Jessie person existed or not, Amélie was quite convinced this was a real girl, and equally convinced this invisible girl stood not three feet from them, listening to every word.

The thought was unnerving, but Julie shook her head in defeat and focused on the task at hand.

"Well, Annie's going to go have a nap now, anyways." Julie reached down and petted the purring kitten in her daughter's lap. "We have to go shopping, remember? Daddy and Adam are waiting for us downstairs, so we gotta get going. If Jessie wants to come, she has to hurry along. Here, you bring the kitty for me, okay?"
~~~~

Amélie turned and stuck her tongue out at the person Julie couldn't see, before trailing along behind her mother, carrying the kitten slung casually over her shoulder, the tiny little arms of the cat hanging limply down the child's back, as though she were a victim being rescued from a burning building. The kitten continued to purr as she they followed Julie to the ensuite bathroom, where Julie placed the small animal securely inside the cat kennel.

"We can't have her wandering around and getting in trouble while we're out, can we?"

Amélie nodded solemnly at her mother and spoke affectionately to the kitten inside, who'd begun mewing plaintively.

"Be a good kitty," Amélie admonished the cat. "I'll be back soon. You should have a nap."

Julie covered her mouth to stifle a giggle. This from the child who refused to nap herself? It was cute how her daughter so easily fell into the role of mother for this tiny creature.

~~~~

Hours later, Julie was grateful to return home. Involving the children in the preparation for the family barbecue had been a bad idea.

"How could I have thought it was going to be fun?" Julie mumbled to herself, as she and Marc carried a seemingly endless stream of plastic bags from the van into the front foyer.

She was looking forward to sitting down and savouring a hot cup of tea, but first, all of this had to be put away. The task was daunting, and Adam had already raced ahead, flinging open the gate at the top of the stairs. Julie heard the TV go on and she knew she'd lost at least one helper.

Amélie was right behind her brother, a true copy-cat. Shaking her head and grabbing a couple of bags, Julie wearily followed the determined three-year-old up each step to the main floor.

She was still putting groceries away in the fridge, when she heard Amélie scream.

"MOMMY! DADDY! MY KITTY!" the child screamed.

""What's going on?" Julie cried out, rushing to her aid.

"What's the matter," Marc called out, taking the stairs two at a time, as his wife rushed down the hall to investigate.

A stricken Amélie knelt on the floor in the ensuite bathroom, tears streaming down her face.
~~~~

The door to the small kennel was wide open.

"Oh no," Julie moaned, fearing the worst. "What's happened here?"

"She's gone!" The child wailed.

"What?" Julie knelt herself and peered inside. The kennel was indeed empty. "Where is she?"

"Dessie took her," Amélie sobbed.

"Now, now I'm sure she didn't," Julie said, trying to think. She couldn't imagine how a tiny kitten could unlock the door of a cat crate. "We probably didn't close it properly," she said to her daughter. "She'll be around here somewhere, let's look for her."

And so, the groceries sat on the kitchen counter and Adam's movie went on pause as the whole family joined in for the great cat hunt.

With her family actively searching, Julie went down the foyer to bring up the remaining supplies, concerned that the newly purchased ice cream would defrost all over the floor while they looked for Ami's cat.

Hands full of bags, Julie paused at the mid-span of the stairs. What was that she just heard? It was faint and high-pitched, like the squeak of a small mouse.

As Julie stood there, all she could hear was the frantic opening and closing of dressers and closets.

"Hey you guys," she called. "Ssh for second, I think I heard something."

In that moment of quiet, Julie heard it again. The noise was very faint, but she followed it to their new computer desk in the corner of the recreation room.

Marc had proudly assembled the brand new desk only a few days before. It was a lot more compact than the big, unwieldy piece of furniture they'd had before, and this one had many compartments where Julie's papers, pens and other office paraphernalia could be stored out of sight and locked away. Even the printer had its own drawer, and when not in use, the drawer shut completely, hiding it away from children with big ideas.

As Julie stood staring at the desk, she heard the sound again.

It was coming from inside the desk!

"She's in here! I found her! Marc! Come quick!" She called. "She's trapped! Her head is stuck!"

Minutes later, as Julie tried her best to fend off the terrified children, Marc lay on the floor underneath the desk, and frantically tried to release the kitten from her dangerous perch. The tiny animal was growing weaker with each minute. Her head was wedged tightly inside a small opening, and she essentially hung from a small round opening in the wood, that was intended to pass printer cables through.

Both children grew more frantic as they heard the kitten struggle for breath.

How had she gotten inside the fully-enclosed printer drawer? When they'd left, it was fully closed, and the only way to get inside would be through that small hole, which was obviously not big enough for her pass through. The kitten must have found herself trapped, and attempted to get out through the too-small hole, Julie reasoned. Clearly, she was only able to fit her head through the hole.

How long had she been there?

It seemed to take forever, but Marc proceeded with great care. Finally, he extricated the tiny body, and quickly wrapped her in a nearby towel.

The kitten was weak, shivering and clearly in shock. Angry red welts showed through the downy white fur on her neck. She was breathing, but each breath came out in a harsh sounding rasp.

Amélie grabbed for her, but Marc evaded her panicked hands.

"My kitty, my Annie. She's died," she sobbed. "My poor baby."

"She's not dead," Julie answered. "Just weak. Daddy will take her to the vet."

"How long was she in there?" Marc asked angrily.

"How should I know?" Julie retorted, going quickly to the kitchen and grabbing the cordless phone. "I was with you remember? She was fine when we left. In fact, she was safely enclosed in the cat crate! Explain that!" Julie angrily punched the phone in her hand. "I'm calling the vet."

"What?" Marc retorted. "None of this makes any sense," he said softly, stroking the tiny body in his arms. "Poor little thing."

Amélie sobbed as Julie spoke quickly to the vet assistant.

The normally energetic little cat barely moved in Marc's arms.

At last, Julie hung up the phone and turned to her husband. "They're gonna wait for you," she said. "They were just closing up for the day but I explained the situation. Let's get you out the door."

Marc headed back toward the stairs immediately.

"Ami," Julie instructed sternly. "Go get the kennel for daddy."

Tears streamed down Amélie's face as she watched her father leave, the small kennel containing her precious, injured kitten inside. There were no words Julie could use to calm the child, as she bolted for her bedroom and slammed the door.

Julie rushed down the hallway after her, and carefully opened the door a few inches.

Amélie flung open her closet door and with hands balled into fists, she shook them in the air, while yelling at the top of her lungs.

"I don't care what you say! I told you not to touch her! You killed my cat!"

Julie just stared. She could see plainly from her vantage point that the closet was empty, except for some clothes and shoes, but Amélie continued to shout. It was clear that to her, Jessie stood in that small space. It was equally clear that Ami blamed the invisible child for this latest accident.

Julie frowned as her daughter continued the tirade but instead of intervening, she let it play out.

What did it matter if she yelled at someone who wasn't there? She was clearly upset, and perhaps this would help her deal with whatever came next. Neither parent wanted to think that the cat would die, but she'd been hanging from her neck for such a long time …

"No! Shut up! You're a liar!" the little girl screamed, her cheeks flaming. "I'm never playing with you again!"

As Julie crouched, peeking into her daughter's room, Adam slowly approached a puzzled expression on his face as he peered past her into his sister's room.

"Casper did it," he said solemnly.

Julie frowned at her son. What did he mean?

The dual reference to their cat's name was an added frustration. Did Adam think that the normally aloof adult Siamese had done this to their little female? Julie didn't think so. Adam knew the cat wasn't capable of opening a locked kennel.

The ramifications didn't bear thinking about. She wouldn't think about it!

With firm resolve, Julie backed down the hallway and went in search of the latest Real Estate Weekly.

~~~~~
~~~~~

In the days and months that followed, Annie recovered and grew stronger. Amélie and her little cat were even more inseparable, now. Amélie was at an age where playing with her brother had become all important to her. Adam, awkward at best and aggressive at worst, avoided his little sister.

Julie felt a stab of guilt. Why couldn't he learn how to play with her? Julie tried every day to encourage the pair, but Adam quickly became frustrated and angry with his talkative sibling.

Increasingly, Amélie turned to quieter forms of play, often sitting in her room, surrounded with stuffed toys. She kept up a constant flow of chatter, seeming to involve another, invisible child in her make-believe scenarios. Julie and Marc knew they should be tolerant, but it wasn't easy.

"Marc, it's time we talked about Amélie's imaginary friend," Julie said to her husband one evening, after an eventful dinnertime.

"What's to talk about?" he asked. "Doesn't every kid have one?"

"Uh," Julie hesitated. She hadn't been prepared for this.

"I mean, it's not like I hadn't noticed, Julie. She's been offering forkfuls of her dinner to thin air, and loudly announcing: *We* don't like it." He chuckled. "How could I miss that? It's no big deal, though right? It's normal for her age, isn't it?"

How could she tell him her fears? Julie thought. He'd say she was just being foolish and worrying about things that were beyond their control.

"Sure," she answered, forcing a smile she did not feel. "Lots of kids have imaginary friends."

Marc nodded. "Exactly, and it's not as though she has an easy time playing with her brother. This is probably her way of coping."

Although she knew her husband was right, she still couldn't shake the suspicion there was more to this than Marc realized. Even so, she couldn't bring herself to share her most heavily guarded secret.

Julie knew the pain of not being believed. She was a child who 'saw things' and 'knew things'. It had been painful trying to find her way in a world that didn't want to believe. Was Amélie's situation similar? Julie had no way of knowing without openly talking about it, and her daughter was far too young for that. She knew very well how her daughter's 'imaginary' friend could seem so real; looking, talking and acting like just a real child.

It was all so complicated, and so frightening. She didn't want that for her daughter, but she also didn't want to stir things up in case she was wrong.

Julie chewed her lip. What she'd wanted more than anything was validation.

But how could they offer validation to a three-year-old?

~~~~

"Adam is out of control!" she fumed. "Depression, anger, negativity, all he says these days are angry quotes from all the worst movie characters he can think of, and I'm so sick of it I could just scream," she complained to her sister. The women were seated in a fast food restaurant, with watchful eyes on their children as they played in the attached playground.

"I thought you were getting some help?" her sister asked. "Last time we talked, you had a new Behaviour Consultant and things were looking up."

"Yeah, well that didn't pan out too well, unfortunately. That darned woman wanted thousands of dollars, and all she was gonna do is write social stories! Can you image that? I can write my own damned social stories. As a matter of fact, I've been doing that already for years, and look at the result? He isn't any better. In fact, sometimes he seems worse. I need someone who can out-think him, and that sure as hell isn't me!" Julie blew the stray hair out of her eyes. "I miss Ariel. I wish she was still allowed to work with us, but the government contract only lasts so long, you know." Julie made a face. "Ariel would know exactly what to do if she were here, but now, we're left without any help at all, and things are going for shit! Marc and I barely talk anymore, except to fight. All I want to do is move and all he keeps saying is no!"

"How come?" her sister asked, her voice deliberately low.

"Oh, he says the house isn't worth enough yet. Apparently, we wouldn't make enough on it if we sold now, but I just don't care. I feel like giving up." She shook her head sadly.

Laura sat back and narrowed her eyes at her little sister, crossing her arms as she did so. "This talk of giving up isn't like you," she said. "You're usually so feisty and full of ideas, you make everyone else feel like a slacker, but hearing this, I don't even recognise you!"

"Thanks," Julie muttered darkly. "Thanks a lot."
~~~~

"Now look, you know what I mean. Where's my fire-cracker sister? You've always got stuff going on! What about your job? How is that going?" Laura, desperate to change the subject, raised her eyebrows hopefully.

"Not enough time, not enough money," Julie answered dejectedly. "Marc hates that I'm working, and so do the kids. I love helping these little kids learn, but every day I just feel the knife going in a little deeper, you know?"

"Explain it to me," her sister said.

"How come I can help other people's kids without issue, but not mine? Mine seem to be on a downward spiral! Adam gets kicked out of class almost every day and last week, I got called to the school cuz he was throwing desks and chairs! Meanwhile Amélie keeps up a running dialogue with a child no one else can see. Can you imagine that?"

"Ah," Laura draped one arm protectively over Julie's shoulders. "So that's what this is about."

"Well yeah, I guess it is," Julie admitted. "I feel so helpless."

From the far side of the room, Amélie suddenly screamed, and Julie vaulted from her seat.

The little girl ran to her mother and Julie gathered her up quickly. Julie caught sight of an angry welt that stood out on the child's forearm. There were perfect indents surrounding it, where human teeth had clamped down on the skin. She didn't have to play twenty questions to find out who'd done it. This was a regular course of action in the everyday of her household.

"ADAM!" she roared at her son. "Get over here!"

A moment later, Laura was behind her and Julie could feel her sister's gentle restraining hand on her forearm. "Take it easy sis. People are watching."

"I know, I know," she muttered. "People are always watching. Well," she emphasized, looking around at all who continued to stare. "*People* can mind their own damn business! Sometimes Autism has an ugly side. They should thank their lucky stars their children are normal!"

"Ri-ight," Laura answered, looking around, her face turning red. "Well, I think it's time to go. Rachelle, bring your cousin please. We're going."

Julie felt the weight of the judgmental stares on her back. She hugged her daughter hard and grasped her son's hand as she fought back tears. Adam's confused, angry cries grew louder as she towed him toward the exit.

"See?" Julie hissed to her big sister, as she stowed her things in the van. "It's always like this. I hate people."

"You don't mean that," Laura said.

"Maybe not," Julie admitted. "I'm just so damned angry all the time, and I'm so tired of being angry. I just want a life again."

~~~~

"Let's go to the cabin," Marc suggested. "I'm sick and tired of this fish-bowl we live in." He waved his arm towards the houses that seemed to press in tightly, on all sides.

"You know what?" Julie replied, her expression brightening. "I would love that."

"Really?" Marc seemed surprised. "No arguments?"

"Did you want one?" Julie quipped.

"No, not really," he chuckled dryly. "I guess I'm just kind of used to getting one whether I want it or not."

Julie decided to let that pass, and instead, she hauled open the pantry doors. "I'd better see what we have in here, *before* I go shopping. No doubt that'll be *my* chore."

Refusing to take the bait, Marc merely shrugged and turned away. A moment later, Julie heard his footsteps on the stairs.

"I'll go grab the sleeping bags and the cooler," he called over his shoulder. "If we work at this together, we can be out of here by the time I'm back from work tomorrow."

"Humph," Julie muttered under her breath. "This will be an interesting experiment. I doubt he even remembers the meaning of together, anymore."
~~~~

Chapter Thirty-eight

"It feels so … safe here, you know?" she said, staring out the windshield at the building just coming into sight. "No one watching us. And my trees! Look at how beautiful they are!" Julie opened her window and felt the bracing wind against her face.

"Yeah, smell that pine!" Marc agreed. "We've come home."

"Mm-hmm, I agree!" Julie replied.

"Oh Marc," she said, climbing the steps of the cabin to join her husband on the front deck. "I don't ever want to leave here. We have a beautiful, modern house with instant electricity and uncomplicated plumbing, multiple bathrooms and a dishwasher! But all I want it to stay here in the woods with you and the kids, and our pets, hiding from reality."

Marc laughed. "Wow! You really needed this vacation, didn't you? I can't say I blame you though. The same thought was going through my head all the way here. The stress in our place is so thick, you can cut it with a knife. And it's no secret you and I have been at each other's throats."

Julie looked up at him cautiously but there was no malice in his honest, open stare.

"But this place?" he continued. "This is paradise as far as I'm concerned."

Julie looked at her husband, and a smile tugged at the corners of her mouth.

"What?" he asked.

"I was just wondering what people would say if they could hear us now," she said. "Would they think we're crazy?"

"What people?" Marc asked.

"Oh just, people," she shrugged.

"I don't care," Marc replied. "Screw 'em!"

Although Adam spent his time in the creek, soaking himself to the skin every day, Julie just smiled at his single-mindedness and dug out another change of clothes.

"Good thing I brought enough clothing for six weeks!" she joked.

It was good to see her smiling again, Marc thought as he absently stroked Casper's silky fur, before going out the back door with his trusty axe to split some more firewood.

Marc chopped wood, stoked the fires and cooked beautiful dinners for them on the old wood stove without complaint. He was in his element there. It was pioneer living, but it was quiet, it was private, and it was safe. There were no dark spirits here, and items never randomly moved while no one was looking. It was a place where they could truly relax.

On top of that, both children slept soundly, including Amélie. At home, she still wasn't able to sleep all the way through the night in her own bed. The deep sense of fatigue they'd brought with them slowly ebbed away as they faced real challenges, like heat, water and food preparation without the help of modern convenience. These rustic simplicities seemed to recharge them in ways nothing else could.

Although his parents had been working with him steadily since the age of three, Adam was still such a creature of habit. Predictability and routine were so important to him that Marc felt sometimes the rest of the family was held hostage by it.

He knew better than to bring this up with his wife. She used to be so logical, so practical about stuff like that, but over the last year or so, Marc hardly recognized the woman he'd pledged to love and honour.

Marc wondered whether it truly was the house that was unhealthy, draining them of all positive energy or was it them? Were he and his wife somehow not good for each other anymore?

The thought chilled him, and he shuddered, pausing on the leaf-strewn path for a moment to clear his head.

Just down from where he stood, Julie was walking hand in hand with Amélie, stopping often as Adam raced ahead to turn over rocks or pluck some moss from a low-hanging branch. Sunshine filtered through the lacy boughs of the pine trees that surrounded the rustic cabin and occasionally a bracing wind danced along the tree tops and whistled through their little valley.

"Home," Marc muttered to himself. "This place *feels* like home."

~~~~

Julie hunkered down on the bank of the creek and opened her spiral bound notebook. It would be good to catch up and do some writing, she thought. Everyone was fed, cleaned and cared for. She stared at the crystalline water as it gurgled past, flowing easily over stones, worn smooth by years of flowing water.

It was peaceful. The tranquillity at such odds with her life, lately.

Opening the book, her eyes fell on the first entry, dated earlier that year.

Dear Diary: Marc and I struggle to find ways to introduce change in minuscule ways for Adam. We're always trying to help him break out of that "autism mold", hoping to re-invent him as a person whose eccentricities won't leave him an outcast in a world that isn't ever going to be set up to his liking. Adam doesn't line things up as much as he organizes his own chaos. What looks like a whirlwind mess to me, seems literally to be Adam's 'sense of order'. To me, it's all lying on his floor, but to him, it's catalogued! He gets so mad when I try to clean things up. I guess that's just me not understanding him. Again. Sometimes I think I should just leave it, but what would Marc say? He's already pissed that I'm working, even though we need the money if we're ever going to move out of that house. I should probably be home, more I know, but I hate it there. It was supposed to be our dream home.
~~~~

Julie gulped and turned the page, her eyes automatically reading the words penned there.

Dear Diary: Explain this? How does clean laundry, dirty laundry, toys, coloring books, reading books, pens, pencils, a coffee cup, crayons, legos, bits of string, paperclips, push pins, bread tags, newspaper pages, and my purse all end up inside Adam's toy box?

I was tidying up today when I noticed the lid of the toy box wouldn't close.

No wonder! All of these things were in there, jumbled together. What next? It's not like Adam to clean up, so it's a bit suspicious, but I'm so tired of unexplained mysteries. I think I'll blame him for a change.

With a loaded sigh, Julie closed the book again and stood up, casting her eyes around for the kids. She soon found them, seated cross-legged together on the front porch, painting large rocks with splashes of vibrant color, equally serious frowns of concentration on their faces.

"Wow," she whispered, as though not wanting to break the spell. Marc emerged from the back door a moment later and placed a finger to his lips as he caught sight of his wife. Julie stifled a giggle as she watched her husband sneak around the edge of the cabin, trying not to be observed by the children, as he captured a photo of this rare moment of togetherness.

He's a great dad, she thought. It's so good to see this side of him again.

~~~~

"I figured it out. We're being manipulated, all of us."

"Excuse me?"

"This thing," Julie explained. "This spirit, ghost, demon or whatever you want to call it. He's manipulating our emotions, controlling our thoughts. All he does is put us against each other." Julie waved her hands as she talked. "Ever since we got home, all we can do is argue and watch things break without any apparent cause! Adam and Amélie freak out and fight over the slightest thing, and utter chaos has become our new 'normal'. Don't tell me you haven't noticed. Where've you been?"
~~~~

"Of course I noticed," he snapped. "Don't drag that sad story out again! I've had a long day at work and I'm tired."

"That's exactly my point! You're always tired!"

"That's not my fault," he snapped. "We've got two kids, a big, fat mortgage and a yappy dog. On top of that, my wife sees shadows and apparitions all over the place! You don't think that's exhausting? Of course I've noticed things are tense around here, but there isn't a damn thing I can do about it, is there?"

"You're digging your heels in where you don't need to, Marc. Can't you just entertain the idea –"

"Look, you don't have all the answers, even though you think you do."

"What's that supposed to mean?" she screeched, her hands balling into fists. "Don't you dare say that to me!"

"Don't you think you're being just a little dramatic?" he asked, hands on hips as he stared her down.

"No, I'm bloody not!" she retorted. "I've seen it, and so have you. How can you blow that off?"

"That?" he scoffed. "That's not a good reason to just up and move, tossing away all of our hard-earned equity! We moved here to get a leg-up, but that isn't gonna happen if we run away at the first sign of something strange."

"Are you kidding me right now?" she argued. "The *first* sign? What about all the hundreds of times things have happened in this house and we have no explanation? And what about my so-called fall? And what about all those unexplained illnesses?"

"Drama," he muttered. "How do you know you didn't eat something you're allergic to? Just because the doctors didn't know what it was, doesn't mean it was paranormal. And as for that fall, we never really established why that happened. Maybe you just tripped. You're always in a big hurry, and wearing those floppy slippers doesn't help you know."

"Argh!" she screamed and threw her hands into the air. "You are so damn frustrating!"

Julie turned away and began randomly picking up toys and dropping them into the nearby toy bin. Marc looked like he wanted to say something, but Julie didn't give him the opportunity. Plowing ahead she continued: "And what about the footsteps in the hallway and on the stairs when no one's there?"

"Julie, look I –"

"And I don't know about you, but it frightens me that this thing messes with our kids. Can you explain the nightmares? And what about our pets? He's more of a master to them than we are!"

Marc pressed his lips together as a spasm of pain gripped his chest. Instinctively, he pressed the palm of his hand to his chest.

I just need to catch my breath, he thought.

He felt like his body was gripped in a vice. Heavily, Marc sat down on the couch. All the fight went out of him as he watched his wife walk in circles. Even as she raged, arms waving for emphasis, she snatched toys from every surface and slid video cassettes back into their sleeves. She was on auto-pilot, Marc realized.

As Marc watched her, his sense of wonder grew. The pain in his chest throbbed as he watched his wife. Although he continued to press against his chest in obvious pain, she hadn't said a word about that.

"And do I need to remind you about the tools in the garage nearly jumping off the wall in front of you?" she continued, stabbing her finger at him accusingly. "Again, no explanation. And the computer! Why does it work fine upstairs, but not in the den? You tell me? Honestly! You make me so mad!"

With the last of the toys put away, Julie stomped from the room, still seething.

"And you!" she shouted at the air in front of her. "I'll bet you're just loving all this, aren't you? The more chaos, the better you like it."

With an expression of detached wonder, Marc sat up straighter. Without realizing it, Julie had hit the nail on the head!

Whatever this thing was, it did feed on negativity and here was more proof!

Marc looked around. Maybe they could sell and get out from under this, he thought. It didn't hurt to try, right?

"Julie" he called. "Where are you?"

"In here," she answered a sarcastic edge to her voice. "With our children. Like you care."

Marc stopped part way down the hall, all thoughts of reasoning with her, now gone.

"Whatever," he muttered, determined not to rise to the challenge. Returning to the family room, he switched on the TV and tried hard not to think about anything.

~~~~
~~~~

Words were Amélie's constant companion, so it wasn't odd to hear language pouring forth from their youngest child's room, but lately it was the types of things she said that made Julie stop and listen at her daughter's door.

"Come on Dessie," Amélie's voice carried easily to the hallway. Her tone was one Julie knew well. Her little girl was irritated.

"Everything okay sweetie?" Julie asked, pushing open the door.

"She won' tell." Amélie answered, folding her arms as she spoke.

"Oh," Julie replied, not sure how to interpret the statement. "Um, what's going on?"

Amélie directed a withering look at her mother. Clearly, she felt the answer was obvious.

"Dessie took my kitty! I'm not gonna play f'her anymore. She's bad. An' she won' go away."

"Oh," Julie blinked at the tiny child. "Is she here now?"

"Uh-huh."

"In this room?"

"In there," she said, pointing at her closet.

The door was closed, and although the young mother should have scoffed at the idea, she felt her heart start to race in fear. With a quick gulp, she reached for the handle.

The closet of course, housed shoes, clothes and few toys but no surly little playmate.

The breath Julie let out was explosive.

What did I expect to see? She wondered. Grown-ups can't see, remember?

"Oh! Gone," Amélie commented, peering past her mother.

"That's a strange way to come and go," Julie replied, trying to calm her rapidly beating heart. "Does she always do that?"

Amélie simply shrugged and turned her attention to the plastic tea set lying discarded on the carpet.

Julie wanted to believe her daughter was merely being creative, inventing a playmate her own age in order to pass the time. She wanted it to be something normal; that imaginary friendship that so many children experience. It was a harmless rite of passage, right?

If only she could bring herself to believe it was that simple.

Julie remembered her own childhood well and it was those memories that made her take these childish statements more seriously than other parents might.

He was a welcome playmate. Someone she could confide in and explore new places with. He seemed to understand what it was like to find yourself in a place where you were a stranger to everyone.

Although he was a lot younger than she, they developed a bond. He was her friend, but her mom, dad and sister called it something else.

They couldn't see him, so they just assumed he wasn't there. Imaginary, they called him.

It wasn't until much later that she'd learned the shocking truth: Her imaginary friend had walked the earth for six years, until a horrible tragedy robbed him of his life.

Somehow, at the age of nine, she was expected to understand, and move on.

Get over it.

Her parents and sister had repeated the phrase often, but it wasn't that easy.

Julie shook her head. Obviously, she still wasn't 'over it' as much as she wanted to be.

Somehow, she vowed she wouldn't make the same mistakes.

Perhaps that's why I'm in this house, she thought. When I first got here, I sensed that it needed me. Maybe that's why …

Oh come on! She chided herself. Thoughts like that bordered on madness, didn't they?

It was this inward struggle that tortured her every time Amélie spoke so casually about a friend none of them could see.

"It was just an accident, Amélie," Julie reminded her daughter. "You mustn't lay blame just because you don't understand."

Amélie narrowed her eyes and pouted.

"Look, if you truly don't want to play with this little girl anymore, just tell her to go home and she'll be gone."

The little girl tilted her head doubtfully, but as Julie left the room, pulling the door closed after her, she heard angry muttering.

Clearly, the advice had done nothing to improve her daughter's mood.

Later, she talked the strange incident over with Marc.

"What do you think?" They were clearing the table after dinner. "Obviously, she's looking for someone to blame for the incident with the kitten. I'm still baffled as to how it got out of a locked kennel in the first place, but to blame an imaginary friend? Isn't that a bit much?"

"Good thing that little fur ball recovered so quickly," Marc said, dodging the question neatly. "Amélie and that little cat have become best friends! She hauls that little thing around everywhere. I've never seen such a tolerant feline."

"Marc," his wife admonished, unwilling to let him off the hook so easily. "You're avoiding the real question here. Should we be worried about this or what?"

"How should I know?" Marc shrugged and looked away. "Amélie does make up some wild stories sometimes. Are you sure that's what she said? You know how she gets."

"Well, I don't know about being sure," she replied. "But she does seem to believe this Jessie person is as real as you and me."

"I thought that was supposed to go away when we put her in preschool?" Marc asked.

"I thought it would, but apparently not."

"What did she say again?"

"She doesn't want to play with Jessie but claims the little girl won't go away. She told me Jessie comes and goes through her closet, for goodness' sake. I'm worried, Marc."

"Her closet?" Marc asked. "That is odd. But then again, she's been moody lately. Maybe there's another growth spurt coming on."

"Maybe," Julie agreed. "She's been secretive, and easily upset, even … oh I don't know!"

"Bitchy?" Marc volunteered.

Julie chucked wryly. "Yeah, that captures it pretty clearly. I know she's only three and a half, but her preschool teacher mentioned it too. It's ridiculous! She goes from being a happy little kid one moment to sad, moody and argumentative the next. It's like she's an emotional satellite dish!"

"I know," Marc sighed. "Adam's like that too, though. Maybe she's learning it from her big brother?"

"I don't know," Julie replied, sighing heavily. "I guess it's a possibility. But you know what? When she's at play dates, it's all sunshine and rainbows. No sign of this behaviour at all."

"Chalk up another 'unexplained' for the scoreboard," Marc muttered.

"My mom thinks its coincidence."

Marc sighed and reached with one hand to rub the back of his neck. "There's no such thing as coincidence," he said.

~~~~

"Get out!! Get outta dose pry-lands!" Adam bellowed, imperfectly repeating yet another phrase from his movies. This time, the angry words were aimed at his sister.

But instead of running away as she'd done in the past, Amélie stood her ground and even stuck her chin out defiantly.

"Take that, you scoundrel!" he yelled at her, throwing a fake punch that landed in the air between them.

Amélie dodged backwards. With narrowed eyes and both hands on her hips, she yelled back. "You're not the boss of me Adam!"

"Why, you!" he growled. "Kill him! Don't just stand there, kill him!"

"Mom!" Ami called out suddenly. "Adam said 'kill'!"

"Adam, Ami, that's enough," Julie interrupted.

"Enough!" Adam bellowed, still quoting. " I'm the king, king, king …"

"Oh no you aren't," Julie admonished, turning her son by the shoulders she marched him into his room. "Why can't you two get along?" she sighed, fending off the affronted four-year-old while she pulled Adam's favourite book from the shelf and sat him down with it on the carpet, and switched on a portable stereo, flooding his room with soothing music.

"Ami," she said, turning back to her daughter. "You need to go do something fun that doesn't involve antagonizing your brother. I don't know what gets into you sometimes."

"He started it," the little girl answered, sticking out her tongue at the big brother she loved to fight with.

Adam, oblivious to his sister's remarks, turned the pages of his favourite book and listened to his music. The change that came over her children would have seemed eerie to Julie if she hadn't witnessed this so many times before.
~~~~

Chapter Thirty-nine

The small cabin was just visible through the interwoven pine boughs. A man stood tall, hands pressed to the small of his back, holding a wicked-looking scythe in one hand. He stood in a small patch of cleared land. The soil was rich and black, a pile of newly harvested grain lying nearby. The man was strong; he was no stranger to hard work. He wore the clothing of a workman. His trousers bagged at the knees, the cuffs tucked into sturdy black boots. The small shack that sat to one side of the clearing was built of tight-fitting, stacked logs. Julie was intrigued by the building and felt herself take a step forward, a welcoming smile on her lips.

But the man in the clearing wasn't smiling. His demeanor changed in an instant from curious to threatening.

Much of his face was cast in shadow due to the wide-brimmed hat he wore, but she could see the line of his jaw, hard and unyielding, and the professional way he held the sharpened scythe told her he would use it if he had to. Julie's smile of friendliness melted away and fear suddenly replaced any feelings of friendship as she realized he was staring at her. There was a challenge in that stare, and a warning. But why? What had she done?

She took a step back, determined to get away from the man, but for every step she backed away, he took a menacing step forward.

The muscles of his powerful shoulders bunched as he tightened his grip on the scythe.

Although the thin lips never moved, a voice that wasn't her own echoed in the forest.

You came looking for me, she heard him say. *But I've been here all along.*

All around her, the land was wild. Where was she? What happened to her house, and the neatly manicured lawns of her neighbours? Everything was gone.

Thick brush, brambles, sinewy saplings and tall grasses choked the earth in front of her, disguising the landscape.

It was all wrong. This shouldn't be here, she told herself. *He* shouldn't be here.

The man who still gripped the razor-sharp scythe had begun to advance on her again. She couldn't let him catch her, she had to run! But where could she go? She didn't know this place.

Julie turned and ran. Brambles tore at her skin with stinging swipes as she fought to break through, aware that he was only seconds behind!

Twigs and branches snapped behind. He was closer now.

Julie's outstretched arms clawed aside the thick branches that slapped her face and head. Which way? It was impossible to see, there was so much undergrowth! Still trying to get her bearings, she swiveled her head as she ran. Was this the ravine near her home? Why had she come there? Could she have been sleepwalking? And who was this guy? Where was her family? Were they in danger from this maniac? What would he do to her when he finally caught up with her?

The questions ripped through her head as the ground suddenly sloped downward and she tumbled head over heels, missing young saplings and boulders by mere inches.

It wasn't real, it couldn't be real …

Julie's breath came in quick gasps and her chest burned. Somehow, she had to be dreaming. That was the only thing that made sense, but the pain in her arms, legs and heaving chest were ever-present reminders that real or not, she was in a fight for her life.

If only she could wake up! Branches and clinging vines reached out to trip her, as she raced on, desperate to escape the madman at her back. Julie realized with a sick feeling that she was too slow to escape him. The sound of his advance was loud in her ears.

Suddenly, triumphant laughter rang out. It was the laughter of someone who knows they are in control. The unexpected sound sent a shockwave up her spine and she whirled around to face her attacker, preferring that to a blind attack.

All she saw was the forest, closing in over her trampled path, erasing it as if it had never been.

Still half-running, Julie stumbled backwards in confusion, the momentum carrying her into the undergrowth. She fell hard, the breath whooshing from her lungs. Spots appeared in front of her eyes as she lay there, dazed.

Vines still clutched at her body and she kicked at them, violently. She had to get out of there! The sky had gone white ….

Julie came fully awake with a start. She wasn't in a forest. This was her room! She blinked at the pristine white ceiling and looked around. The vine she'd been kicking so viciously was actually a tangled mess of blankets and sheets. A sheen of sweat covered her shaking body, and the strange, haunting laughter still rang in her head.

It had all seemed so real. Julie stretched out both arms, and winced. Pain shot through her forearms. In her frantic fight with the sheets, she'd obviously pulled some muscles.

"Oh great," she muttered sarcastically, rubbing her arms. She winced again and pulled her hand away, discovering angry patches of skin on each forearm.

Scratches? Thin white lines stood out in contrast against the reddened skin.

Looking back at the twisted mess of bedding, she tried to make sense of what had just happened. Had she done this to herself somehow, as she fought to escape the dream, or had the cat attacked her out of self-defence as she thrashed about?

Casper blinked lazily at her from the chair in the corner of the room and yawned. Clearly, the scratches hadn't come from him, and Julie knew with certainty that Annie was tucked in bed with Amélie where she slept every night.

"Good thing Marc's out of town," she mumbled. "I haven't got a clue what's going on."

~~~~
~~~~

"Just keep him upstairs when we aren't home, okay?" Julie's dad asked, the frustration in his voice a clear indicator that he wasn't kidding. "Computer glitches are one thing. But when Adam comes in there, he does something to it, I can't seem to get it right again for hours!"

"Sure thing, dad," Julie said. "I didn't realize he was going in there. I'm sorry. Haven't you guys been locking your door?"

"Mother forgets," he said, sighing deeply. "Look, just try and keep him out of my den, okay? That's not his house and he has to learn that! We didn't move in here to have our privacy disrespected."

"Of course, Dad," Julie replied, her voice low. Her dad wasn't usually this demonstrative.

The next day, her parents went out for the morning, and Julie followed her son through the house like a hyper-vigilant detective. She was determined her dad would have no reason at all to be angry with his grandson.

Three times she checked her parent's front door to ensure it remained locked.

But despite her vigilance, shortly after their return, she heard her parent's door open, then slam again with undue force.

"Julie!" Her mother called angrily.

"Yes mom?" she answered. "How was your morning? Did you and dad —"

"Nevermind that," she snapped. "We told you to keep Adam out of here, and not only did we find our front door unlocked, which I clearly remember locking, but when we came in, we could hear the computer whirring away, with Adam's game going! We *asked* you to make sure he didn't come in here when we're gone out! It was such a simple request. Why can't you just watch him?"

Julie was dumbfounded. When would Adam have found time to sneak in there? She was with him every second! And furthermore, how did he manage to unlock their door?

"Just a sec," she began. "I was with him the whole time mom, and your door was locked. I don't see how he could have -"

"Please don't insult me by denying it, Julie." She interrupted. "We can see the evidence for ourselves."

"Mom, I'm telling you," she said.

"And I'm telling you," her mother replied, her tone a clear warning. "If you can't keep your children out of our place, we are going to have a very difficult time continuing to live here."

"Mom, I …" Julie realized there was nothing she could say. She was certain Adam hadn't been in their place. This was yet another example of the insane circumstances they lived with every day.

"And now my parents are pissed at me," she mumbled. "Thanks a lot asshole! I know that was you."

~~~~~

Deliberately, she lowered her voice. "Every day Marc. Every day you and I are fighting. It's not good for the kids, not good for us. Even my parents have been angry and yelling lately. Does that seem like a normal life to you?"

Marc folded his hands in his lap and stared down at them. "I don't want it to be."

Julie felt tears stinging in her eyes. "Neither do I."

"I don't know how to change it though. We've become almost like strangers."

"Strangers who live together," she tried to smile but couldn't.

"We're always going in opposite directions," he commented, still not looking at her. "We can't agree on even the simplest things. We used to agree on everything."

"I know, Marc what happened?"

"We've changed, I guess. I don't know." His words sounded bitter. "People do you know. We were really young when we first met."

Julie's face looked stricken.

"Maybe this place has changed us," he continued. "We're not the same people anymore."

Julie felt an intense stab of pain as she looked at her husband. Oh my God, she thought. This is it. This is when he tells me he's leaving.

"So that's it then?" she found herself whispering. "We're just, incompatible?"

Marc's head came up sharply. "Incompatible? That's a big leap," he disagreed. "I just think we've become different that's all. We want different things, and we keep working at cross-purposes so all we do is fight. We just don't see eye to eye anymore."
~~~~~

Julie narrowed her eyes. "So we're not incompatible, just different. Isn't that the same thing?" she wondered.

"Oh sure," he muttered. "Twist my words again. You think that's helpful? It's no bloody wonder we're always fighting Julie. You can't leave anything alone!"

Julie felt the heat rise to her face, and normally she would storm and scream and probably cry but there was no energy left in her to do that. Instead, she reached out and pressed a folded note into her husband's hand.

"What's this?" he asked suspiciously.

"Just read it," she said. "It says what I can't."

"No," he answered quickly, dropping it onto the coffee table in front of him.

"I see," she muttered, hanging her own head, she stared at her tightly folded hands. She noticed her fingertips had gone white from pressing them together. Her stomach was churning. This was not the conversation she wanted.

Julie didn't trust herself to speak. This was obviously the part where he told her their relationship was over. She stared at the folded piece of paper, wishing she could make him read it. She'd worked on it for days, crafting and re-crafting the words. Her night stand was filled with notes like this one, where she'd worked hard to capture things in exactly the right way. Her words appealed to him as her partner and her lover. Two things that Marc truthfully hadn't been for months.

She'd heard other women describe this moment, but had never dreamed it would happen to her. What would she do without him? How would she raise two kids on her own? How had it all gone so wrong? Julie wanted to scream and run out of the room, but her muscles seemed frozen. It was all she could do to just sit there, waiting for the inevitable.

When Marc spoke again his words almost knocked her over. So tightly wound were her emotions, that she saw spots and almost fainted as her husband spoke again.

"We've got no choice but to sell the house and move."

Had he really just said that? And did he mean they would move together? Or apart?

"Julie, did you hear me?" Marc asked, reaching out to take her hand. "I said we need to move. Get out of this place. It's tearing us apart."

"But you said, uh –"

"You asked what I wanted to do. That's my answer. Don't you want to move?"

Allowing herself a sigh of relief, Julie reached for her husband's hand and held in both of hers. "Yes, of course I do!" Tears rolled down her cheeks and a nervous giggle erupted. So, you don't want a divorce?"

"What??" Marc pulled away and dropped her hand as he stared at his wife. "Divorce? What are you talking about divorce? Is that what the note says?" he asked, reaching for it.

Julie quickly snatched it away. "No, no it doesn't say that at all. I just thought you were going to tell me …" she trailed off, her voice warbling with emotion.

"You want a divorce?" His eyes betrayed the hurt he felt.

"No! No, I don't. Of course not!"

"Then I don't understand," he said.

"Just now, it sounded like you were trying to prepare me," she confessed. "Like you were going to tell me we were done."

"Oh my God!" he exclaimed. "That's what you thought?"

Julie nodded. "I've been thinking that for months," she said. "You've been so distant, and angry."

Marc sat for a few minutes, looking at her. "I can't believe you'd think that I would just leave you and the kids."

"I don't. Not anymore." Julie sighed deeply.

"So, while I've been wrestling with the idea of selling the house, you've been thinking –" Marc stopped abruptly and wiped his eyes with the back of his hand.

"It's okay, I get it now," she reassured him. "It's that whole cross-purposes thing you just said. You've been trying to figure out a way to sell the house, and I misinterpreted."

"It could have caused us to break up," Marc replied, his voice low.

"But we're okay, aren't we? You're not leaving. Right?" Julie craved reassurance.

"I'm not leaving. I'll stay as long as you want me to."

"Forever!" Julie smiled, even as her tears continued. "We're in this together."

"For better or worse. And by the way," Marc reached for her hand again and she took it gratefully. "This is the worse part."

"I love you Marc, but I don't love this house. I never should have tried to."

"There's something going on here, but promise me something, okay?"

"Anything."

"We don't need to stay and figure it out, okay? Let's just call a realtor, cut our losses and get the hell out of here."

"Agreed." These were the words she'd been waiting for. Finally, they would get free of whatever held them prisoner.

~~~~

"I went to the historical society today."

"The historical society? I didn't know this little town had one," Marc answered. "Why?"

"Well, I guess I just wanted to see if I could find out anything."

"About what?" Marc blinked at her, his expression confused.

"Do you remember when we bought this place, and the realtor said it all used to be farmland?"

"Yeah," he said slowly. "It's the same story with almost every sub-division, though. It all used to be farmland."

"Yeah, I know," she agreed. "But I knew there had to be more to the story. I just need to know I'm not crazy."

"Julie, you're not —"

"So, I went looking for answers," she interrupted.

"And did you find any?"

"I'm not sure. You know that dream I've been having?"

Marc nodded. "The one about the guy in the forest, and the log cabin?"

Julie nodded. "It's not a nice dream," she said. "But it's incredibly real. I feel like I'm actually reliving something traumatic, like maybe something from the past."

"I thought we agreed, no more digging."

"Don't do that please," she replied defensively, still not ready to reveal the physical evidence from her last nightmare. "I had to do this. The dream hasn't stopped Marc. It's just gotten more intense."

"Did your research turn up anything?"

Julie glanced into the next room at her children. The movie that played on the screen was a Christian cartoon and both children watched it with keen interest. It seemed so out of place, in light of the discussion she and Marc were about to have.
~~~~

"Yes and no. It might explain a few things."

"Such as?"

"Why we are constantly at each other's throats. And remember when Laura brought the girls over for that wonderful sleepover that was gonna be so much fun?"

Marc nodded, wincing at the memory. "Yeah, little Ava got so freaked out Laura had to come and get them both."

"Exactly, after only an hour and a half! And you know what? My sister says neither of the girls will come over here anymore. They flat out refuse, saying our house is scary."

"Okay, so we have a hotbed of negativity here. We've been over this," he reminded her. "That's why we're moving."

"I know all that," she snapped.

Marc's head came up sharply, his eyes narrowing. "Easy now," he said. "What's the 'and'?"

Julie sighed.

"What?" he said, feigning innocence. "There's always an 'and' so just spit it out."

"This place, this whole area, may have a curse on it."

"What?" Marc leaned away from his wife. This was not what he'd expected to hear. "How do you figure?"

"Let's start with the facts. The land our house sits on was originally all brambles and forest, like my dream. It was eventually cleared by enterprising Japanese immigrants and used to grow crops. They were immigrants, they had very little money. The husband built their first home out of logs."

"Okay," Marc was sitting forward, and Julie could tell he was listening, but his eyes were drawn to his children. "Fact one."

"Fact two," she said. "The man and his wife had several children, and they were farmers. There are records of them living here, acquiring more land acre by acre, until about 1941. By that time, a manor house had replaced their log cabin, and they seemed to be doing well."

"Hmm," Marc commented. "Okay that's fact two, but I don't see how this history lesson affects us."

"It was a manor-style house, Marc. Sound familiar to you?"

"A *manor* house? Around here? Nope."

"Look," she continued, sitting down beside her husband. "Records and maps were pretty scarce in those days, but just going by landmarks and approximate location, that house is right up there." Julie jerked a thumb over one shoulder, pointing behind her.

"The house up the long driveway?" Marc asked incredulously.

Julie nodded. "I found this photograph, published in the local newspaper back in 1940. Houses like that weren't common back then, especially in small towns." Julie handed her husband a folded piece of paper.

Marc unfolded the paper slowly and looked at the copied image for a long time, before re-folding it and placing it on the table top.

"I have to say, that looks a hell of a lot like our neighbour's house," he admitted.

"Yeah," she agreed. "It sure does."

"Could it be the same house?"

"I can't be sure, but I found a lot of real estate ads that look identical, spanning fifty years. There's no more mention of the Japanese family after 1941, but the house itself seems to have been for sale every couple of years."

Marc rubbed his chin thoughtfully. "1941, huh? That's when Japan joined the war. Being a Japanese land-owner here wouldn't have been a good thing back then."

"Oh!" Julie seemed startled. "I guess you're right. I didn't make the connection before. That's probably why there's no more mention of the family after 1941."

"Probably," Marc agreed.

"So, those are the facts," she concluded. Standing up, she began removing the dirty supper dishes from the table, as her husband sat quietly.

"Okay, I'm not doubting you," he said at last. "But these are just circumstances and generalities. Are we any closer to knowing what's going on *here*?"

Julie pushed in her chair and sighed. "There's got to be a better answer. I just need to find it."

"Julie, you promised me," Marc scolded her. "You agreed we would just sell it and get out. I admit, the information you found is fascinating, but where does it stop? We don't have any proof and we're not likely to find it, are we?"

Julie shook her head sadly.

"Then just leave it alone."

"Don't you want to know?"

Marc frowned at her. "No. I just want to take my family and leave."

"But if we understand," she hastened on. "Maybe we can undo this curse and stay here a while longer, til the market heats up. It's not impossible Marc. I've been looking it up."

Marc's sigh was full of the weariness he felt. "Julie, just stop. We're not welcome here. It's time we both realized that. It's my house, but I'd be lying if I said I feel at home here. So, whether this is the original home owner with a deep-seated grudge, or something darker that developed over the years, I don't need to know. I just want to leave it all behind."

Chapter Forty

"Somehow he knows," Julie reported to her husband over the phone.

"Damn!" Marc replied. He didn't need his wife to clarify. "I guess it makes sense that he would. He skulks around watching our every move, after all. Makes sense he would listen in, too. Has he done anything to interfere?"

"Besides mucking up my new paint job in the living room, no."

"Mucking up …what?"

"I re-painted the living room, like we agreed. It looked really nice yesterday."

"Uh-oh. Looked?"

"Yeah. I worked until late last night to get it done, in between dealing with Adam and Amélie. It was well after midnight when I finally got to bed."

"Geez!"

"Yeah, but when I got up this morning, there were hand prints on the walls."

"The kids?"

"Still asleep, *and* highly unlikely in any event."

"What? Why?"

"Well besides the fact that they weren't awake, our kids aren't ten feet tall, and the ladder was still locked in the garage this morning, exactly where I left it. The hand prints were way up high on the walls, Marc. Just below the ceiling. There's nothing in that room the kids could even climb on to get up that high."

"What?" Marc's response was incredulous, but Julie knew he was frustrated by her news.

"The hand prints were child-sized but I'm not fooled. I know it's him."

"What an asshole," Marc commented. "Can you fix it?"

"Yeah, I can fix it. He pisses me off, though."

"Well, this might make you feel happier. I had a chat with one of the local realtors yesterday and she said we won't have to lose money on this deal after all. House prices have finally come up so we might actually do this thing and get into another property, the way we always wanted."

"Marc, that's awesome! Did you make an appointment? How long do I have to finish the repairs?"

"I asked her to come next week."

""What?" Julie looked around at the house. "Marc, I …" She stared at the telephone, unsure what to say next. "Next week? We have so much to do," she finished lamely.

"That's why I said next week," he replied. "She wanted to come tomorrow, but I knew you wanted some time to spruce things up a bit."

"A bit?" Julie's tone was incredulous, as her gaze took in the freshly hand-printed walls.

"Oh! And I didn't tell you the best part," Marc added.

"Okay?"

"Remember when we were gonna sell last time, and we weren't sure what to say to the realtor? I mean, how do you sell a haunted house, right?"

"Right, I remember."

"Well here's the beauty of it," Marc replied happily. "We don't have to say a word about that!"

"What?"

"I'm serious. There's no check box on the real estate forms asking if we believe the place to be haunted."

"You're sure?"

"I checked."

"How did you do that without letting on?" Julie asked.

"I asked to see the forms. Told her I was just being thorough."

"Smart man."

"I have my moments."

~~~~

The realtor arrived promptly at three. She greeted both of them with a firm handshake and a warm smile. Adam happily jogged through the house, from room to room as they led their visitor on a quick tour, and eventually into the formal dining room. The ten-year-old continued to jog, glancing neither left nor right as he continued his circuit. Although the woman had plenty of opportunity to stare or make comments, she casually raised her eyebrows as she unzipped her leather briefcase and transferred a stack of papers to the tabletop.

"Autism?" she asked.

"Um, yes," Julie replied, surprised.

"Is this a good time for you?" the woman asked kindly.

"It's fine," Marc replied. "Believe it or not, this is calm for our household. Besides, we want to get this taken care of as quickly as possible. Is he bothering you? Do you need me to shut the pocket door here?"

"He's not bothering me a bit," she replied. "As long as you're fine, let's get this done."

"Yes," Julie sighed. "We're used to it. He has a circuit he likes to do through the house, you know?"

"Kids will be kids," she commented, smiling. "At least he's happy."

Her wide lips were perfectly outlined with a deep shade of scarlet, and her dark hair was tied back with an intricate gold comb holding the long tresses in place. A variety of bracelets jangled together on her wrist as she arranged the papers between them.

"Now then, let's get some details out of the way, so you can start packing. I imagine you're eager to get on with the next chapter of your lives."

Julie and Marc automatically turned to face each other.

"What do you mean?" Marc asked suspiciously.

"The woman looked up from the paperwork in her lap with surprise. "Most people feel eager for change when they call a realtor. I'm sorry, have I struck a nerve?"

She ducked her chin and looked at them over the rims of her designer framed reading glasses.

"Uh no ... I'm sorry," Julie replied. "We're just a little jumpy."
~~~~

"Oka-ay," she replied. "So, this is a standard contract. Usually a house like yours will go inside of three months. That's what I aim for, but the contract will automatically go for six months, just to be on the safe side. You're good with that?"

Marc frowned. "Six months? Really?" he asked. "We were hoping for a quick sale."

"Everyone hopes for that," the realtor answered, flashing her wide grin at Marc. "Do you have a house already picked out?"

"Ah no, not yet," Marc said. "No sense jumping the gun, right?"

"Sure," she agreed, her tone soothing.

Just then, Adam ran into the room, followed closely by his sister. The two children came to an abrupt halt in front of their parents.

"Give her back!" Amélie screamed. "Mom! He took my doll again! My Suzy doll! Make him give it ba-ack!"

Julie sighed and looked at the floor as Adam bolted from view again.

"Would you excuse me a minute?" she asked, standing up and taking her daughter by the hand she led her away.

"Of course," the realtor replied. "Marc and I will see if we can nail down a date for the open house. Just join us when you can."

"Thanks," Julie breathed, going in search of her son.

"Adam," she said, finding him crouched in his sister's room. "What are you doing in here?"

Julie was just in time to see Adam place a tiny doll onto the floor of Amélie's closet and quickly close the door.

Julie stood in wonder for a moment. "Who's that for?" she asked directly. She'd said the first thing that came to mind, and was about to re-phrase, when Adam spontaneously answered.

"Her," Adam replied confidently.

"Who?" A moment later, Julie hung her head again. He'd turned his body and was staring fixedly at the closet door. Julie shuddered. There was no mistaking exactly who Adam meant by 'her'. This had been going on for months, with Adam hiding Amélie's favorite toys in that same closet. It seemed like he wanted to appease the demanding little spirit that Amélie claimed as her imaginary friend. It was common knowledge that the little spirit girl 'lived' in her daughter's closet.

Only Julie had been able to admit the truth of it thus far and only in the silence of her own heart. Jessie was not a childish invention, but rather a manifestation of spirit energy.

Marc didn't agree, and she didn't push it, but the constant tension over why this was happening and what to do about it wasn't doing their relationship any good.

"Oh Adam," Amélie called to her brother in a high-pitched 'sing-song' voice, suddenly appearing in his bedroom doorway. "You want this?"

Pinched between her fingers was one of his favourite train books, which she wagged back and forth in mid-air.

Amélie knew how to motivate her brother. "Give back my Suzy and you can have it," she announced, her feet wide as she swung the book high over head while rocking her hips side to side.

Adam only had to think about it for a second, before he lunged at his sister.

But Amélie was ready for him. With a quick yelp, she dropped the book and dove under his outstretched arms to haul open the closet door and retrieve her beloved doll.

To the amazement of all, the carpet inside was bare.

Julie wanted to scream but Amélie beat her to it.

"I knew it!" Amélie screamed. "She took it! She always wants it!! Mo-om!"

In that moment, as she stood there with temples throbbing, caught in a scenario she couldn't begin to explain, Julie didn't care what they had to do to make it happen. They had to get out of there!

With a determined step, she left her screaming children behind and returned calmly to the living room as though nothing out of the ordinary was happening. Julie sat down beside her husband, and smiled disarmingly at the realtor.

Marc was worried; she could see it on his face.

The realtor's large eyes blinked several times.

"Sorry for interrupting," Julie said pleasantly, as a counter-point of children's screams echoed down the hallway. "Where are we with the planning?"

"I uh, I think, that I've got a good idea of your must-have list," the realtor said to Julie, struggling to regain her composure. "Are you sure this is a good time? I can call you later if you like?"

"Now is as good a time as ever," Julie replied, her tone still icily calm.

"Alright, let's quickly go through the rest of it then. Do you also work outside the home Julie?"

"Yes, I work part time with special needs children," she said.

The realtor made a note in the open book she held in one hand.

"That sounds interesting, and it strengthens your buying power, too."

Julie and Marc exchanged a small smile.

"Do you think this is doable?" Marc asked. "This is the price range we're looking at." He slid a print-out of several listings across the table so the agent could look more closely at them. "We're ready to make whatever changes you think are necessary."

"This is good, it gives me an idea of budget. May I keep this?"

Marc nodded eagerly.

The real estate agent re-settled her reading glasses onto the bridge of her nose. "And as for changes, unless you really want to, I wouldn't bother. It's nice the way it is."

Marc sat back, clearly impressed with the answer.

"Frankly, it's a nice house in a good location and it's in good repair. At this point, you've got to look at cost versus return. Are you going to get your money's worth if you rip up carpeting, and all that? I would say that's unlikely. My job here is to make sure your home is marketed properly to the right people, and let me assure you, I'm very good at my job. Together, we'll have this place sold in no time!"

"Wonderful!" Julie replied excitedly. "Where do we sign?"

Finally, this was something they both knew how to do.

~~~~

As soon as the 'for sale' sign went up on the front lawn, despite the realtor's advice, Julie became obsessed with change. She poured her creativity into sketches that would help them create a private backyard and although Marc secretly scoffed at the sketches, he pitched in anyway, acquiring potted plants, and strategic pieces of fencing that the young couple hoped would create the illusion of privacy even if they couldn't manage the real thing.

Each night, Marc fell fast asleep almost instantly, while Julie lay awake for hours, sketching feverishly in a notebook she kept by
~~~~

the bed, and casting nervous glances at the doorway and its sinister collection of shadows.

"I know you're there," she muttered. "You know how much I hate that!"

Often, Julie awoke the next morning to find her highly irritated husband, turning off her bedside lamp with a loud click.

"Honestly, Julie. I bought night lights so we wouldn't have to do this," he reminded her one morning as he repeated the task yet again. "We're on a tight enough budget as it is, and electricity is costly. You're not four, ya know. You don't need to sleep with the lights on."

Red in the face, Julie rolled out of bed and stalked past her husband.

"Good morning to you, too," she retorted unhappily.

And this is how it went, day after day until Julie thought she could take no more.

Her bedside table drawer was full of tightly folded notes. They were notes addressed to her husband that Julie had no intention of ever letting him see. She wrote late into each night, as she lay curled tightly into a ball, often sobbing herself to sleep.

"I can't take it anymore," the notes began. "When will the people come? It's been listed for a month already. Is it maybe because they can sense the unhappiness here? We used to love this place together, but that's changed now. I wish I knew how to make it all okay."

As Julie crumbled inside, outwardly, she was the peak of efficiency.

Her Interventionist work doubled, and now she was working until dinnertime, Monday through Friday, with her friend Brenda picking up the days when her mom or dad couldn't help.

"Brenda, you're sure you don't mind?" Julie asked her friend again. "I mean, Adam is a handful! And Amélie is in a very defiant phase right now. You wouldn't believe what the preschool teacher told me the other day!"

"Quit trying to talk me out of this, I said I would do it, and I will. You said it yourself, you need to work. So do I. It's a win-win for everyone."

"And you're okay with that rate, right? I want to be fair."

"Will you stop it? I know you can't afford any more, you're just looking for excuses not to work!" She poked her friend good naturedly in the arm. "Things will be fine, you'll see. Your children love me."

"Now if we could only get some people to start looking at the house," she moaned.

"They'll come," Brenda reassured her. "Aren't you having an open house this weekend?"

"Yeah, another one," she replied. "The first one got rained out."

"Well, the weather is supposed to be grand this weekend, so stay positive, will ya? Things will turn around."

~~~~

Marc arrived home from work, and dropped his duffle bag in the foyer. It made a resounding bang that seemed to echo louder than it should have.

"Hey Julie?" he called. "I'm home!"

His voice resonated in the foyer as he stowed his gear in the closet and carried the rest upstairs.

"You home?" he called. The house was strangely quiet.

Marc grabbed a beer and headed out to the front deck to relax. It was just approaching five o'clock, and he was sure his wife would be home any minute. She was probably at another speech therapy appointment with Adam.

Stretching out his weary legs, he sat back in the lawn chair and looked out over the neighbourhood that would hopefully soon be a distant memory.

Marc took solace in the fact that there was less chance he'd be noticed by nosey neighbours if he sat out front. And besides, the oppressive heaviness he always felt as soon as he crossed the threshold was less palpable out there.

I wonder if he's gonna behave for the open house? Marc thought. Most of his tricks are familiar ones to us now, but I wonder what he'll do with a house-full of strangers?

As the sun set behind his neighbours' rooftops, Marc marvelled at the effect the changing sunlight had on the windows that looked in on the dining room. He watched it through the screen door as the light shifted and danced.
~~~~

Only when the sun had truly set, and the shifting lights continued to spark did Marc sit up and take note.

"What the …?" he muttered. "Well, that's new. I guess that's your answer eh? The old dog learned some new tricks!"

Alone with his thoughts, Marc settled back in his chair to wait for his family and wonder again where they could be. He lifted the now empty can of beer high in the air as he glanced back at the dining room. The lights no longer flickered, he was pleased to see.

"Nice try, asshole," he said. "But we're still moving out, and you're not invited."

Chapter Forty-one

The first day of the open house, Julie and Marc took no chances. Adam and Amélie were safely out with their grandparents for the entire day. Marc had been busy for days, tidying the garage as best he could while Julie scrubbed and polished, paying special attention to floors and windows. The summer sun glinted through the spotless panes and danced across the gleaming laminate floors.

It looked like a perfect home to raise a family.

"What irony," Julie mumbled to herself, as she paused at the head of the staircase.

Julie only had a moment to run her eyes over everything one final time before the peal of the doorbell announced that their realtor Michelle had arrived, to prep for the event.

Marc and Julie climbed into their vehicle and looked back at the front door. Michelle stood, waving cheerily at them from out on the front lawn, where she was working with a small rubber mallet, pounding the stakes of an 'open house' sign into the front lawn. She was impeccably dressed of course, in a pencil skirt, silk blouse and a stylish blazer. The heels of her designer shoes sunk deeper into the earth with each hammer blow.

Marc, ever the gentleman, quickly rolled down his window.

"Hey, are you okay with that?" he called to her. "Do you want a hand?"

Michelle laughed and waved her hand negligently. "Oh, I know this looks ridiculous, especially given my attire, but trust me, I'm fine. I do this all the time."

"Alright," Marc replied. "If you're sure."

"Oh, yes. Totally! There we go," she said, with one final blow of the mallet. "What do you think? Doesn't it look great?" The front porch of the house was festooned with swaying helium balloons and a banner that she'd attached, which proudly proclaimed "Open House Today!"

Marc and Julie had to admit, the house looked spectacular. On Michelle's advice, they'd been busy painting the trim, power-washing the exterior and even planting several flowers in the front garden over the past couple of weekends. The young couple knew the flowers wouldn't last but kept their fingers crossed that the house would be sold long before they succumbed to whatever negativity lurked in the ground.

The realtor was giving it her all, and if her reputation was to be believed, Michelle's 'all' was pretty impressive. If anyone could sell their place with all its quirks and oddities, she was the one to do it.

<div align="center">~~~~</div>

Later that day, as the clock edged towards 4 o'clock, Julie and Marc pulled up into the driveway, where Michelle greeted them with a wide smile.

"Hello, hello!" she said. "Welcome back."

"How did it go?" Marc asked nervously, getting out of the van.

"Oh, we had lots of traffic," Michelle reassured him. "Mostly realtors, which I expected, and some 'looky-loo's' which you're always gonna get, but there were a few serious buyers too. I wouldn't be surprised if we get some offers in the next 24 hours."

"Wow, really?" Julie was amazed. She hadn't thought it would be a success at all, given how important this was to them. The more important something was to them, the less cooperation they got from the entity they now referred to as George. "There weren't any problems at all?" she asked, getting the cat crate out of the backseat.

"Nothing I couldn't handle," Michelle replied cheerily. "Good thing you took the cat with you. That door was opening and closing all day! She might've gone home with someone."

"Yeah, good thing."

"And Marc, thank you for thinking ahead and leaving a key to your in-law's suite. You didn't mention that it tends to re-lock. I couldn't see why it would do that, but maybe I missed something."

Julie and Marc exchanged glances as Michelle leafed through a large black planner book in her hand. Her long, red nails flashed in the fading sunlight as she flicked through the pages. "Okay, I've recorded all the feedback I got from today. Realtors like to write on the backs of their business cards. I have all the info in here, but I thought you might find them interesting, so here you are." She handed Marc a stack of cards. "Keep in mind, you can't please everyone. The take-away is a successful open house. And we have tomorrow to do it all over again, right? So on that note, I'll see you both tomorrow afternoon!"

"Okay," Marc replied, watching as she marched to the curb and got into the elegant, black SUV she always drove. "See you tomorrow."

"I think this calls for a celebratory drink, what do you think?" Marc asked, as they re-entered the house that had never been theirs. Annie howled from inside the crate as if to remind them she was still inside.

"I'm down with that idea," Julie replied, smiling. "And Annie's happy to be back home too, aren't you darlin'?" Grasping the mechanism on the front of the crate, she set down the crate and opened the door, but the cat backed into the far corner and hissed, her eyes flashing dangerously.

"What's her problem?" Marc wondered.

"Oh, she's probably ticked that we took her on an outing without asking for permission. Remember, this one is truly an indoor cat. She actually seems to be afraid of the sky! Can you believe it?"

"With that cat, I'd believe anything," Marc chuckled dryly. "That's our army-boots Annie!"

Julie smiled as they climbed the staircase together.

Army boots-Annie was an inside joke. When visitors came to the house, however infrequently, loud foot stomps going up and down the staircase caused more than one guest to comment.

Julie and Marc became adept at blaming the cat. "Oh that's just Annie" they'd say, with a calm smile. "Sure sounds like a person, doesn't it? Loudest cat we've ever had. We call her Army boots Annie!"

Usually the visitors laughed at the 'inside joke', easing what would have been an awkward moment for all.

"Hey, my parents are taking the kids to dinner so they'll be a while," Julie commented to her husband. "How about let's order in and spend some time just you and me?"

"Alright!" Marc answered quickly, as he chased his wife up the last few stairs playfully.

But as the young couple got to the top, the smiles on their faces quickly faded.

For the open house, Michelle had purchased large bundles of fresh flowers and helium balloons, intended to give the house a festive air, but the air inside the house now was anything but festive.

Vases that had been full of fresh flowers in the kitchen, dining and recreation rooms were now tipped over, water and cut flowers strewn everywhere.

Julie turned her back on the mess, as hot tears flowed down her cheeks.

"He's not gonna let us go Marc," she sobbed, as her husband folded her in his strong embrace and let her cry.

There were no words he could say to comfort her. His thoughts were running along the same path.

Hours later, with order somewhat restored and both children bathed and tucked into bed, Julie laid fresh towels over the still-damp areas of the living room carpet and stepped on each one methodically, trying to draw out the last of the moisture.

"I hope these are gonna be dry by tomorrow," she worried.

"So what if they aren't," Marc grumbled, grabbing the TV remote.

"Let's watch something stupid and brainless, okay?"

"I'm down with that," Julie agreed.

"No home renovation shows, no real estate reality shows and definitely no thrillers," Marc said, as he flipped rapidly though the channels.

"I don't want to watch any dramas either," Julie added. "We've got too much of that in our own house … and nothing sappy. I am not in the mood for a chick-flick."

Marc grinned and kept flipping as his wife stowed the last of the take-out food in the fridge. "You want some popcorn? I think we have some jiffy-pop in the cupboard."

"Yeah! That would be great," Marc agreed. "You might need my height to reach it though. I put it up high so it was safe from little mister."

Marc unfolded his 6-foot frame from the couch and went to the kitchen to help his wife. "Ah! Jiffy-pop. I haven't had that in ages!"

"My parents used to buy it when we went camping," Julie added, turning on the stove burner closest to her. "I love watching it get bigger and bigger until you think it can't take anymore. Funny how stuff like that sticks with you hey?"

"Yeah," Marc replied. "I only hope our kids have good memories of their childhoods. This place hasn't been all bad, but man it's definitely been weird. I guess time will tell how screwed up our kids are from it all."

"Nice," Julie said, making a face at her husband, as she moved the container back and forth on the element, waiting for it to get hot, so it would start popping the kernels inside its tightly wrapped foil package.

A few minutes later, Marc came over to check the progress. "What's taking so long?" he asked. "Is it popcorn yet?"

"No," Julie replied. "That's odd. What's going on?" She held her hand close to the element, but felt no heat. "What's this? It's not even warm."

"Oh no, not this too!" Marc sighed. "Let me have a look."

"Oh, for heaven's sake!" Julie backed away, as Marc lifted the stove top.

"I'll just check the connections first, it could be a blown fuse," he began. "Wait a second! What in the hell? Julie," he called. "Look. You didn't plug the stove element back in after you cleaned it this morning. In fact, all of them are unplugged."

"What?" Julie came closer. Although everything had looked fine at first glance, she now saw that all the electrical prongs were facing away from their sockets, each of them a quarter turn out of alignment.

It made no sense.

"This is impossible," she said slowly. "I used the stove to make the kids lunch. It was working fine, then. I didn't do this, Marc."

The look of disbelief on Marc's face slowly gave way to anger.

"So …he's upping the ante," Julie said, her voice quiet as she watched the heat build in her husband's face. "I wonder what he'll try next?"

~~~~

The sun was setting a couple of days later, as Julie and Marc sank wearily onto the sofa in their formal living room, a place they rarely spent time. The stack of business cards left over from their open house spread out on the coffee table in front of them. Across the backs of each card were handwritten comments.

"This one says, 'shows well. Clean and well kept', which is nice to hear," Julie read them out to her husband, picking them up one at a time. "These next ones are pretty much the same, but oh, I like this one. 'Shows great. A good family home. Just what I'm looking for."

Marc grinned and nodded his head while he sipped his drink appreciatively.

"Okay, this one is a bit negative."

"Michelle did say we'd get those too," Marc reminded her. "What does it say? I hope George minded his manners." The comment was tossed out casually but Julie felt her back stiffen as she read.

"Well, mostly they talk about the lack of yard space and the condition of the back yard. If only they knew what it looked like when we bought it!"

"True," Marc replied.

"This one points out that the garage was too full and didn't afford a full view of the space."

"Marc snorted as he laughed out loud. "No shit, Sherlock! Why do you think we're moving?"

Julie smiled weakly. "Yeah, well there's lots of reasons, aren't there?"

"Not that we're gonna tell them."

"I know, I know," she said, returning her gaze to the last few cards.

But as Julie read, she grew visibly upset. Marc sat forward, a look of concern on his face. "Jules? What's wrong?"

"I knew it!" she muttered angrily. "I just knew he couldn't stay out of it. Remember what Michelle said?"
~~~~

Gripping the card, she got up and stalked out into the hallway, her hands balled into fists.

"Look, I know you're not happy about this, but it's a done deal. There's no going back. If you weren't such an asshole we could live together in peace, but you've got only yourself to blame for that!" She spoke angrily to the empty space, her voice echoing down the stairwell. "You've pulled some nasty tricks before, but I will not permit you to lock any of my doors! That goes too far! This is still MY house!"

Marc's eyes widened at that and he walked quickly to his wife and grabbed the last few cards from her clenched hands.

Flipping each one over, he read: Would have loved to view the master but the door was locked.

Another one read: Door to in-law suite unreliable. Locking mechanism stuck several times.

The third was simply: should replace glass door at back of house. Locking mechanism appears broken. Not a good sign.

"Aw geez, George," Marc muttered. "You're such an ass."

The couple knew with certainty that these things had been his doing.

"I was fully expecting him to flick lights on and off and maybe go stomping up and down the stairs, but randomly locking doors? That's a new one."

<div style="text-align:center">~~~~</div>

Day two of the Open House passed without any additional drama, a fact that Julie and Marc were grateful for, but that night, a tearful Amélie awoke them all with terrified screams.

'What is it? What's happened?" Julie exclaimed, drawing her daughter close reflexively even as she rolled out of bed.

The clock on her bedside table read 4:15.

Amélie, obviously deeply upset, seemed incapable of speech. The tiny girl's body shook as she clung to her mother and sobbed.

Marc, now fully awake just stared at the two, uncertain what to do next.

"Ami, Ami, shh," Julie soothed as she ran her hands over the child's back, limbs and head, trying to assess whether she was hurt or just frightened. "Are you hurt?" she asked repeatedly.

"Stop the noise!!" Adam bellowed as he appeared in his parent's doorway with a deep frown.

With a look that conveyed his sense of helplessness, Marc went to his son and tried to turn him around, but Adam was rooted to the spot.

Clearly, it was going to be another one of those nights.

"Ami, you need to tell mommy what you saw," Julie encouraged her daughter, several days later. "You can't just keep it inside."

But the stubborn child, normally quite talkative, was mute on the subject.

"She'll tell us when she's ready," Marc soothed his worried wife later that evening. "Right now, let's just concentrate on getting this place sold. Maybe Michelle would let you help with the listing description? You are a writer after all. How about you call her in the morning?"

"I don't know," Julie answered. "Wouldn't that be kind of rude? I mean, basically I'm telling her that the description she wrote isn't good enough."

"You really think she wrote it?" Marc replied dubiously. "She probably has people for that. In case you didn't notice, that's one busy lady!"

"I know. I just don't want to offend her."

Marc shook his head and walked away.

Although the house continued to be shown by various realtors over the next several weeks, it remained on the market with no offers.

As the last of the summer sun faded, and October settled in with its grey, foggy days, their realtor Michelle called with an update. Unfortunately, it wasn't the news they wanted to hear.

The purpose of her call was to encourage a price drop on the house.

Crestfallen, Marc and Julie panicked. Would they ever get out?

It seemed everything was conspiring against them.

"No Michelle," Marc said firmly. "Let's just leave it where it is for awhile, okay? It seems too early to drop the price right now."

"Okay," she sighed. "You're the boss but remember I promised you results only if you followed my advice."

"Yes, we understand," Marc replied. "Just give it another month, okay?"

Fall turned into winter and the couple grew more and more unsettled. Although Julie did follow through with Marc's advice and wrote an ad for the house with their realtor's hearty approval, the showings dwindled to almost nothing.

"The time has come, I'm afraid," the realtor said, her voice firm over the phone. "Holidays are the worst time to sell a property, so we need to move fast to avoid that."

Marc pressed the speaker phone button but continued to hold the phone tightly in one hand.

"Hi Michelle, its Julie here, Marc and I have talked it over and we agree with you, we're just nervous, that's all. If we drop the price down too much, we might not get out of here at all, and we have to."

There. She'd said it. Marc looked at his wife and she was shocked to see his handsome blue eyes glistening with unshed tears.

"I understand," Michelle said softly. "Is it okay if I come over so we can talk about this face to face?"

"Sure," Marc answered quickly. "We're home now."

In a few short minutes, Michelle was seated at the kitchen table with Marc and Julie. The overhead lamp cast a warm yellow circle of light over the three people who sat with their heads together. Several sheets of paper lay on the table between them.

"So you see," Michelle said gently. "The way the market is now, we've got to move quickly. I know you're scared but if you trust me and let me do what I know, this will work and then you can get out of here."

The emphasis Michelle placed on the carefully chosen words had the desired effect, and soon the price on their house was adjusted accordingly. A few more showings happened, but interest in their property appeared to have dwindled.

"Don't worry," Michelle advised cheerily when she called for her weekly check-in. "It'll pick up. It always does, just before the holidays."

Julie grew increasingly irritated with the need to keep the house in a spotless condition, lest Michelle call with a last-minute showing. All their emotions were at a fever-pitch, especially Adam, who didn't fully understand why mommy got so mad when he left his toys on the floor.

Amélie was nearly five, and the petulant little girl was frequently out of sorts, stomping off to her room in high drama over yet another perceived injustice.

Julie forced herself to just breathe and let it go.

Wasn't that what Brenda's 'yoga for beginners' video preached? Inner peace was a state of mind, after all.

Despite her determination to take it all in stride, knowing it was just a matter of time now until they were free of this nightmare, Julie was constantly on edge, irritation spilling over at the slightest provocation.

"I don't know how much more I can take Marc," she confided to her husband one evening, as they got ready for bed. "He hasn't let up."

Marc glanced at his wife, noting how haggard she'd become. There were dark circles under each eye and he knew she wasn't sleeping well. He didn't have to ask who she meant by 'he'.

"And the nightmares?" he asked.

"Yup, still there." She tapped the side of her head.

Her voice had lost its cheerful lilt and it was a rare occasion when Marc caught a glimpse of his wife's vibrant smile.

"Hang in there, we're almost home-free," he said, reaching out to squeeze her hand. "Maybe focusing on packing up more stuff will help?"

"What for?" she muttered angrily, tossing the shirt she'd been trying to fold back into the laundry basket. "We're never getting out of here."

"Don't say that!" Marc winced at the sound of his own voice. "We just have to stay positive."

"Easy for you to say, you're never here."

"Julie that's not fair. I have to go to work. We've been over this. You're working now, too. You know what it's like."

"Oh sure, I know what it's like to work with other people's kids and help them learn, only to come home and realize my own kid lacks all those same skills," she replied with heavy sarcasm. "And you know what Marc? I'm too tired to teach him and he knows it! But you know what? My guilt is so heavy that I try anyways, but all I get in return is screaming. Do you know what it's like to be screamed at all the time Marc? Do you?" Her eyes were filled with tears as she faced her husband.

Too uncomfortable to form a reply, Marc simply picked up the stack of folded towels in front of him and left the room.

Folding her arms on the edge of the basket in front of her, Julie rested her head there and cried. She wasn't surprised that Marc didn't return to the bedroom. They rarely went to bed at the same time anymore, and the intimacy seemed to have left their relationship long ago.

My soul mate … my partner. Oh God! Why is this happening?

Chapter Forty-two

"These people are whackos!" Marc fumed.

Michelle laughed good-naturedly. "They may be, but who cares? As long as their money is good, the deal is done!"

"Yeah, but look at this list?" Marc replied, holding up the piece of paper Michelle had brought. "Who does stuff like this?"

"I admit it's a bit unorthodox," Michelle agreed.

"Unorthodox?" Marc repeated. "This isn't a list of requests, it's a list of demands."

Julie took the list from her husband and scanned it quickly.

- Have all carpets professionally cleaned and sanitized
- Must leave ALL draperies and ALL appliances
- Walls to be returned to a neutral color (i.e. family room)
- We are interested in ALL living room furniture and would like it to be part of the offer. (including piano)
- Furnace professionally cleaned and serviced
- Playground structure in back yard stays (this is considered a permanent structure and cannot legally be removed anyhow).

"They are nuts!" Julie agreed, scanning the list again. "Do you they really think we're going to agree to all this?" She handed the list back to Michelle.

The realtor just shrugged and started making notes in her book. "Let's just take it from the top, okay? What are your answers?"

"That was weird about the walls, hey?" Michelle said to them when they talked next. "I've never heard of anyone being so bold as to ask the sellers to re-paint."

"Exactly," Julie agreed. "If it's so important to them, they can repaint themselves, just like we did."

"It's part of owning a house," Marc added.

"Uh, I hate to bring it up, but there's been another request," Michelle said.

Marc and Julie just looked at each other, grateful they were on speak-phone with their realtor so she couldn't see the look of utter astonishment on both their faces.

"What do they want now?" Julie asked.

"They want to meet the neighbours," she said.

"They'll meet them soon enough anyhow," Julie retorted. "But if they're asking us to facilitate that for them? Uh, no. We aren't doing that."

Marc's expression went from incredulity to cold fury as he listened and Julie watched her husband's complexion change from pale pink, to scarlet.

The whole thing felt wrong, somehow. Who were these people?

Even after the purchasing agreement was signed, granting them the backyard structure, all appliances and draperies, pretty standard in most real estate agreements, the demands kept coming.

They wanted the garbage cans.

No.

They wanted the piano.

No.

They wanted the lawnmower.

No.

They wanted the living room furniture.

Again, no.

Julie and Marc soon realized that the purchasers had to be driving past the house daily, adding new items to their list of demands. Was this at all normal?

Julie and Marc's realtor just shook her head, and shrugged. "It seems odd to me that their realtor would even bring these items forward. They must be very convincing."

"Conniving is more like it," Julie corrected her.

"They'll have the place soon enough," Marc answered. "I don't know why they keep making all these demands. The papers are already signed. They aren't getting another thing."

"Yeah," Julie agreed. "Michelle, what is this all about?"

"Amateurs," she replied, smiling comfortingly. "Obviously, the purchasers are panicking a little. They've probably never bought anything this big before. Don't worry, you have professionals on your side. As you know, the contract has already been signed. You already know your legal obligations, and you'll abide by them and not one thing more. What I can't understand is why their agent puts up with them?" She turned to Julie. "Have you arranged to have the carpets done yet? That's their biggest point, as I recall."

"Yeah, it's all set. Being done on the last day so they're nice when the new family moves in," Julie replied.

"That's very conscientious of you. Too bad everyone didn't think that way. Well, hopefully we won't hear any more from them."

"By the sounds of things, they seem to be watching the house," Julie remarked.

"Wouldn't put it past them," she said. "Obviously, they have no class."

~~~~

Moving day had come at last!

Julie eyed the list in her hand.

How was she going to get all of this done in ONE day?

"I must be nuts," she muttered, slugging down the rest of her coffee mug, she washed and dried it carefully, then packed in into a nearby box.

The children were already out with their auntie for a day of fun. The goal was to ensure Adam and Amélie's rooms were all set up at the new house by dinnertime.

Julie moaned again. "What was I thinking? Is that even possible?"

~~~~

Julie paused half-way up the stairs. How could the oven timer possibly be going off? That stupid thing had never worked properly.

Even from brand new it wouldn't allow them to set it for longer than fifty-nine minutes.

The time on her wristwatch proved how long she'd been down in her mom's place. Nearly three hours! As Julie pushed the button that would silence the timer, her hand hovered over the controls.

"I wonder."

Jabbing at the small, round buttons on the control pad, Julie tried over and over to set the timer for longer than fifty-nine minutes, but just as she suspected, the bargain basement appliance refused to cooperate.

'Push?' The command on the digital read-out offered proof of the machine's confusion.

Julie pressed 'start' once more, but again the appliance gave forth a double beep and displayed the same command. *'Push?'*

"Stupid thing," she said. "Good riddance. At least I know I couldn't have done that accidentally."

A moment later, something heavy fell to the floor in the next room, making her jump.

Julie rushed to the living room, to find her antique lamp, one of the last items to be transported, now lying on its side.

"Har-de-har-har," she said sarcastically to the otherwise empty room. "Very nice. That's so original. Is that all you've got?"

Fatigue made her careless.

~~~~

"Not again!" she muttered angrily. "It's impossible. I never even touched it this time!"

Nevertheless, the oven timer was beeping away again upstairs, and once again, she was running to shut it off.

Julie made a face as she jogged upstairs. It felt like she'd been running for years. She sighed as she thought about it. Would there be less running now? She certainly hoped so.

Just as she gained the upper floor, the sound of the front door slamming closed interrupted her thoughts.

Good! Marc's back. Finally!

"I'm up here!" she called to him. Going to the stove, she cleared the alarm and worked at a sticky spill of something on the nearby countertop.

Julie worked on autopilot, even though, in the back of her mind, she knew those counters were spotless an hour ago.
~~~~

As the tell-tale pressure that Julie knew so well began to build in her ears, her shoulders drooped automatically.

Crossing to the staircase, Julie called down its length hopefully. "Marc? Is that you?"

Every minute she spent in there felt too long. Was it her imagination? High blood pressure? Both? The air around her felt as though it crackled with energy. The hairs on her forearms bristled and goose bumps stood out on her skin.

"Cut that out!" she whispered fiercely, hoping her husband wouldn't hear.

The last thing she wanted was more explanations. She was tired of always having to explain.

In a matter of hours, they would close the doors on this place with finality and walk away.

It was going to be someone else's problem then, and she could hardly wait!

As the thought formed in her mind, she was shocked by the sound of the front door opening and slamming shut with force.

"Marc honey? What's going on? Do you need me? I'm coming!"

 Julie jogged confidently down the staircase to greet her husband. Already, she was thinking about the things that were already inside her new house and where each of them would go. A quick check of her watch revealed that she only had a few hours left until Adam and Amélie were due back for supper and she wanted all in readiness by then.

"Marc?" she called out, reaching the bottom. Julie frowned at the front door, which was closed and dead-bolted. "Why lock it now?" she muttered. "I guess he's on autopilot too."

With a growing sense of unease, Julie hauled open the spring-loaded door into the garage and stared at the empty space. Marc and her dad had been busy all day clearing everything out of the previously cluttered space.

"Marc?" she called quietly. "Where are you?"

The garage door was wide open, which seemed unusual, but she guessed Marc had done that for a reason.

The mystery deepened however as she caught a glimpse of the driveway and realized it was empty.

The sounds she'd heard hadn't been Marc after all.

Wanting to cry, but knowing she couldn't afford to, Julie took a deep breath, and returned to her mother's suite to begin the vacuuming that was the final chore on her enormous list.

She could feel someone watching, but that wasn't anything new.

"Enjoying the view?" she muttered with heavy sarcasm. "Boy, am I gonna be glad to get rid of you." Despite the ever-present sense of being watched, Julie just kept on going, running the vacuum over the carpets in methodical sweeps, anxious to be done, and wondering how long Marc was going to be.

Julie had just moved the vacuum to the living room and plugged it in, when she heard noises over her head that made her stop and stare at the ceiling.

Was someone walking up there?

A moment later, Julie heard her name being called. The sound was muffled, coming from upstairs, and she realized with relief that this time, Marc was back… and he was walking on the wet carpets!

"My carpets!" she squealed, bolting for the door. The footsteps were firm and heavy. Marc wore heavy steel toed boots when he worked, and since he'd been at the new house all day, he wouldn't have known the carpets were still damp.

"That is so not happening," she muttered as she ran. "It took me forever to get that arranged."

"Marc? Marc!" she shouted. "Come out of there! The carpets aren't dry yet!"

But as Julie arrived at the top of the stairs, she realized that once again she was talking to herself.

"What the – ?"

"I must be cracking up," she mumbled. George was certainly a nasty prankster, but he'd never called her by name before. "The sooner we get out of here, the better."

She'd been running ever since they'd moved in. Always checking on every noise, running from room to room in a frantic search for someone she could never find.

She had ample reason not to go further, but almost without realizing it her body responded, pointing her feet down the hallway.

The house was quiet. The previous footsteps were no longer audible.

All the furniture was gone, the carpets upstairs had been vacuumed and cleaned, the bathrooms once again immaculate. The newly-laid laminate in the hallway and master bedroom shone. Everything looked beautiful.

Julie shook her head. Appearances certainly were deceiving.

Room by room, she toured the space, reminded of that fateful day when they first saw it and fell in love.

Or so they thought.

With a heavy sense of déjà vu, she peeked into empty rooms, switching on and off lights to ensure all was in readiness for the new owners.

She wondered if the photos this family took would have mysterious white blotches in the centre, too? As she walked through the master bedroom, Julie paused. How many more sleepless nights would there be in that room? She was grateful it wouldn't be her tossing turning, but the thought of handing over the keys to a haunted house still filled her with dread.

These people were weirdos, there was no question about that, and they liked to talk tough, but would they have the guts to sue them over an undisclosed ghost?

With a heavy sigh of resignation, she gave the counter in the ensuite a final wipe. The face in the mirror looked haggard. No wonder her family and friends danced around the subject when she admitted how tired she was. No one wanted to say it out loud.

She wasn't the same energetic young woman who'd moved in just a few years earlier. The face that stared back at her was old. Lines of worry etched deeply across her forehead and around her tired eyes.

As Julie stood there, running her to-do list through her mind, footsteps sounded behind her in the bedroom.

Turning quickly, all she saw was an empty room.

"Oh boy. Here we go again," she sighed. "You're having fun, aren't you?"

As though in answer, the bedroom door closed with a bang.

Jumping back, Julie automatically sought out the windows to rule out a sudden draft.

All of them were firmly closed.

No matter how many noises she heard, no matter how many times things appeared to move on their own she could never get used to this. She didn't think anyone could.

"Damn, I can't wait to get out of here," she whispered fiercely.

Forcing some steel into her voice, she went on. "You think you're always in control? Well soon, we'll be gone and you'll have nothing. What do you think of that? Maybe you were a man once, but now you're just an empty shadow, with no power." she shouted, using adrenaline to build up her courage. "In fact, when my husband gets back I'm leaving here forever!"

Julie pushed away from the wall she'd had her back against and strode purposefully across the room. Gripping the ice-cold door handle, she flung open the door, half expecting to see a menacing figure standing on the other side, but of course there was no one there.

Her heart hammered inside her chest as she fought to keep her panic in check. Although she'd lived in that house for years, it still took everything she had just to keep going.

The oppressive feeling from the bedroom was gone, whisked away like the darting shadow she'd accused him of being. Could it be that simple? Was he finally gone? Maybe he realized at last that this was a done deal?

Chapter Forty-three

Opening the door to the suite, a gust of cool air blew her hair away from her face, just as it always did. Today, the breeze felt good. There was so much to do! Julie turned the lock on the doorknob behind her and heard a satisfying 'snick'. Somehow, she felt better with a locked door at her back.

A few minutes later, on hands and knees, Julie plunged a wet rag deep inside each cupboard, wiping away dust and debris.

Again, the front door banged. With gritted teeth Julie kept working, her head and upper torso still inside the cupboard.

Just try to block it out, she thought.

Moment by moment, more sounds joined the first until it seemed obvious someone else had arrived, and was walking around upstairs.

Yes! The young woman sagged with relief. Any moment, Marc will come looking for me, she thought.

"I'm in here!" she called. Forgetting all about the locked door, she plunged her arm deeper in to the corner cupboard she was working in, twisting her torso so she could reach the back.

But as the minutes ticked past, Julie started to wonder if she'd been duped once again.

"I'm not wasting any more energy on you," she muttered angrily. "Go ahead and slam doors, see if I care."

Taking a deep breath to steady her nerves, she cleaned and packed the last few items from her mom's kitchen. Julie couldn't help feeling exposed, kneeling with her back to the hallway. The energy in the house was building, and Julie still didn't know just what he was capable of. Would he try again to hurt her? At least the children were away from his influence and she would no longer have to fear for their safety.

As she scrubbed, Julie thought belatedly that a radio would have been a good idea. It would have helped to drown out unwelcome noises, if nothing else.

Allowing her thoughts to wander to the details of the new house, Julie wasn't ready for the firm touch she felt on her shoulder.

"Wha–" she yelped, startled at the touch.

Whirling around, she banged her head painfully on the cupboard as she turned, and tipped over the bucket of soapy water at her side.

Standing up, Julie stripped off her rubber glove to touch her head gingerly, her heart pounding as she saw for herself that she was still the only person in the room.

Just as he'd done from the start, the ghost who loved to torture her remained hidden.

"How am I gonna get this done with you messing around?" she exclaimed, frustration and anger masking her fear. These were tricks she had come to know well, and while she would never get used to them completely, Julie was past the point of caring. She just wanted out!

"And now look at me. I'm soaked!" she continued. The knees of her blue jeans dripped with sudsy water, and a large puddle covered half the kitchen floor.

After sopping up the mess the best she could, she grabbed her cell phone angrily from the counter, and dialled Marc's phone.

""Where are you?" she asked when she heard him answer.

"At the new house," he answered. "Are you okay? You sound upset."

"Yeah… you could say that. Are you coming back soon?"

She hated how small and fearful her voice sounded.

"Pretty soon," he said. "What's wrong? Are you almost done?"

"Well, I would be, except for all the shit that keeps happening." She sighed. "I guess I should have known he'd be pissed about this."

"Uh-oh," her husband replied. "What's he up to now?"

Julie noticed she didn't need to clarify who she meant. She and Marc had been talking about this in low tones late into the night for the past several weeks.

"Oh, he's doing the usual, banging shit around and trying to scare me. If I can ever get a few minutes' peace, I've still got to finish wiping out mom's cupboards and vacuuming her rugs. That's the last of the chores on my list, and then I'm getting the hell out of here!"

"Okay," Marc said. "We're just unloading your dad's truck and then I'm coming back. Just ignore him, and try not to yell at him okay? It always makes things worse."

Julie bit her lip and looked around guiltily.

"Can you bring me a clean pair of jeans?" she asked. "I spilled a bucket of soapy water all over myself just a few minutes ago."

"Really?" Marc sounded worried. "Where would I find that? This place is a jumble."

"If you can find our high-boy dresser, check the bottom drawer."

"Okay, I'll try," he promised. "Sounds like you're having a fun time over there."

"You don't know the half of it," she said. "Just get here fast, okay? I don't think I should be here by myself anymore."

Marc sighed quietly into the phone while Julie waited. "Tell you what, I'm just going to come now. Our van is empty. I'll see you in a few minutes."

"Thanks," she sighed. Julie pressed the button to end the call and went to re-fill her bucket.

Julie knew she shouldn't give him the satisfaction, but she still hated surprises. Her work continued, albeit in paranoid, jerky busts of activity. She leaned quickly into each cupboard, made a few swipes with the cloth in her hand, and then sat up, checking over her shoulder and wincing at random sounds, real or imagined.

She knew she was keyed up, but there wasn't anything to be done about it.

At last, the only thing left to do was to vacuum her father's den.

It was a room she'd often felt uncomfortable in, although her parents had felt nothing untoward in all the time they lived there.

Or at least not that they felt comfortable sharing with Julie or Marc.

As she opened the glass doors, and plugged in the vacuum cleaner, all she could think of was getting the hell out of that house!

As soon as she switched on the vacuum, a shrill noise sounded.

"What the hell?" Julie shouted, switching it off right away, she realized it was the smoke detector in the hallway.

Running to inspect the unit, Julie saw the emergency light was on, as it would be during an actual fire, but there was no smoke.

Waving a nearby broom underneath it did nothing to silence the alarm. With no ladder and no chair to stand on, she was simply too short to reach the device.

Escaping the suite to give her ears a break, she stood in the foyer and tried to breathe through the anger that ripped through her.

With the alarm still shrilling away, Julie climbed the staircase with weary legs. It had already been a long day and she wasn't interested in playing more games.

"What next?" She asked, throwing her arms up in the air. "You are too much; do you hear me?"

The house grew mercifully quiet, the shrilling alarm suddenly silenced.

"Look, I know you're upset. We've been together for quite some time. I guess you could even say we've gotten used to you," she muttered. "I've tried to figure out who you are, where you came from and what you could possibly want from us, but I still haven't got a clue. I don't know what you have against us, but don't expect these new people to be any better. They aren't even gonna *try* to understand you."

Julie didn't know why she felt compelled to say these things.

"Well, anyhow, I just thought you should know," she said, starting down the stairs again. "Marc will be here in a few minutes and then we're outta here."

She'd just passed the midpoint of the staircase, when she felt it come at her. Clutching at the railing beside her with both hands, she gasped for breath as a vice-like pressure closed around her neck.

Spots danced in front of her eyes. She was being choked!

She clawed at her own neck but felt nothing beneath her desperate fingers except bare flesh. Julie's throat burned. She realized with desperate sadness that her worst fears were about to be realized. As her vision dimmed, she thought of her children. They would be safe now. Too bad Marc would be the one to find her like this. He was such a good man …

Inexplicably, as Julie felt her body collapse to the hard surface of the staircase, the pressure around her neck released!

She dragged in a lungful of air, feeling the life slowly return to her body. Coughing and choking, she looked around in panic.

It was clear this ghostly maniac had *decided* to let her go. She wasn't strong enough to fight him off and he knew it. This was truly a game of cat and mouse, after all.

Julie's throat burned as she pulled herself up. The house was empty but the air crackled with energy.

"Leave me alone!" she croaked, rubbing her bruised throat. Tears streamed down her cheeks, but Julie knew she couldn't give in to it or she would be even more vulnerable. Marc would be there soon, what was taking him so long?

With careful steps, Julie watched the kitchen doorway. Was it a trick of the fading afternoon sunlight, or was there an oddly shaped shadow peeking out from the corner of the pantry?

Keeping her eyes on it, she backed down each step, feeling her way in wet sneakers, the rubber squeaking in protest against the hardwood stairs.

It was a stand-off and Julie knew it.

The light changed again as she stared at the thing that might be a shadow.

Her eyes widened as the smoky-looking patch of grey coalesced into a dark, elongated mass.

Her legs felt as if they were made of wood, and refused to bend. Is this what fear did to you?

She recalled another moment like this, as she lay in the doorway of her own bedroom, fighting just to breathe.

It was the same story, she realized. An endless loop. He really *did* plan to kill her!

And for the first time, Julie finally understood. The attacks weren't random. They were engineered. This angry spirit wasn't just reacting and lashing out at anyone who stood before him. These attacks were *personal* and until that moment, Julie hadn't realized that the games, the pranks and the taunting messages had all been aimed at her!

With growing clarity, Julie realized that from the first day, he'd selected her as his target.

Swallowing against the new lump of fear that now stuck in her throat, she edged to the next step, aware he was waiting, calculating his next move.

Clearly, his strength had grown, but how? What fed this? Raw energy? Fear?

Julie's mind raced back in time, seeing each incident with new eyes. It had been a training ground, she realized. A chance for him to hone his skills, improve his accuracy and lengthen his reach.

Feeling his ghostly hands around her neck was all the proof she needed that this had gone far enough!

A heaviness pressed down on the top of her head, and instinctively, Julie lifted her eyes. The dark shape that had stood in the kitchen only a moment earlier, now hovered just above her head, undulating like the beginnings of a tornado!

"NOO!" She screamed.

Whirling around, she took the rest of the stairs in a rush, desperate to get outside. Sweat had broken out on her forehead and her hands were slick on the railing, but she clutched at is desperately, keenly aware of the danger.

It wasn't real, it couldn't be real! Let me wake up! She pleaded.

She didn't even feel her feet leave the step as her legs were punched violently out from under her, but a moment later, Julie realized she was airborne, her hand twisting painfully away from the safety of the railing as her arching body pitched forward into empty space.

A sharp stab of pain in her back, told her she'd come down hard on the on the unforgiving edge of the wooden steps.

There was no sense of direction, only spinning, sliding and falling again.

It took only a few moments, but she seemed to be falling forever! Every painful contact with the hard, newly refinished steps whooshed the breath from her lungs. Julie shouldn't have had time to think, but her head filled with the overwhelming sense that this had all happened before!

"Mommy, I flew over the barn!" a child's voice, dreamy and soft filled her mind.

In the space of a heartbeat, she recognised the voice as her own, the innocent statement the only way five-year-old Julie could describe the sensation she'd felt at the moment of impact when an angry stallion kicked her in the face, so many years ago, almost killing her in the process.

The child in her melded with the adult for another moment and then, everything was still.

She'd stopped falling. Crumpled at the bottom of the staircase, her battered body stinging in several places, she remembered her dream:

Her beloved rag doll, tossed aside by his careless hand. Julie had watched, powerless to stop it, as the doll came to rest, her limbs awkwardly twisted at the base of that same staircase.

The irony of it wasn't lost on her, but she couldn't bring herself to be more frightened. A searing pain in the small of her back knifed her over and over as she dragged herself to her feet,

She fumbled to turn and meet her attacker.

Certain he would strike again, Julie pressed her back against the door to her parent's suite and prayed, her breath coming in ragged gasps as she called the rote prayers to mind, taking solace in the comfort of those words.

It hurt to breathe, she realized. It hurt to do anything.

In the emptiness of a house devoid of furniture and living people, every sound was magnified. Julie's own heartbeat sounded like a bass drum in her ears, and her breath whistled through her nostrils as she tried to calm down and remember the words that would protect her.

Our father who art in heaven, hallowed be thy name …

Her frightened gaze took in the front door with the dead-bolt still engaged.

Too far. Would he catch her again before she reached it? This time he might not let go.

She felt tears coming, hot and fast but she blinked them away.

"Come on now, Julie just get a grip, and get out of here," she whispered, the words sounded thick. She licked her numb lips and tasted blood. No doubt she was a mess, bouncing down the staircase, arms and legs spinning.

Julie ran trembling fingers over her arms and legs, expecting to find more blood, but all she encountered was flesh that stung at her gentle touch.

Reaching above her head, she felt the cool metal of a rounded doorknob. Julie slid her hand around it, felt it filling her palm. Decisively, in the space between two heartbeats, she'd opened the door and rolled inside, slamming the door hard behind her.

The sound of her own breath still boomed in her ears as she twisted the lock.

What came next could only be described as a confusion of sound.

Pressing her hands to her ears did no good. It filled the house! It seemed to Julie that it was many sounds, layered on top of each other, confused and chaotic.

As suddenly as it started, the sound stopped, and a new more frightening one began.

Sharp, barking laughter.

The sound tore through her like an electrical surge.

Deliberate, mocking, almost genderless, the ghostly laughter resonated through the house as she scrambled away from the door and down the short hall, on hands and knees.

Julie was ice-cold.

In her mind's eye, she saw his face. She didn't know if the face she gave him was real or taken from her dreams, but the thin lips were parted in a cruel smile and he stared at her with humourless eyes. He continued to laugh, as though this was the moment he'd been waiting for since Julie and her family had moved in.

She shook her head to clear the image but it stayed with her. Closing her eyes, she frowned in concentration.

Didn't she have the ability to make him leave? Why was she so totally overwhelmed?

The eyes that refused to leave her were triumphant; they challenged and chilled her to the deepest parts of her heart. Those eyes told her clearly, there was nothing she could do about any of this.

You really think you're in control?

The words that formed in her mind, were they his or her panicked imagination?

After all this time, you can't tell?

In her parent's former home, back pressed against the farthest wall, Julie willed herself to think clearly. She had to escape. She'd wait for Marc at the curb, if she could get out to the back yard. Neighbours be damned! Just let them talk; she didn't care anymore.

The garden door was a few inches to her left. If she was careful and quick she'd be outside before anything else happened. Heartened by the fact that the house had grown quiet again, Julie slid her back up the wall, the muscles in her legs screaming, and wrapped her sweaty hand around the brass doorknob.

But although she twisted and pulled at it over and over, it simply wouldn't budge!

She saw at a glance that the deadbolt was not engaged. It should have swung freely, it was a door her parents used often and it had never stuck before now.

Was he deliberately trying to trap her here?

Ordinarily, Julie would have dismissed that as absurd and paranoid, but given the events of the past few minutes, it was closer to the truth than anything else. She sank to the floor again, wondering for the millionth time where her husband was.

Bing-Bong, bing-bong, bing-bong! The doorbell shrilled loudly, over and over. Insistent banging seemed to come from the front door area.

Could that be Marc? Or another trick designed to lure her back? She rose on shaking legs, unsure what to do.

Marc banged his fist against the door, irritated that the key would not turn in the lock. What the hell was going on? And where was Julie? She sounded angry on the phone, but surely she wouldn't have just left? He'd done exactly as he said he would, grabbing the keys and getting into the van as quickly as he could. There was no mistaking that things were going on there, but what?

"Julie!" Open up!" he yelled, banging insistently, he pushed the doorbell over and over.

Peering through the oval inset glass in the doors, he saw no one in the foyer and heard no approaching footsteps. Yanking the key back out of the lock, he walked to the garage and pulled up on the handle to open the huge door, but that also refused to yield.

Anger at the situation, and concern for his wife mingled in equal parts as he tried the various keys on his keychain in the lock on the garage door handle. Which key was it? None of them seemed to fit.

Running around to the side of the house, he tried the back door, but it seemed to be locked as well. Jogging to the upper deck, he hauled at the glass door, but it too was sealed, the drapes pulled against the fading sunlight.

"This is absurd," Marc muttered, returning to the locked front door. "Julie, open up! I don't have the key for the garage, and for some reason my key won't work. Julie! Let me in!"

Out of options, Marc thrust the key into the lock once more and desperately wiggled it back and forth. "If I didn't know better, I'd swear that lock was being held from the inside!" he muttered angrily. "Come on!"

Suddenly, with a satisfying pop, the key turned in Marc's hand. The deadbolt gave way at last and the door swung inward.

"Julie!" he called. "Where are you?"

There was no answer. Marc's voice echoed through the empty house.

Had she gone for a walk? What was going on?

"Julie?" he called again. "Hello?"

Again, the house was silent, but as he walked farther inside, the hairs on his forearms arms stood at attention, and a penetrating cold slipped over his shoulders, like a damp sheet.

Recognising the sensation for what it was, Marc took immediate action, and ran up the stairs two at a time. He quickly determined that the upstairs level was empty.

"Julie?" he called again, as he went back down the steps. "Are you down here?"

"Marc?' he thought he heard a voice, but it was small and weak. His heart beat faster. What the hell happened in here? He thought. Was that blood on the doorknob?

He pulled at the door but it wouldn't give.

"Julie?" he called through the locked door.

"Marc!" the relief in her voice was unmistakable. "Is that you? Please say it's you. I can't take any more."

"It's okay honey, it's fine. I'm coming. Can you unlock the door?"

"No," she replied. Again, Marc's heartbeat accelerated. His normally confident, sometimes pissed-off wife sounded like a frightened child! Fumbling in his pocket, Marc dug out his set of keys and found the one for the door in front of him.

"It's okay, I got it," he reassured her.

Marc found his wife huddled against the back door of his in-laws' suite, hugging her knees to her chest.

"Is it really you?" she asked, her voice small.

"Of course it's me," he said. Crossing the room quickly, he helped her to her feet and was startled when his wife collapsed into his arms and hugged him with all her strength!

Marc hugged her back, his curiosity burning. She refused to let go for a long time, and Marc didn't have to see her face to know she was crying. At last she pulled away enough for Marc to get a closer look. Mascara was smudged into dark circles under each eye, and her pony tail had come apart. She was disheveled and shaking. Was that blood he saw glistening in her hair?

"What the hell happened here? What's wrong?" he asked, instantly alarmed. "Are you hurt?"

"I don't know," she answered, shaking her head repeatedly. "Yes, probably, but I just –I have to go. Marc, please? Can we just go?"

"But what about all the cleaning and stuff?" he asked automatically.

"I don't care!" she shouted, pushing away from him, she walked back towards the front door a few paces and stopped suddenly, as though the fear he'd seen in her earlier had taken hold again. "I don't care about anything else," she continued. "It's done. Please. Right now, okay? I have to go now. I can't stay here another minute." Her words came out in a rush, and Marc stared at her as he tried to piece together what happened.

"Marc?" she pleaded.

"Yeah! Okay, of course we can go. Absolutely, but will you tell me what happened? Why are you such a mess? The last time I talked to you, you were telling me there was more cleaning to do, and now ..."

"I don't care," she said. "I'm done. I'm never coming back."

Marc was puzzled, but he knew in his heart something big had happened. His wife wasn't the type to just come apart like this. The best thing he could do was to get her out of there as quickly as possible. If need be, he would come back and finish things off himself.

Marc went up behind his wife and gently urged her forward, but she wouldn't budge.

"Hey," he said. "You said you wanted to go, so what's this?"

"You go first," she said. Clearly, she was still frightened.

With purposeful strides, Marc led Julie forward, through a door that had somehow managed to re-lock itself, and out to the van. He noticed with alarm that she walked as though every muscle was screaming at her.

"You *are* hurt!" he said. "Do you need a doctor?"

"No, I don't want to talk about it," she whispered. "I'll be fine." Julie settled into the passenger seat and pressed the palms of her hands together to stop them from shaking. She watched her husband carefully close and lock the front door.

She knew Marc was concerned, and that she hadn't offered him any explanations, but for once in her life, Julie had no words.

Marc settled into the driver's seat and turned to look at her. Julie avoided his gaze by locking hers on the floor mats.

"You're really spooked," he commented.

Julie tucked her hands underneath her thighs, to quiet the tremors that raced through her body. She shook as though on the edge of hypothermia, but the temperature inside the van was warm and comfortable. Marc shrugged out of his own coat and leaned over to drape over her shoulders, before starting the ignition and backing down the driveway.

Clasping the edges of her husband's coat around her, she said nothing. She didn't trust herself to speak. She knew he was still watching. His gaze felt disgusting as it slid over her, and her stomach lurched in response.

As Marc eased the van out onto the road, Julie couldn't bear to look back at the house she'd once called home.

"Feels weird leaving," Marc commented.

Nervous laughter exploded from Julie's mouth as they drove away.

Marc darted a strange look at her but didn't say anything.

It was just as well. There were a lot of things going on inside of her just then and she wouldn't have been able to talk if she'd wanted to.

Julie didn't lift her head again until they were miles away, driving up the heavily-wooded road that led to their new home. She straightened her shoulders and took a deep breath. It was still moving day, and there were a lot of people at the new house, waiting for them. She didn't need a mirror to know she was a mess. She'd seen the look on her husband's face and that was enough.

Pulling down the small mirror in the sun visor, she winced at her own reflection. But carefully, Julie straightened her pony tail and wiped away the smudges beneath her bloodshot eyes. Her hands trembled uncontrollably.

She hoped this ugly spirit wouldn't be able to follow them to their new home.

"Just let him try," she whispered, feeling more like herself with every passing mile. "Never again."

Chapter Forty-four

Julie noticed the change immediately.

A look of wonder on her face, she stopped short in the entryway of her new house and took a deep breath.

Marc, a step behind, almost bumped into his wife. In his arms, he carried one of the night tables from the master bedroom.

"Jules!" he complained. "Outta the way!"

"Sorry," she mumbled, stepping aside.

"That's okay. I felt it too. Just look out, okay? This is bit heavy." Marc continued inside, up the short flight of stairs to the living room area, where he gently eased the piece of furniture down to the floor. The young man stretched, arching his aching back with a groan.

"Oh man, moving day is such a bitch!" he complained, looking with distaste at the staircase that led to the upper level. "And we haven't even finished up there."

Reaching out one hand, Marc absently closed the partially open drawer on the night stand he'd just brought in. A piece of paper, folded many times over, stuck out at an angle from the partially open drawer. Marc poked it back inside with one finger.

"No wonder it's so heavy. The drawer is still inside it. We should have removed the drawer, before it went on the truck."

"Oh?" Julie asked, trying to sound casual. She'd recognised the piece of folded paper instantly. There was no way she wanted Marc to ever see the contents of that note, or any of the other ones that still filled the drawer.

"This is from your side of the bed," Marc continued." I can tell by all the junk inside."

"Well then, maybe I should bring it upstairs?" she volunteered.

"It's too heavy, I'll help you."

Julie knew that if she protested too much, her husband would become suspicious. She now knew with certainty that all her paranoid wondering was due to the negative influence of the spirit who haunted them, but the words in those letters would definitely hurt her husband and she was determined to take steps so he never saw them.

"Let's take the drawer out first." Marc started to open the drawer, exposing many more, similarly folded pieces of paper and several pens.

"Man, you're such a pack-rat," he said, eying the contents.

"That's okay," Julie said, stepping quickly to the night stand, she closed the drawer and shooed away her husband. "I got this."

"It'll be lighter if you take the drawer out," Marc said, frowning.

"No, no that's okay. No need! Look, see? Here I go!" she chirped. Quickly, Julie moved to pick up the night stand in her arms.

"Don't be silly," Marc protested. "It's too heavy for you."

"I'm fine, Marc really," she protested. Her muscles were screaming at her, as it was all she could do to lift the heavy piece of furniture, but she couldn't let Marc see that.

Chuckling at his wife's determination, Marc raised his hands in defeat. "If it means so much to you, go ahead!"

Julie heard the front door close and let out the breath she was holding as she 'walked' the night stand up each step to the top level and then carried it into the master bedroom.

She was grateful their new house had a convenient fireplace, and vowed to make use of it as soon as possible.

 Those notes were part of a darker time, and now that was behind them. Here, there would be no more talk of divorce and no more unexplained fights.

Mysteriously re-locking doors, randomly moving objects and imaginary friends would be the stuff they might talk about one day, when they were ready, but that dark chapter of their lives was finally closed.

Pausing at the large bedroom window, she stood quietly in the spacious room and smiled.

It wasn't a fancy house, and it needed updating but it was comfortable. It felt like home. And of course, nothing could beat that view!

Mature cedar trees and vast green lawns stretched out behind the house. Julie smiled at grass that looked lush and healthy, even though it was the middle of winter.

"No more black-thumb here," she muttered.

"Well? What do you think?" her husband said, as she descended to the main floor a few minutes later, and stepped into the tiny kitchen.

"I never thought this day would really get here," she said, a note of wonder in her voice.

"Me too," Marc admitted. "It was close, though."

"Closer than you know," she agreed, looking away. "He can't …follow us, can he?" Julie asked timidly.

"He'd better not try," Marc replied, his voice deliberately low. "This time I'll be ready for him. I don't know what he did to you, but right now, if he wasn't already dead, I'd kill him myself."

Julie couldn't help smiling at her husband's protectiveness.

Outside, the air was crisp, nothing out of the ordinary for January, but apart from the temperature, it felt fine. She realized that what drove her newfound delight was something she *didn't* feel.

The air was simply air. Light and refreshing, it wasn't 'heavy' or 'thick'. There were no dark, unexplained shadows, and the noises that reached her ears had easy, *natural* explanations.

Julie walked quickly to the nearest truck, where many hands carried boxes and household items into their new home.

Her own arms now laden with bedding, she made her way back in to the house. Admittedly, the jumble of sheets and pillows was all she could carry after her painful ordeal and the added bravado of carrying that stupid night table up a flight of steps. Julie knew she'd be hurting a lot more in the days to come, but at least she would be safe now, and so would her family.

She and Marc had chosen this property together, after many, many visits. Julie smiled at the memory.

Their bewildered realtor had trailed along behind, a look of intense curiosity on her face as the couple walked the house and grounds with slow, measured steps.

Both wanted to be certain this time, and they weren't taking any chances.

The questions they'd asked would have been startling to some, but Michelle was a seasoned professional.

"No one has passed away on this property that I'm aware of," Michelle reported dutifully, during their last and final visit. "You should be very comfortable here."

And with that, the relieved couple signed the papers that begin their new lives.

Julie found herself humming, a self-satisfied little smile on her lips, as she carried an armload of bedding inside, and set it down in her daughter's bedroom.

"My house," she whispered into the air.

Oh, how *good* that felt!

"It *is* my house!!" she said more confidently.

Her footsteps echoed as she walked through the mainly empty rooms. Furniture and boxes were spread throughout each area of the home, and more was being stacked into the barn out back, but despite the chaos, Julie and Marc were happier than they'd been in a long time.

As Julie walked back to the truck, Marc caught his wife in a quick embrace, a broad grin on his handsome face.

She grinned right back at him.

Home.

They didn't have to say it aloud for husband and wife to know they were both thinking the same thing. Finally, they'd come home.

With every step, Julie felt a little more of the heaviness leaving her, and while she still ached from her headlong plunge down the unforgiving staircase, the young mother worked hard to make the children's rooms and their own ready for their first night in a new home.

The bruises from that last battle would take weeks to disappear, and it would still be months before anyone felt relaxed enough to sleep peacefully through the night. They all knew that those things were just leftovers, psychological bruises that would take time to heal. But each night, as Julie and Marc got ready for bed, the solitude and comfort they felt surrounding them was proof that the healing had already begun.

They were safe. And they were never going back.

Chapter Forty-five

"But mom, can't we just drive by the house?" she asked, her tone wheedling. Amélie was going on sixteen, and her powers of persuasion had only gotten stronger as the years progressed.

"There's nothing to see," her mother replied. "It's just a house. I'm sure you remember it."

"Yeah, mostly, but I just wonder sometimes, that's all."

"You wonder about what?" Julie looked at her daughter sharply.

"Lots of thing I guess, but mostly I wonder if he's still there."

The frank reply startled Julie.

"He who?" she asked, still hopeful her daughter would just drop it.

"The guy who lived there with us," she replied, her tone matter-of-fact. "You know mom, the ghost guy."

Julie's eyes registered the shock she felt at her daughter's calm pronouncement.

"Don't you remember, mom?"

How could I forget? She wanted to say.

"Of course I remember, I just don't see the point of going there," Julie answered. "Someone else lives there now." She shook her head, annoyed.

"What's the harm, though? We're just looking."

"There are laws against stuff like this, Ami."

"Oh come *on* mother, are you talking about anti-stalker laws? Don't be ridiculous. It's not like we're gonna go knock on the front door or anything. I just want to have a look at the house on the outside. Haven't you and daddy driven by? Don't tell me you haven't," she finished, folding her arms and staring defiantly at her mother, eyebrows raised. "Looking is not against the law."

"That's enough young lady," her mother admonished.

"Well, geez you don't have to get mad, I just asked," the teenager replied, assuming a sulky expression.

"Why now?" Julie asked. "Why after all this time? Do you miss it?"

Amélie laughed at that. "No way!" she answered quickly. "I'm just curious, that's all. Aren't you?"

Julie ignored the question.

"And you always say I should ask questions," Amélie continued. "Because that's the way we learn, so again, I say: what's the harm?"

Julie sighed in defeat. Why was she always so logical?

"I hate it when you use my own logic against me," she complained. "Fine, if it's that important to you, we'll go have a look, but I'm not getting out of the car and neither are you, and that's final."

"Deal!" Amélie clapped her hands together and grinned, as though they were going out to lunch, or a day of shopping instead of checking out a house that used to terrify them both.

Julie eased the car forward, aware that she had not been completely honest with her daughter. How could she be? How could she express her fears without putting thoughts in her head? She already knew Amélie had witnessed more things than she let on. Certainly more than a small child should have to, and that was bad enough.

But why was she so determined to go back?

No one must know.

Her mother's phrase came, unbidden.

As soon as the car made its final left turn and she found herself staring at the familiar structure, Julie felt a distinctive pull, and she shuddered.

She didn't need to wonder. She knew he was still there.

"It's not for sale yet, that's odd," she muttered. How did they stay, she wondered? How did they fight it? She could see the house was being lived-in. A small tri-cycle sat just outside the front door, and a few children's toys, visible through the glass railing lay forgotten on the front deck.

Julie followed the curve of the road, and slowly pulled to the curb in front of the house. Julie set the brake and allowed herself to *really* look.

The thought of children living there with that bastard made her hands clench into tight fists.

How could they do it? Surely, they knew he was there! Couldn't they feel it?

Julie sat back and took a deep breath, allowing the sudden burst of anger to drain away. They could just as easily ask themselves the same question, she reasoned. How had *they* stayed so long? It's amazing what you can do when you have to, she thought. Money is money, and real estate is big business. Admitting your house is haunted is probably just as bad for business now as it's always been!

Julie turned off the ignition and pulled out her cell phone and a large map, which she unfolded in front of her and her daughter.

"Uh … mom? What are you doing?" Amélie asked suspiciously.

"Setting up my props," she said. "I told you, the people in this neighborhood don't like it when strangers come around." Julie spoke matter-of-factly. "They're all quite protective, so hopefully they'll just think we're looking for an address and got lost."

"O-ka-ay?" Amélie answered doubtfully. "'Cuz that's not awkward at all, right?"

Julie shot her daughter a sharp look. "I know how suspicious people are in this neighbourhood, Ami."

"Okay, okay, I believe you, but a map mom? Really? No one uses maps anymore. Not when we have a GPS." Amélie shook her head in obvious disgust, and looked around. Suddenly, she sat up straighter, rolling her shoulders with a little frown. "You know, it's hard to explain," she said. "But I think I can feel them watching."

"You mean the neighbours?" Julie asked hopefully.

"No."

Julie was distinctly uncomfortable, and wasn't sure what to say. Wondering if she was opening a can of worms, she chewed at her lip and looked past her daughter through the passenger window. Her eyes fell automatically on the downstairs den window.

That was *his* room.

Closing her eyes quickly, she gripped the steering wheel and faced forward, a familiar sick feeling in the pit of her stomach.

"It feels weird being so close but not going inside," Amélie commented, gazing out the car window. Are you sure we can't just go knock on the door and pretend to be lost?"

"Absolutely not!" Julie shot back, then swallowing the lump in her throat she smiled at her naive daughter. "This is as close as we go. It's not exactly safe … for us."

"You don't have to worry, mom. He can't follow us. He doesn't even want to."

Julie frowned at her daughter.

"Well he doesn't," she answered defensively.

"How do you know that?" Julie whispered.

"I dunno, I just do," Amélie replied, matter-of-factly. "You know what mom? I thought it was gonna look totally different, but it doesn't. It still looks the same."

Julie nodded agreement. The trim they'd so carefully painted before listing the house seemed to be the exact same shade, and the front door Julie had laboriously painted that hot, sticky summer afternoon when Amélie was only two was unchanged.

It wasn't all bad, she thought. We had some good times there. I guess that's why we stayed. We always thought it would get better, somehow.

A gentle breeze blew in through her open window, carrying with it the scent of a barbecue grill.

"Ha!" she smiled. "Someone's cookin' supper! And sure as shootin, someone else is on their back deck, calling out, 'hey neighbor, what's on the grill?'"

Amélie looked at her mother with a frown and a small shake of her head.

"Your humor is so obscure," she mumbled.

"Thanks," Julie replied dryly. "Listen, you had to be there okay? Hey, look at that! The yard still looks the same, too."

"Yeah," Amélie chuckled. "Terrible!"

Several sickly-looking plants dotted the strip of garden that bordered the driveway. The patch of grass that served as a front yard had a distinct hue of yellow amongst the green. "Some things you just can't fix," Julie muttered, as her gaze travelled up to the same gauzy curtains that hung in the upstairs bay windows.

An involuntary shudder rippled through her as her eyes swept over the house she'd once called home.

"I think that's enough," she said, reaching for the car's ignition.

Amélie put forth a restraining hand.

"No, please, not yet. Another few minutes okay?"

Amélie's mood was pensive as she sat quietly in the passenger seat.

What was she thinking about? Why had she wanted to come and look at the house now?

"Mom, what's that?"

Amélie's sharp question brought Julie out of her reverie instantly. She was pointing at the upper windows of the house as Julie turned around.

The face-sized smudge in the dining room window could have been a random patch of dirt. The house was once again in need of a good pressure-washing, but Julie knew with certainty that it hadn't been there a few moments ago.

With a chill that went straight through to her backbone, she was equally sure that shape, indistinct and blurred, wasn't a living person.

"I – I don't know," she replied honestly, her heart pounding.

Hello again, a chillingly familiar voice echoed in her head. Julie's eyes opened wider. What was she thinking, bringing her daughter back to this place?

"Ami," she began, reaching for the ignition. "Let's get out of here, it was a bad idea to come, I –"

"Mom! Amélie remarked sharply. "It's gone! Look!"

Whatever had shown itself in the lower corner of the window was gone.

"So, it was real," the teenager commented, frowning in wonder.

"I told myself it was just imagination," she continued. "That I was just making it up. I used to see it a lot. At first it scared me, and I'd run to tell you and daddy, but you didn't always believe me, so I stopped telling you. Adam believed me though. Sometimes he let me stay in his room a while."

Julie licked her lips nervously as she concentrated on breathing through her panic. Carefully, she started the car and put it into gear. She rubbed briskly at her nose and frowned to stem the flood of emotions.

She wasn't ready for all these sharp memories to return! "You didn't tell me that," Julie replied quietly, as she pulled quickly away from the house.

"It doesn't matter now," she said. "But do you remember I used to get up a lot in the night?"

"Yes, of course."

"I didn't like being in there, especially at night. He used to look in my window."

Julie's fingers tightened on the steering wheel.

"When I got old enough, I just closed the blinds myself so I couldn't see him, and then I'd hide under the covers with my kitty. But I couldn't reach the strings on the kitchen window blinds, so sometimes, if I got up for a drink of water, he'd go to that window instead." Amélie shuddered.

Julie stopped briefly for a stop sign, then took off again, wincing as the wheels chirped from the sudden acceleration.

"Whoah!" Amélie called out, grasping at her suddenly tight seat belt. "Mom! Slow down!"

"Sorry, we just need to get out of here, and you are not to tell your father we did this," she admonished the startled teenager.

"Fine, whatever. I won't."

At the end of the street, Julie cast a frightened glance at the rear-view mirror. The cul de sac with its perfectly manicured lawns and cookie-cutter houses faded from view as Julie cranked the wheel hard to turn the corner.

They drove in silence for a few more minutes before either of them felt comfortable enough to speak.

"It was him all along wasn't it," Amélie asked quietly, looking out the passenger side window. "The little girl? The boy Adam played with? That was all him, wasn't it, mom?"

"I don't know," Julie said. "Maybe. I still don't understand either."

"One thing I know for sure," Amélie replied. "He knew we were there today. Even after all this time, he recognised us."

"I don't know what you mean," Julie lied. Reluctantly, she eased the car to a stop for a red light and waited impatiently for it to change. "But I do know one thing: I'm glad we don't live there anymore, aren't you?"

"Yeah, I like our new house. No visitors."

Julie's eyebrows shot up at the off-hand remark. "Amélie, why was it so important for you to see the house again?"

"I dunno, I thought that if I saw it again, maybe I'd be able to stop dreaming about it," she replied. "I don't want this to sound dumb, but I just want to know who he is and why he does what he does to people."

"Oh baby, I don't think we'll ever know –"

"I'm not a baby mom," Amélie interrupted.

"Of course you're not," Julie replied, automatically. "Do you really dream about it?"

"Lights' green mom," she said, pointing at the streetlight.

Julie launched the car forward once again, happy to put more distance between them and the house they'd never forget, but worrying at the same time that her daughter's sleep was still being plagued by nightmares.

"I wonder if the people who live there now, know about him," Amélie mused.

"Probably," Julie sighed, guiding the car around the last turn, onto their new street. "He's pretty obvious."

"Do you think they're mad at us for selling them a haunted house?"

Julie glanced over at her daughter, surprised by the question. Amélie was playing distractedly with the ends of her hair as she stared out the passenger window.

"Well," Julie answered. "Your daddy and I talked about it a lot before those people bought the house. We really thought hard about telling them, but Ami, something you don't realize is how the adult world works. Let's say we did tell them. Those people might not have believed us. Worse, they might have thought daddy and I were making it up or maybe we were kinda crazy."

"What?" The teenager seemed startled by that. "No way, that's sounds like a scene from a movie."

"Believe me honey, it's about as real as it gets. People aren't always nice. Especially when there's money involved. And what if they did believe us? Do you think they would have bought the house anyway?"

"Oh," she replied. "I didn't think of that. Probably not."

"So," Julie said, as they turned back onto the road that would lead them home. "Are you glad we looked at it?" With every passing mile, it felt like a weight was being lifted from her chest.

"Yes and No. I still don't understand."

"Well," Julie dismissed the topic with a negligent wave of her hand. "Some things just take longer to understand. I think maybe, this can be one of those things."

"I hate it when you do that," the teen objected. "I'm almost sixteen. You don't have to patronize me."

Perhaps one day when she was strong enough herself, Julie would find the courage to delve back into the past. If she looked long enough maybe she'd find those elusive answers.

Julie smiled affectionately at her daughter. How she longed to tell her everything and help her understand, but sixteen was still too young.

Don't search for it so hard baby girl, she wanted to say. It'll find *you* soon enough.

The End

About the story, about the Author

Virginia lives with her husband, daughter and a collection of Siamese cats in Mission B.C. on a quiet acreage, where she pursues her talent for creating spine-tingling stories that captivate readers.

Virginia received her certification in Journalism at Kwantlen Polytechnic University, in 1989 and worked as a reporter for several years before the field of Autism Intervention was introduced with the birth of her son. She went on to work as both a staff writer and a freelance contributor for many weekly newspapers in the various cities of the Fraser Valley in BC, before returning to her first love, creative writing.

Where have these ideas come from?
<u>Hauntingly Familiar</u> and <u>Possessions</u> are both autobiographical accounts from the author's past, and are available at most online retailers in eBook and paperback.
Virginia's future projects are what she refers to as *inspired fiction*. Several more stories are already outlined, inspired by paranormal adventures she and her husband have gathered in their travels.

You can catch up with Virginia on social media to ask a question, post a photo, make a comment or share your own story. Connect with her on Facebook through *Ghostly Publications* **https://www.facebook.com/greatghoststory/**
or tweet the author directly **@ghoststoryV**

Purchase directly from the Authors' webpage and read her ghostly blog at **www.ghostlypublications.com**